HIROONA

Reverend Canon Horatio Nelson Huggins

HIROONA

An Historical Romance in Poetic Form

Reverend Canon Horatio Nelson Huggins

Edited, with annotations
and an introduction
by
Désha Amelia Osborne

THE UNIVERSITY OF THE WEST INDIES PRESS

Jamaica · Barbados · Trinidad and Tobago

The University of the West Indies Press
7A Gibraltar Hall Road, Mona
Kingston 7, Jamaica
www.uwipress.com

A catalogue record of this book is available from
the National Library of Jamaica.

ISBN: 978-976-640-553-3 (print)
976-640-562-5 (Kindle)
978-976-640-571-7 (ePub)

Cover illustration: *The Eruption of the Soufriere Mountains in the Island of
St. Vincent, 30th April 1812*, Turner, Joseph Mallord William (1775–1851) /
© University of Liverpool Art Gallery & Collections, UK / Bridgeman Images

Cover and book design by Robert Harris
Set in Adobe Garamond Pro 11/14.5 x 27
Printed in the United States of America

Contents

Notes on Editing

The first publication of *Hiroona* was produced from Horatio Nelson Huggins's original manuscripts, which were later destroyed. This edition of the poem is based on the first publication (Port of Spain: Franklin's Electric Printery, 1930), thirty-five years after Huggins's death. The greatest difficulty in editing *Hiroona* has been determining whether alterations were to be made to the poet's manuscript or the original editors' corrections. The trouble lies in their assertion that the text is exact.

For this edition, certain emendations have been made. Huggins's original footnotes are included in the notes at the end of the book and have not been altered. Most of Huggins's archaic and variant spellings have also remained unaltered, for example lept (leapt), Arrowack (Arawak), corse (corpse) and sepulture (sepulchre). All uses of "Carib's" in the possessive have been changed to "Caribs'". Rules of capitalization have been standardized. For example, in the original edition, both "leeward" and "windward" were capitalized inconsistently, and have been changed to lowercase throughout. Inconsistent spellings also have been standardized throughout – for example, "Chetwayè" and "Ranèe" were sometimes spelled "Chetwayé" and "Ranée". Rules of punctuation have been retained, except in the case of dashes combined with semicolons, and with exclamation points. Dashes have been retained only when they serve as parentheses. The use of exclamation points varyingly as the end of a sentence has been standardized. Errors have been corrected where it is obvious: "stirfe" to "strife", "troup" to "troop", repeated lines have been removed, and quotation marks have been added where dialogue was present, but there were no marks in the original (V, xix–xxx).

Introduction

Reverend Canon Horatio Nelson Huggins took an estimated sixteen years, from 1878 until the time of his death in 1895, to complete his only significant literary achievement, the narrative poem *Hiroona: An Historical Romance in Poetic Form*. His daughters Charlotte and Evelyn spent a further thirty-five years following his death to prepare the poem for publication. Privately published and distributed to mostly family and friends in 1930, the narrative poem, typed out from Huggins's handwritten manuscript, did not attract a wide readership and it fell into relative obscurity. Due to its limited publication, *Hiroona* was known only by repute. The exact number of copies printed remains unknown and there are currently five copies of its first publication available to the public.[1] Knowledge and critical reception of *Hiroona* outside of St Vincent and Trinidad began to grow when selections of the poem were included in the *Penguin Book of Caribbean Verse in English* fifty-six years later. There are a number of scholars who have recognized *Hiroona* as belonging to a Caribbean poetic tradition, although it still remains marginal to ongoing discussion.[2]

Hiroona is a fictional account of the events of the Second Carib War fought between Great Britain and the Garifuna, then known as the Black Caribs of St Vincent, who were aided by Revolutionary French forces. The struggle between the Black Caribs and Great Britain goes back more than a century before the war, and the mystery of their origin lies at the heart of the conflict. St Vincent, which remained without colonization and unexplored into the late seventeenth century, was likely to have gone the way of the other islands if it not been for the introduction of a group called the Black Caribs. How they got to St Vincent is still heavily disputed, but the consensus is that in either 1635 or 1675, a Spanish slave ship was wrecked off the smaller island of Bequia; the Europeans were immediately murdered by the local Caribs, the

African slaves admitted into the tribe allegedly following a period of servitude, sexual mixing with the Caribs and eventual separation into their own branch of the group.[3] "African intermixture was great enough to bring about a dramatic change in the phenotype", says Nancie L. Solien Gonzalez, so that by around 1700, "a new society had emerged on St Vincent that was radically and culturally distinct from that of the Island Caribs, though undeniably related to it".[4]

Charles I of England included the island in his grant of Barbados to the Earl of Carlisle; in 1672, Charles II granted it to Lord Willoughby of Parham, who purchased it from Lord Carlisle. In 1722, George I made a new grant of St Vincent to the Duke of Montague, but in 1748, with the treaty of Aix-la-Chapelle, the crown forfeited this claim, and St Vincent, along with other relatively unsettled islands became neutral. Britain later declared on 13 November 1763 that in light of France's breaking of the terms of the treaty the island now belonged to the crown of Great Britain.

Sir William Young, who was the first commissioner for the sale of lands in the ceded islands officially granted to the British under the 1763 Treaty of Paris, aimed to force Carib groups in St Vincent to acknowledge the sovereignty of the King of Great Britain, acquiesce to the sale of lands within their district and allow the building of roads, without which "sovereignty in no part could be duly asserted or maintained".[5] In exchange, the Caribs were proffered the full rights of British subjects. In 1773 a treaty of peace between Britain and the Caribs in St Vincent was signed by many of the leaders, including Chief Chatoyer. In 1779, the French returned to St Vincent, and the Black Caribs helped them temporarily regain control of the island until 1783, when the second Treaty of Paris finally and permanently declared the island to be a British colony.

In 1795 revolutions and rebellions spread across the Lesser Antilles on the heels of Victor Hugues's victory over the British. Hugues arrived in Guadeloupe in June 1794 with between one thousand and eighteen hundred men, by various accounts, and the French Republic's slavery abolition decree of 11 February earlier in the year.

> To Hugues' blood-thirst 'twas due—
> That Hugues who, though the outward form he wore
> Of men, the heart of savage beast he bore.
> No hands than his were stained with deadlier dye;

'Gainst none shall blood of vengeance louder cry;
In day that comes when all shall have their meed.
(*Hiroona*, II, vii)

Hugues made an army out of the island's slaves, and drove the nearly twenty thousand British troops and the entire British population to evacuate the island. Hugues sent emissaries to Grenada in 1795, and soon slaves, free mulattoes and Caribs allied under the leadership of Jules Fedon. Fedon and the brigands, as they were called, kidnapped and later killed between forty and sixty British prisoners, including Lieutenant-Governor Ninian Home. Other rebellions and insurrections occurred that year, including the Bush War, or Guerre des Bois, in St Lucia and the Colihault uprising in Dominica. This was also the year of the second Maroon War in Jamaica, which resulted in the banishment of over five hundred Maroons to Nova Scotia, from whence they were later exiled to Sierra Leone. The Coro uprising, led by black generals José Gonzalez and José Chirino, occurred in Venezuela, along with slave rebellions in the Dutch colony of Curaçao and the Demerara region of British Guiana.

In St Vincent, the war began when, on 10 March 1795, groups of Black Caribs led by Chief Chatoyer, along with a number of French settlers and forces from Guadeloupe who were given the order by Hugues, began attacking settlements and plantations along the leeward side of the island. The other Carib chief, Du Valle, and his group of insurgents soon followed by assailing in the same manner down the windward side of the island.[6] The attacks continued until both groups of rebels met and joined with French forces at Dorsetshire Hill on 14 March. It was there and then that Chatoyer died, according to the colonial historians, as the result of ill-advised and seemingly unequal combat with Major Alexander Leith of the West Indian Rangers militia.[7] The war carried on for two more years under the leadership of Du Valle and other chiefs including Chatoyer's son.

Once the Caribs were defeated, the British government decided that deportation was the only way to ensure peace on the island. Embarking on the ship *Experiment* under the orders of Captain Barnett, around five thousand of the Caribs were deported first to Baliceaux in the Grenadines, where the conditions were severe and many died due to famine and disease. Later the survivors, less than half the number who were originally exiled, were transferred to Roatan Island, off the coast of Honduras, where they eventually spread and are currently settled along the coasts of Belize, Honduras, Guatemala and Nicaragua.[8] Not all of the Black Caribs were exiled, and many Caribs who never participated in the war remained on the island in remote villages. The remaining Black Caribs were pardoned in 1805. They were given 230 acres of land, but not permitted to cultivate sugar. In 1812, after the eruption of the La Soufrière volcano left most of their land destroyed and uninhabitable, a number of them left for Trinidad.[9]

Horatio Nelson Huggins

For Horatio Nelson Huggins, the story of the Second Carib War was first told to him by family, friends and the island itself. Private and natural history take precedent over the official record of events. He explains in *Hiroona* the role of history, archaeology and anecdote when gathering material for his poem:

> 'Twas there this bard was born, 'twas there he passed
> His boyish years, too happy long to last;
> And there, in boyish ventures, often found
> Or lying loose, or bedded in the ground,
> Old Carib tools and weapons rough of stone,
> And even time-worn bits of human bone;
> And oft the leaden ball, that told of days
> More recent, and of still more, deadly frays.
> And tales of Carib times and legends wild—
> That lore so fascinating to a child!—
> Oft told to guests around the festive board,
> Were heard, and deep in childhood's mem'ry stored.
> (*Hiroona*, II, iii)

Huggins's paternal grandfather, James Huggins (1752–1837), was born into an English creole family whose past, like many others, helped to form part of the history of the West Indies. The earliest recorded ancestor born in the West Indies was Ensign Robert Huggins (1647–1707), the son of a royalist officer who left England in the aftermath of the Civil War.[10] The family established itself on the island of Nevis for several generations as successful cane planters and members of the navy and military. A legacy of scandalous behaviour on the part of James's uncle Edward (1755–1839) and Edward's sons John and Edward left the family with a damaged reputation.[11] James lived a life less scandalous than his relatives did, although he is known for one alleged incident while serving as provost marshal on Nevis. Fulfilling his duties, James boarded the HMS *Boreas* with the intention of arresting the ship's captain, the young Horatio Nelson, who was there to enforce Britain's Navigation Acts by blockading the trading of American goods to Nevis.[12] Following a standoff that lasted months, Nelson agreed to meet and discuss the matter with the authorities on Nevis, and a friendship developed between the two. Nelson later became the godfather and namesake of James's son, the first Horatio Nelson Huggins in 1787. James moved to St Vincent from Nevis, probably in the late 1780s, where he joined the Queen's Companies, and was present during the insurrection of 1795.

James's seventh son, Daniel (1790–1863), was among the first generation born in St Vincent. He studied medicine at the University of Edinburgh, graduating in 1809.[13] Daniel returned to the island, where he lived and worked as a doctor, an occupation supported by a yearly salary paid by each estate he was contracted to attend.[14] From the late 1820s through the mid-1830s Daniel and his family lived in Rabaca, a village in the north windward side of the island which, until the end of the war in 1797, had been part of the Carib territory. Huggins was able to provide lengthy descriptions of Duvallè's land because this is likely where he grew up. Daniel also served as assistant surgeon and later surgeon in the Queen's Companies in 1814, 1821 and 1828 (his father James was captain).[15] In early 1829 Daniel married Lucy Crichton (1811–1891), the daughter of Patrick Crichton, a young Scottish merchant and accomplished artist who had settled in St Vincent and became a successful planter in Langley Park estate in Charlotte Parish.[16] Like Huggins's father and paternal grandfather James, Patrick Crichton served in the Queen's Companies – rising to the rank of major – and fought in the Carib War, barely surviving a Carib ambush from which few escaped.

Born on 6 September 1830, Horatio Nelson Huggins was the second child (out of twelve) and second son of Daniel and Lucy. He was named after his uncle, the first Horatio Nelson Huggins.[17] During the first ten years of young Huggins's life, the West Indies experienced dramatic social and political changes. Slavery was abolished in 1834, and on St Vincent, where 91 per cent of the island's population were slaves,[18] this meant an end to the slave-worked plantation system on which the society was based. The period of apprenticeship lasted until 1838, ending with the total emancipation of all slaves. While in Rabaca and until abolition, Daniel's household included never more than ten slaves, who worked as domestics, cooks, gardeners and grooms.

Daniel and his growing family did not become planters until after apprenticeship, when he acquired Golden Vale estate in Calliaqua, located less than five miles from Kingstown, the capital of St Vincent. The brief sketch of his life published in the *San Fernando Gazette* after his death mentions that Daniel and Lucy's original plans were to send their son to England for commercial training for a life in the mercantile business.[19] Mrs Alison C. (A.C.) Carmichael, author of *Domestic Manners* and *Tales of a Grandmother*, a loosely biographical novel and the first nineteenth-century work of fiction openly set in St Vincent, reveals that this was a common practice for English creole planter families at the time.[20] It was around this time that Huggins went through his first major life change. Documented in his long poem *The Holiday* (see appendix), he briefly describes being sent away,

> thence, 'midst a mother's tears,
> I crossed the seas for Home and school;
> For such was then th' accepted rule
> And there returned, my school days o'er
> Bright happy days I spent once more.

These plans were never realized, as Huggins matriculated at Codrington College, Barbados, on 12 March 1850 at aged nineteen.[21] At Codrington, Huggins was taught the set curriculum for seminarians at the time, which included theology, classics, logic and mathematics, along with lectures on medical subjects such as anatomy, chemistry and physiology.[22] With the library at Codrington consisting of over twenty-five hundred volumes, he would have been exposed to the many theological and scientific debates going on throughout the nineteenth century.[23] That he had an interest in the earth sciences, like many Victorians, is evidenced in a number of stanzas in *Hiroona* that discuss the nature of various rock formations and the volcanic activity on St Vincent.[24]

After a brief period of missionary work in Trinidad following his ordination in October 1853, Huggins returned to St Vincent to continue his calling as a minister. Not moving from Calliaqua, however, he was posted to St Paul's

Church, and in 1856 he received the appointments of minister official and later perpetual curate of St Paul's.[25] In 1853 Huggins married Adelaide Mary Lacroix, the daughter of his first cousin James Huggins Lacroix (1809–1881), the son of Daniel's sister Ann and Comte Jacques de la Croix, a Royalist who found himself exiled on St Vincent during the French Revolution.[26] Lacroix eventually came to own four large sugar plantations in St Vincent, including the Golden Vale, Evesham and Lacroix estates.[27] Huggins and Adelaide had three children: Henry Daniel (1854); Bertha Marion (1858) and Edwin Bullen (1860). Sometime after the birth of Edwin Bullen, Adelaide died. By 1862 Huggins was married to Charlotte Courtney Wemyss, of the ancient Wemyss family of Scotland known for their Jacobite sympathies and personal losses at the Battle of Culloden.[28] Huggins and Charlotte had six children: Mary Edith (1862), Horatio Otho (1866–1871), Charlotte Emily (1868), Ethel Mabel (1875), Evelyn Courtney (1877) and Lilian Elcho (1878–1879).

Chronic illness caused Huggins to relocate to Trinidad to take up an appointment first at St Peter's and St Philip's parish. In September 1867 Huggins moved his family to San Fernando to become rector of St Paul's Church (rebuilt in 1874), a post he held for the rest of his life. San Fernando, the second largest city in Trinidad, was busy, thriving and cosmopolitan, expanding and flourishing following the initial economic decline brought on by emancipation. Considerably larger than any of the provincial towns in St Vincent, yet smaller than Port of Spain, society in San Fernando consisted of an established social hierarchy. Like all of West Indian society, white elites of French, Spanish, Irish, Scottish and English ancestry dominated the top of the local community in San Fernando. The next major group consisted of the upper- and middle-class black creole population (given the name "coloured" to suggest simultaneous mixture and distance from their African and European ancestors), perhaps the largest group of educated and nationalist black and mixed-race families on any island in the Caribbean. The black middle class in Trinidad were the first to articulate a nationalist identity and ideology, where a uniquely Trinidadian intellectual and literary culture began to develop. Some prominent figures who made up the non-white creole intelligentsia during this period were Michel Maxwell Phillip, mayor of Port of Spain, solicitor-general and author of *Emmanuel Apodaca*; Jean-Baptiste Philippe, author of *A Free Mulatto*; L.B. Tronchin, president of the Trinidad Literary Association; Huggins's friend Samuel Carter, editor of the *San Fernando Gazette,* "the most consistently liberal paper in the later nineteenth century";[29] and scholar and educator John Jacob Thomas, the author of *Froudacity*, a response to Oxford historian J.A. Froude's *The English in the West Indies*, in 1889. Before the publication of *Froudacity* toward the end of his life, Thomas was perhaps Trinidad's first public scholar actively involved in education reform. He regularly contributed to the *San Fernando Gazette*, run by friend and fellow freemason Samuel Carter; he held positions in colonial government, the Board of Education in particular, where he rose to the position of headmaster of the San Fernando High School. Thomas was also known for his philological scholarship, highlighted in his 1869 book *The Theory and Practice of Creole Grammar*, and for a lecture given before the Philological Society in London in 1873.[30] The largely ignored first and second generations of recently freed African slaves who remained uneducated and kept out of white and black creole society made up the third group. The final group were the indentured labourers who arrived on the island beginning in 1845 from the Indian subcontinent and in 1853 from China. This group from the subcontinent, though only brought in to make up for the loss of slave labour, eventually made up about one third of the population of Trinidad during the 1880s.[31] They were mainly the target of black creoles who supported anti-indenture labour laws and Christian missionaries who sought to convert them.

Throughout Huggins's life in San Fernando, social unrest was common. In February 1884 distubances took place during the San Fernando carnival. Later in October, the Hindus and Muslims of San Fernando, mostly indentured estate workers, were forbidden from having a procession through the streets during the Hosay festival. In both cases, the people gathered and celebrated despite the sanctions, which led to clashes with police.[32] These measures were taken after the 1881 Canboulay Riots in Port of Spain and due to the colonial administration's fear that these popular festivals would be used as a cover for revolt following years of economic depression caused by the rise in sugar beet production in Britain.[33]

In spite of the existing tension between the black and Asian workers and the white and black upper and middle classes, worsened by the economic uncertainty of the sugar crisis and continuing water shortage during the 1870s and 1880s, San Fernando became a place where men of learning could thrive. In Trinidad during the late nineteenth century, the intellectual circles incorporated the sciences, literature and politics, and these activities were by no means confined to the white upper class. The black intelligentsia prided itself on its literary and intellectual achievements and boasted of being more cultured than the whites, who were accused of crass materialism. This intelligentsia made its presence felt through newspapers. Men like Samuel Carter and Joseph Lewis, who first ran the *New Era* and later the *San Fernando Gazette,* and George Dessources, who began the *Trinidadian*, were advocates for issues that were important to the black middle class, including education, desegregation in schools, the end of Indian immigration and the opening up of Crown lands.[34]

Huggins and his family appear to have participated actively in the social life of San Fernando. In addition to his duties as rector, Huggins was also chaplain for San Fernando General Hospital; for a short time pastor of St Matthews in Oropouche; a member of the Diocesan Synod; director of the Children of the Good Shepherd, a society for boys and girls at the church school; director of the Society of the Holy Sacrament, for adults and children; warden and treasurer of the Guild of St Paul; and high president of the Order of the Sacred Cross, a social and friendly society.[35] In the early 1870s Huggins directed the reconstruction of St Paul's in San Fernando. The church reopened with two new stained-glass windows, completed in 1875 by the notable firm Wailes of Newcastle, which represented "The Good Shepherd" and "St Paul".[36] Sometime in the late 1880s he was appointed rural dean for his role as the chair of the board of the Diocesan Synod; and in 1893, Huggins was appointed canon.[37]

The Huggins family would have held an established place in society that benefited from the company of San Fernando's privileged English creole families and white intellectuals. One such family acquaintance was Robert John Lechmere Guppy, son of Mayor Robert Guppy.[38] Guppy senior, an Oxford graduate who practised law in England before coming to San Fernando, served as mayor for thirteen years. Lechmere Guppy arrived in Trinidad to work as a civil engineer; within years he became the chief inspector of schools from 1868 to 1891, all the while pursuing his scientific interests. He helped to establish and was named president of the Scientific Association of Trinidad and the Field Naturalists' Club of Trinidad. He was an active amateur naturalist and geologist particularly interested in marine life, instrumental in obtaining for the British Museum the second-largest example of a living species of Pleurotomaria known to conchologists, and lends his name to the *Poecilia reticulata* species of fish he is famous for discovering in 1866. In honour of Queen Victoria's golden jubilee in 1887, Lechmere Guppy founded and was the first presiding officer of the Royal Victoria Institute.

Huggins was a natural scholar who had a profound knowledge of earth history. He was a member of the Victoria Institute, in attendance for at least one of their regular meetings. His father, Daniel, was recognized at the 10 July 1891 meeting of the Field Naturalists' Club of Trinidad, where a list of several different species of bat he collected in San Fernando was "the first records of species in the island".[39]

Newspaper records from the *San Fernando Gazette* help to reveal a man who was unafraid to challenge others, push for cultural reforms in the city and sometimes find himself in the midst of controversy. In 1884, Huggins firmly objected to the building of a new fire brigade station between the town hall and St Paul's Church. He organized a petition and forwarded the list of signatures to the governor, who appeared to ignore the objection and gave the legislative council the right to build in 1886.[40] Huggins, along with others who were so-called men of refinement, successfully bid to establish a public library in San Fernando in 1888. He also battled, unsuccessfully, with the police inspector, Owen Douglas, over a strip of land Douglas bought to build a cab stand that Huggins claimed overlapped onto church property.[41]

Huggins was also unafraid to voice his displeasure in print. On the celebration of Queen Victoria's birthday, he published his protest poem, titled either "A Poem" or "The Grand Usine".[42] The publication of the poem caused a furore that achieved its objective in shaming the owners of the Usine Ste Madeline sugar factory to deal with the immense air pollution it created. During late May and throughout June of 1890, Huggins was involved in a doctrine-based, bitter war of words with Presbyterian minister Reverend Alick Ramsay of the Free Church in Scotland in San Fernando.[43] Ramsay delivered a lecture titled "Presbyterianism" at the Presbyterian Church on 12 May 1890 that was later published in the *San Fernando Gazette* the next Saturday. Starting with an attack on what he believed to be the unsubstantiated claims to spiritual authority made by the Catholic archbishop while on a recent visit, and the regular insistence of the same by the Anglican canons, Ramsay attacked the established principles of the episcopacy, and claimed that on biblical grounds, "the characteristic principles of Presbyterianism are found in, founded on, Scripture, and the other forms of Church government . . . err both by excess and defect; excess as in the case of Episcopacy, where there are numbers of offices for whom no warrant can be found in God's word".[44] The feud began when Huggins responded with a lengthy letter to the editor, printed in the 31 May 1890 issue of the *Gazette*, where he argued against Ramsay's point on historical grounds, namely how the three orders of ministry in the apostolic succession of apostles, elders (presbyters) and deacons are in fact rooted in the traditional Jewish hierarchy of high priest, priest and levite.[45] Ramsay responded the next week with the charge that Huggins had "his own way of reading history".[46]

For the fiftieth anniversary commemorating the emancipation in August 1888 Huggins preached a sermon based on the text "Ye had done right in my sight in proclaiming liberty every man to his neighbour", from Jeremiah 34:15.[47] In honour of the celebrations, Huggins composed the "Jubilee Hymn", which was sung by the St Paul's Church choir at the Wednesday midday service and published a week later in the *San Fernando Gazette*:

> COME, praise ye our God
> This Jubilee day,
> Who broke the Slaves' bonds,
> And cast them away!
> Come free-men, and thank Him
> For all He has given—
> For manhood, for freedom
> And title to Heaven!
>
> Those men had been brought
> From far, and been sold
> As property, bought
> As chattels for gold!
> God spoke in thunder
> The thing should not be:
> Then bonds burst asunder—
> The slave-men were free!
>
> And God brought out good
> To those He had freed,
> As God only could,
> From man's evil deed;—
> A place in His Kingdom,
> The Gospel of Light.

And Heaven's own freedom,
And sonship by right!

For freedom on earth
The millions were paid
For right of new birth
A Ransom was made
Of infinite greatness;
For God gave His Son—
By Christ's very Life-Blood
Redemption was won!

And God, the All-Good,
Who gave us our birth,
Hath made of one blood
All peoples on earth,
All brothers in manhood;
And brothers in love
With even the Saint-hood
In Heaven above!

Then praise ye the Lord!
From father to son
All ages record
The things He hath done.
And tell to the nations
His glorious Name;
With great Jubilations
His goodness proclaim. Amen.[48]

In the hymn, God is the sole reason for the emancipation. It speaks more of thanksgiving, and less of culpability, directly in line with the attitudes of many liberal white and coloured members of Trinidadian society. There are no direct references to African slavery; instead, Huggins says that the slaves were brought from "far". It is a sentiment similar to that in *Hiroona*, when the poet says that the ancestors of the Black Caribs (though never referring to them as such) were a people who came from far away (I, xi). In the latter use of the term "far", Huggins is attempting to distance the Black Caribs from their African heritage in order to further the poem's overarching message of Carib nationhood, legitimacy and autonomy in the face of historians who wished to justify their deportation by connecting them to African slaves and maroons. In the "Jubilee Hymn", however, Huggins's refusal to mention both African slaves and European masters has more to do with the social milieu in Trinidad that began with emancipation and lasted through to the twentieth century. Here, like in *Hiroona*, providential history supersedes all other histories, furthering a message that avoids placing the cause of slavery and its eventual deliverance on the white members of society.

With the exception of a few, many white and coloured elites viewed discussions of slavery and the state of race relations in the aftermath of emancipation to be counterproductive and largely to be dismissed. The editor of the *San Fernando Gazette*, for example, summarizes that during the period of slavery in the West Indies,

> it is not the Negro alone who has been oppressed and debased by this nightmare of absolutism; the weight of its manacles has been greatest around the neck of his master who, by a moral retribution, was chained to the dead soul he had assassinated in his greed for gain, and found his own liberty dying out in the polluted atmosphere and moral poison evolved from the dead carcase of his victim.[49]

The few, in large part, belonged to the Trinidad Literary Association. In contrast to the message of freedom rooted in providential history supported by some members of the white and coloured classes, the Trinidad Literary Association's jubilee celebration was organized and led by Edgar Maresse-Smith, a coloured solicitor based in Port of Spain. Following the church celebration in Port of Spain, members of the association branched off to finish the day with their own banquet and celebrations, which were presided over by Maresse-Smith and Reverend P.H. Douglin, one of the prominent coloured Anglican priests. Of the subjects the association concerned itself with were the ways economic and cultural representation in Trinidad began to include more "people of African descent", a term that became popular among coloured Trinidadians in order to stress their greater connection to their African over their European ancestry.[50]

The emancipation jubilee celebrations served to introduce a national conversation about race and identity throughout Trinidad. Once a discussion held between a few white and coloured liberals on the one hand, and those who supported the planters in the years following emancipation on the other, arguments about the right and wrong of slavery developed into more complex arguments about political representation, legal and economic rights, all strengthened by the question of the role racial (that is, African) identity played in the formation of Trinidadian nationhood. This is where Huggins's "Jubilee Hymn" and the introduction to *Hiroona* enter discussion. The "Jubilee Hymn" is race-neutral. The suffering endured by the slaves is directly compared to the suffering and death of Christ. The redemption offered to all Christians is made manifest in the freedom offered to the slaves.

Throughout the 1890s Huggins suffered from increasingly poor health. In 1893 he took a six-week holiday to St Vincent "for the purpose of seeking that repose of which he stands much in need, as he is an incessant, and zealous worker", says Samuel Carter.[51] In recognition of the anniversary of his thirtieth year as a minister in Trinidad, the Guild of St Paul honoured Huggins, to which his reply is recorded in the *Gazette*: "I certainly do feel the increasing pressure of years, but I rejoice to feel also that I have work in me yet; and I have good hope that in answer to your kind wishes I shall, after a short absence for needful rest and change, return to my much loved work refreshed and invigorated." By April 1895 Huggins was suffering from illness exacerbated by his "already overworked body"; his health had deteriorated to the point where he was unable to perform and attend Easter services.[52]

An often retold story among the family is that there had been an attempt on Huggins's life weeks before his death. A young man holding a cutlass entered St Paul's Church and told Huggins "the masons have sent me to kill you". But, according to Huggins's great-great-grandson Michael Huggins, he was a "strong, wiry man and overpowered his assailant before he could do harm".[53] French and later Scottish freemasons had established a powerful presence in Trinidad since the time of the Second Carib War. Some of the prominent Catholic residents of San Fernando belonged to one of the town's three principal lodges. There is no record of Huggins's membership in one of the Masonic lodges, although in 1886 he presided at the funeral of Philip C. Corrie, borough councillor and right worshipful master of the Royal Trinity Lodge. Corrie was buried in St Paul's with full Masonic rites.[54]

On Tuesday, 23 July 1895, Huggins rode out to the district of Oropouche, a village in the Naparimas, in order to sign papers that were connected with the erection of a new church building. While there he drank a glass of coconut water and ate potted meat, which caused him to suffer severe diarrhoea and intermittent pain that lasted until early Friday morning. His condition worsened until he died from cholerine, described then as a mild form of cholera, on 26 July.

News of Huggins's death made such an impact that the 9 August edition of the *San Fernando Gazette* reported that "no less than 430 extra copies" of the 2 August edition that reported his death were sold within four hours, in addition to letters containing stamps from individuals in different parts of the island requesting copies of the paper. Carter also reported that he was in the process of obtaining a photo of Huggins to send to England to produce a "few hundred reprints, which we would dispose of at a trifle above cost price".[55] This idea never appeared to move beyond planning, possibly due to Samuel Carter's death two months later on 10 October 1895.[56]

Following Huggins's sudden death, *Hiroona* was left as an unedited manuscript read by only a handful of friends and family. The foreword states that the poem was published as an "act of filial remembrance, and at the request of many friends". Huggins's daughter Charlotte Emily (Lottie) taught herself to type, and with the help of her sister Evelyn, worked over the course of thirty-five years during her spare time to type out her father's nearly undecipherable handwriting. Their effort to present the poem as close to the version that Huggins would have published it is laid out in the foreword, where they state that it is issued "without any corrections, or alterations, . . . as he left it when he died thirty-five years ago".[57]

Charlotte and Evelyn's choice to leave *Hiroona* unedited provides clues as to when and why their father wrote the poem. At least one manuscript was distributed to friends, family and Huggins's social network in San Fernando. Based on the textual evidence in *The Holiday*, Huggins's other narrative poem and the only major work to be published during his lifetime, it can be reasoned that he was possibly writing or thinking about writing *Hiroona* before and during his visit to St Vincent in the late 1870s. Toward the end of this shorter poem, Huggins showed an interest in certain historical events such as the 1812 eruption of La Soufrière and the Second Carib War, where he lingered on both recorded events and personal stories. The most notable of these is an entire passage from *The Holiday* reproduced in *Hiroona* – the story of a young slave girl who sacrifices her own safety in the midst of battle to return the son of her master to his family:

> . . . Next morn
> Appeared in Town a slave, all torn
> And soiled, and haggard, and footsore;
>
> . . . .
>
> The sole survivors from the wreck;
> And brave and faithful, thus had won
> Her way, and saved the white man's son.
> (*The Holiday*)

After typesetting the poem, Charlotte and Evelyn turned to their cousin and one of Charlotte's closest friends, the business magnate Sir George Frederick Huggins (1870–1941), for help with publishing. The son of Huggins's younger brother William (whose other son, William Alfred, was married to Huggins's oldest daughter, Bertha Marion), George arrived in Trinidad from St Vincent in 1891, and within twenty years expanded his enterprise into a monopoly of all lighter-to-ship transport in Port of Spain.[58] George financed publication and wrote the preface. The poem was printed by Franklin's Electric Printery, located on Abercromby Street in Port of Spain, in 1930. The printery was owned by Conrade Bismark Franklin, who for a time held one of the sought-after government printing contracts, and published mostly historical works and the *Trinidad and Tobago Year Book*. Distribution of the poem resembled the original circulation of the manuscript in the 1890s – among a small inner circle of friends and family. Because the original premises of Franklin's Electric Printery were destroyed by fire in 1931, it cannot be determined how many copies were actually printed.[59]

Until 1968, the original manuscript of *Hiroona* was kept in Huggins's library in the family home in San Fernando. According to the family, his preparation notes for the poem were also preserved. Unfortunately, after Charlotte's death in 1968, parts of the family home were destroyed by fire. All original manuscripts and notes were destroyed.

Hiroona in the Transatlantic Literary Tradition

Hiroona is 9,410 lines of rhyming couplets mostly in tetrameter separated into 487 stanzas divided into twelve cantos. Other epics and long narrative poems divided into twelve books or cantos include *The Aeneid* (9,896 lines of dactylic hexameter); *Piers Plowman* (2,500–7,200+ lines); *Paradise Lost* (10,550 lines); and *Blind Harry's Wallace* (11,000+ lines). *Hiroona* contains both direct and indirect references to a number of other works and traditions, including the Bible and Greek mythology; earlier works of West Indian history, especially those by Bryan Edwards, Thomas Coke, Sir William Young and Charles Shephard; and nineteenth-century geology. Huggins appeared to have an interest in Viking culture and Norse mythology, with examples scattered in subtle references throughout the poem, as when he compares the barbarousness of the Caribs' ritual blood tasting to "orgies fierce and savageries of eld / When Norsemen Vikings worshipped Tew and Thor" (II, xxvi). Also where Duvallè is called the "true son of Thor, / His name of 'Thunder-bolt of war'" (VI, xiv). A notable allusion is in Norman and his horse Rollo. Rollo is the name of a Viking leader who, during the late ninth and early tenth century, was the first in a series of rulers to settle his people in the area of France that became known as Normandy. Incidentally, Rollo is the great-great-great grandfather of William the Conqueror. This inclusion places a strain brought on by Norman's presence that would otherwise remain unexamined.

Hiroona takes its title from Hairoun, an adaptation of the Carib name for the island of St Vincent. Today, the Black Caribs of St Vincent and Belize refer to themselves as Garinagu which means "cassava eating people". Their ancestral home St Vincent is called Yurumei or Iouloumain/Youroumaÿn, which appears to be the origin of the word Hairoun. The poem details the key events of the war and parallels the official histories with local, usually apocryphal, oral legends that the poet collected from those who fought on British and Carib/French sides. By the end of the poem, Hiroona the beautiful, "blessed land" has been transformed, through bloody war and the forced exile of its people, into St Vincent, an island foretold in Warramou's curse to be destroyed in fire and ash by nature and left with an uncertain future. It is an attempt to reclaim the history of this significant event away from the detached and unsympathetic official accounts and insert the lives and experiences of all involved into a literary record.

Historical fiction like *Hiroona* was created to serve as an alternative means of telling the story of the island and its peoples. Yet *Hiroona* is more than just a literary performance of a moment in St Vincent's history. By merging the problems associated with empire, national identity, religion and modernization (primarily accessed through scientific knowledge), Huggins's poem offers a meaningful contribution to the evolution of a unique kind of West Indian consciousness at the end of the nineteenth century.

Hiroona contains an elaborate narrative metaphor of the Fall of Man that runs parallel to the history of colonialism in its relation to the end of Carib presence on St Vincent. This metaphor corresponds to the poem's exploration of the relationships between public and private history, and of God the Creator and humanity the Created in a New World established through old principles. Huggins portrays the Caribs as living in a prelapsarian natural world; their "discovery" by Columbus is a disastrous fall into history, while their expulsion by the British is a second fall, punished by God working through nature. Utilizing a biblical framework in telling Carib history, Huggins introduces the poem before the *beginning* that is recorded in history, before Columbus, and discovers a New World and its inhabitants as if through the eyes of God. The final canto concludes the poem with the end of the Caribs' connection to the island – their deportation or forced exile by the British government, which Huggins represents as a post-apocalyptic rebirth of the world (in this case, the New World that is renewed as colonial space). Completing the eschatological framework, canto XII foresees the destruction of St Vincent by the eruption of the La Soufrière volcano in 1812 – fifteen years after the end of the war. Warramou is able to issue this prophetic vision as retribution for the colonial government's exile of the Carib nation.

Perhaps even stronger than his scientific interests, nurtured by his father and emulated by scholars such as Lechmere Guppy, was Huggins's acceptance of the need for a national story. Surprisingly, he turned not to Trinidad but to St Vincent, and instead of telling the story of the nation's growth he told of its downfall. What brought him to this decision is unknown, but its origin is likely connected to *The Holiday*. Years before the *Hiroona* manuscript was circulated, Huggins wrote the 813 line poem that details his first holiday returning to St Vincent in August of 1877.[60] *The Holiday*, published privately as a miniature booklet and distributed to extended family and friends, celebrates his return to what he calls his native home after a sixteen-year absence spent ministering in Trinidad, and recounts a family history, both past and present, in verse.[61] This poem was Huggins's attempt at retracing the life of the poet as it was united to his natural environment, a sentiment often employed by Romantic poets. Though never reaching the descriptive length and depth that Wordsworth reached in laying out his growth as a poet and priest of nature, the poem captured the moment where Huggins began to understand what he believed to be the universal connectivity of earth history and natural presence (existing here without fully articulating his sense of providentialism) to the history of St Vincent as told through the lives of its citizens. Written in the same verse structure as *Hiroona,* Huggins managed to parallel his personal history as a member of a prominent English creole family and priest with the official history of an island still in the aftermath of a war ninety years prior, a violent volcanic eruption, and the emancipation of slavery that changed the visual, natural, cultural and political landscape.

Huggins's decision to write *Hiroona* was influenced by his exposure to the literature produced on both sides of the Atlantic. The most famous of these, *The Song of Hiawatha*, written by Henry Wadsworth Longfellow in 1855, is an epic poem in trochaic tetrameter. The story is based on a combination of wrong ethnography and jumbled mythology grounded in the work of Henry Rowe Schoolcraft, an American geologist and ethnologist known for *Algic Researches* in 1839, which includes the original story of Hiawatha and other American Indian stories told to him by his second wife, Jane, who was of Ojibwa descent. Incidentally, Longfellow weathered a storm of criticism that alleged that he borrowed the organization and metric form of *Hiawatha* from the *Kalevala*. The *Kalevala,* the national epic of Finland published first in 1835 and as a complete edition in 1849, is really a collection of epic poetry, ballads and proverbs compiled by Finnish physician and scholar Elias Lönnrot.[62] It was published at a time when Finland was a grand duchy of Russia and the formation of a national epic gave validity to the idea of a nation. Translations soon followed, including Franz Anton Schiefner's 1852 German edition, which caught the attention of Longfellow. *Hiawatha* went on to become one of the most popular poems of the nineteenth century.[63]

The self-taught Anglican missionary, Reverend William Henry Brett, was one of the first to apply Longfellow's formula for preserving in literature (with no attempt to maintain or retain) that aspect of Amerindian religion and myth that persisted in the culture. Brett was born in Dover, England, in 1818 and, funded by the Society for the Propagation of the Gospel in Foreign Parts, travelled to British Guiana in 1840 to begin nearly four decades of missionary work among the indigenous peoples there.[64] Brett's purpose was to "preserve, and to give at one view, the more serious traditions – religious, mythological, and historical – of the four aboriginal races [Arawaks, Waraus, Caribs and

Acawoios] who live nearest the shores of Guiana" on account of the passing of "many time-honoured legends".[65] The result was his *Legends and Myths of the Aboriginal Indians of British Guiana* published in 1880.

An author who is rarely mentioned and whose work provides a clear inspiration is Henry Hegart Breen and the lasting contribution of his novels and histories. Breen was from Ireland and spent thirty years in St Lucia holding various posts in the colonial administration from 1832 to 1862, when he moved to St Vincent to serve as provost marshal. He is the author of *St Lucia: Historical, Statistical, and Descriptive* in 1844, a book of poetry, *The Diamond Rock and other Poems* in 1849, and *Modern English Literature* in 1857. While in St Vincent, Breen was an associate and co-worker of Huggins's younger brother, Patrick Foster, who held the posts of revenue officer, registrar of births marriages and deaths, and acting colonial registrar in succession. In 1876 Breen published his final work, *Warrawarra, the Carib Chief: A Tale of 1770*.[66] The story is set on the fictional island of Sidonie, based on St Lucia, in the Lesser Antilles (St Vincent is represented by the neighbouring island Sablonia). Since he had been living in St Vincent for fourteen years at the time of *Warrawarra's* publication, it is reasonable to assume that certain details and experiences are inspired by Breen's life on both islands. An example that supports this can be found in the novel's title, which appears to draw from Warrawarro (also spelled Warrawarou), the name of a Carib valley and a river that extends into one of the bays south of Kingstown. The novel includes an entire chapter (outside the narrative direction of the novel) of ethnographic descriptions of Carib customs and culture. In later chapters, the story of the Carib insurrection is awkwardly interwoven with the stories of Irishman Henry O'Neil. His experiences in the island and romance with the governor's daughter dominate the novel at the expense of the eponymous hero Warrawarra (son of the dead Carib chief Marabou), and his journey from Carib chief to Catholic priest and back again. This all happens during an insurrection on the island that is similar to the events of the Carib war in St Vincent. Breen's way of storytelling is standard for the late nineteenth century. It is simplified and largely dismissive account encased within a fictional story – the kind of representation Huggins was interested in improving.

Where acknowledged, Huggins and his poem are generally associated with the writings of white creole West Indians such as Nathaniel Weekes and M.J. Chapman, who both wrote long poems about their home Barbados, and Guianese poets Henry Gibbs Dalton and Egbert Martin.[67] Works such as these give scholar Laurence Breiner reason to begin his discussion of West Indian poetry by saying that "apart from oral poetry and some scattered early publications, Caribbean poetry in English begins around 1920 – long after colonization, the colonial wars, slavery, emancipation, and indenture".[68] *Hiroona* takes a much different stance to its subject matter and audience while managing to maintain traces and imprints of the Romantic and epic traditions throughout. Paula Burnett feels that many if not all of the poems composed in the West Indies before the twentieth century are only of interest today for their "insight, however incomplete, into a unique society and into that society's growth towards moral and cultural integrity".[69] She places Huggins somewhat apart from his colonial literary successors and counterparts, saying that he was the first to attribute the guilt of the extinction of the Caribs to the British, "the first to question the whole role of empire".[70] This is disputable, given Burnett's and others' reason for the delay in *Hiroona*'s publication is what they see as Huggins's presumed attack on colonialism.

Huggins did not make the claim that *Hiroona* was written or should be read as an epic, opting instead to subtitle it "An Historical Romance", the epic's successor as envisioned in the work of Sir Walter Scott and James Fenimore Cooper. Huggins replaces the traditional epic question with the question faced by many West Indian writers. That is, how to make sense of the sublime beauty of the landscape in its relation to the political landscape made natural by centuries of European presence, and how the former is in truth shaped by the latter, posing a challenge to the question of whether an authentic Caribbean epic is possible. If epic is what Huggins had in mind for his poem, then he would have undertaken the project knowing that epic "locates what a culture struggles most to find, and it encapsulates the values of that culture for future generations to practice and future societies to study and understand, often to appreciate and occasionally to incorporate, though seldom to emulate".[71] It was much later that scholars like Burnett, Selwyn Cudjoe and Louis James describe *Hiroona* as the first authentically Caribbean epic, perhaps with stress placed on substantiating the poet's Caribbean identity and apparent commitment to exploring the same themes as other Caribbean poets of the twentieth century. James ends his survey of early West Indian literature with a brief note on *Hiroona*. With the publication of *Froudacity* by John Jacob Thomas in 1889, James believes a unique style of writing emerges. Thomas's defence ends with a call for independence that "defines and defends its culture".[72] According to James, this is where *Hiroona* steps in as an illustration of this new "historical consciousness". *Hiroona* is thus placed in a linear chronology of Caribbean epic that ends with Derek Walcott's *Omeros*.

Selwyn Cudjoe claims *Hiroona* to be one of the "most important and sustained poetical work[s] written in Trinidad in the nineteenth century".[73] Considering that the non-white middle class was at the forefront of many intellectual and literary circles in Trinidad during the late nineteenth century, the question arises whether there could possibly be a connection between Huggins's way of writing the poem and the readership – that is, were non-white readers exposed to his manuscript, and in what ways might that affect the poet's narrative decisions? Cudjoe believes that because of his closeness to the freedom struggle, Huggins was able to depict the Amerindian in an authentic and sympathetic light.[74] He also believes that Huggins's Amerindians are equal to Europeans and possess strength and bravery not articulated as strongly in earlier works about the Amerindian presence in the Caribbean. "Thus, in *Hiroona*", Cudjoe continues, "the Caribs are depicted as individuals who possess free will and have their own outlook on the world".[75]

Over the years the Second Carib War has become the central moment in the history of St Vincent. More scholarship has been devoted to this event than any other historical moment and to the Black Caribs than any other cultural group in St Vincent. Cudjoe writes that Amerindians figure prominently in the nationalist ferment taking place in Trinidadian society at the time. He includes *Hiroona* among a set of novels produced in Trinidad that were influenced by the popular feelings of romanticization of Amerindian culture during the 1880s. Works such as L.B. Tronchin's *Inez* (1885), and Jean-Ch. de St Avit's *Les Deux Premiers Martyrs de la Trinidad* (1885) were motivated by the "romantic inclinations of the time and [Pierre Gustave Louis] Borde's [*History of the island of Trinidad under the Spanish Government*]".[76] These sentiments were in turn incited by a new-found sense of Trinidad nationalism. While this explanation is appropriate for Tronchin and St Avit, it does not fully explain Huggins's motivations for writing. Though he lived in Trinidad for most his adult life, he lived along the margins of the both white and coloured creole society, which remained dominated culturally by a strongly Catholic French-Spanish creole class. It was his holiday home in the late 1870s that ignited the idea of applying the already articulated nationalistic feelings in Trinidad to his own home of

St Vincent. Unlike the Trinidadian authors mentioned, Huggins did not use the figure of the Amerindian as a narrative tool. George Huggins stated in the preface that Canon Huggins "committed to memory the many stories of the Caribs as handed down by tradition. In later life, having the desire to perpetuate the memory of that ancient tribe, he set himself to the somewhat unusual task of doing so in poetic form." He turned to the history of the Black Caribs and their brief expression of nationhood in the late 1790s as a story that tells of both foundation and loss. As the island is destroyed by natural disaster and the planter class eventually falls, *Hiroona* ends with a future that ultimately lies beyond the island.

On its publication in 1930, *Hiroona* emerged into a Trinidadian society that was continuing to articulate its own anticolonial voice in the literature of authors who seemed to have little time for what appeared initially to be imitative fiction, much less verse written by an amateur poet whose race and vocation automatically, if unintentionally, is a reminder of the often rigid social, political and intellectual period of Trinidadian history during the late nineteenth century. Writers who were now associated with literary societies, such as the famous Beacon Group, sought to break away from derivative European styles by identifying whatever appeared before them as separate from a distinctly Afro-Caribbean version of West Indian literature. Reflected in the years leading up to the labour revolutions that swept the entire Caribbean beginning in the early 1930s, many Caribbean writers "dedicated themselves to establishing authentic national literatures based on working-class and peasant culture" which was often "referred to this national, folk literature as the soul of the nation or of the people".[77] When producing literature, writers from both the white and black middle classes in the Caribbean may well have been colonialist and often imitative, but that does not negate their interest in self-representation. "What comes across clearly is [a] profound middle-class desire to see their own cultural reflection, a desire manifested in the stories and other features of Caribbean newspaper and magazine culture from the late nineteenth century through the 1920s and 1930s."[78] For early Afro-Caribbean writers in particular, the struggle against rootlessness had to be fought against popular opinion in Britain from a century earlier.

The efforts of writers throughout the nineteenth century to establish a distinctively Caribbean voice culminated with the publication of Claude McKay's *Songs of Jamaica* in 1912. The 1920s and 1930s experienced an explosion of Caribbean literature: McKay, with H.G. De Lisser and Una Marson, who published her first book of poetry in 1930, *Tropic Reveries*, in Jamaica; Alfred Mendes, C.L.R. James, Albert Gomes and C.A. Thomas in Trinidad; Eric Walrond and Walter Mac A. Lawrence of British Guiana. All are remembered as part of the first generation of twentieth-century poets and writers whose work focused on the need for creating a national and native culture through literature. By 1930, the year of *Hiroona*'s private publication, Mendes, James, Gomes and others were in the midst of a literary revolution. Their goal, laid out in the pages of one of their two major publications, the *Beacon*, was to "break away as far as possible from the English tradition", which saw many West Indian writers "still slaves to Scott and Dickens" because they lacked "the necessary artistic individuality and sensibility in order to see how incongruous that tradition is with the West Indian scene and spirit".[79]

For Huggins, however, historical romance was a simultaneously imitative and nationally significant literary style. The presence of the poem in the twentieth century presents an anomaly for scholars of Caribbean literature. It would take another forty years before Huggins's poem went from being recognized as imitative of European literary styles to a significant contribution to West Indian literature worthy of study. It was in the midst of this cultural and literary revolution that *Hiroona* was published, but it appears to have been overlooked by those seeking to establish a West Indian literary type. No reviews were written, and there is no reference to the poem in other works. The closest to a reference is G.C.H. Thomas's *Ruler in Hiroona: A West Indian Novel*, published in 1972, which utilizes Huggins's distinct spelling of the Carib name for the island in order to depict a fictional story of political intrigue in St Vincent during the 1950s.

It is inequitable to judge *Hiroona* against the development of Caribbean literature during the twentieth century. For men like Huggins, the recognition of a national identity in the West Indies should never include a rejection of Britain, since he and others like him viewed the origin, history and culture of all West Indians inextricably tied to the United Kingdom. While the poem omits a considerable representation of African and creole slaves it does sympathetically represent the Black Caribs. His choice to omit the accepted African origins of the Caribs was strategic. It allowed him to work the transition in his narrative from Columbus to insurrection. His nineteenth-century readers would not have considered the Caribs, through their partial African origins, to have more claims to the island than the settlers; they were dealt with by the colonial government as maroons.

Huggins did not belong to any influential literary group. Although he belonged to one of the old and large planter families spread out across the West Indies, and was the rector for his church, he appeared to resist holding a high position in society. He did not go to a top public school or an English university. His personal reasons for spending the last quarter of his life producing a long narrative poem about the nearly forgotten indigenous people of St Vincent can never be fully explained. But the poem reveals that Huggins understood, as many West Indian writers of the twentieth century throughout the region understood, that literature and not history provides the fullest means to record the connectedness of transplanted and destroyed cultures, of the destructive forces of nature and empire. Romance is singular as a genre in that it effects the resolution of real political conflict in the realm of the imaginary.[80]

The final passages end with the question of who benefits from progress. *Hiroona* is an attempt at shaping a collective identity through the merging of history and narrative. The epic question is really a reflection of the concerns of the society that produced it. For Gilgamesh, it was the search for immortality; Achilles asks what is the best way to achieve honour and heroism; while Beowulf searches for the means to maintain that heroism; by the age of Milton, the epic question is the search for an answer to the problem of theodicy. The search in *Hiroona* is for an answer to the lessons of history.

This is what makes *Hiroona* so interesting and unique. Unanswerable mystery and impenetrable privacy are aspects of both the poem and its author. Areas of Huggins's life, his personal motivations, remain unexamined and the notes and manuscripts for *Hiroona* are lost forever. As for the protagonists of the poem, the Black Caribs, or Garifuna, their true origin and appearance on the island remain a mystery for descendants, historians and anthropologists. The details of the 1795 war between them and the British, including the circumstances that led to the death of their leader, Chatoyer, and their surrender and deportation are encountered as a mere footnote within British imperial history, part of the revolutionary wars, not worthy of their own official history. For years, the telling of this story remained in the hands of amateur historians. But as far as Caribbean literature is concerned, *Hiroona* shows that its seeds were planted before its actual publication in 1930. The poem reveals a story of tragedy and loss hidden within Caribbean history that has been long overlooked.

Due to its subject matter, *Hiroona* is either doomed or blessed with the burden of having a life beyond the original publication. While scholars still refer to the insurrections of 1779 and 1795–97 as the "Black Carib Wars", the Afro-Amerindian group who were both heroes and villains of *Hiroona* have been referred to as Garifuna for most of the twentieth and twenty-first centuries. The presumed traditional name for St Vincent, *Hairoun,* was corrected into the remotely sounding *Yurumein* in a further attempt to indigenize and authenticate pre- and post-encounter Kalinago/Garifuna presence.

The original or intended readers of *Hiroona* or what they thought will never be known. It is likely that the poem was not meant to stir up feelings of injustice on behalf of an indigenous deracinated people, or a sense of ethnic nationalism in colonial Vincentians or Trinidadians. Any moral judgement made by the poet remains implicit. The Christian symbolism of the Fall, of sacrifice, exile and the end of history stand out above any specific political message put forward by the author. In the end, it seems Huggins's narrative goal is contained and remains in its full title *Hiroona: An Historical Romance in Poetic Form.* The poem is an attempt at telling different histories using the familiar genre of romance, understood within its own established parameters, and using Huggins's own words, a history that records

> sad, shamefaced,
> In tears, with pen, reluctant, traced
> These records dark, that blur her page,
> And shame an else enlightened age—
> (I, ii)

A work like *Hiroona* initiates the uncomfortable conversation that failed to take place between the groups of white West Indian and black and brown Caribbean writers about the future of Caribbean literature. The poem lies somewhere between the view of Huggins's descendants Rachel Ley and Nan Peacocke, who express the belief that he *chose* to see himself as West Indian in spite of his white Englishness,[81] and the generally accepted view initiated since the days of the Beacon Group, that the literature is authentic and serious if it springs from the voice and experiences of people of African (and sometimes South Asian) descent. The most fitting summary of the experience of *Hiroona* and its author is found in Daryl Cumber Dance's analysis of the work of Francis Williams, the Cambridge-educated eighteenth-century Afro-Caribbean poet: "The diction is of England, but the vision draws from Caribbean life."[82]

Characters

In *Hiroona* the characters fall into one of four categories. The first are the known historical characters: Chetwayè, Du Valle, Governor Seton, General Abercromby and Major Alexander Leith. The second group are those partly derived from historical sources but given fictitious names such as Barbette and Warramou. The fictional "local" characters, those whose names are mentioned but normally have no place in the written record, make up the third group. Characters like Nannette and Chetwayè's wives, Waroutie and Winnie, possibly inspired by the popular painting of Chatoyer and his five wives by Agostino Brunias, are given speeches before their own deaths; and even in some part Ranèe, whose act of heroism in saving the life of a planter's child is really the retelling of similar incident: all these are the characters whose stories Huggins derived from oral sources. The final group is made up of the small number of semi-fictitious composite characters. These are partly inspired by real people known to Huggins, such as Norman and Crayton, who, according to Michael Huggins, were based on Huggins's grandfathers.

Principal Characters

Chetwayè: Leader of the Caribs. Based on the historical figure Joseph Chatoyer. Declared the "Paramount Chief" of the Black Caribs and in 2002 St Vincent's first national hero, he is the most iconic and recognizable figure from this period in Vincentian history. Historical records document his death at the hands of Major Alexander Leith. The life of the historical Chatoyer remains obscured by the scattered nature of European and Caribbean historical records and equally by the romance of his legend. *Hiroona* is the first and longest fact-based accessible work of fiction to attempt Chatoyer's story and present him as a complex character both romantic and historical. Renamed as the less French-sounding Chetwayè, he is introduced early in the poem in canto II, as the cautious and calculating leader of the Black

Caribs awaiting the arrival of Victor Hugues's emissary of war, Barbette, and the blessings or omens from the volcano god, Qualeva that will determine the Caribs' involvement in the war. Throughout the poem, Huggins attempted a description of Chetwayè's character – a feat never attempted before – by focusing on his reserved nature and bravery in battle. His death at the end of canto VII signals and represents the death of Hiroona.

Warramou: Son of Chetwayè. The poem's most complex character. He is both hero and villain. His rage at the beginning and curse at the end serves as framing devices for both the narrative and for history as envisioned in the poem. He is engaged to Ranèe, but she is reluctant to marry him because of her unrequited love for Scottish settler Crayton. This disappointment, combined with his acknowledgment of the inevitable loss of the island propel Warramou into a role more tragic and heroic than his father or uncle Duvallè. Huggins connected Warramou to the historical figure John Dimmey (spelled "Demmy" in *Hiroona* III, xiv), the son of Chatoyer mentioned in Thomas Coke's *A History of the West Indies*. Dimmey was instructed by the Baxters, Methodist missionaries stationed in Antigua from the 1760s to the end of the eighteenth century. In 1788 Dimmey unsuccessfully attempted to introduce Coke and Baxter to both Du Valle and Chatoyer.[83] In his recent study of the Black Caribs, Christopher Taylor introduced the overlooked detail that Chatoyer had more than one son. Highlighting the close ties that existed between Chatoyer and Sir William Young, Taylor writes that one of the chief's sons lived in Young's household, while Chatoyer himself was a frequent guest at Young's estate at Calliaqua.[84] Governor Seton mentions in a letter from January 1789 that Chatoyer had two sons living with a gentleman's family who had the intention of bringing them to Europe, but could not due to his being detained on business matters.[85] Combining these findings together with the notes by Coke, it is reasonable to assume that these were two separate young men, who, when the war began, returned to their father's side.[86] Huggins appeared to have borrowed from the historical record when documenting the words and thoughts of Warramou. This speech attributed to the son of Chatoyer, appears in and is similar to Warramou's speech in canto XI, xxxiv–xxxv. After Chatoyer's death, Shephard notes that the "young Chatoyer", sometimes called "the orator", took up leadership of the Caribs and was among the nearly five thousand who surrendered and exiled in 1797. In his account of the war, F.W.N. Bayley wrote that during one skirmish in Calliaqua, "the son of Chatouay was taken prisoner and butchered by the negroes [possibly soldiers in the Sixtieth Regiment]", after the English took control of the Carib camp.[87] Huggins appeared to have at least one of these men in mind in creating Warramou.

Duvallè: Carib chief and leader along with Chetwayè and later Warramou. Some historical and oral traditions connect him as a member of Chetwayè's family, in most accounts his brother, but Huggins does not connect them.

Ranèe: Daughter of Duvallè and the only character with a whole canto devoted to her. In creating Ranèe, Huggins drew on the accounts of two legendary figures with the purpose of presenting a character able to personify a nationalized archetype of the powerless, submissive and willing native woman as a New World subject. These two well-known figures, Pocahontas and Yarico, are, like Ranèe, embodiments of the native woman as the innocent, beautiful and yielding noble savage whose closeness to nature became increasingly romanticized.

Nannette: *Hiroona's* only true villain. In creating Nannette, Huggins relied on popular and negative perceptions often attached to African female slaves and their descendants: unattractive, unfeminine appearance; masculine strength; ignorance and intellectual inferiority in the form of superstition; vengefulness; and violence. In her is all that personifies an opposition to civilization and the natural patriarchal order. In addition to being a fierce and feared warrior, she is also an obeah priestess. At the same time, Nannette symbolizes all the wildness and violence of the Carib unseen in any other character in the poem. From the passages of her first appearance through to her death at the hands of the nameless slave soldier, Huggins's alternating descriptions of Nannette as both Amazon and witch, and the way in which she fulfils each characterization, help to push the narrative further and supplant the role traditionally assumed by Chatoyer.

Kodanda: The only Afro-Caribbean character given noteworthy attention in *Hiroona*. He is introduced in canto IV, a Mandingo slave revealed to Norman as one of the three survivors (the others being the mistress of the plantation and her three-year-old son, who is saved by Ranèe) of the attack and massacre at the Planter's Hope estate, which unofficially starts the war. Kodanda later joins the St Vincent Rangers and performs many heroic deeds; he is responsible for organizing an attack that mimicked the Carib style of ambush; unfortunately, the result was that he was mistaken for a Carib by the English and shot at (X, xxii). As a result of his bravery, he is awarded his freedom from Governor Seton in his final mention in the poem (X, xxiii). The story of Kodanda's heroic act is similar to the story of Tamaun first told in Thomas Coke's *A History of the West Indies* (1810, 232–33). This appears to be the extent to which the character can be studied. On the one hand, Kodanda is used by Huggins to present a character who exemplifies the success and organization of the plantation system in that he is loyal to his master's memory and the victory of the colony and crown over the Caribs. On the other hand, Kodanda, like Norman, Crayton, Warramou, Chetwayè and Ranèe, is given the opportunity to exemplify the potential for individual bravery. He is "A negro slave / Than whom there breathed no truer man" (X, xxii). However, in a way that is also similar to the other characters mentioned, Kodanda embodies one of the significant and essential themes that persist throughout the poem: the dialogue between recorded past and lived history. In the *Registry of Slaves* for St Vincent is a man named Codanda. Alternately spelled Cadanda and christened Isaac, he was estimated to have been born around 1801, and listed as belonging to the household of Huggins's father Daniel Huggins beginning in 1817 when he is sixteen, through to the final *Registry* in 1834 at the age of thirty-three where he served the family as a groomsman.[88] While it is impossible that Codanda fought in the war,[89] what remains intriguing about the actions and adventures of the character is his inclusion.

Norman: Principal English hero in the poem. Norman is based on Huggins's paternal grandfather James Huggins, who was a captain in the St Vincent Militia's branch of the Queen's Companies. Norman is not presented modestly; Huggins portrays him as a successful plantation owner, decked out with diamond ring, all-white linen clothes, all to "mark" a "man of culture and of wealth" (III, i). Norman served as doctor to Chetwayè and agricultural advisor to Duvallè on the cultivation of his coffee estate (III, v–vi). Right after the slaughter of a group of slaves by Caribs, Norman has an outburst where he understands the anger of the Caribs (IV, xviii). He is inserted in many battle scenes and often serves as the voice of the poet in his assessment of other characters or situations.

Crayton: Based on Huggins's maternal grandfather Patrick Crichton. Not as fully developed as Norman, his presence is primarily in Ranèe's narrative. Crayton is introduced angling alone by a pool, and at other times he is seen through the eyes of Ranèe, who spies on him through the trees. Crayton is the major commanding the St Vincent Rangers. His rescue by Ranèe that resulted in her death is based on an allegedly true incident.[90]

Governor Seton: Colonel James Seton, governor of St Vincent from 1787 to 1798.

Barbette: Victor Hugues's emissary in St Vincent. Not a historical figure, Barbette stands as a mouthpiece for Hugues, who was not in St Vincent. The name of the French commander sent by Hugues was Touraille.[91]

Ledru: Carib leader who only appears in canto X. In an apparent rejection of traditional Carib culture, he is the only bearded chief.

Leighton: Lieutenant-Colonel Baldwin Leighton (1747–1828) of the Forty-Sixth Regiment. Leighton fought in the American Independence War and the Peninsular Wars; he commanded the Forty-Sixth Regiment from 1795 to 1801. In 1819 he inherited the title of Sixth Baronet of Wattlesborough and served as governors of both Carrickfergus, Northern Ireland and Jersey.

Black-hawk-wing: Mentioned as the "old-boyez" earlier in the poem. His one named appearance is in the role of wise old Native American sage at the end of canto XI. Not only does Black-hawk-wing's name sound the most American Indian of all the characters, the "aged priest" is an example of the Vanishing Indian trope made popular by American writers of the early to middle nineteenth century. His name, character and pattern of speech in canto XI is evidence of Huggins's open pastiche of American writings of the Native Americans. In Black-hawk-wing, the Vanishing Indian is symbolically imagined as the two aspects of Cooper's famous American Indian character Chingachgook, in *The Last of the Mohicans* and *The Pioneers*; first as the last of his people and second as an old man with nothing left to hope for except death.

OTHER CHARACTERS

Abercrombie: Lieutenant-General Sir Ralph Abercrombie, 1734–1801, commanded the British forces in the West Indies during the Napoleonic Wars, recapturing St Lucia, Grenada, St Vincent and Trinidad, where he served as governor in 1797. He died fighting in the Mediterranean.

Waroutie/Winnie. Two of Chetwayè's wives. Each gives a speech before being buried alive with his body at the beginning of canto VIII.

Clare/Greaves: Based on two slaves owned by Daniel Huggins. In a possible reference to Clare, Daniel discusses an old slave woman who nursed generations of Huggins's in his correspondence in Prichard's *Researches into the Physical History of Mankind*: "My father will be eighty-four years old in May next, and the negro woman who carried him about as a child is still living, and at the age of ninety-six enjoying good health, upright in figure, and capable of walking several miles."[92]

The Young Boyez: Carib priest who plays an important role in causing the Caribs to declare war. He ignores the warning given by Qualeva.

Victor Hugues (1762/1774–1826): French military leader of the forces in the Caribbean during the revolutionary and Napoleonic Wars. Hugues, described by some accounts as mixed-race, was a member of Robespierre's Jacobin party. He has remained, according to written histories in English, a mysterious figure. According to Harry Johnston, Hugues was born of poor parents in France and went to Guadeloupe as apprentice to a hairdresser, afterwards becoming innkeeper, master of a small sailing-vessel, and then lieutenant in the French Army.[93] Returning to France, he was elected a deputy to the National Assembly and attached himself to Robespierre, who in 1794 sent him as commissioner to Guadeloupe. Alan Burns says Hugues was a former innkeeper, and C.L.R. James, in his monumental study *The Black Jacobins*, makes two small references to Hugues, saying that he was "taken from his post as public prosecutor in Rochefort and sent to the West Indies".[94]

Qualeva: Huggins's invented demon god of the Caribs. Qualeva is the malevolent god who "reigns lord paramount of earth and air" (II, xxviii). He is the personification of the Soufrière volcano, as well as the "god of wrath and harm" (X, iv). It is Qualeva in the volcano who decides the Caribs' fate early on when the boyez is given several signs by him warning them not to engage in war against the British, which they choose to ignore. This warning is in the form of supernatural signs in the Crater Lake. Qualeva has no historical basis in Amerindian religion or beliefs. A wholly reliable source that identifies Qualeva as the god of the volcano or the spirit of malevolence within an Amerindian religion has not been found. While several varied sources support the knowledge that the Caribs believed in, and in some instances, deified both a supreme being and an evil spirit, there is little supporting evidence for Huggins's identification of this evil spirit as Qualeva. The name shows up once, in Sir William Young's *A Tour through the Several Islands of Barbadoes, St Vincent, Antigua, Tobago, and Grenada, in the Years 1791 and 1792*. Young's journal entry dates from 16 March 1792, when he visits his estate on Tobago, and calls on and makes note of "the radical words and language of the Indian red Charaibe (Louis)", the chief of a group of Caribs who, according to Young, escaped the persecution of the Black Caribs. Huggins would have understood this group to include Chatoyer and his people.[95] Young reads out twenty-one phonetically spelled Carib words, which Louis repeats back to Young in French in order to ascertain their meaning. The final word "Devil", translates into "qualeva".[96]

Major Alexander Leith: Based on a historical figure, although less is known about him than is known about Chatoyer, who he allegedly kills in combat on 14 March 1795. A memorial inscription placed under the main chandelier in St George's Cathedral, Kingstown reads: "Alexander Leith, Esq born 4th June, 1752 left Scotland his native Country in 1771 and died 13th February, 1798. He lived highly respected and beloved for his integrity and humanity and died most sincerely regretted. His death was occasioned by the great fatigue he endured during the Carib War in which as Colonel of the Militia he bore a distinguished part, the Carib chief Chattawae 'falling by his hand'."

Hiroona

An Historical Romance in Poetic Form

Reverend Canon Horatio Nelson Huggins

Original Foreword

As an act of filial remembrance and at the request of many friends, this poetic work, the humble effort of our dear father, has been published.

Its issue without any corrections or alterations, is as he left it when he died thirty-five years ago. It is therefore a posthumous work and many of the fine touches which may have been added, had he been spared to edit it, are unhappily not made.

Lottie & Evelyn Huggins
Trinidad, 1930.

Original Preface

The little island of St. Vincent is one of the Caribbean group in the West Indies. It is but 18 miles long by 11 broad and at the last census (1921) boasted a population of nearly 51,000 souls. The chief town is Kingstown with a population of about 5,300.

At the time when Columbus discovered the island (1498) it was inhabited by Carib Indians. These people were left in possession down to 1783 although Charles I. granted the island to the Earl of Carlisle in 1627. It was re-granted to Lord Willoughby in 1672. In 1779 the Island was surrendered to the French but was restored to Britain in 1783. In 1795 the Caribs, aided by the French, rebelled against the British rule, and after many conflicts, with varying fortunes, Sir Ralph Abercomby arrived with reinforcements and subjugated them. On 11 March, 1797, Caribs to the number of 5,080 embarked at Bequia and were deported, as a tribal nation, to Rattan Island in the Bay of Honduras.

St. Vincent is traversed from north to south by a chain of mountains, that rise in the volcano called the Souffrière to 3,000 feet. This volcano erupted in 1812 and 1902 with very disastrous effects, the volcanic ashes on the former occasion fell on the nearby islands within a radius of one hundred miles, whilst on the latter it erupted simultaneously with Mont Pelée, on Martinique, and caused 1,600 deaths.

The Indian name for St. Vincent was "Hiroon," which means "The Blessed," but for poetic euphony and "for endearment sake," as the author tells us, the word "Hiroona" has been substituted almost throughout the entire work.

The author, Canon Horatio Nelson Huggins, was born at St. Vincent, and in his earlier years heard and committed to memory the many stories of the Caribs as handed down by tradition. In later life, having the desire to perpetuate the memory of that ancient tribe, he set himself to the somewhat unusual task of doing so in poetic form, recording their many heathen practices, their dauntless, though savage bravery; the thrilling episodes of battles won and lost; the changes of fortune; and the final curse on their conquerors, pronounced by their last Chief; and, to lend a greater interest to the sometimes harrowing details, he weaves through the whole the love story of a beautiful Carib maiden, thereby adding charm to the recital of these incidents.

The poem has so often been favourably commended by those who were privileged to read it, that at length, after many years, the family have decided to have it published. As a descendant of the author I am diffident, yet proud, to assist in carrying out what would have been, no doubt, one of the greatest ambitions of his life.

Geo. F. Huggins [George Frederick Huggins]

Hiroona Discovered

I

The sky was clear, the air was mild,
And Heaven in kindliest aspect smiled
On tranquil seas; the light sea-bird
With sunlit wing but scarcely stirred
Few drowsy circles round the spot
From whence her scaly prey she'd got;
And scarce the flying-fish, with spring
In air-like flights on silver'd wing,
Light ripples o'er the surface threw,
So soft reflecting Heav'n's own hue.
The man-o-war, most gallant sight,
With moveless wing's majestic flight;
The tropic-bird, and albatross,
Which shun the seas when tempests toss,
And landward on prophetic wing
Of coming storm the tidings bring;
The pelican with gullet full,
And cormorant, and white-winged gull,
And other denizens of air,
All ignorant yet of man-made fear,
Were circling in the mid-day sun,
Content their morning meal was won.
The lumbering porpoises in troops,
A playful race, in sportive groups

With lazy plunge just turned in air.
And e'en the greedy shark was there,
The scourge and terror of the deep,
But milder then than now—Asleep,
And rocking with the wave he lay,
His fin just peeping into day.
The clear transparent sea with light,
Which poured from sun in noon-day height,
Was full. In gradient depths below,
In sun-illumined brilliance glow,
(Ablaze in every gorgeous hue
From molten gold to azure blue),
A thousand scaly forms of life
In peaceful rest, or playful strife.
And as the astonished eye passed through
One group, another came in view
In lower depths; and lower yet
The sheen and glow of others met
Th' unwearied eye, to view displayed
In living strata, grade o'er grade;
And ever where, beyond the view
The peerless light but just pierced through,
Some finny one would catch the beam,
And flash in momentary gleam.
  II
On scenes of life and peace like these
In sky, in air, in teeming seas,
Yon glorious orb would daily rise:
And ah! 'Twas surely Paradise
As yet in those primeval seas!
Not yet the keel of Genoese—
Grown now through new-born science bold,
In greed of fame and fabled gold,
Adrift from old exhausted world,
With sail to untried winds unfurled—
Had thrust profane intruding prow

O'er those fair seas, so scared now
To plenty and to solitude,
To waken with awakening rude!
  III
But now the fatal keels draw near
With freight of misery and despair,
To fray these islands of the sun
With darkest deeds that e'er were done,
Colon! Thyself a righteous man,
Ah! Could thine eye prophetic scan
The vista dark of coming years—
The wrongs, and agonies, and tears,
The black man's chains, the red man's ban,
That follow fast thy leading van—
Thyself, appalled, would surely shrink
As from some dreadful crime's dark brink;
Or, on thy knees, at least thy tears
Would mingle freely with thy prayers!
  IV
'Neath sky, which nowhere rival knows,
From seas surpassing beauty, rose,
In virgin robes of Nature dressed,
Hiroon, in Indian tongue "The Blessed",
The name a tenderer form would take,
"Hiroona", for endearment sake.
'Twas then the Heaven-sent month of May;
And sun, superb in cloudless day
In all imperial splendour dight,
The unpaled glory of his light
Poured down upon the lovely isle,
Which gleamed it back in sunlit smile.
  V
High mountains, wooded to the peak,
(With here and there a silvery streak,
That told of crystal stream, which lept[2]
One moment into light, then crept

Unseen to depths of gloom and shade
Of rock-hewn glen, or leafy glade,)
Would seem, with Nature's rarest grace,
To hold in loving arm's embrace
(Now opened wide, now closed again)
The shrinking vale, or facile plain,
While through those glens and round those hills
Soft music floats from murmuring rills.
There, loftier mountains Heavenward rear
The moss-clad range, or summit bare,
The while their granite feet they lave
In grateful cool of ocean's wave;
And here, dark rocks with one huge leap
Plunge down some fifty fathoms deep.
There, nestling trees in sheltered cove
Would meet in leafy roof above,
And deep luxurious shade would throw
O'er calm and placid tide below;
There, grassy knoll of velvet green,
With verge of feathery palm, is seen;
Or flowered carpet, richly gay
In Tropic sun's intensest ray.
And there, in miniature morass
O'ergrown with weeds and tall rank grass,
Some mountain-stream would idly end,
Unwilling yet with brine to blend!
And there the red flamingo[3] stalked,
Or blue or snowy gauldens walked.
There flitted humming-birds, ablaze
In emerald, ruby, or topaz:
Or there, the golden berries found,
The gaudy parrots screamed around;
Or hawk, with screeches shrill and clear,
O'erhead pierced through the quivering air.

VI

The bold Italian's searching eye
The signs of man could now descry;
Light curling smoke on hillside, seen
In faint blue cloud against the green;
And soon the frequent hut appeared.
There on some breezy hill-top reared,
Or here along the circling bay,
The scattered hamlet snugly lay
Beneath the bearded fig-tree's shade
By huge and columned branches made.[4]
Or there were groves of plantains grew,[5]
The single huts were peeping through
The giant fronds, or fields of maize,
The simple crops which Indians raise;
While, guardian over each low hut,
There waved the graceful cocoanut.
And all along the sandy beach,
But just beyond the flood-tide's reach,
Were corials, those light canoes,
Which handy Indians deftly use
Alike in calm or stormy sea,
Each hewn from out a single tree:
Protected from the scorching day,
Beneath a leafy branch each lay.

VII

The men themselves had fled to height
Of wooded hills, at startled sight
Of Colon's ships. No cravens they,
They soon stept boldly into day
To face the strange thing, friend or foe,
And meet their chance of weal or woe.
And soon the conch-shell's warning sound
Aroused the wakeful echoes round;
And soon the whoop and wild war-shout
From distant woods came answering out;

And now to every bluff and hill
The Indian files came crowding still.
All armed with weapons frail and few,
Yet fit for all the war they knew—
A bow, and arrow-heads of bone,
And tomahawk of smooth-hewn stone,
With shield of plaited leaves of palm
To guard the naked breast from harm;
With huge knarled club, and sword of wood,
And bamboo spear—they dauntless stood:
With hurtling stone and arrow's flight,
(Poor weapons for the coming fight!)
With bold war-shout and gesture brave,
They hurled defiance o'er the wave.
Alas! Hiroon, too eager far
To measure strength with Europe's war!
  VIII
Ay! Savages they surely were!
Yet man's own royal form they bare:
A fine and well-formed race, high-souled,
With love for kith and kin, and bold
To admiration to defend
Their hearth, to save or serve a friend.
Them Colon claimed, but claimed in vain,
For Holy Church, for conquering Spain.
As gage of right, and Spaniard's love,
As pledge of mission from above,
He sent resounding to the shore
The cannon's fulminating roar
And, terrified, the Caribs fled—
By mercy, or by prudence led,
He landed not; but gave command
To bear away from th' hostile land;
Then shook his sails to favouring breeze,
And wandered on to further seas.

IX

Ay! Go, Columbus, on thy fated way
Nor dream a nation's doom thou'st seal'd this day!
Go! Proud Civilization's pioneer,
And carve in new-found worlds a new career!
Yet know thy well-meant zeal, that led thee here,
Doth bode th' unmeasured grief, th' unnumbered tear!
O'er those fair lands shall havoc's deluge sweep;
And while recording Angels write they'll weep!
Mysterious fingers trace, as on the wall,
Spain's misused day of grace, and Spain's downfall
Alas! If willed, there's no retreating back,
And fast the hell-hounds follow in thy track
Dark horrors, from thy pious soul concealed.
To my prophetic eye are seen revealed:
Dark spectral forms, like phantoms of the night,
In weird procession sweep before my sight—
Some monsters, gluttoned, yet insatiate,
And others, victims of their lust and hate.

X

There mid-night murder prowls with blood-stained hands;
There stalks red war with gory reeking brand;
There Agony in forms unseen before.
In tears and sweat of blood at every pore;
There Panic, terror-struck, now rushes by;
There ghastly Famine stands with glaring eye;
There Manhood, pillaged from his native land,
And outraged Womanhood as chattels stand,
While Freedom, shackled, shrieks in wild despair,
And calls on silent Heaven in hopeless prayer.
There, sordid Greed in quest of Inca's gold,
For which his tarnished name the Spaniards sold!
There, preaching truths in Heaven's own sacred name,
Tonsured Hypocrisy, devoid of shame,
Lifts up on high the holy crucifix,
Then stoops on convert's feet slave-chains to fix!

There, most appalling spectres in the line,
(Say ye, ye wise, 'tis Heaven's decree divine?)
The wraiths of nations soon to be no more,
Whole peoples, doomed to dark oblivion's shore—
The races urged by some resistless fate
The stronger man the weak to extirpate.
And even where they've neither fought nor bled.
The robust white prevails, the weaker red
Succumbs, retires and vanishing, gives birth
To scoffing phrase, "Improved from off the Earth".
  XI
And now, in fierce contention for the spoil
Just pillaged from the lust-invaded soil,
Are Europe's blood-stained navies sweeping past.
With cannon-shattered hull and shivered mast!
And there, death-freighted rafts beneath the blaze
Of burning skies, and sun's unpitying gaze.
There, rakish privateers like falcons fly,
And trade of licensed theft and murder ply;
They scour for prey the now-polluted Main,
And sell their souls and reckless lives for gain!
And there, in yon secluded shallow cove,
Or there, in creek of tangled dark mangrove,
Those human sharks, the hellish pirates lurk:
Thence issue forth to urge their damnèd work,
To hoist their terror-flag to tainted breeze,
And carry death and havoc o'er the seas!
  XII
And where, O vaunted Freedom, now thy boast,
When lo! From ravaged Afric's bleeding coast
The cursed, thrice cursed, hell-sent slaver comes!
With human freight from plundered village homes?
See! Motionless, like stricken thing of death,
The laden slave-ship lies becalmed beneath
The blazing fires of Heaven, in burning air,
On glassy sea reflecting back the glare—

For days now sweltering there; and now but few
Of e'en her guilty, famine-stricken crew
Are left—By those now sits a spectre Death;
Himself, to snatch their last polluted breath;
While down beneath the battened hatch below,
In deep untold unutterable woe,
Poor wretches lie, as laid in living grave,
Denied e'en light, kind Heaven so freely gave!
I will not wring the bleeding heart to tell
The speechless woe that fills that man-made hell;
How shacked, starved, with darkness closed around,
In untold filth, with undressed festering wound,
The living, midst the dead now rotting there,
Lie gasping in corruption's poisoned air!
Can vengeance, patient, wait on wrongs like these?
Rise, Heaven! And sweep such demons from the seas!

 XIII

And see, on sunny plains where palm trees wave,
How men will use the power that Heaven ne'er gave!
See crouching negroes bend to shrink the blow
Of bull-hide thong, or lash of long Mahaut,[6]
Then lift their fettered hands, O Heaven, to Thee,
And ask for death that so they may be free!
Alas! Polluted seas and blood-stained isles,
In vain for you your endless summer smiles!
Alas! For other nations, filled with greed
Like thine, shall follow, Spain they guilty lead!

 XIV

What bring'st thou, Colon, here as gifts to these
Bright, gemmy isles, that bask in peerless seas?
Civilization, say? To elevate
The savage breast, and teach to emulate
The virtues, ay! Alas, and vices too,
Thou bringest from an old world to a new?
Give easier means to live man's little day,
Or e'er he moulder into kindred clay?

More joys to have, and more of ills to know;
A stronger, deadlier skill to strike a foe?
Alas! Thy higher culture's power is such,
That at its soft yet scathing, withering touch
(Like their own upas' soft but treacherous shade)
Their feebler life will shrink, their manhood fade;
And tribes and nations wither day by day,
Sad victims of mysterious decay;
Till swept from off the earth, to live at last
Alone in fading memories of the past.

  XV

Wilt bring philanthropy? I tell thee nay!
But dawn of Tyranny's own darkest day,
To bind on freeborn necks th' unwonted toil;
As slaves to till their own embondaged soil;
Then fill these fairy isles with other groans,
When Afric's exiled sons lay there their bones.
Religion? Nay! Mock not the sacred name!
Let Europe hide her face for very shame;
For every soul begot for Heaven's new birth
Then thousand perish off the weeping earth!

  XVI

Intrepid voyager! Such events shall roll
With onward rush beyond thy small control.
Perhaps, as in those vast Silurian ages,
(Of which in Earth's primeval rocky pages
We seem to read) some mighty deluge swept
O'er submerged continents; and these then slept
An æon; to wake with increased powers rife,
To teem with new and higher forms of life;
So 'twas by God's decree that human flood
O'erswept these isles and continents for good;
In lapse of rolling centuries to raise
A type of life and man of higher phrase:
If so, we deem 'twas Heaven's own gracious plan,
All wrongly worked by erring hand of man.

End of Introduction

Early History of St Vincent

I

Saint Vincent[7]—so the new-found isle
Columbus named—was left awhile
Untrod by stranger's foot; for years
Yet spared that avalanche of tears
And blood, that torrent deep and red
Which followed aye the Spaniard's tread;
Which swept fair isle and continent
Where'er his murderous footsteps went.
Meanwhile Hispaniola bled
From every pore; her life-blood shed
Like torrent of her tropic rains
Downpouring on her teeming plains;
For treachery, leagued with Hate and Lust,
First taught the guileless Cazique trust,
Then seized Destruction's bloodiest brand,
And wrought with red, relentless hand
Till that depopulated shore
Her slaughtered millions knew no more.
'Tis Spain's eternal foul disgrace,
A stain which time will ne'er efface;
Whose guilt, like Cain's won fadeless brand,
Is stamped by Heaven's recording hand
To bide the sure though lingering hour
Of vengeance' Own resistless power.

And o'er fair Cuba's palmy plain
The Invader dragged his tyrant chain,
And taught his brute, the fierce bloodhound,
To track the slave by dripping wound.
Now o'er the Aztec's Mexico,
Her smiling vales, and wide plateaux,
And City nestling on the lake,
Swept war with rapine in his wake.
And o'er the Eden-like Peru
Black murder's human vultures flew,
To gorge, by right of Papal gift—
O Heaven! Avenging arm uplift,
Chastise the sacrilegious claim
To kill and ravage in Thy name!
  II
While truthful History, sad, shamefaced,
In tears, with pen, reluctant, traced
These records dark, that blur her page,
And shame an else enlightened age—
At thought of which unhallowed deeds
E'en yet compassion, heart-rent, bleeds;
And Pity owns to shuddering Truth
She ne'er shed tear o'er sadder ruth,
Or darker crimes than these, that stain
Thy once most gallant Knighthood, Spain;
And honest Manhood burns with shame
To own with thee one kith and name—
Our happier isle, too small and poor
To tempt the plunderers to her shore;
Whose guard of warrior-sons most bold
For Spaniard's greed had war, not gold;
(Their greed was not by mercy curbed!)
Was left in peace and undisturbed.
  III
Her sons, and Autochthonic race,
(Whose stirp and origin to trace

Ethnology hath sought in vain
Throughout her broad, world-wide domain,)
Sole masters of their little world,
Not deck'd with gold, nor ring'd, nor pearl'd,
All ignorant of Mammon's power,
Lived on in Nature's simplest dower;
Their brief and careless span passed through
With pleasures simple, wants but few.
Born on, and dwelling by the shore,
And nursed midst ocean's ceaseless roar.
At home alike on land and sea,
Amphibious, they claimed to be
The children of the ocean-wave;
Their nation's Crêche some coral cave.

   IV

A wattled hut of roseau bands,
Well thatched with neat though savage hands;
A hammock-bed (both name and thing
From them did Europe learn and bring)
A hammock, slung from plate to plate;
A few flint-tools, a fishing-crate,
A bow and arrows, club and sword,
Rough bowls of calabash or gourd,
Or goblets, formed of earthenware
With skill in savage men most rare;
Tobacco tube of bamboo reed,
For fumes of rank narcotic weed;
And last not least, their loved canoe,
(Both weed and boat, to Europe new,
Soon found a facile way to please)
Their worldly all, their riches these!
They drank the beverage of the brook;
Their simple food the fish they took
With crafty hands and Indian skill
From open sea, or sparkling rill;
Luxuriant Tropic's starchy roots,

And Nature's own spontaneous fruits;
Or dove or parrot, won as game
With sling, or arrow's dext'rous aim;
Opossum,[8] crouched on leafy bow,
Or "Goutie,"[9] earthed 'mongst roots below;
Or "Guana,"[10] chased with nimble feet
From rocks, where Dare and Danger meet.

V

In grass-spun garments sparse and rude,
With stalwart limbs all free and nude,
They roamed through densest forest shade,
O'er wood-clad hill, or sunny glade;
Or climbed the mount's volcanic height,
Secure and safe by day and night.
No dangers hovered near: to fray
The night no noxious beast of prey,
By day no serpent in the grass[11]
With threatened death to all who pass.
Or, on the sea they loved, their day
In toil or sport was passed away;
Their rarest sport to quit their bark
For fearless combat with the shark.

VI

Midst ramparts dark of frowning wood
In every village, central, stood
A monster hut, where youth and age
Alternate met—for counsel sage
The one, to learn the other, came—
Hear legends of barbaric fame,
Or train the youthful arm to throw
The smooth sling-stone, or bend the bow
His share of food not his until
His shaft with Balearic skill,[12]
Shall pierce and strike it to the ground,
And practice be with triumph crowned.

VII

Dark mysteries passed within that hut
When youths were through their ordeals put.
Boy-babes were there baptized in blood,
In blood which welled in purple flood
From out the father's opened vein,
Who gloried in the deed and pain
Which thus his boy true warrior made,
Through sparks of his own soul conveyed.
And youths and braves, whose fiery souls
Would reach ambition's furthest goals,
There dared, and won the Chieftain's meed,
The right in battle-front to lead
Hiroona's sons in fierce attack
And victory o'er the Arrowack.[13]
That youth, whose hero-soul can bear,
In haughty conquest over fear
And mortal pain, the flames that burn
To very bone, or blade in turn
That tears his tortured flesh, and leaves,
Within a breast which scarcely heaves,
But half its life; And yet no groan,
No anguished sigh, no smothered moan,
No look, nor faltering sign, nor sound
To hard unpitying crowd around
The untold agony reveals,
Which yet in every nerve he feels—
That youth, who thus his manhood proves,
Midst chiefs and giants henceforth moves,
Is leader of his tribe proclaimed,
And 'mongst his country's heroes named.

VIII

One strangely fierce and mystic rite
Endowed the youth with conquering might.
While low, weird chant of medicine-man,
With wild refrain from all the clan,

Bestirred and fanned the fierce war-flame,
And sent it leaping through the frame,
A Boyez—so their priests were called—
With rites enough to have appalled
The weak, with forehead crowned with leaf
Of Manchineel,[14] approached the chief,
And smeared his naked limbs with oil,
Of last war's raid the horrid spoil—
An unguent drawn from fatty brain
And flesh of foes in battle slain!
With limbs by this to pain inured,
Unflinching fierceness this insured,
The chief no fear, no mercy knows,
The scourge and terror of his foes.

  IX

When favouring winds in season blew,
They'd launch the well-filled war-canoe,
With souls by hero-dreams inspired,
By venture's restless ardour fired;
Would skirt the Caribbean chain,
Or dare the terrors of the Main,
With nought but trusty oar to sweep
The seas, and cleave the swelling deep,
For scourge of war and plunder raid.
Alas! They knew not peaceful trade:
They thought—and who can greatly blame,
When cultured men have thought the same?
That might is right, and that for prey
Before the strong the weaker lay.
When fates propitious hailed them back
From slaughter of the Arrowack,
A human freight, alas! They bore,
Purchased from Hayti's ravaged shore;
The maids to slavery's doom consigned.
The men for sadder fate designed,
When morn of gala day should rise

For feast of human sacrifice.
Through cannibals they were, at least,
'Tis known, in this their horrid feast
It was not thirst for human blood
That chose this most unnatural food:
By superstitions dark down-trod,
They thought t'appease their demon-god;
But Nature taught them to abhor
The flesh of victims slain in war.

  X

Thus, since had passed those ships of Spain
Like meteors onward to the Main,
A century fled; none dared intrude
On Hiroon's sacred quietude;
And while events were rushing fast
Elsewhere, here tranquil years were passed.
Her sons in lifetime basked their day;
In death in peaceful graves they lay.
They lived free as the air they breathed;
Their soil to sons as free bequeathed,
Secure in their unconquered isle,
Where none dare tread with foot hostile.
But thus it was not aye to be!
There came a day, by stern decree
Of Destiny—(that Hand that guides,
As ebb and flow of ocean's tides,
So tides and waves of human life—)
The peaceful Isle awoke to strife.

  XI

Adrift from far-off, unknown seas,
On wings of some ill-omened breeze,
Was cast on Hiroon's sacred ground
An alien race.[15] They welcome found
As friends; but this in evil hour;
For soon they rose to strength and power.
Of darker hue they were, and bold

With passions fierce and uncontroll'd.
A strife of races then began,
In which prevailed the darker man.
He won for home and domicile
The leeward portion of the isle,
The tranquil sea, the placid bay,
The West where sleeps retiring day:
The Caribbee, to instinct true,
To bolder windward side withdrew,
Where winds and waves are strong and free,
And sea asserts his majesty;
And where, to greet their sacrifice,
From out his depths the mornings rise.

  XII

Then came a darker day of fear,
The bold and outlawed Buccaneer,
(An exile for his crimes from home,
Or led by reckless choice to roam,
To flaunt his pirate flag unfurled,
And lift free-lance against the world,)
There sought and found a safe retreat,
Beyond the Warships' usual beat:
Then Hiroon learnt, through sword and flame,
To fear and hate the white man's name.
At length from France's courtly race,
Won by her beauty and her grace,
There came some bold adventurous bands,
As settlers to her virgin lands.
They claimed th' invaders only right,
The barbarous claim of greater might;
They seized the lands, yet feigned to buy
With worthless toys and trinketry;
Yet came to cultivate the soil
With honest labour's fruitful toil;
And thus a truer wealth unfold
Than silver mine, or nugget gold.

XIII

But grasping greed was never still!
Not long content to simply till
The field, which Honesty had bought,
For more than due the Frenchman sought,
The Caribs, warlike, strong and proud,
With mutterings ominous and loud,
And flinging fierce defiance, viewed
The stranger on their soil intrude:
Flashed forth the spirit of their sires,
And Fury fanned the kindling fires—
Alas! The cannon's echoing boom
Presaged a valiant nation's doom!
The Carib's broad, but naked breast,
His heaviest sword, his arrows best,
Though steeped in poisonous manchineel,
Or winged with flame, to gun and steel
Opposed, which hurl their death so far,
Were toys and playthings for such war.
Yet Frenchmen found the Indian brave,
Too proud and strong for serf or slave;
And oft in fierce and doubtful fight
They felt the Carib warriors' might;
While they, in multitudes untold,
Their lives, but not their freedom sold.
At length by treaty bonds of peace
Th' unequal strife was made to cease:
The Carib saved his manhood still;
He kept his hold on mount and hill,
And, what he loved and treasured most,
His fatherland, the windward coast:
He left his foes the leeward shore,
Long lost to alien race before.[16]

XIV

Anon, as rolling years advance,
And England's navies follow France

With war all round the world, where'er
Her bold pursuing ships can steer.
Hiroon was doomed to feel the throes
Of war thus waged by alien foes;
Now held and garrisoned by one,
Now, spoil of war, by other won.
On every sea-bluff cannon frowned,
And wakeful sentry walked his round;
And every hill and valley knew
How gory war his victims slew;
Knew every bay the thunder's roar
Of privateer, or man-of-war.
Thus years with varying war rolled on.
Till England final victory won.

  XV

The while these giant nations strove,
Our Caribs unsubjected throve.
Three hundred years their vigorous race
Had looked the white man in the face,
And had not quailed before his glance;
Scarce shrank before his slow advance.
Their ancient tribal feuds had burnt
Their embers out: The tribes had learnt
Their interests; and dread of France,
And healing Time, and circumstance
Had o'er their feud a victory won,
And two had welded into one.
The darker men, the younger race,
But else to older Red the young
Had given way—had learnt their tongue,
Their own forgot, had learnt to claim
The Carib rites and Carib name.
And (though it brought them doubtful dower,)
Civilization's silent power,
And Frenchmen's culture, side by side
Their savagery, had modified

Some fiercer rites of other days,
But yet their manhood could not raise:
(Without religion never could!)
They learnt much evil, little good;
Some few French words slow Time had taught
To clothe the new idea and thought.

  XVI

From rocky ridge of Byëra,[17]
To surf-resounding Owia,
And Tarraty[18] embathed in spray,
Their Chieftains held their sovereign sway
Where granite rocks are rent in twain
And awful terror holds domain;
Where savage glens, like jaws of death,
Are lost in horrid depths beneath;
And mountains rise high over head,
Where scarce the foot of man can tread;
And where in deep and gloomy wood
Grim vengeance seems to lurk for blood;
Where spirit of the Souffrière bird[19]
In witching notes is faintly heard,
Mysterious echoes fill the air,
And danger bristles everywhere—
There, where no feet e'er freely trod,
Abode, they thought, their dreaded god;
And then those wilds would furnish sure
Retreat, and for their braves secure
Strong fastness in war's adverse day,
To hold pursuing foes at bay.

  XVII

They made no friendships; native pride
And hate all overtures defied.
The patriot flame ne'er ceased to burn
Within their injured breasts; they'd spurn
To give or take the sheltering roof,
But sternly, proudly, held aloof:

Their freemen's right would ne'er forego,
Nor cease to deem the intruder foe;
Save when their great sea-lore, and craft
Of perfect boatmanship, (which laughed
To scorn the heavier English skill,
And Afric' slave's oar heavier still,)
O'ercame all feeling else; then pride
Beheld itself with thrift allied.
They shipped the English tuns on board
Their fleets of heaving billows moored,
On which could live no English boat,
Where nought but Carib skiff would float.
And thus their skill on th' ocean wave
To culture's fruitful labours gave
Those rich, but wave-beat coasts, till now
All profitless for hoe or plough.
'Twas thus alone the Carib sold
His toil; but took the planters' gold
To buy his powder, gun, and shot;
The coming vengeance ne'er forgot!
  XVIII
Their ancient gods they worshipped still:
No feet, "so goodly on the hill,"
That "bring the Gospel" news, had trod
Their soil, to tell of Christ and God;[20]
But seeds of alien vices sown
Grew fast, and mingling with their own,
Produced fresh faults, and crimes not few,
And bred diseases foul and new.
With white-man's war familiar grown,
With skill not far beneath his own,
And sturdy courage quite as good,
They handled Europe's tools of blood.
Sometimes their warlike aid was sought,
And gold their wild alliance bought;
And oft, with savagery untamed,

By real or fancied wrong inflamed,
Marauding forays boldly made,
Or prowled in murderous midnight raid;
And oft would startled tidings come
To fray the peaceful settler's home;
And oft at eve the tale was told
That made the shuddering blood run cold,
And oft to hush her child, the dame
Would use the dreaded Caribs' name.
  XIX
When, part of England's diadem,
Hiroon, a small but glittering gem,
Had sparkled in Britannia's crown
Till thirty tranquil years had flown;
Then Frenchman's envy, Indian's hate,
Dark passions close confederate,
Aroused the sleeping war. The French
Had given the world a mighty wrench;
Their monarch slaughtered, God denied,
But Lust and Reason deified,
Had Terror's bloodiest reign restored,
Decreeing myriads to the sword;
And scattered seeds of discord far,
To ripe in universal war.
To these fair isles, by evil chance,
One of those monster-sons of France
(To whom her agonies gave birth,
To be hell-demons here on earth,)
Had come to Hugues,[21] whose cursèd name
Almost excels his master's fame,
The great Arch-demon, Robespierre.
He sent his emissaries here
To scatter seeds of hate. To hale
Old England's flag, and vilely trail
It in the dust, the Frenchman thought;
The Carib for his tool he bought,

And held before his patriot eyes
Restored Hiroona for his prize.
Then sleeping war arose once more
And deluged deep the isle with gore.
 XX
And now by long and devious path,
My verse hath reached the point that hath,
From outset been the minstrel's goal
From whence his story to unroll
Of tragic war and desperate strife,
Which wrecked at last a nation's life.
Sure o'er the wreck recording Truth
Will drop the gentle tear of ruth.

End of Canto I

MUTTERINGS OF COMING WAR

I

From rugged mountain's foot and easy plain,
E'en down to wide Atlantic's surfy main,
(To where his restless, ever-rolling waves
Break round Hiroona's coasts and sea-worn caves)
In gentle lines of graceful beauty glides.
Abrupt there rises thence, with bold steep sides,
A single hill, like tower that stands alone,
Or islet-rock from open sea upthrown.
But this no barren steep: With verdure clad
It rose, and ever pleasing aspect had,
A range of lofty mountains stood around;
Anon in smiles, anon in gloom they frowned.
There Ocean spread before the well-pleased eye
And arc of far horizon swept the sky—
Most beautiful that panoramic view,
The hills so brightly green, the sea so blue,
The sky so exquisitely clear and bright,
With fleecy clouds so soft on pinions light.
While morn brought balmiest breath from over sea,
The even brought mountain-breeze so cool and free!
A spot for lover's choice: When there to dwell
Came two, "The Happy Hill," they named it well.[22]

II

But in the pathway of the storm it lay;
Yet scarce the Tempest lingered on its way,
As wildly in the pride of strength it flew
To genial heights and peaks of Morne Garou.[23]
Ah! How the big loud thunder round the wold
"In scale of Heaven's own diatonic rolled!"
And how the rushing winds hurled by and roared,
And rains from Heaven's now broken cisterns poured!
Black clouds on wings of terror seemed to fly,
And in great rolling masses hurtled by;
And how the lightning, almost blinding sight,
That darkness cleft with streaks of living light!

III

'Twas there this bard was born, 'twas there he passed
His boyish years, too happy long to last;
And there, in boyish ventures, often found
Or lying loose, or bedded in the ground,
Old Carib tools and weapons rough of stone,
And even time-worn bits of human bone;
And oft the leaden ball, that told of days
More recent, and of still more, deadly frays.
And tales of Carib times and legends wild—
That lore so fascinating to a child!—
Oft told to guests around the festive board,
Were heard, and deep in childhood's mem'ry stored.

IV

The hill in time of war was stronghold fort,
Impregnable; in peace the fond resort
Of youth and revelry. In darker hour,
When gloomy danger o'er the Isle would lour,
There wary chief and grey-haired sage would meet,
And dark designs of threatening Harm defeat.
A sacred hut the narrow summit crowned;
Beneath the brow few straggling cots lay round.
In one a boyez, hoary-headed, dwelt,

Who daily to returning sunrise knelt;
While waving fronds of two huge grugru trees[24]
Flung round the muttered prayer to morning breeze.
   V
'Twas there, while o'er yon Souffrière's ruddy crest
The wearied sun was settling down to rest,
Nine Carib chiefs for great war-council bound,
Had met in circle, seated on the ground,
All sat save one, Chetwayè[25] stalwart chief,
Of height gigantic, strength beyond belief,
With flattened brow, to art not nature due
(For Carib infants such their usage, grew
With brow between two tightened boards compressed)
And savagery in every line expressed.
Away superfluous clothing he had flung;
On naked breast a silver gorget hung,
The gift of William, England's sailor-prince:
The gift retained, the pledge forgotten since.[26]
   VI
With foot set firm on rough-hewn block of wood,
From which he just had sprung, erect he stood.
His hawk-wing plume was waving in the wind,[27]
His long black hair 'scaped trailing down behind;
His muscles huge with every movement played;
With one hand clenched on hilt of naked blade.[28]
And one arm stretched extended to its length,
He stood, a grand embodiment of strength.
"They come," he said: his quick instinctive ear
Had caught a bugle note, though far yet clear;
"The Frenchmen come! Now, Caribs, play your part,
And meet the cunning Frenchman's art with art.
Command yourselves; let all their seats retain;
Let no one speak—let silence hold domain."
His seat resumed, his eagle-eye swept round,
Till every voice was hushed, and every sound.

VII

At length the sound of drums and bugles shrill
Came mingling up the pathway round the hill;
And then with flag of truce in far advance,
And waving high the tri-color of France,
The strangers come emerging into view,
An embassy. To Hugues' blood-thirst 'twas due—
That Hugues who, though the outward form he wore
Of men, the heart of savage beast he bore.
No hands than his were stained with deadlier dye;
'Gainst none shall blood of vengeance louder cry;
In day that comes when all shall have their meed.
And they the whirlwind reap who sowed the seed!
Fair Guadaloupe he'd just o'erwhelmed with wave
Of blood, the patriot blood he'd sworn to save!
Some British prisoners also wounded lay,
And sick in crowded hospital: they pray
For medicine, food, and room for stifling breath;
His answer is a warrant for their death!
Alas! For France's once chivalric name,
And pride of martial glory turned to shame!
Her honour's shield by craven deeds now gored,
And murder-stained her sword! Once gallant sword,
It struck not save in Honour's cause till then.
But butchers children now, and wounded men,
And gorges horrid feast, unknown before,
Of infant's brains and pregnant women's gore!
And here to work his diabolic ends,
His emissaries hither Hugues now sends—
Would Hiroon's sons to bootless war beguile,
Set murder rampart o'er a peaceful isle;
Would pile the slain in useless hecatomb,
And hurl a trusting people to its doom.

VIII

No eye smiled welcome; and no sign they gave
(Still silent sat the chieftain's stern conclave;)

That they were conscious of the slow approach
Of strangers who with foot profane encroach
Upon their sacred hill, whence, heretofore,
The foot that dare'd encroach came forth no more!
No curious head is turned aside to gaze,
Through, every eye the scene askance surveys.
Their presence seems so utterly ignored,
The astonished Frenchmen hesitate; no word
Is spoke until they reach the silent ring.
The envoy silence broke, "I greetings bring,
Chetwayè chief, and all this noble group,
From brother chiefs in France and Guadaloupe."
  IX
The chief had lived his boyhood's years among
The French, and fairly spoke their fluent tongue:
And when the envoy spoke, he raised his eyes
With cunning look of well-assumed surprise.
He bade the Frenchmen halt by wave of hand,
And still outside the mystic circle stand.
And then, obedient to his silent nod,
The clumsy image of a demon-god,
(A limbless thing of clay, most rudely wrought,)
From out the hut the grey-haired boyez brought
With toil, and placed erect before the door.
For Caribs deemed it needless to adore
The Kindly Father God, *Tamousi* called,
Regardless of gifts; but bowed appalled
Before the powers of Harm, which seemed to reign
Supreme in storm and darkness, death and pain;
And thus by false, degrading terrors cowed,
Before the demon-god *Qualeva*, bowed—
His mischief powers they sought to deprecate,
Yet not the Father Spirit supplicate.
With fruit and flowers before the image placed,
The Caribs deemed themselves now safe, and graced
To meet their foreign guest with confidence.

Thus then the chief began the conference;

 X

"The Frenchmen send us greetings; this is well!
We would be friends; but lest some charm or spell,
Some jumbie,[29] ghoul, or demon of the air
Be working round us, by your God now swear,
No thought of Carib hurt hath brought you here."
The Frenchman answered—not without a sneer.
For, child of monster Revolution, he,
From "Superstition" claiming to be free,
Had effaced God, as far as mortals can;
The Carib was in faith the better man—
The Frenchman said, "On honour I declare,
S'il plait, by what men call their God I swear,
That sacred friendship brought us to your isle,
And in our hearts no treachery lurks no guile."
Chetwayè rose, "Your thoughts now, chieftains, tell";
A murmur round the circle went, "'Tis, well!"

 XI

The use of words to hide the mind's intent,
(That mask to eloquence by treachery lent)
Was art beyond to simple Caribs' ken:
"Yea" still was "Yea" to such untutored men;
And deeper, subtler treachery scarce knew they
Than panthers use to circumvent their prey.
To thrive, the lie a soil more cultured needs:
It is not one of untrained Nature's weeds;
In Art-made soil it strikes its vigorous root,
And bears its upas crop of baneful fruit—
The vice of cultured, not of savage man;
Ye moralists, explain it as ye can!
Chetwayè feared no foe of human kind;
'Twas fears of demon-craft possessed his mind;
But blunt, and offhand in his savagery,
And stranger to refinement of a lie,
He took at once, as offered without guile,

The Frenchman's Oath and answered with a smile
"Then welcome, Frenchman, to Hiroona's land!
As pledge of friendship give me now thy hand
And sit thou here, where chieftains only sit;
Your errand say: we will consider it."
 XII
The priest (full well he knew the chieftain's mood
Had brought another block of Almond wood
Within the ring; a grass-wove mat he set
Thereon; and there Chetwayè placed Barbette.
Religion's code had long fore-planned that seat:
It formed the mystic ring of *ten* complete.
None else could venture there: it ill had fared
If foot, o'er bold, to cross that ring had dared,
Aloof and far, the followers stand around,
Or fling their idle limbs along the ground.
Alas! Hiroon! 'Twas done in evil hour:
Thou'rt helpless now in crafty tempter's power!
 XIII
Barbette then rose—a fortune's soldier he,
Yet cursed with gift of fatal fluency
Of honied words to sway the fickle mind
Of vain Parisian mob; no less to find
To simpler Carib hearts a ready way;
To treachery of his art to easy prey!
Barbette declaimed with soft persuasive tongue,
While on his words absorbed Attention hung.
Unbounded love for Hiroon he pretends;
Protests the French had ever been her friends;
Had never robbed her lands in days of eld,
But only what her Caribs sold had held,
And held by double right—at first had bought
At Red men's hands, and when the dark men fought
Against the red, and won the doubtful day,
Had been compelled at arrow's point to pay
Again. Their settlements had ne'er been traced

Beyond the boundary lines which treaties placed.
Not so the grasping Englishman had dealt
With them; no such punctilious honour felt.
The Frenchman's cultured lands they'd won in fight
Then claimed the Caribs' untrod soil by right
Of war; and dared those lands to seize and use,
Which Frenchmen never owned, so could not lose.
Then drove their pillaged tribes from Calliaqua
Back step by step to lines of Biëra.

  XIV

His soft but treacherous periods then proceed
(The Caribs drinking all with fatal greed,
As spell'd by witch's eye, or wizard's wand)
T'enlarge on Hiroon's wrongs at England's hand;
Till facts by prestidigitating touch,
Where mingled little truth with falsehood much,
Were conjured into shapes so strange and new,
Hiroon herself had never dreamt nor knew.
The Caribs saw their Island's features changed;
O'er all her glens and dales, (where once had ranged;
The sisters Peace and Freedom hand in hand,
And found content all through the Mother-land)
Saw shadows of some awful presence brood,
May be of Death, or worse, of Servitude;
And Hiroon's fair and whilom smiling brow
Deep lined with woe and gloomed with sorrow now—

  XV

They saw, or war with England to the knife,
Or slow Decay's more fatal scathe—their life
By English life in all directions crossed;
Their country's rites and customs changed or lost;
Their gods dethroned; their very manhood crushed
(A cheek less bronzed by crime at this had blushed!)
Their Nation's freedom gone; their choicest lands
Despoiled; their tribes, (erst numerous as the sands
On Ocean's beach and lords of Ocean's main,

As far as sweeps th' Antilles' Island chain
From North to South,) like captured hawks in cage
Which lean at last to tame their useless rage,
In-barred in this one island and confined,
They chafe indeed, but still a prison find.
And through diseases all unknown before,
And ills their fathers' manhood never bore,
They see their millions shrink to thousands now,
And Hiroon, once the proud, unconquered, bow
To yoke of England's king.
  XVI
                Such words went straight
To depths of Caribs' soul, where slumbering hate
Lurks low; as lurks the dreaded Mapapee[30]
Beneath the roots of some old forest tree,
Asleep; and yet its quick alertness such,
That instant on the first light, springy touch
Of some poor hunted deer, or lapo's feet,
That leap unconscious past its dark retreat,
It lifts its horrid head, as though it sprang
From out the earth; unsheathes its angry fang,
Through which the deadly poisons swelling rise;
And hissing out its rage, through burning eyes
Sends fury flashing far in every glance;
With forkèd tongue, as though quivering lance,
Far flings at every glance the threat of death,
And chokes the air with poison of its breath:
Then caution bars the interrupted way,
And dogs and startled huntsmen stand at bay.
  XVII
Barbette watched well the Caribs' kindling eyes,
And marked with glee the slumbering demon rise;
But deemed it wise to lay it for awhile,
So changed his ground with ready tact and guile.
In France, he said, a mighty change had run
Its matchless course: her favoured sons had won

For wronged and suffering man an era new;
While round the world the hopeful Gospel flew,
That man is free from slavery's cursèd ban,
And equal brother with his fellow man;
And *now*, from vicious laws of tyrants freed,
And terrors of an antiquated creed,
('Twas so he termed the Christian Faith!) *men live.*
The while Fraternity and Freedom give
To man's down-trodden energies new birth;
They cast oppression prostrate to the earth,
And fat Hypocrisy and strutting Pride,
Which rough-shod o'er the low-born crowd would ride;
They banish Need and Want from out the world;
And having Wealth and Rank and Lordship hurled
From off their long usurped and gilded throne,
To every man give manhood all his own;
And thus the Golden Age, at length begun,
Shall last while Time's unending eyeless run!
And now, redeemers of the human race,
The French go forth on glorious work of grace,
To give the nations still enslaved around
The Freedom and the Light themselves have found.

XVIII

A splendid dream! But vainly wise, ye fools!
Not such accursèd means, and not such tools,
As ye in bold and vaunted Science used,
With right and wrong in medley wild confused,
Shall Wisdom, in Her own good time, employ
To usher in the coming peace and joy;
And prove at last, in Heaven and Earth made new,
Man's noblest aspirations more than true!

XIX

"Those English"—so the soft persuasion ran—
"Those English are chief hindrance of our plan,
The foes alike of progress, God and man;
They spend their nation's gold, and wield her might

To stay the onward march of conquering right.
They meet us everwhere as stubborn foes;
On continents they step by step oppose
Our way, and ancient tyrannies uphold
With armed battalions bought with lavish gold;
And where a craft can float, where'er the breeze
Can waft a sail, they meet us on the seas!

XX

We French detest them with a mighty hate;
You suffering Caribs ought to know as great!
With many-handed outrages you they've wronged,
Your rights betrayed with falsehood many-tongued
Have robbed your lands, and here imprisoned keep
Your freeborn tribes impenned like flocks of sheep;
And aim at shackling you, the free, the brave,
With bonds like Yorouba or Congo slave!
They send you preachers; trust them not! They're spies
The worst of foes are those in friendship's guise.
Amongst the nations, England's name is this,
'Perfidious Albion,' uttered with a hiss!

XXI

And now, brave Caribs, hither we have come
To give back freedom to your island home;
To make you free as Frenchmen are to-day:
Your English tyrants help you drive away;
Cast off your servitude's ignoble chain;
Give back your own, and make you men again!
We seek no gain: by Friendship's sacred laws
We've come to aid you in your patriot cause;
Your warrior sons to marshal, and to train
With equal skill of war to wage campaign
With England's best-trained troops successfully;
And arms and furniture of war supply—
And more; to ask as boon, (and give you thanks)
A brother's place beside you in the ranks.
With you all England's vaunted powers we'll dare,

Your conflicts and your coming triumphs share;
Our blood with yours shall mingle as we bleed—
Guns, soldiers, ammunition, all you need,
All lavishly supplied from France's stores,
E'en now the winds are bearing to your shores.
We'll meet our foes with more than equal powers;
And soon shall Victory's pæan shouts be ours;
And never shall our march of triumph cease,
Until the vanquished English sue for peace.
Our only terms of truce shall be, 'Restore
Your spoils, and quit this land for evermore!'
  XXII
Unless to these our worsted foes agree,
At bayonet's point we'll drive them to the sea,
Hiroona in her might of wrath shall rise;
With aid of France's sons, her true allies,
Shall hurl the hated English from her strand,
And, wiping from her now-polluted land
The English occupancy; now her shame,
Exterminate them; till their very name
Shall linger in your children's days at last
Alone in old men's memories of the past!
And then, our work of liberation done,
Your Isle reconquered, and your freedom won,
We'll leave you to your own; but o'er the sea
From yonder sister isle of Sainte Lucie,
Your life renewed will foster, and will guard;
To watch your nation's growth our sole reward.[31]
  XXIII
And now, great chief and friend, I pray you rise.
I've heard the far-famed prowess of your eyes.[32]
There stand the blue-green hills of Sainte Lucie,
Look well, and tell me what you yonder see."
He rose, and measured with his gaze awhile
The double-coned and Sugar-loafèd isle.
The isle was more than twenty miles away,

But clear in beams of evening's light it lay—
The rain had fallen much that morn, but clear
And soft was now the evening atmosphere;
The isle seemed floating nearer with the tide;
Through lens of densen'd air much magnified,
With every vestige gone of cloud and haze.
Chetwayè looked with keen yet careless gaze,
Expecting little; and indeed no more
Across the leagues, that stretched from shore to shore,
Than crested billows rolling slow between,
Could be by common eyes unaided seen.
But soon, with start and sudden shout, that rang
With many echoes round the hill, he sprang
Upon a rock that furthest view commands;
And making telescope with both hands,
"I see" he cried, "along yon coast I see
A fleet of ships; and count them, three times three—
And from the hills a frequent, glittering light
Like lightning flash at times, it gleams so bright."
   XXIV
His hand with frantic gestures Barbette grasped,
And, wild with French ecstatic joy, he clasped
Him to his breast, "I give thee joy, my friend!
"Those ships are ships of war; they hither bend
Their heaven-directed course from Guadeloupe:
Deliverance comes at last! Our eagles swoop
Upon their English prey, as though from far
They'd sniffed the carnage dire of coming war.
But till your passive or your warlike views
They learn, beneath yon sheltering coast they'll cruise,
Beyond the reach and sight of England's fleets.
The moment that our proffered friendship meets
Acceptance, they will spread resistless wing,
On favouring winds exulting forth will spring;
The foe they'll vanquish on the lands, then sweep
His vaunted warships from their native deep.

Those flashes on yon distant cliffs, which seem
Like lightning sparks, they are the bayonets' gleam
Of marshalled troops of France, that line the hill,
Manouv'ring there in usual evening drill."
  XXV
Till now, by sternest self-control repressed,
No passing thought by smile or frown expressed;
The Carib chiefs had sat; but now a change
Most sudden seized the group, complete and strange—
Like pent up waters of some dam or pool
In upland glen, which lie all still and cool
And innocent beneath the grateful shade
By hanging rocks and spreading branches made;
And vales, and glens, and meads below, meanwhile
Secure in peace, in happy sunlight smile:
When sudden bursts the barrier frail which held
The stream—perchance some tree by woodmen fell'd
Which spanned the gorge from side to side, and then
Some fall of earth had dammed the narrow glen—
The barrier bursts, and lo! With one huge leap
The placid waters spring, and wildly sweep
Before them every vestige of restraint,
And every mass which makes a moment's feint
To bar their way; then down the glen they pour,
And mad in fury, rage and tumult roar.
E'en rocks and tree and helpless beast are borne
Through yawning gulf, erstwhile the peaceful vale,
To cumulate the morrow's mournful tale.
  XXVI
E'en so, the Caribs, in whose stolid soul
All passion seemed fast bound in stern control
Of coldest apathetic self-command,
As sudden burst through every bar and band.
All grave decorum gone, their council broke
At once; at once their slumbering furies woke.
They sprung upon their feet; their weapons flashed

And leapt in air, in wild war-dance they clashed;
With shouts they filled the welkin high; they gnashed
Their teeth with hideous sounds; with knives they gashed
Each man his own and brother's quivering flesh
'Cross breast and arms, and not skin-deep; till fresh,
And not by drops but fast in flowing flood
There gushed the swelling torrent of red blood.
The reeking blades each lifted to his lips,
And lapped the horrid stream with frequent sips;
And by that tasted blood each chieftain swore,
His blade should fatten soon on English gore!
Inhuman rite! Yet scarce more barbarous held
Than orgies fierce and savageries of eld,
When Norsemen Vikings worshipped Tew and Thor,
And wrought their souls to fever heat of war.

  XXVII

Chetwayè stood aloof; his stronger mind
In nobler mould was cast, and more refined,
More trained to measure facts, the future scan,
And meet approaching fate with counter plan.
The wild proposals which the Frenchman brought,
Had seized and filled his mind with anxious thought;
And while he weighed the peril with the gain,
Some cautious doubts perplexed his throbbing brain:
His nation on a dread volcano's brink,
He only saw the void, and paused to think!
Fair auguries he sought ere answer made
For peace or war; and lo! From deepening shade
Of grim Souffrière and gloomier Morne Garou
Two companies, approaching fast, now drew
His quick attention—first some women, led
By one who fiercely strode some yards ahead.
Well known at glance, Nannette the amazon,[33]
Of those dark glens the dreaded denizen;
The others men—as thought good news they'd got
They came in Indian file at Indian trot.

XXVIII

To Souffrière's sacred summit they had been,
O'er rocks and steeps; where scattered wreck is seen
Of dread Qualeva's wildest work; and where
He reigns lord paramount of earth and air.
There, midst the splintered crag and horrid gorge,
He sets his thunder-bolt and lightning's forge.
Where shattered mountains part with riven sides,
And leave the yawning gulf between, there rides
Qualeva on the whirlwind and storm,
With clouds and mist wrapped round his awful form.[34]

XXIX

Beyond, and deep beneath the loftiest range
Of Mount Souffrière (a sight both fair and strange)
A lovely placid lake there lay, and slept
In deep repose. But not so once, when lept
Volcanic fires from out the nether world,
Immensurate, and half a mountain hurled,
In air as though 'twould strike th' astonished sky!
When ceased at last the throes of agony,
And those dread fires in slow subsidence died,
Deep down the disembowelled mountain's side
There lay a crater, horrid, huge, and fell,
And sulphurous, like opened gates of hell![35]

XXX

Time sped, till gentle Nature's healing hand
Had swept o'er all her more than magic wand—
The headlong precipice with sharp, clear brink,
From which the very eye would shuddering shrink;
The crags, which everywhere in wildest freak
That rage of fire had flung; the splintered peak—
Had Nature moulded these and softened those
To gentler lines and angles of repose.
The blackened rocks she'd clothed in softest green;
Where chasms remained they scarcely could be seen:
Her hand had flung across the leafy bridge,

Which deftly spanned the chasm from ridge to ridge.
Meanwhile the depths with limpid waters filled
From loftiest skies and purest clouds distilled;
Till thither Peace and Beauty chanced to roam,
And, liking well the spot, had made it home;
And Peace reposed and Beauty safely slept
Where mountains once had burned, and flames had lept!

  XXXI

Yet once those fires from sleep of ages woke,
From gneissoid depths and granite prison broke;
And bursting through their subterranean caves,
To hissing vapours turned the frigid waves.
When all had lapsed once more to quietude
A cone of sulphur, high and golden-hued,
The centre of the lake was seen to fill,
While lay around the waters deep and still.
So peace and Beauty came and dwelt once more,
And found there charms e'en greater than before;
Yet charms for weak-souled man of slight avail,
When Superstition dragged its serpent-trail,
And laid its slimy coils in the fair spot,
And o'er the whole its dread possession got.

  XXXII

Qualeva, demon dark and terrible,
Fierce wielder of the powers of earth and hell,
And havoc-maker both in sea and air,
Was thought for rest to seek retirement there.
That sulphurous cone was thought his chief delight;
And from its peak across, at fearful height
Above the mere, to jutting rock was slung,
His hammock huge, and there mid-air it hung!
When weary-limbed, Qualeva, dreaded one,
Would seek repose from wreck and havoc done!
When all was still and calm 't was thought he slept,
Yet dreamed dark dreams. Then shuddering Caribs crept
To reach the water's edge, o'erawed with dread,

With trembling feet, with bared and oft-bowed head.
In light canoes they'd steal across the lake,
Each moment fearful lest the demon wake;
Around the sulphur islet they would steer,
And down the dark and silent depths would peer,
To note the shadows passing far below,
The misty harbingers of weal or woe.
For shades and forms reflected there, it seems,
They thought were dread Qualeva's passing dreams,
And shadowy germs of dark intents, that crossed
That soul, that restive ocean, tempest-tossed!
They searched, and through such signs they sought to steal
The secrets Fate herself would not reveal.

XXXIII

On such an errand went that band of men
We saw emerging from yon darksome glen.
With them a priest—not he of hoary head,
Whose powers (alas, Hiroona!) long had fled,
And left the sage too feeble-kneed to climb
Those Souffrière steeps and rocky heights sublime;
Far younger man was this enthusiast!
Most headstrong he in all he did, and cast
Far more in warrior than in priestly mould;
To win his ends unscrupulous and bold.
The future's course he thought to regulate,
And not to follow, but to govern fate!

XXXIV

They gained the mount, crept down the slippery steep,
And stood beside the mere so dark and deep;
And, filled with awe, one moment paused to pray.
All rippleless and mirror-like it lay;
No sign of life was there, no voice, no sound
To stir the death-like stillness reigning round;
And few and bright the shadows passing there,
For air and sky above were calm and fair.
Qualeva's sleep was fast, he scarcely dreamt;

The happy hour, propitious, seemed exempt
From influence, so seldom wrought in vain,
Of that o'er-restless mischief-working brain.
The men, scarce breathing, launched their frail canoe
To cross the awful lake; it held but two.
The bold and crafty boyez seized one oar,
And one a friend; the others lined the shore.
  XXXV
They glided on, and scarce their paddle-blade
A ripple on the sleeping waters made.
Twice round the cone they rowed; they spoke no word
But looked, and then by silent signs conferred.
All augured well: the fates all seemed to smile,
No ills to prowl around Hiroona's isle.
Their task was done; yet, ere they turned to go,
The boyez's quicker eye saw deep below
The oncome of a gloom, portentous, vast,
Some coming dread event's foreshadow cast;
While two dark clouds enmassed themselves on high.
The Form's dim outline only met the eye:
He saw, but would not see! "'Tis well! 'Tis well!"
He said, "Against Hiroon there works no spell."
His friend content, they struck the ready oar,
And soon were standing with their mates on shore
That secret, hidden in his own dark soul,
The boyez kept, and held possession sole.
  XXXVI
One other augury there yet remained,
Before th' assurance sought was fully gained;
Could they but reach the plains or ere were heard
The plaintive notes of dread Souffrière bird—
Mysterious Songster, which had never been,
And could not be, 'twas said, by mortals seen,
From inmost shades, where deepened solitudes
Enthral with strange still awe the gloomy woods,
Thence weirdly sweet yet mournful notes would swell,

And send the thrilling warning though the dell,
O'er wold, round bluffs and heights of grim Souffrière,
Till th' echoes floated faintly o'er the mere.
Those phantoms notes the Caribs heard with dread
As voice of warning sent them from the dead.[36]

XXXVII

The mere now left, the steep ascent began;
They crept at first, the summit gained, they ran.
Qualeva slumbered still; the threatening cloud
Had passed, and freed the mount from vapoury shroud.
"The signs are good, my men," the boyez cried;
Then bade them shout, as down the mountain side
They lept o'er boulder, crag, or gorge, and sprang
From rock to rock; and then the mountain rang
With shout and laughter high, and warrior song,
That filled the glens with echoes loud and long.
'Twas done with craft, to drown the fatal note
That haply on the mountain-air might float.
With daring strangely mingling with his fear
The priest, who would not see, now would not hear;
Would coming fate by human craft disarm.
And alter Heaven's decree by counter-charm,
(As Balak thought of old![37]) and deftly cheat
Qualeva, and his dreams of harm defeat!
Hiroona wrecked now rues that daring deed;
For well in what he willed he did succeed;
For thrice the silent forest's depths were stirred
By three long plaintive notes—but no one heard.

XXXVIII

The men came on at steady Indian pace,
And stood before their chief's enquiring face.
Their tale with panting breath, in words most brief,
They told: "The omens all are good, O Chief!
No cloud across Hiroona's future sweeps;
In dreamless slumber dread Qualeva sleeps;
No shadows dark alarm the peaceful mere;

No note of phantom-bird has reached our ear."
Their errand told, a moment's smile was seen
To fling its light across that gloomy mien.
  XXXIX
But ere he spoke, the fiery Nannette strode
Upon the scene. Her presence could forbode
No words for peace: Her wildly straggling hair,
Her starting eyes, and almost maniac glare,
Her head erect, and breadth of shoulders vast,
And limbs in more than woman's mouldings cast;
Her loins in scantiest garb, two kerchiefs tied,
And cutlass hanging from her belted side,
An arrow-sheath, and bow of Indian yew—
The priestess proved and woman-warrior too.
  XL
Th' attendant women gruesome burdens bore,
Ghastly and pale, the severed members four,
The thighs and arms, with red blood trickling fresh,
Of some poor slaughtered Englishman—the flesh
Contrasting clear and white, though stained with gore,
With those all bare and swarthy arms that bore
The mangled limbs; another held in arms
A child, but gagged to still its wild alarms;
And these they brought and laid with reverence meet
(Three were his wives) at chief Chetwayè's feet;
And then retired in modesty and fear.
Not so the amazon; for she drew near
The council ring, and there she took her stand
With sybil's right[38] of presence and command—
Unquestioned right, and gesture suiting it.
She bade the much excited chieftains sit,
Resume the council, and their will declare
At once for craven peace, or manful war.
  XLI
Herself relentless, hate intense possessed
And filled with frenzied lust of war that breast.

No Carib she of late degenerate days:
She spurned these softer thoughts and milder ways;
And oft in dark and gloomy solitude
O'er disused rites and altered times would brood;
Her one life-aim (it yearly stronger grew)
"Revive the ancient ways, oppose the new";
And claiming now an ancient sybil right
She'd brought barbaric orgies, to incite
To war. She now commenced her wild harangue
In high-pitched tones, which round the welkin rang.

  XLII

In rapid, ceaseless shriek of words she told
Of Caribs' hero-deeds in days of old,
When their resistless war boats used to sweep
The seas, th' unconquered chieftains of the deep;
And then the wrathful story fierce and long
Of loved Hiroona's agony and wrong
At white man's hands; of battles vainly fought
Against a war which Hell itself had taught.
And thus those warriors' inmost souls she wrung,
Her own heart-strings to highest tension strung.
With woman's skill and tact, and not in vain.
She wrought those fierce but simple hearts to gain
And with her own enthusiasm fill.
And heart to heart responsive beat, until
Full sympathy of rage and fury flew
From hers to theirs, and filled them through and through.[39]

  XLIII

And such her madness of ungoverned rage,
Beyond out northern ken, beyond all gauge
Of our more sluggish Saxon temperament,
(She cradled under fiercer firmament!)
She seized a knife and gashed, and gashed again
Her living flesh, unconscious of the pain;
Till o'er her swarthy limbs the purple flood
Had spread most hideous war-paint of her blood!

With blood grows thirst of blood with man and beast,
And lust of war by slaughter is increased.
  XLIV
Thus Nannette's furies fed yet fiercer grew.
Across the space she ran, she almost flew,
To where those human limbs meanwhile had lain,
By her own sacrificial dagger slain.
She seized and tore them with her teeth, then flung
Them one by one, now bleeding flesh, among
The crowd of wild infuriated men,
As flinging food to wild beasts in their den.
Some caught them as they fell, and, horrid sight!
Each licked the trickling blood, with snap and bite—
Each tore the flesh, then passed the mangled limb
To the impatient savage nearest him.
But not to eat: from that shrank even they;
With hate and rage they spat the flesh away,
And spurned and trampled it upon the ground;
Then danced the frantic war-dance, whirling round
To wild war-chant, "Qualeva to our foes."
And thus o'er Hiroon's now-doomed hills there rose
That cry her warrior-sons so loved of yore—
It rose that eve, but rose again no more!
  XLV
Chetwayè; first of chiefs, he shouted, "War!"
Duvallè caught the cry and sent it far;
Joyette,[40] Codron, and chief by chief on high
Sent up the shout to rasp the patient sky!
"War! War," the passing breezes bore amain.
"War! War," the labouring echoes brought again:
But hark! Between that war-cry rolling out
And yon approaching echo's answering shout,
Just filling in that waiting moment's pause,
And floating on the West wind's fitful flaws,
There came "Ha! Ha!" half yell and mocking half;
It may have been Qualeva's demon-laugh!

XLVI

Meanwhile the frenzied woman-fiend had watched
Her time, and now the white man's infant snatched
And bore him to the front. An altar stone
Stood 'neath those gru-gru trees, with moss o'ergrown,
Unused for years, but whereon once had bled
The human sacrifice; whose blood was shed
To turn Qualeva's dreaded wrath aside,
Whose flesh the sacrificial feast supplied.
That fierce unhuman rite of days long gone
The fiend for years had gorged her mind upon.
And now the long-hoped hour had come at last
To break her people's long inflicted fast.

XLVII

She laid the child upon the stone: the knife
Was raised on high to take its baby-life;
Its keen edge flashed and glittered in the light
Descending to the stroke—but ere it quite
Had reached its fatal aim, the eager blade
By sudden touch of unseen hand was swayed
Aside; the hard cold stone received its stroke—
It shivered and to shining fragments broke!
Th' astonished fury turned, and by her side
Duvallè's maiden child, the destined bride
Of Warramou, Ranèe, the pure and good,
With trembling heart but mien undaunted stood.
All speechless Nannette gazed; and strange effect
Of maddened pulse and passion roughly checked
Was seen: she tossed her arms and then with yell
In strong convulsions cataleptic fell!
The chiefs and women gathered round dismayed,
Too terrified to think, or render aid.
The swoon soon passed; but now, surprised anew,
They looked—the child was gone and Ranèe too!

End of Canto II

CANTO III

French Intrigue and War Begins

I

Along Grand Sable's low and sultry plain[41]
A single horseman rides; his slackened rein,
But barely held in grasp of idle hand
Relaxing from its wonted strong command,
Lies swaying loosely on the horse's neck,
(Which silver tags, in Spanish style, bedeck.)
Hangs by the rider's side his other arm
With hand and glove; from whence with life-like charm
A splendid diamond ring flings forth its gleam;
And golden seals flash bright in mid-day beam,
His wide straw hat, and garments all of white,
Of spotless linen, glisten in the light;
While every air and feature tell of heath,
And mark the man of culture and of wealth.

II

The sun, intense in fiery Cancer, pours,
And deep in Earth's grand laboratory stores,
As light and food of life to be, such rays
As threaten, in the fierceness of their blaze,
To slay the life that is. From all around,
From tree, from field, from rock, and parchèd ground
And burning sand, the heat reflected flies,
And tremulous waves of simmering ether rise.
The heavy air is still, as still as death,

Not e'en from o'er the ocean comes a breath
To stir the fronds of yonder palm, that spread
In plumes superb to crown the royal head.
The sickened flowers are shrunk, with petals paled;
The leaves are drooping, lustreless, and quailed;
The weary dove has ceased to feed her brood,
And silent are the voices of the wood.
The lizard on the bank, or rocky steep,
Scarce opes a lid from lazy eye to peep.
The very flies have fled to sheltering shade,
And e'en mosquitoes ceased their hungry raid.
The horseman's head is bowed, his eyes are closed,
(And, if the tale be rightly told; he dozed.)
The horse, the only thing that moves, moves on,
Yet barely drags his draggling steps along,
Too somnolent to pluck the blades of grass,
Which brush his very footsteps as they pass.
All nature, sympathetic, owns the power,
The drowsy influence of such an hour:
'Twas calm profound in earth, in sea, in air—

   III

Sudden from out the slumbering atmosphere—
Or from lethargic earth itself it came—
And blinding e'en the sunlight with its flame,
And startling Heaven, a sheet of lightning flashed;
While instant with the bursting light there crashed
The horror of the tearing thunder's roar!
Astounded Terror wakes along the shore,
And startled echoes wakened roughly roll
From hill to mount, from trembling earth to pole!
The rolling waves of sound first struck Mount Young.
And thence upon Mount Bentick's[42] heights were flung;
And then rushed back, with scarce diminished roar
To frowning heights of ghastly Byëra[43]
From thence they rolled to distant Morne Garou,
Whence, fainter now but restless still they flew

Once more to green Mount William's[44] further hill,
Then back again, reverberating still;
And reaching last the crest of bleak Souffrière
Flowed faintly back, a murmur on the ear;
And yet, when seemed the great disturbance done
There came one thud, like boom of distant gun.

IV

With one sharp cry our startled rider woke;
With one wild leap his horse from slumber broke,
And would have bounded onwards if he could,
But paralized with fear, he trembling stood,
Ah! Gentle Norman, heed the omen dread,
Of unseen dangers gathering overhead!
'Tis peace to-day, the warders shout, "All's well";
But shriek of sudden war shall break the spell;
Electric shock from out yon cloudless sky
Shall sudden burst, and carrying havoc, fly—
Shall wake the slumbering hates of peaceful men,
And raise War's wreckful thunders once again
And round the shuddering mounts and weeping hills,
Where floods of dewy tears Hiroon distills;
O'er drooping plain, through trembling glen and dale,
The echoes of her people's war and wail
Shall rise and fall; nor cease their lingering moan,
Until is heard that people's dying groan;
Until with agony's last sob and sigh
Her sole remaining patriot's struggles die.

V

But why rides Norman here? Why rides alone
In Caribs' dangerous lines, and where 'tis known
Malignant fury crouches in her lair,
And woe to all her gloomy haunts who dare?
For he who dares invade their sacred soil
Shall find the Caribs' steel no fencer's foil!
Who ventures through the pass of Byëra
Has ventured through the open jaws of war.

But he as "Caribs' friend" has long been known;
And powers of manly kindness all his own
(A master he of healing art divine—)
Had found a way to enter, and entwine
Around the Carib heart—it so was thought.
From very gates of death his art had brought
The huge Chetwayè, Hiroon's mighty chief;
And more than once again had found relief
For ailments past the Caribs' skill; or bound
The sabre cut, or desperate gunshot wound.

  VI

Duvallè too had often named him friend,
And found him apt his ready aid to lend
In nobler aims, which floated through his mind,
When, turned from dreams of war, he sought to find
Some means to raise and civilize his tribe;
(Ideas which he had helped him to imbibe;)
Or sought, with hand untrained, to cultivate
In Coffee plant his virgin-soiled estate.
And often in the Island council too,
A noble stand our doctor took, when few
Were found from ingrained prejudices freed,
Or from unreasoning love of gain, and greed
Of Caribs' land; and, grand exception bright,
For England's honour stood, and Caribs' right.

  VII

And once Chetwayè bold, and King of men,
In Iambou's[45] rocky gorge and sacred glen
On which Petit Bon Homme and Grand Bon Homme[46]
Gaze down through mists from Heaven's darkened dome;
Where stands the Caribs' holiest altar-stone,
On which, in ancient times now long since flown,
Beneath the opening eye of pitying sun
The darkest mystic rites were freely done,
That ever held enthralled the human soul
In gloomy superstition's fierce control;

Where human victims poured the pleading blood,
And yielded flesh for sacrificial food,
To deprecate the bane of demon-power,
When hovering o'er their Isle in evil hour—
  VIII
Here once, while purple light of fading day
Hung lingering o'er the hills in fond delay,
Ere, eve on Vigie's[47] ridge of mounts had set,
Chetwayè bold in chance encounter met
His noble English friend; and here he swore
By spirits of his fathers gone before
To be his friend for aye; and gave the pledge
Of Carib troth upon his cutlass edge,
And thus his tribe's most graceful compact made.
For holding in his hand the keen bright blade
With point to naked breast, he bent and gave—
'Tis thus the brave alone can treat the brave—
He gave the hilt to Norman's loyal hand,
With grace which chivalry could scarce command.
  IX
No craven-souled submission's token this
In self-respect of Carib pride remiss—
(That pride to Hiroon's Indian souls inborn,
Rejecting claims of Kings of lords with scorn—)
But pledge and token, meant and understood,
That man to man in equal manhood stood;
That Honour plighted troth upon that brand,
And placed its very life in friendship's hand:
And breach of friendship's bond no Carib knows,
Though treacherous, implacable to foes.
One moment Norman held the proffered sword,
Accepting thus the troth; and then restored
The pledge. His own good word he gave with clasp
Of honest hand, the hearty English grasp.
The shades of night were deepening fast around,
Before the friends had left the sacred ground.

X

'Twas thus, with honest trust his bosom filled,
Good Norman traversed freely as he willed,
Secure from hurt, or chance of evil trap,
The Caribs' country. When that thunder-clap,
Presaging tumult, crime and blood, had rolled
Its terror round the mount, and hill, and wold,
And shook both rocks and hearts of oak with fear;
And when at last the startled atmosphere,
With sob subdued, like sigh from troubled breast
Of glad relief, subsided into rest,
And not till then, did horse or rider stir.
Both then regained their breath. The urgent spur
Struck deep on either flank the high-bred steed:
He needed not such prompter to his speed;
But with one bound, as startled bird will fling
Itself in air with nervous frightened wing,
He flung himself away—

XI

Along the sands
Where rock or frequent boulder stands;
Along through tangled glade of roseau-brake;
Where lurks the manicou or conger snake;[48]
Beneath the shade of dreaded Manchineel,
Where wearied travellers treacherous languor feel;
Through groves of Caribbee, or "Sea-side grape,"
Where trees of every strange fantastic shape
Entwine the crooked branch from tree to tree,
Like huge distorted arm, or bended knee;
Along the sea-worn, cave-indented shore,
Where ocean's voices murmur evermore,
Our traveller sped. Through Warrow's[49] silver stream,
Whose waters flashed like light in noon's clear beam,
He dashed; and up the slippery steep hill-side;
Where oft in vain the struggling footsteps slide;
Along the riven mountain's craggy brink;

Where e'en the boldest sometimes shuddering shrink.
Through rugged paths in sombre dark defile,
Where never enters Daylight with his smile;
Through dim primeval forests gloom and shade,
Where awe-struck spirits oft have knelt and prayed—
Beneath their feet a down-like leafy bed,
A floriated Gothic arch o'erhead;
O'er saddle-ridge, where one false step would leap
Down chasms which right and left were yawning deep
Through such the narrow Indian pathway led,
Through such our traveller, struggling onward, sped.
  XII
At length, to blood and mettle be the thanks!
His steed with panting breath and reeking flanks,
Has climbed the ridge of rugged frontier height,
That spot where bursts upon th' enchanted sight
The Souffrière plain, which glides, a meadow lea,
In Beauty's lines from mountain foot to sea
The Carib barrier this, which marks the line
Where jealous nations meet, but not combine;
And here the dreaded paths of Byëra,
Which gloomy wit had named the "gates of war";
A citadel, where Nature's own rock-towers
Defy invading Warfare's utmost powers.
Down through the gorge, where shaggy mountains stand
Like champions huge, on guard on either hand,
With greavèd legs and crested head superb,
Bold Norman rode with tightened rein and curb.
  XIII
But far he had not gone when out there stept—
Or from the splintered rocks above they lept,
Or rose from lichen-covered floor beneath—
Three Carib warriors armèd to the teeth;
The young Chetwayè one; in French so named,
But *Warramou*⁵⁰ for Carib name he claimed
The two on guard in rear, he forward strode,

And with his person barred the narrow road.
He stood with sword in hand, but bared his head,
And spoke; "The Englishman must halt," he said;
The word and action stern, but mild his look,
Now sheer defiance Norman would not brook,
Although unarmed: Just startled at the word,
And apparition of a naked sword,
But self-possession not one moment lost,
He drew his rein to heed the strange accost.

  XIV

"What ho! Chattoyer! You, my friend, what now?"
Grew dark with gathering shade his swarthy brow
Before he answer made, "Not e'en from you,
I'll hear a foreign name—I'm Warramou!
Chetwayè, like my father, I might claim
To be. But Chattoyer, the barbarous name
Is French. 'John Demmy,' that the English gave.
These tainted names I bury in the grave.
E'en from my youth to bear them I was loth,
But from to-day renounce and scorn them both.
I'm Warramou! My blood was pure and red
As ever Hiroon's warrior-sons have shed.
I tell thee England's reckoning-day has come,
And Carib war hath quit his mountain-home."

  XV

He said. In noble mould his frame was cast,
In lines of manly grace, by few surpassed;
And, one of Nature's royalty, he wore
Right princely aspect on his brow, and bore
A countenance, when in repose, refined,
Index of noble, though untutored, mind,
But now fierce passions swelling seemed to rise,
And flash in strange wild fury through his eyes;
And uncontrolled emotions seemed to roll
In very hurricane all through his soul.
His bosom, struggling with its energy,

Upheaved like rolling billows of the sea.
His head, his arms, his sides, his pillared thighs,
Bereft of every cumbrance and disguise,
Were quivering o'er, as though in every limb,
His very passions were consuming him.
His features glowed, as though the imps of hate
Had filled him with their rage infuriate.
All milder human elements, 'twould seem,
Had left the man: the savage was supreme!
And there the cultured English gentleman,
And nature's own untutored typal man
Gazed face to face, a strange and wild contrast;
Until the Carib's paroxysm was passed:

  XVI

And soon it was. As o'er the sunlit hills
Aglow with light, swooped up a storm, and fills
The atmosphere with sudden gloom and awe:
Anon sweeps up the wind in fitful flaw;
And soon the hills are wrapped in watery shroud;
Now rush the rains with footsteps wildly loud;
And now with one fierce flash the sky is riven,
While thunder rolls across the startled heaven.
And now the storm is on in all its power,
Supreme in awful grandeur for an hour—
The thick air trembles with electric light;
One moment seems it day, next moment night;
Continuous thunder rolls along the ground,
Which quakes responsive to its ceaseless sound;
For ere one peal in falling echoes dies
Another bursts from out the riven skies:
And rush of falling water's wild down-pour,
And thunder's roll, and fierce wind's maddening roar,
Before whose blast the palms' straight columns bend—
These all their sounds in one huge volume blend:
All Nature heaves and groans in agony,
And tumult of excited energy.

For one half-hour the storm's wild throes thus last:
'Tis gone: As sudden as it came 'tis passed!
The exhausted lightning's corruscations cease;
The winds and rains are silenced into peace
And sudden calm, save waters murmuring low
With muffled sound in yonder vale below.
From sky serene the sun now smiles again,
And brightening in that smile are hill and plain.

  XVII

So through this untamed child of Nature rolled
That furious storm of passions uncontrolled;
So came and went the rage of Warramou—
One moment into frenzied madness grew,
And then as swift subsided into calm;
As though his soul were sport of spell or charm,
Through which his better manhood struggling broke.
Become his better self again, he spoke:
"Hell's demons bade me slay the Caribs' Friend;
Bon-dieu better thoughts from Heaven doth send—
'Tis well: I own my father's plighted word
Once given, as Caribs give, on naked sword.
I hold it sacred; else thy forfeit life
Had been to-day first victim of this knife."

  XVIII

Not wont was Norman's lofty soul to bear
Such speech as this, nor unresented hear;
But being unarmed, he curbed his rising ire;
Yet flashed from out his eyes their native fire.
"Small thanks requite scant courtesy, my friend!
What least we spoil by words we easiest mend.
But, Warramou, what means all this? Those arms?
That paint? And round thy neck those hideous charms
Of bones and teeth? Not so in peace we walk.
What means it all? What means that strange wild talk
Of taking life? Of Freedom's day that's come?
And Carib war that's left his mountain home?"

XIX

"It means, our Nation has declared its war,
Has drawn its sword, and flung the scabbard far,"
"Ha! Say ye this? What rash and monstrous thing!
Foul traitors ye, and rebels 'gainst your King."
"Beware thy words! How can that treason be
Where wars a nation never else but free,
And owners of the soil? My father's chief
And King, if King we have! No royal thief
Shall rob us of the rights our fathers gave,
Who sprang from Hiroon's womb and ocean's wave.
As free as e'er our fathers were before,
No slaves are we, and never fetters wore."
"How now! Ye did yourselves your fetters forge:[51]
Ye freely vowed allegiance to King George.
Your father's name and many chieftains' more
Upon that loud are writ, whereby ye swore
To be our England's subjects liege and true,
Prepared to yield all loyal service due.
You call it war: it is rebellion now,
All worthless is 'tis said, a Carib's vow;
To combat that I've often stood your friend;
But after this such protestations end."

XX

"No friendships now we need, and none we ask
With England's King, with whom we war—our task,
By Hiroon's Gods whom we, her sons, adore.
To drive you English strangers from our shore."
"Ah! Warramou! You know not what you say;
And, ill-advised, you'll rue this evil day.
Your demon-gods, your tribes deluding, mock.
Our England's power is like yon granite rock,
Against whose sides, with all the force they come,
Those huge green waves but dash themselves to foam.
But what mischance, or what delusion strange,
O'er peaceful minds hath wrought such sudden change?

Lived not your people thriving and content,
Dealt kindly with by England's Government?
Your country's rites, your laws and lands secured,
What harm or wrong for years have ye endured?
Why then this fruitful peace so madly break,
And cursèd War's now slumbering horrors wake?
Why hurl Destruction like a surging flood
To fill Hiroona's isle with tears and blood?"

XXI

The Carib's brow flushed o'er with darker scorn
Than any yet that guileless brow had worn;
"Tell Christians that! Think you we do not hear
Of Christian nations warring everywhere?
The guilt of war no Christian peoples dread;
None deem a brother's blood too pure to shed.
We know that floods of war had deluged France;
And now its surging waves of blood advance,
And burst through every barrier in the way
To other lands that round her peaceful lay.
You English too, e'en now your hands are dyed
With English blood that flowed like rivers wide—
Your great war-thunder o'er the seas ye brought
To your own Colonies; and there ye fought
Not alien foes, but brothers of your blood;
And fathers 'gainst their sons as foemen stood.[52]
When, like our fathers then in older time
Our Indians wage their war, why, call it crime?
That treaty with King George? Why, those who make
Rash bonds in fear, they such, when strong may break.
What paper bond can our great wrongs atone,
Or make it sinful fighting for our own?"

XXII

"All this is worse than foolish, rash and wrong!
Were you ten times as numerous and as strong,
What could you do against the English might?
What end but one to such a madman's fight?

As still your people's friend, I'd save your race
And name from extirpation and disgrace.
I counsel you to bide by England's laws;
To England's honour trust your scared cause.
How true to friends you Caribs are, we know;
But England, not to friend alone, but foe,
Is just, and never fouls her glorious name
With stain of broken faith, or falsehood's shame.
Your nation's right her solemn words secures;
The land from hence to 'Wia[53] ever yours:
Do you but keep the peace you'll find, by Heaven,
She'll never break the sacred pledge so given!"

  XXIII

"By Heaven, I say, Hiroona all is ours!
And ours shall be *malgre* all England's powers.
To trust in England's honour you invite;
But red men know they dare not trust the white,
Destroyers of our race—Do we not know
(The time is long, some thousand moons ago,)
How Caribs swept these seas from isle to isle,
The bold unconquered lords of all the wild?
From fair Iëre,[54] land of birds, of palms,
(Amidst whose placid seas and softest calms
The hurricane first draws his infant breath,
Then growing rushes forth on work of death;)
Past fifty isles of mounts and vales and streams,
Of which each isle in fair succession seems,
In soft repose and beauty's chastened hues,
More lovely than the last,—our bold canoes
Would sweep in fleets, until their long drawn track
Far Hayti reached, where dwelt the Arrowack.

  XXIV

And all was ours: our seamen met, where'er
They went, our conquering people everwhere.
Our nation filled those wide and many lands
With war-like people numerous as the sands.

And all came back, life's toil and wandering o'er,
To Mother-land, Hiroona's happy shore,
The centre of the world, the paradise,
The Caribs' home of bliss where'er he dies,
But then in evil day the white man came,
And brought from hell itself its brands of flame.
Such hell-born powers our war could not withstand;
And soon with Desolation's bloodiest hand,
In sheer barbarity, not e'en for gain,
They filled our writhing isles with rotting slain.
Sometimes in open war, more oft with guile,
They drove our shattered tribes from isle to isle:
They drove from land to rock, from rocky height
To all engulphing sea, with no respite,
Until the merest remnant refuge found—
On this our own Hiroona's sacred ground.

   XXV

In yon Grenada, so you name it now,
Before the holy cross, with prayer and vow,
The murderers knelt and took the Sacrament;
Then rising, straight to slaughter's work they went;
Their vow (could sacred things be more defiled?)
To leave alive nor man, nor maid, nor child.
They lost scarce one, while they their thousands slew;
For what could bow and feeble arrow do?
Until the few they left, like helpless sheep,
Were driven and huddled on a rocky steep
O'er hanging far the breaking surf below;
And when drew near the unrelenting foe,
With one long wail their cruel faith they wept,
And then adown the yawning abyss lept.
That fatal rock, where perished thus a race,
But where they left for aye the crime's sad trace,
(Its granite cheeks are trickling down with tears,)
The heartless conquerors, mocking, named "Sauteurs".[55]

XXVI

Hiroona's self, in this her sacred home,
Where spirits of our ancient fathers roam,
Has seen her children bear ten thousand wrongs;
And we, to whom the whole land still belongs,
In spite of all we manfully have striven
To one mere corner have been slowly driven;
And here, in this the stronghold of our race,
You, sir, would have us live by England's grace!
But no! Our Island cannot hold us both,
And though to break our bond for one I'm loth,
Our Chieftains see the nation's coming doom
That soon will bear it withered to its tomb,
Unless we drive the white man from our shore,
And breathe Hiroon's untainted air once more,

XXVII

Than in the past we now are stronger far:
We use your weapons, and have learnt your war.
Know this besides; by compact firmly made
We have secured the valiant Frenchman's aid.
Our blood is up, our spirits lashed to rage
And naught but death or victory can assuage
The fury of our war. And if we slay
And spare not, as we go our conquering way—
If blood of man and maid and child we shed—
Remember what the white man did the red!
The mem'ry of those deeds, our country's woe,
With every gush of blood will fiercer grow;
Devouring swords the more in gore will steep,
And maddened with the blood, will drink more deep,
Till very Vengeance, wearied, ceased to gorge.
Now tell ye this to him ye call King George.
Hark hark! The war-shells sounding o'er those hills!
Hark! How those woods the piercing echo fills!"[56]

XXVIII

Norman essayed to speak, but ere he spoke
His quick eye sees two columns rise of smoke,
A darker and a paler one,—he knows
At glance, the pale from burning houses rose—
The dark? 'Twas smoke of canes that dimmed the sun:
The war was out: the carnage had begun!
His spurs that instant strike his horse's sides,
And forth, like rush of thunder-bolt, he rides.
Ah! Speed thee, Norman! Rouse thy friends, arm! Arm!
And gallop on to spread the wild alarm!

End of Canto III

A Carib Raid

I
Like arrow bursting from the bow-string freed
Sped on our Norman's gallant steed
Adown the bridle-path, which wound,
Rock-hewn, beneath steep bluffs that frowned
With dark and lowering scowl o'erhead;
Whence rock and branch protruding spread
Around a shadowy gloom, which made
The fiery day to twilight fade,
And clumps of pendant roots appeared
Like monstrous tufts of grisly beard,
Down which the trickling waters flowed
Like tear-drops on the slippery road.
II
That road no more than rocky ledge,
From whose unparapeted edge
There lept the headlong precipice;
While rocks in equilibrium nice
Seemed waiting but a breath as lunge
To hurl them on their fatal plunge.
A fearful sight: but Nature, kind
And beauty-loving, sought to find
Some friendly vail, some screen provide,
The horrors of the Fall to hide:
By aid of Tropic suns and showers
She curtained them with shrubs and flowers.

III

Adown such paths our Norman flew,
Nor spared the spur, nor bridle drew;
In Rollo fullest trust he put,
So sound in limb, so sure of foot.
Below, the Byëra (the name
Of mount and mountain-rill the same)
No petty streamlet flowed that day;
A broad and silent pool it lay.
The swell was rough, and high the wind
Had been; and gale, and waves combined
Had piled along the beaten strand
A bar of driftwood, weeds, and sand;
So turned the streamlet back again,
Refused it entrance to the main,
And forced it in recoil to make
A small but deep and dangerous lake

  IV

If danger lurked, no time to heed,
No power to stay that downward speed
Had Norman now. With uncurled leap
His faithful Rollo plunged: so deep
The tarn, so high the slippery bank,
At once both horse and rider sank.
But horse with rider rose again
Still seated, clinging to his mane:
Each the other knew. A score
Of strokes regained the further shore,
And, dripping from their dangerous bath,
The struck again their forward path.

  V

Along a grassy down, their way
Quite close the open sea now lay,
Where rolled an ever-glorious surf;
Beneath their feet a springy turf.
He twice encountered passers-by,

And twice he bade the tidings fly.
And soon his wistful eye could see
The green-clad banks of Colonarie;[57]
Whose waters, always bright and cool,
Through many a mullet-teeming pool,
Through rapid, reach, and cascade flowed
Hard by his homestead's sweet abode:
But o'er its waves how soon, alas!
Shall hideous metamorphose pass;
And mingling streams of human blood
To crimson change its limpid flood!
  VI
Along those fair and flowering banks.
At maddening speed, with reeking flanks
All gashed with barbs of spurrèd heel,
(Unwonted pain for *him* to feel!)
Now Rollo bore; for mighty dread
O'er Norman's soul its horror shed,
And made him wish for wings of wind,
And Rollo's pace so faulty find.
For near now lay his cherished home,
And thence, O God! Now seemed to come
The smoke he had been watching rise
In thickening volumes to the skies,
And spread on high in gloom glare.
What deeds of woe were doing there!
A mother, wife, and children two
Were unprotected there, he knew;
And in that anxious moment's span
A thousand imaged terrors ran
In wild confusion through his brain,
Which almost maddened with the strain.
  VII
But turned the road, and brought to view
His smiling home: one glance he threw—
The buildings yet were safe. He bent

His reverent head, and Heavenwards sent
A word of thankfulness. But though
His own was standing safe, not so
His neighbour's humbler home, erstwhile
"The Planter's Hope," but now a pile
Of blackened, roofless masonry:
The wreck of Carib savagery,
It stood a kiln of living fire!
Around in desolation dire,
Where lately canes had waved the sheen
Of silvery plumes o'er fields of green,
The flames a hideous waste had laid
And now their all-devouring raid,
With mighty rush and roar, o'er hill
And plain was fiercely driving still.

  VIII

Around, and scattered all abroad
The Homestead's desecrated sward,
(A scene the pen can scarce portray)
The charred and littered fragments lay
Of household furniture and store;
And, grimed with smoke and smeared with gore,
The severed limb and mangled corse[58]
Of negro slave, and mule and horse.
And yonder, midst the fire and smoke,
Whose volume for a moment broke,
The hideous forms of Caribs glide,
Ghoul-like, and hugely magnified!

  IX

A cautious rein then Norman drew
Beside a friendly bank, with view
To learn, or ere he hurried on,
If need or room for help were gone;
And scarce had paused, when from beneath,
With trembling limbs and chattering teeth
And blackness terror-changed to white,

A negro slave emerged to light.
He caught and held the rein, and tried
To speak, but struggling utterance died
Upon his lips; no words would come,
For terror made the negro dumb;
Until the fear-spell Norman broke
By some kind, cherry words he spoke.
He then, in broken fragments, learned
The truth his fiery soul had burned
To know: his home had felt no harm
Beyond the hurt of wild alarm.
"On 'Planter's Hope' they all were dead,
Except the few, like him, who fled."
   X
As caution now forbade to ride
In th' open, Norman turned aside
To cross the stream, and seek the shade
Of cocoa grove, and orange glade;
And thus to reach his home unseen
Beneath the woodland's leafy screen;
While on his ear continuous fell
The crash of fire and Caribs' yell.
With hand on bridle-rein still ran
The terrified Mandingo man;
Who thus, with blood still running cold,
His wretched tale of butchery told;
   XI
How "Master," in the early morn,
Before indeed the day was born,
Had ridden to the woods. "By eight"
He said, "You meet me by the gate."
Alas! He spoke those words in vain:
He never had been seen again!
And how his mare, at past mid-day,
Now riderless, was seen to stray
From out the nearest upland wood.

Upon her saddle-bow was blood—
Not single drops, but copious stain,
And clotted o'er her neck and mane.
She whinnied to the servant's call
At once, and trotted to her stall,
The whole plantation in dismay
Soon heard the story, and away
Man, woman, every one that could,
All rushed to search the darksome wood.

XII

And so it chanced, by evil fate,
No man upon the whole Estate
Was left; the forest held them all.
With shout, and whoop, and Indian call,
They searched its utmost depths around:
No answer came, no trace was found
The Mistress could not stay within,
Nor bide at home—it looked like sin!
Her husband dying in the wild,—
Could she sit still? She seized her child,
Her noble boy of three, her one
Remaining child, her only son.
Such hideous horror filled her mind,
She could not leave her boy behind.
"I look for father too," he cried,
And trotted bravely by her side.
Together they were seen to pass
Up through the field of guinea-grass,
Near where the double Black Rocks stand,
He holding fast his mother's hand.

XIII

Of what then fell no tongue can speak.
All sudden rose a piercing shriek;
At first like Terror's startled cry,
And then long-drawn in agony.
Himself, Kodanda, was first

From out the tangled wood to burst,
And forward to the succour press.
To know his mistress in distress
Had lent his eager spirit spurs;
For well he deemed that scream was hers.
Ten seconds scarce, it seemed had passed
Since now he'd heard its echoes last;
But when he gained the low hill's rise,
There flashed before his startled eyes
A sight, which made his spirit quail,
And trembling heart and courage fail—
Nannette, the dreaded Carib queen,
The obeah-working fiend, was seen
To pass across the open space,
Not run, but glide with rapid pace.

  XIV

The hag had seized the Master's boy,
And bore him fast away. A toy
In such strong arms, she'd flung
Him o'er back, and thus he hung
With downward head, one foot each side
Her neck, across her bosom tied.
The hag's waist-cloth was stained red:
The boy was senseless, if not dead.

  XV

All this in but one moment's flight
Was printed deeply on his sight—
When passed the fiend between the blocks
And shadows of the double Rocks,
And sudden seemed to disappear!
The mother's self was seen nowhere;
But yonder lay a straggling mass
Of draggled drapery on the grass.
That spot, with Nannette lurking there,
No one, alone, would venture near—
Such dread her very name inspired:

But four just heart enough acquired
To steal across the green, and found
The mistress weltering on the ground
In swoon—a faint and faltering breath
Just feebly proved it was not death!
  XVI
But Nannette and the child? They thought
To find them by the Rocks, but sought
In vain: no vestige could be seen,
Beyond, along the shining green,
Or near beneath the darkening shade,
Although most eager search they made,
Around, between, above, below,
Where eye could reach, or foot could go;
While frowned the dark forbidding rock,
And seemed their fruitless search to mock.
Cold horror held them torpor-bound:
Nannette had vanished under ground,
Like Soucouan[59] dissolved in air,
Or sunk beneath the Black Rocks there!
The thought unmanned them with its dread,
With one loud yell they turned and fled,
Alas! And left their mistress there,
Forgotten in their abject fear.
  XVII
And now from all the forest round
There rushed a mingling roar of sound;
The yell of fear, the shriek of pain, the shout
Of savage war; and then the flying rout
Of Caribs and of slaves from out the wood;
The slaves by Caribs close pursued.
No cravens were those slaves, but apt for war;
And all were armed, and bill or cutlass bore;
But then, not always men their manhood keep—
Surprise and panic drove them on like sheep.
They fled, the Caribs following fast behind,

More fleet of foot, and sounder far in wind,
And dealt with dagger-blade the fatal blow,
Or sent pursuing death from out the bow:
The doom of one to die, and one to slay.
And Death made bloody sacrifice that day;
And not till victims ceased that Priest forbore,
But now the reeking steel can do no more;
So flames with incense of foul vapours rise,
Completing thus th' unhallowed sacrifice.
  XVIII
"O Heaven! Espouse our slaughtered people's cause!
Lay bare Thine arm: avenge Thine outraged laws!
And yet—'fore Heaven's Tribunal which is worse?
Which wrought in these Antilles greatest curse?
The unkempt dark man's savage code of blood,
As from his fathers learnt and understood;
Or polished Europe's tale of Indian wrong?
The boor was weak, the European strong,
And blessed with Heaven-sent gifts to lead him right
The Creed of love, the Gospel's guiding light!
There's justice in thy taunts, O Warramou:
Humiliating, yet I own them true!"
So Norman thought, and thinking reached his home.
'Twas well: one half-hour more too late he'd come.
  XIX
He doubted not Chetwayè's oath
For self; but wife and children both,
And mother far advanced in age:—
For those beloved he dared not gauge
His loyalty; nor trust, forsooth,
To Carib clemency and truth.
Besides, they'd tasted human gore,
And tiger-like would rave for more,
  XX
"Papa! Papa!" Then quick steps pattering run;
"Thank God! You've come! I breathe again, my son!"

A scream of joy, outbursting from a breast
For hours by silent agonies oppressed—
Such sounds of honest welcome greet
Our Norman's ears, before his feet,
Though swift, have crossed his threshold o'er
A moment lingering at the door,
Fond arms are thrown around his neck,
And tears, which nothing now can check,
Are flowing free and fast: that breast,
Its anguish passed, has found its rest!
"O husband mine! Where hast thou been all day?
Since quitting us, an age has passed away!"
His answer an impassioned kiss:
No time for explanations this!
  XXI
"Be bonneted, my love! And quick!
One shawl, or wrapper warm and thick
For self and Mother you will need,
But nothing more: we've scarce, indeed,
One moment's time to lose! What ho!
Bring out the horses, there below!
The Grey, and Nell of gentle pace—
On them the ladies' saddles place;
Leave Rollo saddled there for me;
Get one horse ready more; and see
The girths and straps are right, d'ye hear?
You, Pompey, call the overseer!
The stock? Set everything at large!
Those fowling pieces there discharge:
We'll let the Caribs know we're armed,
Go! Call the negroes out by gong,
'Tis well to let them see we're strong."
Thus sharp and fast the orders flew,
Obeyed at once; for all well knew
When such commands their Master made
He sternly meant to be obeyed.

XXII

At once the welkin rings with sound—
Reports of fire-arms echoing round,
And iron gong's incessant din;
While shouting slaves come rushing in,
And opened pens are pouring out,
In terrified tumultuous rout,
The varied stock which planters keep,
Ox, mule, ass, poultry, pigs and sheep.
The well-trained horses, even they,
With startled and enquiring neigh,
Excited, scarce are kept in hand
As saddled at the block they stand.

XXIII

"Now Mother! Mount old faithful Nell,
Be nervous not; she'll bear you well,
Now, wife!" With action light and neat
He placed her gently in her seat.
"I mean for you, McLean, that mount,
Upon your prudence I can count;
You've been a faithful overseer,
To you, I trust this charge so dear:
My boy upon your saddle-bow
You'll carry safe with you. And now
'Tis time you're gone, Away away!
You'll keep the Royal Road, nor stay
For rest, till all are safe with you
Within the lines at Biabou."60

XXIV

A mother's glance he caught and read;
"The girl will go with me," he said;
"I've still some needful things to do,
And then I'll quickly follow you.
Rollo is fleet, ere half your ride
Is o'er he'll bring me to your side."
A smile of love, content and trust,

With nothing of reluctant *must,*
In one long lingering look she threw,
Then waved a kiss of fond adieu;
And soon the dark-leaved cacoa glade
Received within its fragrant shade
His well-loved fugitives.
  XXV
                Meanwhile,
The Caribs round the burning pile
In dark and threatening numbers stood,
Prepared for further work of blood;
But paused in consultation long.
For Norman's guns and clanging gong,
And sturdy negroes mustering still,
Well armed with cutlass or with bill,
Bade caution hold their lingering feet,
With dubious thoughts of safe retreat.
  XXVI
Then Norman to th' assembled slaves:
"There's now no fear those Carib knaves
Will dare attack, at least by day.
Perhaps like prowling beasts of prey,
In darkness of the coming night,
When moon and stars withdraw their light,
They'll come again. No common raid
Is this; their plans are deeply laid
To spread their war and ravages
All o'er the land, poor savages!
The cunning French are here to lend
Their aid, and men and arms they send
From Guadaloupe. The Caribs swear
No man, nor maid, nor child to spare,
That owns the white man's skin or blood.
But *you,* except in first fierce flood
And tumult of mad rage and war,
They will not hurt: they'd sooner far

Not kill, but make your men their slaves,
And keep your women for their braves.
They will entice you to forsake
Your duty to the whites, and make
With them a common traitor-cause
Against your country, King and laws.
  XXVII
The French will be your tempters too
To break from your allegiance due
With all the blandishments and lies
Their ready tongue so well supplies;
With all the craft their hatred finds
They'll seek to poison deep your minds;
They'll place the weapon in your hand,
And tempt you join their rebel band;
Away all truth and honour fling;
Betray your country and your King,
And load your souls with all the guilt
Of all the needless blood that's spilt.
What say you then, my men, will you
To England and King George be true,
And trust! Howe'er the warfare goes?"
  XXVIII
"We will! We will!" In mingling notes
From ten-score male and female throats,
At once spontaneous bursting out,
Upraise a mighty loyal shout.
"We're English, master, live or die:
If any say we're French they lie!
For master, and for mistress too,
We'll freely shed our blood; for you
Are next to God; and rather we
Would be your negroes than be free."
Thus one, a stalwart negro spoke;
Assenting acclamations broke
From every side—Their speech uncouth,

English and French *patois*—but truth,
And loyalty as pure as gold,
Disdaining to be bought or sold
For flattering hopes or threatening fears,
Full filled those honest hearts of theirs;
And sure was Norman he could trust
His slaves; to doubt would be unjust.

 XXIX

"Well said, my boys! Right well I knew
Your hands were strong, your hearts were true.
So *you* be true (you need not fight)
No fear from all the Caribs' might,
Not all the weapons France can forge.
Three cheers for England and King George!"
With heartiest will the cheers were given,
And by the evening breeze were driven
Far o'er the hills and woods, till clear
And soft upon the lady's ear,
Like cadence of some far-off bell
Like voice from other world, they fell.
She paused with listening ear intent;
A prayer in answer Heavenwards sent,
And angels blessed it as it went.

 XXX

Then issued forth some brief commands;—
They might remain upon the lands—
All those, at least, who had no fear
Of Frenchmen's sword or Caribs' spear—
And guard their cots and grounds; all those
Might go who would, or stay who chose,
And do their best some watch to keep
O'er wandering mules and scattered sheep;
Until the English troops arrive,
And to their dens the wild beasts drive;
While those who went should rendezvous
Upon th' Estate at Coub'marou.[61]

XXXI

Now came two ancient grey-haired slaves,
Old Clare the nurse, and butler Greaves;
Most faithful honest pair. The one
Regarded Norman as her son;
Had nursed him thirty years ago,
And now she nursed his babes; and so,
A strangely privileged old dame,
And slave in nothing but the name,
She deemed herself, good soul, to be
Head member of the family.
E'en more important still, old Greaves
Looked down upon his fellow slaves;
Mere *negroes* they, worth so much pelf,
But *he*, his master's second self!
And by that master humoured much:
The country's customs then were such.

XXXII

Now staggering forth beneath the weight
Of heavy chest of household plate,
(Unthought of by their master then)
A load almost for two strong men,
The old folks came. With hoe and spade
Beneath a tamarind tree they'd made
A hole (poor souls they'd done their best)
They dragged and buried there the chest.
'Twas done in open-face of day,
For none would steal, and none betray;
And Norman watched the scene and smiled:
To loiter thus he'd been beguiled.

XXXIII

'Twas growing late; the setting sun,
Through masses gloomy, dark and dun
Of cloud and smoke-encumbered air,
Threw o'er the skies a strange red glare;
The vapoury masses seemed all tinged

With blood, with dormant lightning fringed.
The Heavens, o'ercharged with darkening gloom
Seemed laden with some dreadful doom.
On such an eve none unimpressed
Could gaze—a shudder, ill suppressed
Ran through our Norman's sturdy blood,
As he one moment lingering stood.
He shook it off, and lightly lept
To horse; and yet again it crept
As coming ague creeps all through;
Or was it chill of evening dew?
His child, a pretty petted girl,
With bright blue eyes and flaxen curl,
He raised, and on a pillow placed
In front; for smooth and gentle-paced
Though Rollo was, the roads were rough,
To rack the maiden quite enough.

 XXXIV

Then Norman gave the spur and rein,
And bounded on o'er hill and plain;
Through rippling stream, through mossy dell,
Where Rollo's foot-prints noiseless fell;
O'er rocks, where, in the growing dark
His swift heels struck the frequent spark;
Till soon was heard the ocean's roar,
And soon he'd gained the high-cliffed shore.

 XXXV

By now the Tropic brief twilight
Had deepened into moonless night.
And came the night-breeze down the hill,
Which, after fiery day, felt chill,
Not silent was the hour, nor dull;
The air with life and sound was full—
The scintillating bright fire-flies
In millions flashed before his eyes;
Labelles,[62] with unmatched lamps of gold,

In hundreds issued from the wold,
And trailed across the glowing night
Their trains of green phosphoric light;
Like living meteors cleft their way,
And almost turned the night to day!
In piercing notes the strange *shack-shack*;
Rang out its ceaseless clatter-clack;
Night-beetles hummed, and crickets chirped—
And thus their myriads usurped
Night's sovereignty; and o'er all those
Shrill, high-pitched, piercing notes, there rose,
Just harmonising all the noise,
The bass of grand old Ocean's voice.
  XXXVI
At length by Massy's[63] noisy brook
Our horsemen joyfully o'ertook
His fugitives, near Biabou:
The lines were reached, and soon passed through.
He found the troops alert and armed:
Two hours ago they'd been alarmed
By his own messages—At length,
With wearied limbs and wasted strength,
The travellers sought and found a friend
And brought their troubled day to end:
Beneath the hospitable roof
They put that friendship to the proof.
But all night long (next morn they knew)
Whole families were passing through
From all the country far and near,
In trembling haste and helpless fear.

End of Canto IV

RANÈE

I

While Havoc waved in one relentless hand
The blood-stained steel, in one the fiery brand,
With every terror savage war could wield;
And laid o'er desolated home and field,
Where Peace and Hope that morning smiling stood,
The horrid trail of ashes and of blood,
Ranèe, a father's pet, a chieftain's pride,
And maiden pure, along the river's side
It chanced was wandering all alone, near where
The cascade's leaping waters filled the air
With soft and murmuring music of their fall,
And formed the deep dread pool, which some would call
Le trou demon, some, "Mermaid's Pool." The maid
Knew nought of Havoc's work and Murder's raid
On "Planter's Hope" near by; no hostile sound
Amidst the song of falling waters found
Intrusive way, with tidings of red war.
Her mind was swayed with gentler motives far:
She loved with strange deep love, but knew it not,
No stranger she to that romantic spot,
Some tender memories for her lingered near:
'Twas their soft influence now brought her here.

II

Of tall slight form, in Carib maiden rare,
And crowned with coronet of raven hair
In queenly plait across her brow, yet free
To flow behind, and trailing to her knee;
Dark skinned, with red blood flushing clear beneath;
With eye-brows arched, and peerless teeth;
With splendid bust, which gently swelled and heaved
With many maiden thoughts, and just relieved
By snow-white robe, the which with modest charm
Revealed one breast, left bare one rounded arm.
Her flowing skirt, not Carib-like, was deckt
In stylish Martiniquan, striped and checked,
Of pensive mien, yet oft for pleasant while
O'er brightened with the gleam of sweetest smile:
Such Ranèe was, Duvallè's only child,
Acknowledged beauty of those mountains wild,
And worthy well, if such her fate had been
To be redeemed Hiroona's future queen.

III

Among the Europeans by chance much thrown
In childhood's day, she'd happily outgrown
Her people's sterner hates and fiercer traits,
Imbibing much of white men's thoughts and ways.
Her heart brimful of tender patriot-love
Was in her native hills; yet far above
Those native hills, she loved her people well:
For them her freedom or her life could sell.
Duvallè's child in high designs was she
And longed to lift them from their savagery.
But o'er her pensive soul ('twas passing strange!)
There seemed to creep, she knew not how, some change:
She felt not as she used and wished to feel,
Across her soul a feeling new would steal,
Which with her older self would strangely jar,
Whene'er the angry chieftains spoke of war

Against the whites, and aired their gloomy hate.
She felt small sympathy with this of late;
Retiring she would sit alone, and muse,
And question with contending thoughts, and lose
Herself in strange perplexity—She ought
(A thousand times she owned the duteous thought)
To be at heart with all Hiroona's woes
Or weal—to love her friends, to hate her foes,
And startled now to find it was not so,
The reason why she vainly sought to know.
  IV
She loved, but knew it not. To Warramou
Long while betrothed; yet circling seasons flew
In vain. Her father's will, her plighted troth
She held as sacred, yet to wed seemed loth;
And when the youth would plead to have his bride,
"Not yet! Not yet!" with smiles or tears replied.
  V
Young Crayton loved that river's shading banks
And peerless water's rhythmic flow, and thanks
To gentle "Izaak's" art,[64] with silver fly,
Cast light with well-trained hand and practised eye,
Would draw, with joy which only anglers feel,
Some luxuries for his frugal planter's meal.
  VI
One angling day, some half-score moons agone,
The maid as now, was wandering all alone
Along the banks, near where the tangled brush
The darkest lay; when thence with yell and rush
A Carib sprang. She fled, but he pursued.
She knew him well; an ancient Indian feud
Had made the man her father's mortal foe:
He thought through her to strike the vengeful blow.
She fled in vain, and shrieked for hopeless aid;
She fell; but ere the threatening stroke was made.
A white man from the stream with athlete bound

Had sprung, and struck the savage to the ground
And pinioned him for Justice' tardier hand;
Then raised the fallen girl: she could not stand,
For ankle-joint was sprained; and so he bathed
The limb with gelid waters, and then swathed
It with his handkerchief; then tried to cheer
With kindly words, and soothe her shrinking fear.
He bade her there no longer lingering stay:
She thanked him much, and limped her homeward way.

  VII

'Twas Crayton. But few words in French were spoke,
But manly grace and word and act awoke
Most strange emotions in the maiden's breast:
They woke and never since had sunk to rest.
Since then not once nor twice her restless feet
Had drawn her there; and twice she'd chance to meet
Her rescuer then striding homewards fast:
With pleasant smile and kindly word he passed.
But oft beneath the banks' arboreous shade,
Herself concealed, the timid modest maid
Would gaze for hours, with heart and soul aglow,
Upon his movements in the stream below,
Her footsteps following his where'er he went.
Thus feasted to the full, with heart content
She sought her home by light of cold moon-beams,
And went through all again that night in dreams.

  VIII

Yet oft she made in vain her secret quest
And carried home but chagrin in her breast.
She loved no doubt; and yet no wanton jilt
Was that fair Carib maid; all free from guilt
Her strange attachment was. Too far above
Her humbler being for thoughts of earthly love
The white man's higher nature seemed to be:
Her heart might love; her soul would bow the knee,
And would, while worshipping the ground he trod,

As soon have thought of wedding with a god!
But heart and soul e'en now began to vie
In painful struggle for supremacy.

  IX

She'd seen him angling in the Pool that day
Had seen him restless early go away,
And turned but half contented from the stream;
Then wandered on in fanciful day-dream,
In which her hero filled the whole foreground,
Half conscious now of stranger sounds, 'twould seem
Than fall of waters mingling in her dream,
The charm was broke, she wakened startlingly
To sterner scenes and dread reality.
The yell of murderous war, the shriek of fear
Fell now distinctly on her wounded ear:
And then soon burst the scene of devilry
In sight, in all its hellish revelry.

  X

True Carib though she was, too much dismayed
At such a scene to venture near, she made
A circuit round the hills; and thus by chance,
As on she fled, her footsteps' swift advance
Approached that gloomy-shaded Double Rock;
But there aghast, with sudden, startled shock
Arrested stood. Across her very way
The body of that English mother lay—
Unseen by Carib eyes, or left for dead
'Twould rather seem; for many footsteps tread
Had laid the grass around. Poor Ranèe stood
Half petrified; but, soon recovering, would
From sight of Death on wings of fear have flown,
But as she turned to fly, a low faint moan
Was heard, which once more chained her where she stood
And brought back all her truest womanhood.
That sympathy, which makes all kith and kin,
And glows alike 'neath fair or darker skin,

Had found in hers, an untamed Carib breast,
Congenial home to do her high behest.

XI

She knelt, and bending o'er the prostrate form,
She touched the limbs, and found they yet were warm;
And blood was oozing still from open wound;
Whence life had freely flowed until she'd swooned.
At once by instinct not experience taught,
She hastened to the brook near by, and brought
Delicious draughts to cool the lips and now
A copious stream to bathe the fevered brow:
Huge tania leaves,[65] which lined the water's side
With simplest art the needful bowls supplied.
And soon her kindly efforts met reward,
The opened eyes, the faintly murmured word;
And while in pity's tenderest tones she spoke
Full consciousness from out its slumber woke—
Awoke at first to agonies of fear
To find a Carib woman standing near;
But Ranèe looked so kind, so sweetly smiled,
She quickly felt at ease and reconciled.

XII

Each other's tongue unknown, they thus compelled
By signs, and some few words in common held
Of French *patois,* their converse brief to hold.
And thus midst choking sobs the mother told
Her tale-told how the hag had snatched her boy,
Her only child, her sole remaining joy,
And left her life a blank—"Oh! Would they'd ta'en
That life, and left her, as they thought her, slain!
She'll surely kill, and—" but no mother dared
To speak the dreadful thought: which Ranèe shared.
"I'll save him if he lives," the maiden cried;
"Duvallè's daughter never is denied!"
And full of high resolve to dare and do,
On anger 'gainst such heartless outrage too,

She turned in haste to go; but first she led
Her English friend along the streamlet's bed.
To where a cave afforded hiding-place:
There bade her safely rest by *Bondieu's* grace,
And there, till evening's shades descend, await;
Then seek, in sheltered night, the next estate.

  XIII

The boy is saved! As Nannette's glittering knife
Was flashing down to take its baby-life,
Fair Ranèe touched her arm and foiled the stroke;
The fatal blade just swerved aside, and broke
In fragments on the sacrificial stone:
A moment more and girl and child were gone!

  XIV

God speed thee, Ranèe, on thine errand pure!
God speed thy nimble feet and footsteps sure!
The while the swoon holds Nannette still in thrall;
The while surprise holds chained the chieftain's all;
The while they search the hill-side far and near
In vain suspicion thou art hiding there;
Make good thy vantage time, as fleet as wind,
By pathway too those demons may not find;
Thy flight away from English frontier, where
Those Carib warriors prowl around, for there
Nannette would deem thou'rt gone, and follow thee
With mad and tiger-like ferocity:
But seek thy father's 'rock-built fortressed home,
Where none would think or none would dare, to come.

  XV

And now she's safe! Where Rabaca[66] (the queen
Of Hiroon's streams in olden times, I ween)
Rolled down her silver tide o'er pebbly bed
Between high fern-clad banks, and wide o'erspread
Of lavish, wild luxuriant foliage,
Scarce rivalled since the Miocenic age—
Romantic stream! Most beautiful and chaste;

Ere Mount Souffrière in throes had hurled her waste
Of lava, sand, and scoria, and turned
A stream, like those of Paradise, to burned
And blackened plain, Sahara-like; below
Whose arid sands the buried waters flow
In unseen depths, and unseen find the sea—
Where Rabaca then bounded full and free,
Ranèe's swift flight was run, secure beneath
The leafy umbrage; staying scarce for breath
Until she gained the boulder-covered beach.
There lay her own canoe in easy reach
Of water-line: she'd left it there that morn.
'Twas easy task for her, the ocean-born,
Unhelped to launch it down the sloping shore
And through the surf. Well used to wield the car
Was she, to urge the boat as thing of life
Through ocean's calm, or ocean's billowy strife.

  XVI

Fast faded now the day's remaining light:
Long ere her lonely home was reached 'twas night.
Then safe within that home at Owia
The wearied maid succumbed to nature's laws;
While night, like gentle mother, fondly laid
Her mantle o'er the child and sleeping maid;
And ocean, modulating now her roar,
Sang softened lullaby along the shore!

  XVII

Now Warramou had noted long the change
In Ranèe's fitful love. 'Twas hard, 'twas strange
Th' impatient chieftain thought, and well he might
His plighted bride should show such constant slight.
Next morn his skiff came dancing with the tide:
He came to woo once more his coyish bride.
Some strife anent the rescued child arose
That pallid offspring of detested foes!
He chid her for her English sympathies,

And waste of love and care which should be his!
And tortured by his green-eyed jealousy,
He fiercely charged her with inconstancy.

 XVIII

She answered not. Though eyes were flashing fire—
For self-reproach had checked her rising ire:
She answered not for self; but for the boy
She bravely spoke; "I've sworn, and sworn with joy,
That I will save that baby-life; and he
Who thinks to injure him is foe to me!
I've sworn; and with my life I will defend
The boy. He is by oath a *Carib's friend*;
And Warramou should help me keep my oath."
He gave his word; and regretful both,
She blaming self for slights and words unkind,
They sauntered forth, with hand in hand entwined,
Where grassy mead sloped down the slippery steep
To grotto hanging o'er the foaming deep:
Well chosen spot to lover's thoughts inspire!
And there, in presence of their ocean sire,
He strove his long-betrothed once more to woo
And vows of love and plight of troth renew;
And long their converse was, long lingered they
Unmindful of the hours that slipped away!
His earnest pleadings of a lover's woes,
Of passion full, sometimes to pathos rose:
That old-world tale, that never weareth old!
Such fragments here, as needs my verse, are told.

 XIX

What ails thee, Ranèe mine? Thy ways are strange—
Thus pleaded he—'tis long I've marked the change.
You're not yourself, nor I myself to you.
What wrong I've done that wrong I would undo
A thousand times! But say the wrongful deed,
And on my knees I will my pardon plead.
Ah! Ranèe, what would I not dare and do

To prove how faithful is thy Warramou!
I'm thine by every vow and pledge; and thee
The gods themselves have given as bride to me.
Oh! If not yet my lavished love has won
My Ranèe's heart, at least the deed I've done
Should win; but yet I will not boast, as though
I'd claim thee as a debt thyself doth owe;
I own 'twas gods, not I, that did the deed—
And yet my hand was there! Yes! Yes! I'll plead
My claim with that!

   XX

             'Tis moons and moons ago
When last the dread Qualeva went to row
His storm canoe, and wake the sleeping winds
For sport, and loose the chafing chord that binds
Them to their prison rocks and coral caves,
Like hunting dogs, his playthings and his slaves;
And forth they sprang from out their deep sea-cage
With howl and screech, and with joy and rage.
I then was fishing on a stormy sea,
While maidens sang some merry songs for me
From off those rocks near yonder Indian Cove:
So calm the sea below, and sky above.

   XXI

A war-bird[67] overhead with flapping wing
Was first to warn, and startled tidings bring
Of coming gale: with terror in her cry
She flew from sea, and hasted screaming by:
The echo-sprite scarce caught the falling, sound
To toss it back, before it touched the ground,
When Obi's far-off thunder faintly rolled.
And quick almost as can no words be told,
The fair blue sky to deepening gloom o'ergrew,
While fitful gusts of wind around me blew;
And soon from out the darkening sky then fell
The first big drops the coming gale that tell.

XXII

They hailed me from the shore: I laughed, aha!
As then I sniffed the coming squall from far,
We love the gale, we children of the wave,
Whose sire th' Sea our life and being gave,
Nursed by the storm, and rocked upon the deep,
Where spirits of the night wild dances keep,
We free-born sons of Ocean and the Isle
Are born to welcome danger with a smile.
We love to ride the storm, and ride with ease:
As some ride prancing horses, we the seas!
Ah! How the fires of heaven lept round and danced,
As Obi's wheels on rolling clouds advanced,
And scattered quivering sparks on every side,
And thundered in the skies; while earth replied
Re-echoing back as loud, yet shook with fear,
As though it knew the dreadful god was near.
Ah! How the fierce winds drove the flying cloud
In wild war-hunt, and shrieked and roared aloud!
And how the terror-spreading water-spout,
In foam and fury joined the flying rout!
Just as the wild black sheep of Morne Garou
Outrun the fleetest hounds of Washlibou;[68]
While fierce and lumbering boars (which dogs with ease
Outspread with lighter foot, and bite and tease,
And chase along the banks of Rabaca)
Will turn with foaming tusk and gaping jaw
Upon their foe's pursuit, and turn again
And yet again, in fury fierce but vain—
'Twas thus the wild winds chased the spout,
Cheered on by Obi's wildest shout.

XXIII

And how in storm and chase fared Warramou?
Out on the deep alone in frail canoe?
No Frenchman's bark, no English Man-of-war
Is safe on such a sea, but *our boats* are

In sea-born Caribs' hands. My dear old boat
But danced upon the storm like corkwood float.
I sat and sang the sea a wild war-song,
As with the flying waves I swept along.
But when the rains were gone, and gone the wind,
Yet left the havoc of their work behind;
And ocean's roll and swell had come at last,
(Till then kept down by fury of the blast)
First sinking down to hideous depths below,
To where the Mermen dwell, and sea-nuts grow.
Then lifting me on mounting waves on high,
As though to fling me helpless to the sky—
My sea-born spirit rose; for then I knew
The dangers which I loved around me drew,
Yet to our father-spirit of the deep
One prayer I sent, his child to guard and keep.
Tamousi, great and wise, cares not to know
(So say our tribes) his creatures' weal or woe;
But he, our father of the bright warm seas,
To watch his children's weal will often please;
Like great *Bondieu,* who loves his Christians well,
Of whom I've sometimes heard my Ranèe tell.

  XXIV

Swept now beyond the cliffs of Biabou,
(So far had drifted down my brave canoe)
I saw those bluffs from base to crest were white
With foam and spray, a grand and glorious sight!
And English soldiers, so it seemed to me,
From off those bluffs were gazing out to sea;
Yet scarce on me they gazed, a tiny speck
Upon the waves; they watched a drifting wreck,
Some grand old ship, some English sloop of war
A helpless wreck, for gone was every spar.
The waves, which would but play with me and pass,
Upheaved against the poor wreck's helpless mass,
A moment paused, then lept in seas aboard,

And then through open ports in torrents poured.
It drifted on a dark and spectral form,
Be-ravined, yet still worried by the storm—
As when the tiger-cat has seized its prey,
Yet tortures it in sheer and wanton play.
No living freight that foundering ship did bear;
For all its crew in terror and despair
In boats, perhaps on planks, had left the wreck,
For Solitude and Death to walk that deck.

  XXV

A wild thought seized my mind to board the hulk:
So quick as thought beside the massy bulk
I rode my boat, beneath the safer lee
Where sails and cordage draggled in the sea.
I sought not white man's gold— it hath small, charms
For Caribs' eyes—I sought the white man's arms,
The musket, sword, and pike for use in war
Which all our chiefs then thought could not be far.
For that I'd brave a hundred deaths, nor fear
To mount the sea-washed decks—for that I'd dare
Qualeva's wrath. My boat secured, I sprang
To lofty poop, while from the cliffs there rang
An English cheer; they cheered the Carib boy,
(The brave admire the brave!) I laughed for joy,
And sent them back their cheer; then sought my prize
With eager gaze below; but horror met my eyes!
Within that awful cabin's narrow span,
Half filled with waves, the features of a man
With ghastly staring eyes there glared on me—
Once boastful lord, now plaything of the sea!
But Death and I too oft have met, for fear
Because I see or feel his presence near!

  XXVI

The glittering dirk, and sword and murderous gun
Well ranged in view; my prize was quickly won,
While those now rocked beneath the deep salt main,

Who owned them once, but ne'er should own again
I gained the deck, but paused and gazed around
There seemed to come some strange soft murmuring sound,
Which reached me through the hissing swell, and roar
Of breakers sounding loudly from the shore.
Was it some voice of spirit of the deep
That came to mourn? Like those who come to weep
The slain of war, in night of battle-day.
While yet the dead are still unburied clay?
Or tender souls that linger round the dead
Until the hours of death's first day have fled?
To me it seemed to murmur near and say,
"Not yet, my son, oh! Go not yet away!"
  XXVII
I paused; but on that instant there uplept
O'er deck and poop a huge green sea, that swept
Me from the ship. Qualeva sent that wave
The spiteful foe of all that's good and brave,
Hiroona's foe! But in the deep below
In battle with the waves I'd not forego
My treasure trove: I swam yet held it fast,
And reached my boat with half my prize at last,
And soon was rocking safely on the deep.
One moment only; for with mighty leap
A monster wave was on my brave canoe;
First flung it quivering into air then drew
It down in whirl-pool deep beneath the foam.
Small hurt from this to Carib boy could come;
But guns and swords were gone; yet quick as thought
I followed them, like flash of light, and caught.
Though sank already, many fathoms deep,
This dirk, this very one, in walk or sleep
My comrade ever since, my trusted blade
In hunt, in battle fray, or plunder-raid.

XXVIII

And when from Ocean's caves I rose to air
My boat capsized was floating idly near.
To right her, fling the waters to the sea,
And gain the oars was easy task to me.
I'd lost—the *Bondieu* had his reasons why—
I'd lost my hard-won spoil; but win or die,
I vowed at once I'd have again as good.
In presence of the grinning dead I stood
Once more, and seized again some arms of death:
This time with beating heart and trembling breath;
For some new fear, some unfamiliar dread
Held fast my soul, as faintly overhead
I thought I heard those low and mournful moans,
Suppressed like Agony's expiring groans.
They seemed to float, like spirits in the air,
And to express not mortal man's despair;
Yet seemed to shape a voice I strangely knew,
And formulate my name "O Warramou"!

XXIX

From Fear's cold grasp I struggled to be free,
And turned with terror-driven foot to flee,
My only thought to spring with one wild leap,
And find my safety in the friendly deep!
But on the deck my flying feet were held,
When I, my fears all gone, a sight beheld
My eyes had missed before. At first amazed,
Soon Pity seized and held me while I gazed!
For hanging, lifeless, from a broken mast,
And bound by circling cords that held her fast,
With drooping hands and head, and long black hair
That draggled dripping in the cold wet air,
The sport of heartless winds and billows wild,
Was Carib girl, in years no more than child;
And while I gazed, those heaving billows flung
Their cold, salt spray, and washed her as she hung.

XXX

A storm of thoughts went through my head:
But fury rose supreme, and pity fled
In wrath as only outraged Caribs feel
When in an enemy's breast th' fatal steel
They bury deep, and drive to very hilt,
Then drink in very hate the blood they've spilt.
A kidnapped Carib maid! I cursed the hand;
That dragged her there from Hiroon's ravished land;
Who, when avenging Heaven the scourge had found
To pay the deed, the fiend had left her bound,
Forgotten in his craven haste to fly—
May be the dastard willed her thus to die!
Then rage and horror almost burst my soul,
And like the swell around me, seemed to roll
In heaving mountains through my breast. *"Bondieu!*
Abandoned, murdered by a heartless crew,
(For so it seemed: I knew not then the truth)
Because a dark-skinned Carib girl, forsooth!
The whites have bound and left her thus to die,
And rot abandoned on the deep; but I,
The Indian boy, will nobler be!" So ran
My furious thought in one short moment's span.
"I'll save the corpse, not leave it there to be
The food of sharks, or monsters of the sea,
Which haunt the sunken ship, with hideous claw
To rake the dead, then gorge with glutton maw."

XXXI

'Twas done as soon as thought; and sure I heard
That voice again, distinct in every word;
"The ship is settling fast; no time to waste,
O Warramou! Oh speed with flying haste
To 'loose the cord with love's own eager hands,
They will not yield? Quick! Cut th' unwilling bands.
And seize, and bear away thy fragile load,
With all the strength Tamousi hath bestowed;

Then fly from th' yawning gulf thyself to save
Cast off thy rope, and fly on flying wave!"
'Twas done! I know not now, I never knew
How e'er I reached at last my good canoe—
With burden safe in such a dangerous sea:
'Tis all like dream confused and lost to me.

 XXXII

The ship had vanished to her deep dark home,
And left to mark her grave one moment's foam!
But at my feet there lay a helpless form—
My dirk and *that* sole salvage from the storm!
And as I looked, strange memories from the vast,
Dim, shadowy, more than half-forgotten past
Came creeping through my slowly-waking brain,
And, mingling with the living, lived again:
And as the misty shadows crossed my view
I scarce could tell the dreamy from the true.
Across that death-bound brow—was that a dream?
There seemed to play a momentary gleam,
As though the soul still lingered near the dead;
Or lept from angel's wing flashed round her head.
But as I gazed with wistful dreamy eye
She moved her lips, and breathed a feeble sigh.
At once from dreamy mists my mind sprang free,
With floods of light the whole truth flashed on me;
"It is! It is my chieftain's long-lost child,
Not dead!" I shrieked, with frantic joy now wild.
Ah! Then I knew whose warning voice I'd heard
Upon the wreck, and which so strangely stirred
Thy shuddering soul, as not of mortal men:
I knew the *Bondieu's* gracious purpose then.
Before the open Heaven's high-vaulted throne
I bowed my knees, and thanked the Great Unknown!

XXXIII

You lived! For, Ranèe, you it was! 'Tis true
That, much you know, but all you never knew.
You lived: there just was breath; but death's cold grasp
Might any moment stifle life's last gasp;
'Twas like the flicker of a dying fire,
Which may be fanned to flame, or may expire.
To give you warmth I laid you to my breast,
And to your poor cold cheek my own I pressed.
I chafed the shrunken hands and wet cramped feet;
And listened for the poor chilled heart to beat.
But all too slow the longed-for warmth returned
And all too faint the flicking life-light burned.
I thought of white man's life-restoring drinks;
And though my haughty Carib nature shrinks
From asking those I hate for gift or boon
(And these I hoped to meet in battle soon)
For you, my chieftain's child, I choked my pride,
And humbly sought where oft I had defied.

XXXIV

The cliff where English soldiers lined the height—
So far I'd drifted—now was out of sight;
But land was very close, and curious eyes
Were there, and following me; and with loud cries
And friendly signs men hailed me from the land.
I paddled closer to the foaming strand;
But through such furious surf with *you* I dared
Not venture—Yet alone I had not feared.
To leeward of a rock, where bristled guns,
I rowed, and there to England's warrior-sons
I showed my freight, and made them understand,
In such few words as I could then command
My pressing want. I scarce had need to ask;
With cords one flung me from the rocks a flask
Of spirit; and, O sight most strange to see!
He drew his cloak, and flung it out to me!

The white men's God doth bid them treat their foes
Like this—but treatment such no Carib knows.
If aught could win me from my country's god
To bow to England's faith and England's rod
'Tis deeds like this! I thanked the noble man,
And vowed to pay the deed if e'er I can;
In planter's 'garb, tall, with open brow,
Though unseen since I yet would know him now.

  XXXV

With spirit to your lips, and warm dry cloak
Around your arms and breast, you soon awoke
To consciousness. I waved my thanks anew,
And English cheers brought back their last adieux.
And then I turned my bow for homeward run.
The sea went quickly down with setting sun,
Then rose at full our glorious queen of night,
And flung o'er each wave-crest her silvery light.
And soon of Batt'wia[69] we'd seen the last;
And soon, the cliffs of Biabou repassed,
The long white line we now could clearly see
Of surf that washed the beach of Colonarie,
At last with clouded moon we crept with awe
Beneath the frowning bluffs of Biëra.

  XXXVI

The while, recovered now from swoon and cold,
Your own strange tale to eager ears you told;
How on that day our chieftain lost you two,
Your brother and yourself, a large canoe
Just off the beach at Rabaca lay moored;
In heedless play you swam, and loosed the cord;
And then by aid of treacherous winds, that blew
In freshening gusts from slopes of Morne Garou
You swiftly rowed to sea; but when, at length,
You sought the land, you found your childish strength
Could make no way against the envious wind;
And from your play you woke at once to find

Yourselves lost waifs, blown helpless out to sea!
And evening closed; and then the agony,
The hunger, cold and tears of long dark night,
When all of home and hope was lost to sight,
Except a fire which waved in mountain breeze,
And twinkling torch that glanced amongst the trees,
And told where grief-full father vainly sought,
And mother watched for tidings none e'er brought!
How through the long night hours you sat and wept,
And how at length exhausted nature slept.
And how (so fast had you been borne along
By wind, and wave, and tide, and current strong,)
When lingering morning came in mist and rain,
For home, for land, your young eyes sought in vain.
"Lost! Lost upon the sea!" Th' appalling truth
Quite crushed all life from e'en your hopeful youth.
You laid you down on that unpitying deep,
And hand in hand you wept yourselves to sleep;
Till, when in evening's hour you startled woke,
Strange men were peering in your boat, who spoke
In words whose sound was strange to you. By chance
They'd seen you drift, those warrior sons of France.
Had turned aside and stayed the waif to save.
And rescued you from worse than watery grave.
  XXXVII
To their own distant isle of Martinique
They carried you; and there you learnt to speak
Their foreign tongue, by Captain's wife caressed—
Of pale-faced race the kindest and the best.
All this you told; and how in those long days,
You learned to know and liked the white man's ways,
And e'en to bow to Christians' God, and pray,
To handle beads, and Paternoster say;
And even learnt their books; yet all the while
You grieved and pined for dear Hiroona's isle.
And when two years had gone how Ronlou died,

And all the more for home you pined and sighed.
Then came a day the wife would not refuse
The husband's prayer to go with him a cruise.
She took you too, that o'er the great blue sea
You might our own dear Island chance to see;
But how it rather chanced an English sloop
Of war came down, like ravenous hawk, with swoop
Upon its prey; and how in short fierce fray
Your Captain fell, and England won the day.
The English sent the ship and captured crew
As prize of war, and sent the lady too;
But you she gave to kindly Captain's care,
An English gentleman, and made him swear
That, as he passed our Isle, he would restore
You to your people on your native shore.

XXXVIII

And then you told of sudden hurricane,
When all of England's seamanship was vain
Their proud and gallant sloop-of-war to save
From wreck, and foundering to an ocean grave.
The sailors took to boats, with little hope
That with such huge wild seas those boats could cope.
Some perished as they touched the waves' wild foam,
And others were capsized in air, and some
From off the davits swept with all their crew;
But how the Captain fared you never knew.
Some few got clear the wreck, and went their way,
But yet what fate was theirs none live to say.
But you, half dead, some rough but kindly hands,
To broken mast, with garments used as strands,
(Lest seas should sweep you from the deck) had bound.
And then you must have swooned, for what befell
From that your failing memory could not tell.
The foundering ship—'tis so I love to think—
As though expecting me had ceased to sink.

XXXIX

'Twas thus your thrilling tale you told, while night
Rolled on her moonlit hours in rapid flight;
Yet long before the dawn of coming day
We reached the sheltered cove of Indian Bay,
And then your father's camp. I need not tell
The rest—chief part yourself, you know it well.
But, Ranèe, from that day my life was bright;
For you became then mine by double right—
I'd won you from the all-devouring deep;
I'd won your father's faithful word to keep
You sacredly as mine, my plighted bride,
Until you'd passed your childhood's morning tide.
You're meant by Heaven's decree for Warramou;
And that Qualeva's self may not undo!

XL

Much more he said of e'en more tender kind
As, lover-like, they sat with arms entwined;
The while the waves from rolling surf beneath
Send ceaseless chant, and ocean's perfumed breath
O'erhead amidst the leafless branches floats,
Or round the rocks, in soft æolian notes.
No rude barbarian he, of speech uncouth.
Prince like, and foremost of the Carib youth
And far beyond his people and his age,
He'd spent a year in English pupilage,
And spoke both French and English fluently,
Though filled with Caribs' fierce antipathy.
Much more he said, to urge his eager suit,
Than for the bard to here record 't would boot,
And Ranèe's heart was won. But flashed across
Her soul one burning thought. She'd be at loss
To say from whence or why at all it came—
That he, her river-champion, was the same
As he, the hero of the rock, who threw
The cloak: there scarce in Hiroon could be two

Such Englishmen; and glistening tear-drops filled
Her eyes: she could not help them had she willed.
But Warramou had won. She gave her word
She would be his from next new moon the third.
But oh! That now this hateful war were done!
That victory, or, at least, that peace were won!
Alas! Ere to the Past one week had fled,
Hiroon was weeping o'er her mighty dead!

End of Canto V

The Caribs Sweep All Before Them

I

E'en gentle streams will hurl their tide
When storm-fed down some mountain's side
O'erleaping banks—where Culture's hand
Had made a little faëry land,
Of vines and palms and orange trees,
And other plant-gems fair as these,
With bower and bed, and bright parterre
Of scented flowers rich and rare;
While, nestling cosily between,
The trellised half-hid cot is seen;
And toil had won from yonder plain
Rich promises of golden grain—
The waters o'er all barriers leap
And in o'erwhelming torrents sweep
The open field and sheltered nook:
(With force no human power can brook.)
Where life and smiling hope they find
They leave but woe and death behind.
So down each craggy mountain side
There poured a headlong human tide,
With no less devastating force
Than marks the swollen torrent's course;
But this a darker deadlier flood,
Red-hued with affluents of blood.

When o'er her fields they made their sweep
Hiroona, shuddering, stooped to weep
Her ravaged lands and slaughtered dead;
And silent desolation spread,
Black-robed in Death's funereal hue,
Where homes once stood and harvests grew.

   II
Down east, down western slopes they poured
Resistless, merciless; each horde
With trusted chieftains at its head,
Half disciplined, but bravely led;
Their arms the musket, bayonet, sword,
The best that Europe could afford—
Though some still bent the ancient bow
With arrow-head ("for deadlier blow")
Of jagged wood instead of steel,
The point well steeped in manchineel.
Such deadly wound the splintered shaft
Would deal, the best skilled surgeon's craft
Could scarce the fragments all withdraw,
And foil the dreaded foe, lock-jaw.

   III
Duvallè—Hiroon's fiercest child,
In action vehement and wild,
Cruel, in war infuriate,
For England full of deadliest hate—
Led down a purely Carib host
To devastate the windward coast,
Where English settlers mostly lay;
His only thought and creed to slay.
Chetwayè, e'en more fell and bold
When roused, was cast in different mould;
He would his acts premeditate,
And would forecast the coming fate:
The one excelled in council far,
The one was thunder-bolt of war.

Some few maroons, a few half-caste,
Some discontented French, and last
Not least, Barbette's own little band,
Had joined them to this chief's command.
Adown the vale of Wallibou[70]
Chetwayè led this motley crew.
His plan of well-designed campaign
To spare, not devastate—to gain
The old French colonists as friends;
And when he'd won his grandest ends,
Exterminating England's power,
In that exultant victory's hour,
Retain the whole for self as prize:
At worst, admit his French allies,
Till better days, to share the spoil.
If no ill fate his plans should foil,
Again he'd wield his conquering arms,
Destroy the French and seize their farms:
Then Hiroon's soil from mount to plain
Should Hiroon's sons alone sustain!

IV
But so the fates did not unfold,
The Caribs' plans were wise and bold:
To Dorset Hill[71] each verging line
Should trend, and there their troops combine;
Then sweep, an avalanche of death,
Upon th' unguarded Town beneath.
And all was nearly won! The crash
Of Hiroon's sudden charge, their dash
On England's feeble lines was such,
They broke and scattered at the touch;
And ere one half-week's course was run,
Th' exulting Caribbees had won
The Isle, all save the trembling town.

V

As thunder-clouds come darkling down,
Enmassing on the hills, and whirl
Around, as gathering force to hurl
Their storm's full fury down the plain,
In thunder, lightning, wind and rain;
So Caribs swarmed on Dorset's height,
Then hued with evening's purple light—
For setting sun had flung a glare,
Which tinged with blood the sickened air;
While ponderous clouds athwart the Heaven;
Portentous, and surcharged with levin,
(Forecast of perils drawing near!)
Weighed down the stifled atmosphere—
Came Caribs grouping on the hills,
The darkening mass aye gathering still;
Yet scintillating with the sheen,
That flashed from out the gloom of keen
Bright bayonet point, or naked blade;
As though electric sparks had played
Athwart the surcharged atmosphere,
While yet no thunder struck the ear.

VI

The startled town, bewildered, dazed
At such an apparition, gazed
In dread suspense. With trembling feet
In groups assembling in the street,
Each told his neighbour in the throng
His whispered fears with stammering tongue
"We have no force that can protect
The town—by night we must expect
The worst, those hordes come pouring down."
Wild terror held the shuddering town;
And Heaven recorded many a tear,
To many a hurried vow lent ear!
Yet night dragged on till morning broke

And hope, renewed with dawn, awoke.
But had the Caribs been more bold,
Far different tale the bard had told;
But caution, coming now too late,
For re-inforcements bade them wait.
Had they but kept their counsel still
Had Patience curbed their fury, till
The French had brought their promised aid,
And, full equipped, they then had made
Their onset without halt or pause,
Lost would have been old England's cause:
Their rashness, brooking no delay,
Near won, but really lost the day.

  VII

The minstrel's song too fast doth flow:
And back the stream of time must go;
Must tell of rout our countrymen saw
At thy red stream, O Massarica![72]
Tell how our troops no better did fare
On deadly field of Chateaubelair.[73]
The day had risen in mist and in rain
Through which the sun had struggled in vain,
Yet all not mist that clouded the air,
But smoke which rose from many a fair
And comely home, and many a field,
Which, golden crops no longer shall yield.
For all night long that tragical scene,
Which "Planter's Hope" had yesterday seen,
When whites and blacks together were slain,
And thrice-told woes were acted again.

  VIII

Duvallè 'twas commanded the force;
His martial spirit directed its course,
Four thousand strong reputed to be.
And this rolled on—as when from the sea
Some tidal wave, or huge rushing bore;

Upflows some stream, and sweeps all before;
While on it rolls resistless, and grows
More huge more fierce each mile that it flows,
Until it reach some affluent stream;
Then swerves in two, each fiercer 'twould seem,—
So this tumultuous wave, as it rolled
With freight of woes and horrors untold,
Each moment seemed new forces to gain,
Until o'ercharged, it parted in twain.
One stream held on its southerly bent,
And gathering force as onward it went,
Aye fiercer yet and swifter it grew
And sweeping on past Conbiamarou,[74]
Impinged at last on Calliaqua.
The other made for Marriaqua;[75]
To threaten with wreck the beautiful vale,
And fill its homes with weeping and wail.

IX

And where was England's vaunted power,
Meanwhile, in danger's anxious hour—
The ever ready, ever strong,
To aid the weak, avenge the wrong?
See yonder streak now glancing red!
It is th' advancing column's head
Come creeping round the windy bluff;
Where ocean's tides and billows rough
Are surging fifty yards below;
Above, some thirty yards or so,
The cliffs like mighty walls uprise,
Rock-ramparts towering to the skies.
Now, winding round some angle sharp
On such huge rampart's slippery scarp,
The column creeps; while over-head
The cliffs throw down their menace dread,
And make the nervous heart-strings quake.
For splintered peak and severed flake

Of worn and weather-beaten rock,
All mined by frequent tempest's shock
Would seem, in airy heights above
'Midst moving clouds themselves to move,
And oscillate before the eyes;
As though the sea-gull as it flies,
Could loose them by its passing wing,
And on that march below could fling

   X

But bold and confident their tread,
Like troops so oft to victory led;
To them it seemed but sport of war:
What Carib hordes could stand before
Their threatening front much less be targe
For fire, or wait the British charge!
They march with easy, careless gait,
As men whom certain victories wait;
No caution shown, no scouts outflung,
Their goal the frontier post Mount Young,
Their task, with merely warfare's frown,
To put an Indian rising down!
And Expectation soon fulfils
That task, and hunts them to the hills:
Alas! When evening closed that day
The hunters were themselves the prey!

   XI

And now th' advancing column seen
Far flashing red on hill-side green,
The Caribs pause to fling on high
Such yell, as fills the lowering sky,
And from the hills and mountain's flanks
Upon the startled English ranks
Rolls down in one continuous roar—
Grim challenge of the coming war!
Along those ranks a tremor thrills,
And terror more than one heart chills.

At conch-shell's can and bugle's note,
Whose long-drawn undulations float
Upon the heavy, smoked-filled air.
Come pouring in from everywhere
The Carib hordes—from yon estate,
And yonder smoking pile, where late
Grand sugar-works and mansion stood;
From o'er the hills, from out yon wood;
From yonder fields of standing cane;
From yonder low and blackened plain,
O'er which the withering flames have swept
Or cocoa piece, through which they've crept
To reach yon hill with wooded brow,
Round which they're fiercely rushing now—
From every side the Caribs pour;
And still the conch shells call for more.

  XII

They quickly fill the open ground,
Where hills stand semi-circling round.
Where floats a banner from a lance
A blood-stained battle-flag of France;
And there upon a mound, just high
Enough that thence his hawk-like eye
May scan his warriors far and near,
And voice may reach the furthest ear,
Duvallè stands. His broad deep chest
Is bare; but arms of Europe's best,
Cartouch, and pistol, dirk and sword.
Depend from belt of scarlet cord,
And bristle in barbaric taste
In horrid circle round his waist.
He makes one signal with his hand;
All own his prowess to command,
And quick the barbarous pass-word flies,
"The man who fails Hiroona dies!"

The conchs and bugles cease their clang;
And thus he makes his brief harangue:

  XIII

"Hiroons! See there your foes advance!
See yonder how their bayonets glance!
They're England's well-drilled troops, you see;
But then they fight for pay; while we
For country, freedom, and for life
Itself, have drawn the warrior's knife.
The men who war, as we, for right,
Are doubly armèd for the fight!
The memory of your country's wrong
Shall make each heart and arm more strong;
Shall give more keenness to your steel,
And drive more home each blow ye deal.
With this ye need no shield, no charm
'Twill lead to victory, guard from harm!
At last has come Hiroona's day:
Comrades, your manhood now display!
To ravage as in common raids,
To slaughter mothers, boys, and maids,
Or sabre unarmed men and slaves,
Is play, not work, for men and braves!
Cease that awhile: go meet the foe
With foot to foot, and blow for blow,
And make those English boasters learn,
That Caribs *can* do more than burn
And pillage lands—that, brave as they,
They fight and win in open day.
Upon your swords let be no rust;
And when we've won, as win we must,
We then, by Victory's fair award,
To heart's content shall glut our sword!
Now shout and send our challenge far,
Hiroona's shout and yell of war!
Ha! Ha! They hesitate—they halt.

They look unsteady, seem at fault!
And hark! Their drums some order beat.
Again!—It is! It is, 'Retreat!'
They face about - they flee! They flee!
And leave us unbought victory![76]
Caribs! We must their flight pursue,
And of that corps escape shall few."
  XIV
His plans were bold, and quickly made,
And no small soldier-skill displayed
He won that day, true son of Thor,
His name of "Thunder-bolt of war."
Joyette, as second- in command,—
'Twas so his skilful war was planned—
He should, with cautious steps and slow,
Pursue the now retreating foe;
Should not engage, but hover near,
As threatening his disheartened rear;
Spread out his men o'er plain and hill,
Displaying them with care and skill,
And so manœuvering, deceive
And make the Englishmen believe,
That all the Carib force is there,
Half timid, hanging on his rear.
Himself with far the greater force,
Would shun the coast-line's winding course;
Would cross the hills by paths well known,
But trod by Carib feet alone;
And thus the enemy outmarch,
As by the chord that spans the arch;
Then halt on banks of Mass'rica,
His troops within its gorge withdraw.
The trees, that cluster in the glade,
Would cover yield for ambuscade.
The English thus way-laid, pursued,
Impending fate could not elude!

XV

Compact and close, with measured beat,
The British Infantry retreat.
Around huge bluffs the roadway creeps,
Or round the circling valley sweeps,
Where 'tween two headlands bold it dips,
Which stand apart like parted lips;
Or, past the high cliffs' threatening frown,
Now trails along the grassy down.
How soft that velvet green! Ere night
That mead shall show a different sight—
Its green empurpled with blood-stain,
Its softness rough with mangled slain;
For ambush, war and slaughter lurk
Hard by, impatient for their work.

XVI

And hark! That cry, which from the rear
Like demon laughter strikes the ear!
And say! Yon plain was bare, when last
Its well known slopes our army passed?
Not there those shrubs and sapling trees,
Which close it now? See in the breeze
They sway, as though there blew a gale,
While here the sleepy zephyrs fail
To stir the sultry air, too weak
To bathe the brow, or fan the cheek!
And see yon clouds of watchful foes
Descending from the hills! They close
In gathering masses on the rear,
And bring the threatened onset near.

XVII

'Twas here the highest cliffs o'erhung
The road and gloomiest shadows flung—
That road itself but narrow ledge
Two fathoms wide, from whose bare edge
(O'er which one peeped with shuddering fear)

The frightful precipice fell sheer
Into the foaming surf below:
Terrific spot to meet one's foe!
Round this the cautious columns wind:
Be sure that none now lag behind;
Be sure that many an anxious eye
Has scanned those threatening bluffs so high;
And many have glanced, to quickly shrink
Back shuddering from the path's sheer brink.
A strange deep awe bespells each breast.
No flippant laugh is heard, no jest;
Where rang the oath, or boast o'erbold,
The whispered thought is scarcely told.
Below the ocean moans a dirge.
  XVIII
At length the leading files emerge
Upon the green: keen glance is cast
Ahead. "All's well!" Cries one, and fast
Along the ranks the murmur flies,
Till on the rearmost lips it dies:
Unseen the foe's approach in rear,
Undreamt aught else of danger near!
But now a yell; and such a yell!
As though from deepest dens of hell
It burst, and rent the stagnant air
As if a thousand fiends were there!
And then a crash and tear of rocks,
And showers of stone and massive blocks,
Beneath which many a soldier brave
At once found both his death and grave.
"An earthquake from the depths profound
Hath shook the trembling mountains round!
Or asteroid hath burst, and hurled
The fragments of a shattered world!"
'Twas so in first surprise it seemed
As down that rocky torrent streamed;

Yet nought unearthly there befell,
From demon, riven sky, or hell!
 XIX
Where sea-birds wing their airy flight,
The Caribbees had lined the height;
And now upon their foes beneath
With rocks and crags, were hurling death!
Yet, though on death's dread mission sent,
Full many a crag in its descent,
Attracted, struck the cliff's straight wall,
And thence, repelled like tennis ball,
(For England's troops indeed 'twas well!)
O'erlept the ledge-like path, and fell
Down plunging to the sea below—
Else none had 'scaped the huge o'erthrow!
 XX
When Panic found more threat than harm,
He rallied from his first alarm.
But yet in vain, the gallant stand!
In vain rings forth the loud command!
In vain they fire 'gainst crag and peak!
The leaden missiles vainly seek
The lurking foes! While they, secure
Beyond Revenge's reach, still pour
Down death, and all approach defy:
The English unavengèd die,
Then from such hopeless war away!
It is but massacre to stay:
Here flight is no dishonour; gain
More room for war in yonder plain!
 XXI
Then forth the broken battalion rushed,
While still the falling boulders crushed
Some few, who wounded, lingered still
Escaped from that o'erhanging hill,
As from a slaughter-pit, or vault

Prepared for sepulture,[77] they halt,
Reform their broken ranks, and count
Their loss, and mourn the sad amount.
But fast the thickening war draws near;
The foe comes thundering in the rear:
The "Forward at the quick!"
                              Ha! Flash
From out yon trees in front, and crash
Of musketry some foe betray,
In ambush there to bar the way!
And see! At that death-signal dread,
From rock, from tree, from river bed,
The swarthy Caribs spring to view!
Ah! England, now thy folly rue!
'Tis fatal to despise a foe.
All hope now hangs on one strong blow.
With sword and bayonet cleave the way:
An English charge may save the day!
Give them your fire. Saint George for you!
And steady be your aim and true:
Then give them home the bayonet, boys!
  XXII
Too slow! Too slow the line deploys!
Why lags the lingering fire? Why pause
Before destruction's open jaws?
"Charge! Charge!" Too late! For now outburst
The Carib volleys crashing first
Before the English fire one shot.
Fall scores of English on the spot;
And when they fire, their volleys fail,
And harmless falls the leaden hail;
For heart and hands unsteady grow.
And now, when gleams the glittering row
Of bayonets levelled for the run
Ere yet ten yards of ground are won,
Their foes step forth to meet the shock;

While still from every mound and rock,
From every tree, with deadly aim
There bursts the death-propelling flame.
And lo! The trees themselves advanced
And seem to join in war's wild dance!
From yonder, where but now they stood,
Huge shrubs and saplings come, a wood
Of walking, leaping trees! But some
Cast off their branches as they come
And thus, that umbrage gone, reveal
The foes they did so well conceal![78]
  XXIII
The foe along the river's bank;
The foe in front; the foe on flank;
And yelling in the closing rear,
Where on the hill-tops they appear—
The English now perceive their fate:
They slacken pace—they hesitate;
And numbers fall, and numbers die.
Great God above! They break, they fly!
They leap the precipice! For death
Though everywhere, yet down beneath
Those heights, midst rocks, perchance on sand,
Death *there,* than death by Caribs' hand,
Less terrible! That fatal coast
Has seen Duvallè win his boast
And win at England's fearful cost—
Her prestige gone, her honour lost!
Ah! How it fell that dreadful day,
'Tis strange that any lived to say!
  XXIV
No prisoners made, no quarter given.
Before the hastening sun had driven
His glowing wheels one half-hour west,
Where downy beds await his rest,
Their work was done, the carnage o'er;

And yet, to make e'en death more sure,
The Caribs traverse all the plain;
And trampling on the yet warm slain,
With sword and bayonet thrust them through,
And glut their rage and hate anew
 XXV
Then tidings of the great disaster
(Than evil news no news moves faster;
And this on wingèd foot-steps flew)
Soon reached the camp at Biabou,
With many horrors added on.
Then Panic seized the garrison;
And urged by its resistless dread,
The troops in huge disorder fled.
"Defenceless settlers left to fate!"
The thought had scarce one atom's weight:
The warrior's master thought that day
How best to get themselves away!
 XXVI
Abandoned thus, the whole sea-board
Was swept by rapine, fire and sword—
Near half the isle, if line you draw
From Mount Young point to Calliaqua.
Duvallè kept his wrathful word,
And gave to mad debauch his sword.
Extermination all his aim,
The whites were slaughtered as they came
To hand, nor age, nor sex was spared,
And negro slaves scarce better fared.
The old, the young, the newly born
Alike were doomed; the infants torn
From mothers' very breasts and dashed
Upon the ground—the victims, gashed
And mutilated, left to die
In slow unpitied agony.
The sky rained down the dewy tear,

But mercy, aye to Heaven so dear,
On other mission sent that day,
To unchecked fury left the way!
From cane-fields, homesteads, factories, burned;
From smiling plains to deserts turned,
Whence every living thing had fled;
From valleys strewed with rotting dead;
Exhaled a rank and poisonous breath;
While o'er the blackened void now Death
And Solitude, allies of eld,
Confederated empire held.
  XXVII
'Twas thus the fierce Duvallè warred,
With havoc's bloodiest scath and sword,
Along where ceaseless trade-winds urge
The wide Atlantic's untamed surge
On Hiroon's wave-beat Eastern shore.
See how those rolling billows pour
Against some bold out-standing rock
Their floods! Though staggered by the shock,
They leap and whiten with their spray
His crown (with brine not ages gray);
Then down his stiff, black limbs they flow
In robes of grace, as pure as snow.
Or loud as thunder, lash the strand—
Not where there lies the pliant sand,
But granite boulders, turned and ground
By ocean's constant friction, round
Like monster cannon-balls, or sized
As skulls of giants fossilized:
These flung in rage, or tossed in play,
And rattling 'neath the surf and spray,
Resound, and thus add two-fold more
To ocean's own majestic roar.
There, stunted trees, (and few will grow
Where winds so keen and constant blow)

Which sparsely line the cedared hill,
Are clipped, as though by gardener's skill,
By gales of salt-encumbered air;
The rocks left e'en by lichens bare.
Along this never silent shore,
Where storms, (long gathering up, from o'er
A thousand leagues of open sea,
Their vast reserves of energy
And stores of meteoric force.)
Sweep down their fierce resistless course,
In flood and thunder black as night,
And lightnings more than noon-day bright—
There swept that fiercer human tide
Of passion wild, intensified.
By memories brooded o'er so long—
Three centuries of crime and wrong!

XXVIII

Meanwhile along the leeward coast
Chetwayè leads his conquering host;
From where the Souffrière rears so high
His massive piles to meet the sky,
That downy clouds perpetual rest,
Like shroud of snow, on head and breast,
To where the bold St. Andrew[79] ends
The lofty mountain chain, and trends
In hastening slopes and falls to meet
The sea, and bathe his naked feet.

XXIX

Ah! How long the whole coast-line,
The grand and beautiful combine!
How smiling seas intensely bright,
And scintillating with the light,
Dissolve through every shade of blue,
Until they wear jet's deepest hue!
And screened by lofty piles of hill,
(At water's line they're mountains still)

The resting ocean's heaving cease;
No boisterous winds there break the peace,
And scarce the playful evening breeze
Makes ripple o'er those placid seas.
　XXX
By rocks all bare and stratified,
That rise like walls from out the tide
Immensely high, profoundly deep,
The currents strong but noiseless sweep;
Yet flowing on from year to year
Those stubborn rocks they cannot wear.
There sea-birds, undisturbed, find rest,
There raise their broods in peaceful nest;
There 'thwart the bare rock's slippery side,
Chameleon-like, iguanas glide;
Assume at will their robes of light
Or gloom—in gold and emerald bright
In glittering splendour there displayed
Or gloaming there in deepening shade.
　XXXI
And here, from off this rocky steep,
To eye deceived an easy leap
'Twould seem for plunge and swim, although
The tempting waters really flow
In treacherous depths so far beneath,
That leap or fall would sure be death.
And there, the well-pleased eye surveys
The widening bights or narrowed bays,
Where culture lines the fertile reach
Or wild luxuriance holds the beach
And cove, (where reigns perpetual calm)
With almond trees and cocoa-palm,
With guava groves and sea-side grape,
(Strange trees of most fantastic shape!)
With cactus on yon sandy bed,
With frangipanni, (white and red,

Which waft around their breath perfumed,)[80]
With royal palmiste crowned and plumed.
With clusters here of huge bananas
And on yon rocks the wild ananas;
While, proud with coronet and spear,
Rise aloes on the craglets there.

XXXII

And yonder, 'neath that hanging cliff
Where noiseless glides that Carib skiff,
All dark the glassy waters lie
There, mirror'd on the deep, are sky,
And cloud and rock, and passing boat,
And birds on airy wing that float,
And frowning bluff, and pendant tree,
All reproduced so faithfully,
(Ideal with true so closely blends!)
Where rocks begin and water ends
No eye can tell-which Nature made—
As solid rock, which watery shade!
And there the sombre rocks above
Close round, to form the narrow cove;
And hanging trees their branches spread,
And stretch so far to reach o'erhead,
That shades of almost night they throw
Upon the sleeping tide below.
So cool that shade, so dim that light,
'Tis exquisite relief to sight,
When wearied with the glare of day,
And fevered with its burning ray.
There owls scarce sleep, to rocks scarce cling
The bats, but flit on restless wing.
With cautious oar and noiseless skiff
The boatman glides beneath that cliff;
For jombie[81] coarse, or classic fay
There lurks, and wide awake all day.
Perchance some blood-stained pirate there

Had made of old his 'customed lair,
And there his dark unshriven soul
Still haunts, though ages onward roll.
  XXXIII
Yet just beyond its darkening frown,
A mass of glowing light pours down,
And spreads abroad a brilliancy,
Like molten sun upon the sea.
But where, refracted, burns less fierce
That blaze, the eye undazed can pierce
The volume of the mighty deep,
And scan some treasures in his keep
May be, some sparkling coral bed;
May be, some sea-weed gardens, spread
With flowers and silvered fronds, midst which
Ten thousand creatures, rare and rich
In hue and form, disport and play,
Or eager seek th' abundant prey
And ever where no eye can sound
Those depths so vasty and profound,
Yet through the watery strata low
With mellowed sun-beams all aglow
The scaly tribes in shoals are seen;
And glittering with their silver sheen,
Their maze of merry measures thread—
Or *silk,* or *snapper,* flaming red,
Like flashing-meteor leaves a line
Of gold and silver in the brine.
Or parrot-fish, which sparkles through
Transparent seas a brilliant blue;
And other swimmers numberless
(Of which yet Science scarce has guess)
Through that pellucid medium sweep;
Or here and there take flying leap
In air, the silent waters lash,
Then, falling, make the frequent splash;

When mimic rainbow-colours gleam
A moment in the dancing beam.
 XXXIV
And then the endless chain of hill,
With valley, rivulet, and rill
Alternate, clad in fadeless green—
Each adds its beauty to the scene.
Oh! How fond memories linger o'er
The glorious beauties of that shore!
'Twas down those sunny hills and bays,
By wooded paths and devious ways,
The wiley chief Chetwayè, cold
And serpent-like, and self-controlled,
With cautious noiseless footfall crept,
Like panther crouching ere he lept;
While round the coast his war-canoes,
With boys and women for their crews—
Not marshalled then for war and blood,
But laden deep with stores and food,
And spare munition for the fight—
Came creeping stealthily by night
From Fancy Bay,[82] and e'en beyond,
To wait events beneath Morne Ronde,[83]
The while he led his warriors down.
 XXXV
Chateaubelair, the old French town,
Extending round the narrow bay
And up the glen, low nestling lay,
Each flank commanded by a hill.
There brooded Discontent, Ill-will,
Disloyalty in no small part,
In many an old French settler's heart,
And Rumour, like the scarce-heard roll
Of far-off thunder, while the whole
Blue vault of Heaven is yet serene,
Nor sign of coming storm is seen:

The listening hinds look up and wonder
If what they hear be really thunder—
So Rumour's mutterings, faintly heard,
Were floating in the air and stirred
Some vague suspicion in men's breasts,
That treachery, that worst of pests,
Was leaguing French and Caribbees
With England's foemen o'er the seas;
But few then really thought much harm
Could come: most deemed it weak alarm.
  XXXVI
Brave Seton,[84] then the Governor,
Though trained in acts of peace, not war,
Alone foresaw the storm would break,
And set himself at once to make
Best disposition in his power,
To meet dark danger's coming hour;
Called out Militia bands, who all
Responded promptly to his call;
And loyal confident and bold,
These yeoman-troops marched down, to hold
Chateaubelair, to re-inforce
Its garrison's then feeble force;
But scarce had occupied the ground
When, creeping down the hills all round
The Caribs on the green wood's verge
In fast increasing mass emerge.
  XXXVII
"To arms! To arms!" The bugles sound;
And trembles now the hollow ground
To soldiers' quick and heavy tramp.
And horse-hoofs to and fro the camp,
Urgent on flying errands sent.
With sound of coming battle blent;
The sharp command, the ring of steel
From belted sword, or armèd heel,

Or flint-edge proved by hammer's fall,
Or ram-rod driving home the ball

 XXXVIII

Short time for preparations given:
Short time, alas! For souls unshriven!
For now the Caribs, with a yell
A thousand-tongued, and fierce as hell,
Rushed forward from the sheltering wood.
Not in battalioned ranks they stood,
Nor charge in columned mass their foes,
(Scarce disciplined enough for that) yet close,
And man to man; and so they rush;
One moment, Expectation's hush;
The next, upon th' expectant car
There bursts the English fire and cheer.
Too far the foe! The volleys fail,
And harmless falls their leaden hail.
The troops were raw in warfare's art,
Untrained the eye, though brave the heart.

 XXXIX

Derisive shouts then rent the air,
With rush the Carib hordes drew near,
Nor from the close encounter shrank;
First paused to hurl their fire point-blank,
Then dropt to earth to load again:
Their foes: dropt *they* in death and pain!
Ah! Then there raged for one half-hour
The flash, and flame, and leaden shower,
And rattle fierce of musketry,
In small but fatal mimicry
Of thunder-blasts of angered Heaven,
And flashes of its awful levin.

 XL

Not long did Doubt the balance hold
Between the hosts; events soon told
Which way the arduous fight would go;

Which fate would aid, and which o'erthrow.
Diverse surprise had seized, 'twas clear,
Both hosts, surprise of hope and fear.
This one had thought, in easy fight
At once to turn their foes to flight;
And *that*, for desperate work prepared,
The potent dread of England shared.
Surprised at vigour of th' attack;
At fault for means to hurl it back;
At every round the foe more near,
Who showed no sign of flight or fear,
The war on England's yeomen frowned
Though stubbornly they held their ground
Each moment fell their spirits lower,
Their nerves each moment spent their power
Not so the warlike Caribbees:
Each passing moment gave to these
More confidence, more hope inspired,
Cheered on, and more their fury fired:
The more that victory seemed in view,
Their onset more audacious grew.

  XLI

Outnumbered far, outflanked as well,
Before Death's scythe the English fell
As autumn's harvest falls; at most
One half of that once gallant host
Now stood. All heart and courage broke,
At last th' un-English word is spoke,
"Retreat!" The remnant face about,
Then fly in helpless, hopeless rout.
The foe their broken flight pursue,
And Death, the Reaper, gleans a few.
The Caribs, crowding o'er the field;
No mercy show, no quarter yield.
The wounded die; and o'er the plain
Lie thick the mutilated slain.

XLII

Some stragglers from the worsted band;
Some fugitives along the strand;
Some pack-mules up the hilly road,
Slow toiling 'neath the household load;
Some laden ·slaves with "massa's" goods,
Now creeping 'neath yon shadowy woods;
Some boats with ladies 'long the shore,
Which ply a nervous, unskilled oar;
All flying now in mortal fear
Of Caribs following in the rear—
Such frightened groups, such sights as these,
For hours the lingering day-light sees;
Till friendly shades of night close o'er,
Yet add some unshaped terrors more.

XLIII

The first to reach Queen Charlotte's Fort,[85]
And there that fatal field report,
Was slave, on mule: he'd cast his load,
And mounting, terror-driven, rode.
And all night long, and all next morn
Came fugitives, footsore, and worn
With toil, with cheeks assoiled with tears,
Or furrowed deep and blanched with fears—
From leeward and from windward came;
The maid, the boy, and courtly dame,
And gentleman of honour too,
With gartered knee and powdered queue.

XLIV

Each had adventurous tale to tell
Of hair-breadth 'scape, that there befell
From some most hideous form of death—
From death that, torturing, lingereth,
Or death that slays at single blow;
From fire, or sword, or Indian bow;
From lead that sought them o'er the plain,

From torrents, threatening watery grave,
Or desperate chase on th' ocean wave.
Some told Chetwayè's sure pursuit,
To reap his signal victory's fruit;
Some spread the direst of alarms
Of fierce Duvallè's conquering arms.
Two streams of fugitives; from East
Came pouring most, from leeward least
For many French their fealty broke
Shook off, they said, proud England's yoke,
And seized the hour, with Frenchman's brag
To join Chetwayè's bloody flag—
Two streams that poured in ceaseless flow;
Each wavelet bringing in new woe.
  XLV
So passed that long, long weary day
Its terror-laden hours away.
Meanwhile the Carib hordes converge
From north, and east, and west, and merge
Their conquering hosts in one and gain
Their plan of well-devised campaign.
Noon saw their van on Dorset Hill,
And evening saw them mustering still.
There stood the trembling Town aghast,
And hundreds deemed that night their last!

End of Canto VI

CARIBS REPULSED: CHETWAYÈ FALLS

I

That night fell not th' expected stroke:
The threatened Town next morn awoke
To hope revived. The wily foe
From unknown cause reserved his blow:
And Seton, always brave and true
To high emergency, all through
That anxious terror-weighted night
Had seized each moment in its flight;
Had summoned all the well disposed,
And organized a force, composed
Of royal troops, militia men,
And many volunteers; and then
Had marched them in the dead of night
To camp on Sion Hill[86]—a height
Far less than Dorset's towering steep;
But yet securing power to sweep
Th' approaches leading from the East
Into the Town—a point at least
From whence to watch the daring foe,
If by the open road below
He sought the Town, or sought to creep
By craggy pathways down the steep.

II

When vigorous deeds are promptly done
In danger's face, half victory's won!
To many a bosom anguish torn,
To many a manly breast, that morn,
So welcome, brought intense relief;
For men then felt they had a chief
With heart to dare, and do, and caught
The fire from him, as brave men ought.
Then hundreds freely volunteer,
Who neither now despise, nor fear,
But so much respect, their savage foe:
Would God it had been always so!
To do the all, resolves each man,
That England's sturdiest manhood can.

III

But all along the circling Bay,
Round which so picturesquely lay
Th' endangered town, the whole night long
There ebbed and flowed an anxious throng.
The matron, maid, and babe were there,
And feeble age with silvered hair;
The European, high-born or base,
And slaves of swarthy Afric's race.
Some still, with awe which feels, not speaks;
But others piercing night with shrieks;
For maddening fears of Carib sack
Their wild imaginations rack—
Such fears as make the blood run cold
And blanch the cheeks of e'en the bold
Are driving all that crowd to flee,
And seek some safety on the sea.

IV

Confusion, gathering more and more
Of terror, swayed the crowded shore;
While to and from the water's side

All night the sturdy boatmen plied
Their weary oars in frequent trips,
To ferry to the sheltering ships
Or stores of gold and valued plate,
Or, mostly, helpless human freight—
The English mother, new-made wife,
And maiden fair, who fled for life,
And more than life—from what than death
A hundredfold more terror hath.
The *men*—their country's hour of need
Required of them to fight and bleed:
What tears and anguished partings then
'Tween those who ne'er might meet again!

   V

Among the throng who went and came,
Conspicuous by his manly frame,
Was courteous Norman: when he knew
That children, wife, and mother too
Were safe embarked upon the wave,
Contented, then he turned and gave
His splendid powers, with no reserve,
His country and his King to serve.
But some, who flung themselves on board
The boats, and shamelessly implored
To stay, (though form of men they bore,
Poltroons!) were sternly thrust on shore.

   VI

Now, when our troubles seem to fill
Their utmost measure up, there still
Are troubles worse than ours behind,
Worse in degrees, and worse in kind.
Thus while upon the friendly deck,
Bewailing loss of wealth, and wreck
Of home (expected in their fears,)
Some women, mingling briny tears
With ocean's deeper brine, bemoan

As hardest of all fates their own;
One delicate, refined as they,
And formed of just as pure as clay,
A high-caste stamped upon her brow;
A wife, but widowed, childless now,
And homeless too (for all was gone!)
Half maddened, helpless, all alone,
Through wild and wold, o'er hill and brae[87]
Two fearful nights, one dreadful day
Had passed, all through Duvallè's raid;
Death hovering round each step she made.
 VII
She'd seen the hopes of years o'erturned,
Her crops destroyed, her homestead burned,
Her slaves all killed, and all her stock,
The lowing herd, and woolly flock,
Yet this, though great, the lightest blow
Of her accumulating woe:
Her husband, glorying in the wealth
Of manly and exuberant health,
Had ridden forth, most miserably
By hand of woman-fiend to die.
By chance she'd seen him pass beneath,
Where leafy branch and flowering wreath,
Entwining overhead, had made
Such scented and refreshing shade,
As there had tempted him aside
To give his mare the rein, and ride
With lingering steps; and thus decoyed,
A dear-bought lux'ry he enjoyed,
While gentler musings filled his brain
Than cotton-pods or sugar-cane.
 VIII
The fiend (in hell such hags are hatch'd)
With glistening serpent-eyes had watch'd
Him pass, and formed her purpose dread.

She glided with her noiseless tread,
And sweeping past her victim, made
One stroke with ten-inched dagger-blade—
A back-hand stroke, which opened wide
A fearful wound from side to side
Beneath his belt: At once the man
Succumbed to Hecate's dread ban.[88]
For second stroke like that no ned;
That fatal one had done the deed;
And yet the hag, to instinct true,
That moment vanished from the view.

   IX

"My wife! My child!" These words alone
Come mingling with his dying groan:
He swooned, and falling to the ground,
His life fled through the hideous wound.
Come Caribs then, and quartered him;
And women bore each bleeding limb
To where th' assembled Chieftain's still
Where holding council on "The Hill."
Thus widowed, next her eldest born,
And sole remaining child, was torn
From out her arms' own mothering hold,
As in these rhymes hath erst been told.

   X

But midst the torturing fears that filled,
And with their agony nigh stilled
For e'er that mother's heart—midst cold
Hard things which Reason's whisperings told
Against all hope, that heart still clung
To one unreasoning hope; it hung
On what all else had deemed absurd
But her's, the mother's heart, the word
An unknown Carib damsel gave
She would her child, if living, save;
And clinging to such hope, she clung

To weary life, which else she'd flung
In mad despair away—
          She thought
To linger near her home, and sought
A neighbour's house at dusk, but found
A band of Caribs prowling round,
And fled into the moonless night,
And lost herself. In piteous plight
She wandered on through wood and brake
For hours, till, stiff with toil and ache,
Her weary limbs would do no more.
Where drooping plantain-fronds spread o'er
Some shade, she just had strength to creep,
And there she wept herself to sleep.

  XI
But ere the 'lated sun had broke
Next morn through clouds of mist and smoke,
She'd sprung with start and ringing scream
From out the horrors of a dream:
She'd seen a white-haired boyez priest
Presiding o'er a drunken feast
And rout, by watch-fires' lurid light,
Whose glare made visible the night,
And played, in hideous phantasies
Of ghostly light and shade, on his
And hundred others' features, foul
And swarthy-hued as his, with scowl
As dark and terrible as e'er
Made human beings like fiends appear.
The Caribs yelled for warrior-food;
And he with gory hands, imbrued
In human blood and dripping yet,
Unhung a heavy caldron, set
To seethe besides a blazing hearth,
Or altar, built of baken earth.
When thence its wooden lid he took

Within she might, but dared not look—
Her fancy saw it all, and through
Her mind the dread conviction flew
What kind that caldron held of meat:
They'd slain her baby-boy to eat!
  XII
Half maniac, with frightful scream
She woke; but haunted by that dream,
Her heart scarce less of anguish knew
Than if the dream had all been true;
And scarce could Reason's weakened power
Dispel th' illusion of that hour.
Then forth she rushed in aimless flight,
With mind unstrung, tear-blinded sight,
And weary bleeding feet, all day—
Self-lost, yet guided on her way
Through all by Father-hand that sent
Her woes, but in them mercy meant.
She saw the country fired all round;
She heard the war's not distant sound,
The fierce war-shout, the musket-shot
On every side, except the spot
Her flying footsteps chanced to tread
She came across the weltering dead;
She passed the desolated home;
And once she even chanced to come
Upon a Carib village, mid
The forest's deepest umbrage hid;
Some dogs rushed forth to chase her flight,
And harass her with bark and bite;
But human for not one, nor yet
One friend, in all her wanderings met.
  XIII
O'ercome at length with toil and pain,
Beside a field of ripened cane
She flung herself and prayed to die;

And Death himself indeed was nigh!
From yonder blazing fields the flame,
Swept on by morning breezes, came
Most fierce, and with resistless force—
Like crescent moon of fire its course
Until its sweep embraced the spot
On which she lay, but heeded not.
And when from swoon-like sleep she woke,
And some new sense of danger broke
Upon her mind, on either hand
The horns had crossed the path: and fanned
By rising winds, now downward bore
The flames with rush and hideous roar
Like charge of fiery cavalry.
Beyond the path where cane-fields dry
And parched, from last year standing still,
Sun-burnt, scarce fit for th' reaper's bill,
Like tinder ready for the spark,
Yet dense, too close for flight; and hark!
That crackling as the canes ignite;
Like laughter of the fiery sprite.
  XIV
She saw the flames all around her now;
She felt their breath upon her brow,
And then the fearful truth she knew.
In Reason's last sane act she threw
Herself beneath the sheltering lee
Of some drift rock, that chanced to be
Since glacial times left stranded there;
Some yards in length, yet low, and near
A hollow, ditch-like, in the ground,
With grass, still green, not canes, around;
And there the lady senseless lay:
Fear, hope alike had passed away!

XV

Still on the flames devouring swept,
Nor at the roadside paused, but lept
Across with hungry searching tongues,
And hideous noise of panting lungs,
Expecting, but for vain, more prey;
In vain, for younger flames than they,
Whose cracking laugh was heard before,
Already far careering o'er
The field, had left a void behind,
On which pursuing flames could find
But blackened stalks, subsistence none:
So there their cruel chase was done!
But yet their breathing close and hot
Swept o'er and scorched, yet injured not
The swooning mother where she lay
As senseless as her kindred clay.

XVI

When fell the balm of evening's shade
Upon the waste the fire had made,
The sleeper's consciousness came back;
She rose, but rose a maniac,
And fled, as chased by elves of fright,
Herself like spectre of the night;
But what her wanderings none could tell,
Nor what the long night hours befell.
By noon she'd straggled into Town,
With mud-soiled skirts and tattered gown,
With bare and lacerated feet,
Which bled, and left along the street
Their impress on the flinty grail;
With hollowed cheeks, and features pale
And hunger-famished; yet her tread
Was firm, her tramp unwearied,
While flashed with fire her sleepless eyes:
Such force insanity supplies!

XVII

And all day long, where'er she went
Along the emptied streets, she went
All through the echoing void her wild
And hopeless wail, "My child! My child!"
Or if perchance she sometimes met
Some passer by, who lingered yet
Along the ways, (but they were few;
For whites were out on service due
The State, and blacks, by terror scared,
To meet a maniac scarcely dared)
She'd rush upon him fiercely, and,
With murder in her eyes, demand
Her boy; and so the story flew
Till all the Town her ill-fate knew.

 XVIII

All night the fierce war-fiend still curbed
His fretting steeds; and undisturbed
The hours all uneventful passed:
Portentous calm before the blast!
The active foe on Dorset Hill
Was urging preparations still;
And moving to and fro, seemed bent
On some great work of deep intent,
But what the English could not guess.
While they, upon defence no less
Alert, spent well the hours of grace,
Each man now burning to efface
The dark dishonour of defeat,
And deal the foe chastisement meet.

 XIX

Next morn—before the duteous Dawn,
Attendant on the day, had drawn
The dark night-curtains of the skies,
For waking lord of day to rise—
Came creeping on her cautious way,

Beneath the cliffs, which guard the bay
With rocky ramparts high, and through
The anchored ships, a light canoe.
Sometimes 'twould creep quite slowly by,
Sometimes like frightened sea-bird fly;
Not oared by masculine strength or thew,
But paddled by young maidens two—
Young maids of Carib's swarthy skin,
But true their woman's soul within
As glows in England's maidens fair.
A noble errand brought them there,
And no small bravery, to trust
Themselves within such risk, and trust
Their perilled life in midst of those,
Of whom they could not but suppose
(When judged by standard of their own,
As handled from their fathers down;)
That dark revenge and deadly hate
Must pledge them to retaliate
With blood, which only blood repays,
The slaughter of the last two days.
It was a truly gallant deed,
And worthy of the hero's meed.
  XX
Quite noiselessly they crossed the bay,
And though the roadstead stole their way
Without or paddle-splash, or speech;
Until they struck the sandy beach,
Just when the earliest rays of light
Began to pierce the shades of night.
Their nimble feet soon touched the shore;
One held the boat, the other bore
In tender arms with gentlest care
A sleeping babe, whose features fair,
As, kissed by waking morn, they smiled,
Proclaimed at once a whiteman's child.

With noiseless haste, as though she fled
From guilty deed, the maiden spread
Some matting on the open sands,
A woof of plantain's silk-like strands;
There laid her charge, while still he slept,
Twice kissed his warm red lips, then lept
Aboard. Fast now the paddles flashed,
And far the flying waters splashed;
As fast, with every vigorous stroke
They made, the dreaded daylight broke
Ah! Ranèe, ply thine utmost might
To hie thee from the dangerous light!
And Heaven forefend thee in thy need,
To save thee for thy gallant deed!
  XXI
Now nearly has she won her way
Across the yet unwakened bay,
To where yon furthest ship is moored,
A dark and silent mass. On board
The drowsy watch sees nought, except
The mate, whose curious eye has kept
Far straining through the morning haze
Upon the skiff: its haste betrays
Suspicious flight. At once from out
The stillness bursts the challenge shout
And hail to "stop": that heeded not,
Outrings the startling musket-shot,
And sharp command to "man the boat"
Belayed astern as wont, to float
The idle hours, till need should rise
At call of duty or surprise.
The watch on deck with shouts arose
Their mates, and soon from taffrail, bows,
And ratlines eager sailors peer
With searching eye and listening ear,
To catch in that imperfect light

Th' uncertain object in the bight;
While bullets flying thick pursue
The misty, phantom-like canoe:
These, hissing, pierce the murky wave;
But harmless pass the maidens brave.

 XXII

Meanwhile, from lee-side of the ship,
Like eager hounds for chase let slip,
Two boats from out the darkness shoot,
Six-oared, and eager for pursuit.
Twelve sturdy English arms give way;
Their bending oars fling far the spray;
Their keels cleave fast the yielding wave:
What power can now their quarry save?
But Heaven be praised! Their chase is vain;
One foot, one inch they cannot gain
One boat soon yields the bootless race;
And though the first maintains the chase
With force of six oars' vigorous sweep,
Those maids their vantage distance keep.
Their skiff, like floating, airy thing,
As if each paddle-blade were wing,
Not through the denser water swims,
But, as through air, the surface skims,
Like flying-fish on wings of speed,
Pursued by barracouta's[89] greed:
And Fortune holds the scales, to weigh
The chance whose strength shall first give way.
But soon she needs the scales no more!
For snaps one labouring English oar,
And then the chase is done; for now
The chagrined English cease to row,
And by the lifting daylight see
But girls the fugitives to be!
The baffled men then homewards steer:
The maids fly on, and disappear.

XXIII

Some early passers by had found
Meanwhile the boy in slumber sound.
Their touch and acclamations broke
The charm that held him fast: he woke;
But kindly words soon calmed his fears,
And changed to smiles the coming tears.
Then soon adown the waking street
The rumour ran with hurrying feet.
They bore the boy through all the ships
Where mothers were: though many lips
Caressed the child, none owned the waif—
Each mother saw her own were safe;
And none remembered then that wild
And weird-like cry, "My child, my child!"
Which yesterday send such a thrill
All through the day and evening still;
In timid hearts such terror threw,
Such tears from gentler eyelids drew.
Till now upon th' encumbered beach
The maniac herself, with screech
As much like terror as like joy,
Has seen and rushed upon the boy;
Has thrust the awe-struck crowd aside,
Who, shrinking back, leave passage wide;
Has raised and clasped him to her breast,
And long and rapturous kisses pressed
Upon the red lips of the boy,
And wept and moaned in speechless joy;
While he around her neck has flung
His arms, and there had fondly hung:
And now through all the crowd 'tis known
The lost has found at last his own!

XXIV

And when at length the mother spoke,
Her reasons as from trance awoke,
And Intellect resumed his reign—
The power of joy had made her sane!
Her tale—at least what memory knew—
She told to those who round her drew:
They praised (and well their praise was due!)
That Carib maid so brave and true.
The soul within that Indian girl
The proudest English lord or earl
No nobler soul for maid of his
Could wish! And Heav'n they thanked for this,
Those musket-balls had missed their aim!
But none had learned the heroine's name.

XXV

Another day of fear and doubt
Its weary length had now dragged out.
Already in the glowing West
Fort Charlotte's guns and frowning crest
In outlines bold, stood out in high
Relief against the purpling sky.
Those lofty heights and cannon gave
Command unchallenged o'er the wave:
Alas! Mount Dorset, held by foes,
Beyond their range defiance rose.
That foe had more audacious grown,
It seemed, and now the cause was known;
For up the steep and craggy hill
With labour huge and crafty skill,
(The French Barbette had taught them how)
They'd dragged and planted on the brow
Some guns, which now were gaping down
With open mouths upon the Town,
Left undefended to its fate
Now, will th' exulting Caribs wait

For morning's lingering light to break?
Or else themselves, impatient, wake
The slumbering demon of their war,
Their guide red Mars' own fiery star?
  XXVI
While terror held the townsmen dumb,
Brave Seton saw the hour was come
To deal one great and desperate blow;
He must anticipate the foe—
His only hope, ere morning's light,
To storm and win the threatening height:
On th' instant such conclusion true
His untaught martial instinct drew.
But all was staked on that one blow;
So weak his force, so strong the foe.
It was a hold and desperate feat,
And ruin hovered o'er defeat.
But timely, Heaven's o'er-ruling hand
Brought aid; two frigates, manned
With England's sea-kings, proudly sailed
Into the bay, as daylight failed;
And, casting anchor, shook the shore
With their saluting cannon's roar,
And sent to friend or foe around
The welcome or the warning sound.
Ere eight bells struck, a gallant band
Of fourscore tars had lept on land.
  XXVII
The new-born day was two hours old.[90]
From Dorset's height poured, damp and cold,
The heavy, mist-encumbered air
Down slopes all treeless then and bare:
Its mountain breath so keenly blew
It sent a wintery shiver through
The English sentry on the beat—
So great the change from mid-day heat!

Deep silence reigned in either camp:
No bugle's blast; no measured tramp
Of squadrons making earth to quake;
No shout commanding war to wake;
No clink of arms; not e'en a word
No sound above the night-wind stirred;
Yet creeping to th' assault and storm
Are Seton's troops in columned form;
Each soul with smothered vengeance filled,
And yet to sternest silence drilled.
The lion roused is stealing there
With noiseless foot-fall from his lair!

XXVIII

First marched a corps of regulars,
The veterans of England's wars;
They claimed as theirs by soldiers' right,
The post of honour in the fight.
The man-o-war's men next, men who
Had passed a score of battles through,
Well used to win for England's fame
Through charm and magic of a name—
That master-spirit's of the deep,
All conquering Nelson's—taught to sweep
As sea-kings o'er the subject wave.
Their field of victory or their grave:
Resistless on the seas, on shore
May be they'd never warred before.
Then came the brave militia last—
With volunteers as brave, scarce classed
As troops, yet doomed to bear away
The honours of the war that day!
One company by Norman led,
As though to war not medicine bred;
And one by Leith, the gallant Scot—[91]
And none as they such honour got.

XXIX

Thus on the cautious columns creep,
Still noiseless, up the grassy steep
On either hand—the soldiers here,
The eager, clambering sailors there,
And Expectation thinks to win
The hill unchallenged; for within
The Carib camp a silence deep
Prevails, like midnight's heaviest sleep
There seems no sentry at his post,
No night patrol to guard the host,
No sleepless watcher on the height
To cast an outlook on the night;
Secure and careless seems the foe.
The English then less cautious grow,
And mount the height with hastier thread,
By ardour not by prudence led.

XXX

Then suddenly the challenge came:
No human voice, but tongued by flame,
That spoke with fiery sulphurous breath,
And *sent*, not only *threatened* death!
At first one single musket-flash,
Next moment bursts of flame and crash
Of volleyed thunder rolling round.
And many a fateful bullet found
In English breast its billet then,
As told by groans of dying men!
The Caribbees, most wily foe,
Prepared, were first to strike the blow,
From all their fortressed height then came
A shower of lead, and sheets of flame:
Nor only Caribs manned the height;
A corps of French were in the fight.
Though well th' assault was organized;
Th' assailants were themselves surprised.

XXXI

That blast of death the English met
With cheers in English style; and yet
Though veterans who knew not fear,
There seemed a quaver in the cheer—
Some faltering indecision shown?
Confusion in their column thrown?
Some error in their orders made,
Misunderstood, or ill-obeyed?
What was it? Why that needless pause?
That dubious cheer? What ill-fates cause
That halt? Or such mistake inspire
As lingering to return the fire
Instead of charging? None can say.
The sailors too have missed their way,
Misled on yonder flank too far:
'Tis trembling crisis of the war!

XXXII

Just then, with rush and ringing cheers,
The gallant corps of volunteers
And brave militia gain the front,
And take, perforce, the battle's brunt,
By Leith and Norman ably led
With sabres flashing overhead.
With that one dash the height was gained;
But then the desperate fight remained
For bayonet and for sword to do:
And ah! Those deadly weapons drew
The life's red blood most greedily
Of those appointed there to die,
Exulting, in that morning grey,
In work of making human clay!
And chief in all that revelry
Chetwayè's broad sword seemed to be:
Where'er throughout the doubtful field
His Caribs seemed to shrink or yield,

To rescue there Chetwayè flew,
And there the battle fiercer grew;
And there, new heart and courage found,
His rallied Caribs held their ground.
  XXXIII
And once, they sought it not, but yet
Had Norman and Chetwayè met:
It needed not the dawning light
To know that voice and stalwart height.
Arrayed as foe each met the friend,
With whom a friendship without end
Was sworn. Each felt to such a foe
He could not deal the mortal blow.
The Englishman, the Christian bred,
Had felt such blood he could not shed:
The Savage in his way, 'twas seen,
Had felt reluctance quite as keen.
"Chetwayè, yield thee!" Norman cried,
"The day is ours, the fates decide:
So yield! Thy life is safe. Resign
Thy sword: I pledge my life for thine!"
He answered, "No! Till death we'll fight.
We twice have put red coats to flight.
If victory now from us should fly,
Chetwayè will not yield but die!"
He said; and where his troops distressed
And broken now, and hardly pressed
By fiery Leith, were giving way,
He rushed and plunged him in the fray—
While Norman gave the word, "Advance,"
And charged where waved the flag of France
Where spurious chivalry, allied
With fealty false, fought side by side.
  XXXIV
The chieftain with impetuous rush,
Through awful tumult, shouts and crush

Of struggling and of dying men,
Now gained the battle-front, where then
His lines were shrinking from beneath
The onset of th' impetuous Leith.
The leaders met, and face to face
They stood, and gazed a moment's space.
"Are you Chetwayè?" Leith then cried
With leaping heart; and he replied
With exultation scarcely less,
"Ten thousand maledictions, yes!"[92]
And then their flashing swords were crossed.

  XXXV

The rock where thus they fought was mossed,
And slippery for booted feet;
Chetwayè's gain was this: defeat
To staggering Leith it almost brought,
Who thus at disadvantage fought;
Yet being better swordsman far,
This fault but equalized the war.
Short, sharp, and desperate was the fray;
And twice, his foot-hold giving way,
He tripped, and twice was made to feel
The keenness of Chetwayè's steel.
But now the great chief's hour ill-starred,
Alas! Had come: his unskilled guard
Had twice his faulty fence betrayed,
And twice had Leith's most eager blade,
On which his utmost force was flung,
Unchecked drank deep in either lung.

  XXXVI

He yielded then; but not to pain—
Such weakness Caribs could disdain:
But from his wounds the gushing flood
Had now suffused both lungs with blood;
And suffocated thus—and drowned
In his own blood—he staggered round,

And wildly gasping for his breath,
He struggled furiously with death;
Then falling without cry or groan
He rolled, in huge contortions thrown
With head thrown back and limbs contort;
A frightful struggle, though but short.
'Twas well such anguish could not last:
His bosom's swelling throes soon passed;
With one vast sigh they ceased to heave:
So loath that spirit was to leave,
So loath to herd it with the dead!
And when to Hiroon's bosom fled
That soul, she knew that not alone,
Was battle lost but freedom gone!

  XXXVII

At once outrang the English cheers,
And Panic with its wildest fears
Seized both the Caribs and the French.
They lept o'er parapet and trench;
Or where the crags and rocks o'erhung
The fallen precipice, they flung
Themselves, and some their lives, away;
While some there bruised and mangled lay.
The hill was ours! Our banners waved
On high: the trembling Town was saved!
Th' exulting victors count the dead;
Some prisoners, traitorous French, were led
To speedy justice: hanged, cut down,
Refused interment in the Town
And flung to sea to find their graves,
Dishonoured corpses, in the waves.

  XXXVIII

But o'er Chetwayè's prostrate form,
Still through such vigorous life-blood warm,
Stood Leith in flush of victory
And pride of conscious gallantry;

And gazed upon his fallen foe
With reverence such as brave men know.
Around the chieftain's shoulders lay
(The gift of England's prince, they say,
Who thus in sort had dubbed him knight)
A silver collar, glittering bright.[93]
With reverent hand unclasping this,
The victor claimed it now as his.
"A splendid soldier here has died
Of honours due be none denied
A soldier's grave refuse him not:"
With glistening eyes thus spoke the Scot.
But Caribs crept, how none can say,
And bore the honoured corpse away.

End of Canto VII

Victory Fluctuates

I

’Tis morning in the Carib camp
Amongst the hill; but morning damp
And sunless, all o’erhung with clouds.
No rain has fallen; yet heavy shrouds
Of mist envelope woods and hills;
And this, condensing fast distills,
And mingling with the heavy dew
The leaves have gathered all night through,
Now drips upon the sward all round,
Like tear-drops falling to the ground—
Like tears from all those weeping trees,
Which heave and sob with each light breeze.
It is Chetwayè’s funeral morn;
A day in tears and anguish born!

II

No camp for active war is this;
But set in mountain fastnesses,
It was Chetwayè’s home whene’er
His restless spirit drew him there,
To seek some brief repose; and far
From scenes and sounds of recent war.
Midst locust trees and angeleens
(Hiroona’s forest kings and queens)
An ancient clearing had been cut,

Where stood th' accustomed sacred hut.
Another hut, Chetwayè's own
Was also there; these two alone
Within the cleared inclosure stood;
But nestling near, within the wood,
Lay twenty more, but lay unseen
Behind the brushwood's leafy screen.
  III
Now, rising with the lingering morn,
The sound of muffled drum and horn,
And dirge of death-chant wild and weird,
From out the forests depths are heard;
Far off indeed, yet sounding near
Through dense and moisture-laden air.
The mournful dirge—now ceasing quite,
Now loud from yonder winding height,
Now soft from depths of narrowed dell—
In undulations rose and fell.
The Chieftain's roll of valiant deeds;
His death; how wounded Hiroon bleeds;
His home, where Hiroon's warriors go,
One voice in mourning chant sang low;
A thousand swelled the loud refrain
"Qualeva hoot Hiroona wane!"
While sword and cutlass flung on high,
And brandished round defiantly,
Proclaim how each untutored breast,
Where passions seldom are at rest,
Of rage and hate hold equal share
With kindred passions, grief and fear.
  IV
The tortuous line for full a mile
Crept round the hills in Indian file;
Till serpent-like it glided through
The brake and slowly came in view.
No vain display, no pageant this,

To mock the human littleness,
Which passed for greatness in its day,
And puffed with pride its strutting clay:
No marshaled pomp of death or war,
No cavalcades; no gloomy car;
No steed now rider-less and draped
In heavy folds of velvet, craped
Or, may be, silver-fringed, and, shame!
The poor beast pricked to make him lame;
No slow-drawn hearse with shuddering plumes,
As when your purchased grief inhumes
The dead, when tears are bought and sold,
And hireling woe is paid in gold:
But sterling grief, unpriced, is here—
A nation's grief is round that bier.
Not only bore they to the grave
Their chief belov'd and nobly brave;
They went to pay th' unpitying tomb
A double debt, a twofold doom;
For when the foe their Chieftain slew,
That blow struck down their freedom too!
  V
A hammock slung on poles was all
They used, for bier alike and pall,
Wrapt closely round the slumbering dead;
And thus, with slow and reverent tread
Two pairs of stalwart warriors bore
The mangled fragments ruthless war
Had left them of the chief they loved.
And so the slow procession moved,
Until its trailing length had made
A circuit of the sacred glade.
  VI
In centre, covering half a rood,
The palisaded cottage stood:
In life Chetwayè's chosen home,

In death his destined tomb become.
His widowed wives had dug a grave
Beneath its roof—a pit, with cave
Within, their own unaided toil
Had delved beneath the stubborn soil,
The while the hours with labouring flight
Had winged them slowly through the night.
This task by ancient rites were due
Their lord, but claimed as honour too.

  VII

By Hiroon's laws a Carib's wife
When widowed, widowed was for life.
But when the Reaper filled his sheaf
With richer spoil, with King or chief,
At once he thrust his scythe again
To reap the relicts of the slain.
The wife, or wives best loved were doomed
By cruel rites to be entombed,
Yet living, in their Chieftain's graves,
To be in other worlds their slaves
As here; to toil and bear the load,
And be companions on the road;
And wives, not shrinking from their doom,
Were rivals for the living tomb.
Thus, while Chetwayè's wives, whose zeal
Nor faint nor weariness could feel,
Had wrought all night with willing hoe
Their lord's last resting place below,
They had, as well themselves they knew,
Prepared their own death chamber too!

  VIII

And now the hour is come. Outside
The hut, and round in circle wide,
The war-dance whirls its frantic maze;
And hundred deep-bassed voices raise
The battle-song; while play of arms

And mimic warfare's mock alarms,
With conch and drum, produce a din
Most horrible to hear. Within
The hut the funeral rites, meanwhile,
Proceed in Indian pomp and style.
  IX
Within the inner, smaller grave,
Which opened from the first—a cave
It was of eight feet square, or more,
O'er-arched, with well-smoothed walls and floor,
And plastered o'er with kneaded mud
Vermilioned slightly as with blood—
In each far corner had been put
To stand some fronds of cocoa-nut;
In centre of the floor was spread
A frugal feast; cassava-bread,
And eggs, and yams, and water-cruse,[94]
Such articles as Caribs use
On long sea voyages, or trail of war;
Not least the well-filled spirit-jar;
While from a niche a tiny light
Threw down its rays, dispelling quite
Th' abysmal horrors of a tomb:
It rather seemed a dwelling room.
Within the lighted vault the chief
Was placed, with every sign of grief
And woe removed—the body placed
Upright in sitting posture, faced
As though to greet the rising sun;
And round him spear and shield and gun.
  X
At signal, dance and drum outside
Subdued in fitting pause subside.
And then the chosen pair of wives
(Woe worth the wife whose fate survives
Her lord, of life-long troubles sure!)

Prepare them for the sepulture.

  XI

Waroutie first, the young and fair,
Whose rich and coroneted hair,
And gay attire, and stately mien
Befitted well the Carib queen.
Up to the yawning pit she stept,
But paused ere down its gulf she lept—
Yet not in new-found fear to shrink
With horror from its crumbling brink:
Her fate one moment thus deferred,
She turned to speak the parting word:
"You, noble chiefs! You, Hiroons all,
Before the dead and Heaven I call
To witness to my faultless life,
As great Chetwayè's favoured wife.
Now, how I die for him go tell
Your children's children. So farewell!"
A burst of cheers and shouts avowed
The prompt approval of the crowd.

  XII

And now, equipped her life's last path to tread,
Waroutie turned to greet her waiting dead;
While silence, which no whisper broke,
Had spelled the crowded; and thus she spoke;
"Chetwayè's, noble chief and lord!
In life time followed and adored,
Thine own Waroutie—follows still,
Through all the good and all the ill
That death can know. Qualeva thought
By that foul deed of woe he wrought,
To leave thee on that cold hill-side
Where thou with all thy bravest died,
To lie and rot unburied there,
Devoured by beasts and birds of air;
Or leave thee, fouled in filth and stench

In some half-covered pit or trench,
Where English foes had flung thy corse
With burial of a mule or horse—
Thy spirit doomed to tread alone
Death's paths, so dark and so unknown!
 XIII
But dread Qualeva failed! Thy brave,
True sons have won for thee a grave
As well befits a Carib chief,
Let be the gods refuse, or lief
Had given the boon; for higher laws
Than they can wield have judged thy cause.
Waroutie with thee, now thy path
Through untrod ways no longer hath
The curse of loneliness, no power
Shall now death's demons have to lower
Around with hurl or threat; for though
Qualeva wills it not, I go;
And goblin sprite can do no harm
If one stand by to watch the charm!
I'll bear thy load, I'll smooth thy way,
Through cold by night or heat by day.
And now, companion of thy death,
I'll breathe on thee my latest breath.
In beauty of my youth's full bloom
I come, the help-mate of the tomb,
To share with thee that dark cold bed;
And thus with thee once more I wed."
 XIV
And then upon the brink she stept,
And pausing not one moment, lept
Into the chasm, and passing then
Into the lighted vault within,
She knelt, and laid her head to rest
Upon her dead lord's still, cold breast.

XV

Then scarce less willing, Winnie came,
Of coarser mould and rougher frame
She was, yet no less faithful found,
Without a word she threw around
A tearful glance, which said adieu:
Her spoken words were always few.
Then at the yawning brink she stood,
And spoke brave words, as best she could.
With gaze transfixed, with hands outspread,
She slowly called upon the dead;
"Chetwayè! Leave not, leave not me;
Thy Winnie's hastening after thee!
Since thou are gone, I hate my life.
Thou'lt not forbid thy slave, thy wife,
Where'er thou goest there too to go."
She said; then she too lept below,
Approached the dead, and, as most meet,
She knelt down humbly at his feet.

XVI

No moment now has lost; a score
Of strong-limbed men with hoes, and more
With only eager hands, as fast
As hoe and hand could work, now cast
The loose earth back to fill the pit;
And soon their zeal accomplished it.
The chasm—so worked they were a will—
Took scarce two minutes' space to fill:
Two minutes more and heaped a mound
Some feet above the earth around.
And then they turned to leave the dead
With life entombed! They turned and fled;
As though at terror at the deed,
The whole crowd fled with panic speed;
And, scattering in their senseless flight,
They vanished quickly out of sight;

As though some vengeful doom pursued
With power o'er life and limb endued.
  XVII
And thus they left the dead alone:
All gone, and now forever gone!
There Solitude henceforth shall reign;
No human footsteps tread again
That sward, that desolated hearth,
Save those no longer now of earth.
The hut, forsaken and unrepaired,
Beneath the withering hand of Time
In Hiroon's moist dissolving clime,
Shall crumble soon, and disappear—
Till now the chieftain's homestead, where
His life's more peaceful days were spent,
But now his tomb and monument!
  XVIII
The routed foe, from Dorset Hill
Retreating, rallied not until
Their travel-worn divisions saw
Their own rock towers of Biëra.
Yet England reaped no victory's fruit
That day, attempting no pursuit.
Content t'have beaten back the foe,
She deemed that one decisive blow
And loss of chief of such renown
Had broke the Caribs' spirit down,
And thus the insurrection quelled:
A vain delusion soon dispelled!
Of sterner stuff those warriors bold,
Their courage, now as e'er high-souled,
With failure rose: their chieftain's fate
Had but embittered more their hate;
Ambition's arms had grown no less;
No hope had failed; their first success
And late reverse alike had taught

Them much experience, doubly bought.
They vowed to leave no feat undone
To win the prize so nearly won.
The serpent in the grass laid low
Recoils to strike the deadlier blow.
His father's place young Warramou
Had claimed, and all his fitness knew:
He claimed (and so by all 'twas willed)
To fill that place, and nobly filled.
  XIX
Now raged such furious scourge of war
As made the colonists abhor
The Caribs' very name. Two years
It drenched the land with blood and tears;
Two years of ceaseless strife; for here
Perpetual summer claims the year.
No winter with its glacial laws
Compelled the combatants to pause
For one brief interval of peace,
To stanch the blood, and hold in leash
The chafing dogs of war. Besides,
Like equinoctial tempest tides,
Which rise and fall immensely far,
So rose and fell that tide of war:
And Fortune, having spite to wreck
On either side, wrought elfish freak;
And baffled Victory went and came
Like battered foot-ball in the game.
  XX
One moment, almost at the bound,
The ball is balanced off the ground
In Mêlée of contending feet,
Where Hope and Desperation meet;
One moment more hurled forth again
Into the open field, to gain
Almost the far opposing goal—

Driven on in one unbroken roll
By chance, or well directed blows,
Which skill and speed in vain oppose:
The almost conquered conquering now!
Not yet! The mocking fates allow
The ball to bound across once more,
The fight to be all battled o'er.
  XXI
'Twas so that frightful warfare rushed
Across the Isle; one moment crushed
The Caribs with a whelming blow,
Next moment hurled a huge o'erthrow
Upon the English arms, Defeat
From neither host would far retreat;
With neither Victory long abide,
But, mocking, rush from side to side.
Three times th' insulting foe swept down,
And almost won the helpless Town,
Their banners tauntingly unfurled
On Dorset's height—three times were hurled
Their still unconquer'd hordes across
Their frontier lines with frightful loss.
Three times th' invading foe pursued
And thrice seemed Hiroon's sons subdued.
But thrice rolled back the tide of war,
Back through those rocky gates ajar,
And thus each blood-stained hill and plain
Beheld the marshalled troops again
The hard-fought stubborn fight renew:
Each field a second battle knew.
  XXII
No sooner fierce Duvallè knew
No foe was venturing to pursue
His flying bands—that none did dare
To face the tiger in his lair—
Than, on emboldened plans intent,

His swift-foot messengers were sent
With order strict and stern command
To blow the war-shell through the land;
The scattered chiefs and tribes recall
For fiercer war, and summoned all
Hiroona's last reserves and powers.

  XXIII

Their feet outran the hastening hours
Of morn; for ere the earliest caught
The sun's first orient rays and brought
To watching boyez priest the news
That out from darkness, chills and dews
The blessed morn was come once more,
The Carib hordes began to pour
In scores and hundreds from the heights;
Both veterans from former fights,
And youths in e'en more eager mood
To plunge the untried sword in blood.
By noon, the bands, some thousands strong,
Had mustered and defiled along
The glen, and precipice, and bluff,
Where foot-hold space was scarce enough
For me to move in Indian file;
And halted where they lofty pile
Of hills, surmounted by Mount Young,
Some semblance of a plain o'erhung.

  XXIV

And then came runners from the South,
With panting breath and open mouth,
With tidings "that the land was free
Throughout from British soldiery,
Save in the Capital itself:
All unprotected lay for pelf
And arson at the Caribs' hands:
Abandoned were the cultured lands,
And ownerless; there had not been

Throughout the land on planter seen—
No white man, maid, or woman met
As food for sword, except in yet
Unravaged vale of Marriaqua,
Rock Duvernet,⁹⁵ and Calliaqua,
From which there frowned the threatening gun.

  XXV

"Hiroona ours! Hiroona won!"
Duvallè screamed ferociously;
"Our watchword and our fierce war-cry!
Now, warriors, let the flying word
From troop to troop be loudly heard,
'Hiroona won! Hiroona ours'!
Then on with all our banded powers:
Our task, which gods have set, to be
To drive the English to the sea.
When on the hill our hordes appear
Like Obi's storm-clouds in the air,
Like sheep before the storm they'll fly,
The Town they hold so tremblingly
Shall yield a war-feast to the flames,
To glut Qualeva's hunger-claims,

  XXVI

To lead the young men down the coast,
Where plunder least but honour most
May be, and there the war pursue,
I'll leave to you, young Warramou.
Myself shall choose the Iambou pass
Where grows still green th' untrodden grass;
Where still untouched on hill and plain
Stand thick the crops of ripening cane;
Where yet in homesteads undefiled
Are still the maiden, and the child,
And matron, if not bearded man;
And these shall yield, and yield they can,
Such sport of raven and of blood,

As best shall suit my savage mood.
Let each pursue his way, until
Our forces meet on Dorset Hill."
 XXVII
The deed fulfilled the cruel thought.
When dewy midnight now had brought
Its deepest slumber all around
And cast its darkness most profound
O'er Iambou's almost peerless vale—
The hour when Night's last vices fail,
And myriad piercings, high and shrill,
Of evening insects cease to thrill;
And tropic Night at last, oppressed
With weight of sleep, sinks down to rest—
That hour the cleft rock-pass (that rock
Erst reft in twain by earthquake shock)
The grim Duvallè's Caribs drew
Their line, snake-like and trailing, through,
 XXVIII
Thus while th' unconscious valley slept
Secure; the prowling Caribs crept,
With neither moon to guide, nor star,
The bloody foot-steps of their war—
So settlers' old traditions say,
They crept like midnight beasts of prey,
And sprang, as savage and as wild,
On helpless woman, maid, and child;
They sprang ferocious in attack.
Alike on white man and on black;
They spared no life that night, but gave
To death the master and the slave.
 XXIX
Ah! Then from out that startled vale
How rose to Heaven the midnight wail
Of vengeance and of woe! Next morn
Appeared in Town a slave all torn,

And soiled, and haggard, and footsore,
In bleeding arms a babe she bore;
(The father, he to Town from home
On service with the troops had come)
The babe she'd snatched from midst the dead,
Her master's infant child, and fled
The vale of massacre, through blood
And fire, and night, and river's flood,
Through mountain-path and wood; her prize,
The babe and darling of her eyes,
Held fast, close clinging to her neck,
The sole survivors of the wreck!
Most brave and faithful thus she won
Her way, and saved the white man's son.[96]
　XXX
The Caribs led by Warramou,
With yet unblooded hands, passed through
That desolate and ravaged shore
Duvallè's scourge had swept before;
Encountering no whites, but slaves
Now master-less, but these his braves
Were forced to spare against their will:
Their alien blood he would not spill;
But with some small success he tried
To win them to his country's side:
And there sound policy he showed.
　XXXI
Avoiding then the royal road,
O'er Carapan and Ribishi,[97]
And sterner heights of bleak Vigie
His nimble Caribs climbed; then poured
Like lava-streams—but *they* flow broad,
Not leaping torrent-like, but slow,
And creeping down the slopes, as though
To warn the trustful vales, that lie
In peace below, of danger nigh;

Reluctant yet to hurl their death,
And blast with fiery sulphurous breath
Frail things, which on their touch expire;
But these were streams of living fire,
Of mortal hate and wrath, with less
Than molten rock of tenderness.
In Caribs' hearts no pity's grace
For foes in war e'er found a place

 XXXII

But now they pause, and check their rush,
To creep through sheltering scrub and bush.
Not that they shrink from murderous deed,
Or hearts with some new pity bleed:
But they detect the bristling gun,
And yonder, glistening in the sun,
A line (they knew it well!) of red:
This fills them with a wholesome dread,
And makes them thus their tactics change.
They pause beyond the cannon's range,
Whose threatening boom their ardour damps;
Yet halting, form three separate camps
On neighbouring hills—thus curb their hate,
As though th' attack themselves to wait.

 XXXIII

Meanwhile, with horrid whoop and howl
Their overflowing numbers prowl
All round, for prey, for fire and sword;
And find in Greathead's factories stored
Full half the crop of Arno's plain,[98]
Rich sugars, bright with golden grain.
To these, and all to very foot
Of Zion's fortressed hill, they put
The burning torch; while from the height
Th' insulted English view the sight,
Surprised too much to interfere,
Or daunted by the numbers there.

XXXIV

Next morn, in bitter anguish, saw
The bloody field of Calliaqua—
To England almost fatal field,
Although compelled at last to yield
A tardy victory to her arms;
Mistakes, and Panic's wild alarms,
Had near lost all; and without doubt
That field had almost been a rout.

XXXV

Some marshalled movements of that fight
Uprise before my shuddering sight.
I see the English forces come
With flaunting flag, and rolling drum,
With bayonets flashing in the light,
And all in war's red splendour dight:
See seamen from the ships combine
With bronzèd soldiers of the line:
And next a strong militia force
Sustain th' advancing column's course;
See Highland Campbell[99] last appear
With kilted warriors in the rear;
And there, true soldier born, beside
The creole corps see Norman ride.
The moments linger on their way
While Expectation waits the fray
With beating heart and quickened breath:
Ah! Who is marching there to death?

XXXVI

And now bursts forth the war; a flash
Of fork-tongued flame and ere the crash
Of musketry and rolling roar
Of arms can reach the ear, a score
From out the English foremost rank
Have fall'n and left the gaping blank.
Then volleys, following volleys fast,

And sheets of flame, and withering blast,
And rushing storm of fire and lead
Sweep down the wounded and the dead.
  XXXVII
No childish work, no battle-play
Has England on her hands to-day!
Strong hands, bold hearts, cool heads she'll need,
Or else her soldiers vainly bleed!
Too well the Caribs have the range:
"On! On! My lads, push on! Now change,
Your front! Your Rangers open rank
Engage the enemy on your flank
Column, prepare for charge, my boys,"
Rings forth the chief's commanding voice
  XXXVIII
Beneath the murderous fire 'tis done,
But done in haste—too late begun!
Or what? Did ear or heart detect
In that command some slight defect?
Some doubt, or quaver in its tone
Revealed to craven ears alone?
Or some strange spell infatuate
Our troops? The blunder, hesitate;
And thus in much confusion thrown
Their broken ranks like hay are mown
By Warramou's incessant fire:
And midst it all a shout, "Retire!"
  XXXIX
At once they raw militia wheeled,
And fled disordered from the field;
Wheeled too the corps of British tars,
The yet unconquered sons of Mars;
Wheeled too the infantry in front
Who bore alone the battle's brunt:
They too, although to fly they spurned,
Confused and unsupported, turned.

Then Panic drove the rear outright,
And soon retreat became a flight.
The martial courts in vain demand
Whose voice had given that false command.
　XL
In vain the all in manhood lies
To stay the flight good Norman tries:
In vain, and frantic in his wrath
He flings himself across their path,
And would the great disgrace atone:
But courage, honour, reason gone,
Nought could their senseless terror bate,
Till, Kingstown reached, they each relate
Th' exaggerated tale. Their shame
The truthful Chronicles proclaim:
And had but Warramou charged out,
That flight had been disastrous rout!
　XLI
But Campbell with his Highland men
Is coming up, and well I ken
The metal of those warriors grim:
Old England's honour's safe with him!
The rout scarce wasting glance upon
He meets, upbraids, and passes on.
But meets the broken infantry
With strong appeals to gallantry;
In cheering words, which wring their hearts,
New shame and honour new imparts:
Their faltering manhood comes again;
They rally, and once more are men!
　XLII
And Norman, he, in high disdain,
And rage he could not then restrain,
Discharged his pistols at the rout,
And hurled them after; turned about,
And sprang from off his Rollo's back.

Not needing now that faithful hack,
He threw his bridle on his mane,
And sent him bounding o'er the plain,
Then seized a musket from the ground,
Where one had thrown it; with a bound
He placed himself, with spirit fine,
As private in the Highland line!
Then on at quick the columns sweep—
At quick, but steady, trained to keep
Their wind, and well reserve their breath
Until the charge and rush of death.
And soon the Caribs' nearest camp
Can hear the thunder of their tramp.

 XLIII

The column's head in sight, once more
The Caribs' deadly musket pour
Their storm of leaden hail, and flash,
And bolt, and mimic thunder-crash.
But on the bayonets go without
A check, and high the leader's shout
Is heard, "My lads! That camp we'll storm.
We'll give it them short, sharp, and warm:
Charge! Charge! And on them with the steel!"
But ere the rush and shock they feel
The Caribs, terror-struck, retire,
And, flying, yield their camp. "Now fire!
And give the flying foe the lead!"
At once the field is strewn with dead.

 XLIV

And then, without a breathing space
Allowed, at steady charging pace
The conquering hill-men cross the plain
Five hundred yards; and there again
At bayonet's point a camp they win,
And yet no prisoners make within;
For none await the bayonet's thrust.

Then on through heat and smoke and dust
Still rush pursuers and pursued,
To where the third encampment stood.
One moment's struggle sees it fall!
One splendid charge has carried all:
In twenty minutes all is won,
And grateful England cries, "Well done!"
  XLV
Retrieved the honour of the day,
Its sheer disgrace now wiped away;
The worsted Caribs now all fled,
Compelled this once to leave their dead;
At last from such a rush of death
The panting English pause for breath:
They fling themselves upon the ground,
And spread their heaving limbs around
Thus fell the fight at Calliaqua:
Next fight was fought at Owia.
  XLVI
The beaten foe fell back at once.
Disaster but one moment blunts
The keenness of a brave man's spirit;
And Carib courage had this merit,
Recovering quick their manhood, though
Much staggered by a sudden blow,
Duvallè's hordes in their retreat—
Their murder-instinct, passion-heat
And rage had risen (as wild beasts thirst
For blood, mere appetite at first,
On taste of blood to fury grows)
From beats of common pulse to those
Of frenzied madness, since their taste
Of blood and ravin, fire and waste.
In Iambou's ravished vale that night—
His hordes, now on their homeward flight,
Were passing Norman's country-seat,

Which all alone, amidst complete
Surrounding waste and solitude,
Still smiling in its beauty stood;
And when they came outbursting through
The woods, it burst upon their view.
A savage yell from savage throats,
And shouts and cries in answering notes
From those within the forest's shade,
Its yet unbroken peace invade.

  XLVII

"The torch! The torch! It all must burn!"
Cried most, yet pleaded some in turn
To spare it still; when with a shout
Came fierce Duvallè rushing out.
"The Caribs' friend! Does someone say?
Chetwayè's oath? I tell you nay!
Chetwayè's dead, by white men slain—
Not he nor oath can come again.
And Norman fights amongst our foes
Against us. Hiroon only knows
Him now as enemy, not friend.
Let all such woman-talk now end!
I know he fought in Dorset's height;
I hear in Calliaqua's last fight
He surely was—the only twice
The English showed no cowardice.
No white man's house shall ever stand
By will of mine on Hiroon's land.
'Twas passed and spared by Warramou,
But so shall not Duvallè do.
So burn it must!"

  XLVIII

           While yet he spoke
Was seen to rise the curling smoke;
And soon fierce tongues of leaping flame;
And long ere sultry evening came

The monster had consumed its prey;
And nought but blackened fragments lay
Where mansion, factories, crops had been:
Then Night's own blackness hid the scene.
  XLIX
Now follow fast th' avenging meed
On broken faith and savage deed;
It followed then in coasting sloops
And schooners, which, well filled with troops,
(Through flush of victory now brave)
Came breasting up 'gainst wind and wave
On Hiroon's surf-bound windward coast;
Their aim the Caribs' stronghold post
At Owia, Duvallè's own,
And now to great importance grown.
For there upon the craggy hill,
With European art and skill,
And not a little Indian craft
Upon that higher skill engraft,
He had entrenched himself, and raised
A stronghold e'en by foes much praised.
Dark cannon bristled on the height,
And open-mouthed, commanding quite
The zigzag paths that climbed the side,
Approach of every foe defied.
Well manned, and stored, munitioned well,
'Twas deemed by him impregnable.
  L
The transports nearing Sandy Bay,[100]
(Not anchoring, off and on they lay)
Sent reconnoitering boats ashore,
To guard against the tricks of war.
No signs of living beings appear:
No trace of Indians lurking near,
Save distant barkings of a dog,
And here a huge sea-drifted log,

Some cork-wood tree, or Indian oak
From Amazon, or Orinoque,
Half finished as a boat; around
Some tools and fresh chips on the ground,
As though, disturbed at work, in fright
The craftsmen dropped them in their flight.
The hills with telescopes were scanned
Most carefully: they seemed not manned
But tenantless, though 'Wia mound
Was seen by gaping cannon crowned
  LI
The commandant, elate, surmised
(And hoped it much!) he had surprised
The settlement; perhaps had won
Without the firing of a gun;
And yet (for well their craft he knew)
Neglected no precaution due.
He formed his troops on reaching land
In two divisions on the sand,
Each in a small secluded bay—
On either side the point they lay,
The famous Sandy Point—their plan
In two well-timed assaults to scan
The dangerous height; prepared to storm,
The place of needful, in due form.
And well 'twas so, for else I ween
Completely massacred had been
The whole of th' English force. For there,
Like wild beasts crouching in their lair,
A thousand hidden Caribs lay.
And calmly waited for their prey.
  LII
One party was t'approach in front,
And bear the coming battle's brunt;
And one approach by flank, by path
Which even now its terrors hath:

To pass that treacherous way was then
Like entering Danger's darkest den.
It led o'er slippery marsh o'erhung
With walls of solid rock, which flung
A gloom, and with the dubious shade
Of trees an almost twilight made.
On *that* hand walls of rock, on *this*
The sheer and awful precipice;
Where he who fell, fell straight to death.
(Not few have fall'n, tradition saith;)
With scarcely foothold for a kid;
Yet treacherous shrubs, that clung there, hid
The dangers and some semblance gave
Of safety, which it did not have.
One peering o'er the ledge could see
Beneath the glitter of the sea.

LIII

The troops advanced with cautious feet,
Prepared for any foe to meet
Them on the earth, but not to rise
From hell, or pour down from the skies!
So on they moved; and then the road
Abrupt turned round to left, then showed
Decline of ten-score yards or so,
Then turned again to right; below
Th' Atlantic rolled; and there the ridge,
Like some unparapeted bridge,
With hideous precipice was bare:
Not even shrubs were clinging there!
And here the troops made startled pause,
Yet saw for fear no human cause.

LIV

So on they went—at once there burst
A crash of musketry, at first
From rocks in front, and then from rear,
From flank, o'erhead, from everywhere;

And 'midst it all, and sounding o'er
The musket's voice, and crash and roar,
Upon the English ears there fell
The Caribs' well-known hideous yell.
Fast fell the wounded and the dead,
Fast filled the path with carnage red;
Ay! Quicker than the words can tell.
Then, adding horrors still, there fell
A rushing mass of stone, and rock,
Of boulder, crag, and splintered block—
Hurled down by Caribs from the height,
While yet no Caribs were in sight!

    LV

Death now in front; death in the rear;
And death o'erhovering in the air;
Death on the left; death on the right;
Death at their feet; death on the height!
Yet nobly were our soldiers led,
Their leader's coolness never fled.
"To stay here, soldiers, is to die!
If e'en we would we cannot fly.
The foe is strong in front, but there,
Beyond the foe, our comrades are.
Then forward at the double, men!
Hold well together, clear the glen.
Should foes in forces before us lay,
God help us cleave through death our way!"

    LVI

With bayonets at the charge they rushed,
While bullets pierced and boulders crushed
At every step. The cleared the den;
But there they left one half their men.
They met some foes, but cleft their way,
And, breathless, reached the "Sandy Bay."
That ambuscade not yet forgot,
Tradition marks the fatal spot;

And passing travellers hold their breath
While treading o'er that "Bridge of Death."
  LVII
Meanwhile, the second English corps
With rush had carried all before;
And now their banners, burning bright
Were gleaming on the captured height;
They'd won the Carib stronghold fort.
The battle had been sharp but short.
Our men had gone up with a dash,
Midst showers of musketry, and crash
Of tearing grape and shell, which burst
From out the Carib lines, at first
So silent, as though tenantless—
Had burst, but grew each moment less;
For on the dreaded bayonets rushed
Along the zigzag path, or pushed
Their way through sheltering scrub and rock.
The Caribs staggered, shunned the shock
So well sustained, so bravely led;
And, turning from their ramparts, fled
  LVIII
They'd heard the firing on the right,
And some had rushed to join the fight,
(The column creeping to their nest
They had not seen as yet, nor guessed;)
Thus weak'ning their defences much.
They saw not this advance, and such
Their trepidation and surprise,
When flashed before their startled eyes
That dreaded line of red and steel,
It made their wonted courage reel,
Th' attack had thus less arduous way,
Their comrades had not died in vain;
Their death had been their country's gain!

LIX

The fortress razed, its guns upturned
And spiked; Duvallè's village burned,
Its site become a blackened void;
His vast provision grounds destroyed,
And twenty large canoes reduced
To ashes—such results produced
A triumph for the day; repaid
In sort had been Duvallè's raid,
And blow for blow been dealt; but nought
Beyond that hard-won victory brought.
Their dead they buried, but 'tis said
The English found no Carib dead:
They'd bravely borne their dead away;
Or none had fallen in the fray!

End of Canto VIII

The War Continues. England's Star Ascending

I

Events moved on with hurrying feet:
Recording all, methinks, would meet
Small guerdon in my Reader's mind,
Most patient though he be and kind.
Yet though I leave the most untold,
Some threads and skeins must be unroll'd,
Lest through the tangled mass he fail
To find coherence in my tale.
And if, when lightened thus, my theme
Like jaded pack-horse still should seem—
If e'en my lighter pencill'd sketch,
His suffering patience too far stretch,
He has full means of self-defence
And need not give nor take offence:
To skip the page will be rebuke;
Or else lay down the offending book.

II

The French poured in from Guadaloupe
Their promised aid—the furnished troop,[101]
Fire-arms in full supply, and store
Of all material of war.
Within Saint Lucia's sheltered bays

Their ships had lain concealed for days;
And watching for their chance, had shunn'd
The English frigates, twenty-gunn'd,
Which cruisèd, blocking off the Isle.
The day was breathless calm; and while
The English, seized by currents, fell
To leeward far, the French guessed well
Those very currents would avail
Their cause; so setting scarce one sail
(In fear such sail seen far away
Their presence and design betray)
From out their hiding-place they crept;
And venturing out to sea were swept
By tides and gentle winds, that blew
Anon yet fitfully and few;
And aided too by sweep and oar
Bore down upon Hiroona's shore.
The cruisers whom they dreaded most
Eluded thus, they gained the coast
And found no forces to oppose
Their landing anywhere, so chose,
As suiting best their plans that day,
The Calliaqua's forsaken bay.

III

To fortify Vigie they'd brought
Some thirty-pounder guns, and sought
The least of arduous paths to gain,
To lessen the tremendous strain
Of dragging ponderous guns so high.
With these they crown and fortify
Those Vigie heights, which rise like walls,
And from whose breezy summit falls
On either side the steep descent,
Where never human footsteps went.
Small fear such heights should e'er be stormed
Yet barricades the Frenchmen formed

Of what there readiest came to hand,
Huge sugar-hogsheads filled with sand,
And trees, upon the summit grown
Midst wind and clouds, cut down and thrown
Across the Ridge's narrow crest.
From thence their great ship-guns depressed
Could hurl the plunging fire below;
Or from the ridge could sweep the foe
With grape and shell point-blank. Their skill
And enterprise had crowned the hill
With three redoubts. The Caribs mann'd
The other two; the chief command
And third redoubt, which much excelled
The rest, that fire-brand, Barbette, held.
  IV
To Calliaqua came English then,
Molesworth[102] with scarce one hundred men:
They held the lines of Ratho-hill[103]—
With base upon its foot-like mill—
And then like wolves upon the Town
The French came fiercely pouring down,
In numbers to annihilate
Those English few; yet hesitate
To make the rush—like wolves at bay,
Afraid though yelping for their prey.
  V
No soldier bred, but trained among
Civilians, trusting more to tongue
Than arms—to suasion to seduce
Than war to win; to flag of truce
Than battle's fierce but doubtful test—
Barbette with crossed hands on his breast
Steps forth, and shouts across the field
A summons to surrender "Yield
Your arms, and unmolested go!"
The while Duvallè, treacherous foe,

Has crept an ambuscade to lay
Across retreat's one only way—
In yon well chosen spot t'impen
And butcher the defenceless men.
Barbette knew this, yet pleading stood
To save, he said, the needless blood!
Broke Molesworth fiercely forth "Retire
At once, you scoundrel, or I fire!"

  VI

Next moment sweeping down the reef
Quite unexpected comes relief;
The sloop of war, *Alarm,* with guns
Run out for action, and at once
Her broadside belches out its flame;
And shot and shell with deadly aim
And roar are rushing through the air.
The English raise a mighty cheer:
The French a wholesome prudence fills,
And sends them scampering to the hills.

  VII

The sun went down; the soft sea-breeze
Came freighting night from o'er the seas;
And soon o'er mountain, plain and dell
Its slumber-bringing shadows fell;
But yonder wily, active foe
No soldier's couch, nor sleep shall know,
Save that from which no martial drum
Shall rouse, no wakening ever come.

  VIII

'Tween Vigie's range and Dorset's height
Some miles of roadway crept: as flight
Of bird's might wing the shortest way
There scarce three miles of distance lay.
That space was crossed in early night
(While Hesperus gave the only light)
By Caribs and their French allies,

With well-plann'd project of surprise,
Conceived with boldness and with skill,
The midnight prowlers gained the hill,
And up its sides they crouched and crept.
Meanwhile the cold night air, which swept
The Hill-side, moaning as it went—
Or screech of owl, which signal sent
To yonder denser shades, where lay
Her owlets hungry for their prey—
Was all the drowsy sentry heard,
Alone the sleeping silence stirred;
Nor reached him on his lonely beat
The stealthy tread of naked feet.

   IX

But list! What's that the night-air brings?
Was that the swoop of some owl's wings?
Or that the distant rainfall's sound?
Or earthquake's rumble underground?
He paused and peered into the night,
But nought could take by ear or sight;
The sky was clear, the stars were out:
He turned and flung away his doubt.
But when his short-beat's term again
The sentry reached, and looked, no strain
Of peering eyes was needed then—
The slope was plainly filled with men
Just closing for the final dash.

   X

In vain the musket's warning crash;
Awakes the midnight's wild alarms!
And rush of startled men to arms
In vain! The furious foe is on;
No precious moments given to don
Accoutrements or arms! Half dressed
Half armed, at Terror's stern behest
Or e'er ten minutes' space had flown,

And night those minutes older grown,
Our men so roughly waked from sleep,
Were flying Town-wards down the steep—
The foe exulting (well he might!)
Allowèd unmolested flight:
He waited for the dawning day
To shell and fire the Town, (which lay
At mercy, helpless at his feet;)
And then make victory complete.

  XI

Brave Seton paced the room: the strain
Of anxious thought upon his brain
Had wrung his nerves, and banished sleep,
And made him unwilled vigil keep.
Though ached his still unpillowed head
He scorned to press an useless bed;
And when that musket-shot awoke
The sleeping garrison, and spoke
That startling soldier-call to arms,
Some instinct told him whence th' alarms;
And rushing to the open sash
He heard the roar and saw the flash
Of hurried broken musketry
In which that first shot found reply.
Then noting how from sudden height
The turmoil fell to silence quite,
With much presentiment of ill
He guessed some mischief on the hill;
Yet hoping 'twas but false alarm
He drove away the thought of harm.
But still the very air seemed full
Of dread expectancy, and dull
With weight of some catastrophe,
Like clouds with thunder hanging heavily

XII

And soon along the wakened street
The gallop of some horse's feet
(Suggestive of ill news such pace!)
Brings many a pallid frightened face
Regardless of the chill night-breeze
To windows and to jalousies;
And many a hail, "What news? Pray tell,"
Upon the night unanswered fell.
'Twas Aide-de-Camp from Sion Hill,
Which was th' advanced headquarters still,
And strongly garrisoned; though quite
Commanded now by Dorset Height,
And useless when the foe held that.

XIII

The horseman reached and reined up at
The Governor's guarded gate, and sprang
To ground; but ere he reached and rang
A summons on the warning bell,
Stept forth, as seemed, a sentinel
With challenge sharp and brief, "Who's there?"
"A message for the Governor's ear;"
"And I am he! Here, guard, unfast
The wicket; let this man be passed."
'Twas Seton's self, the Governor,
Always alert and first astir—
The first when danger seemed at hand,
The first at Duty's least demand.

XIV

Th' unwritten message soon was given
In brief, "Our troops from Dorset driven;
The hill by French and Caribs stormed."
His prompt decision Seton formed
At once; and minutes flying fast,
Yet scarcely wingèd ten had passed
Ere mounted aides were spurring on

To camp and field and garrison
To th' officers commanding there
With urgent orders to repair
At once to council's board of war,
Which pressing need was calling for;
Yet leaving orders most express
To hold all troops in readiness
In arms, to meet attack, advance
To front, or whate'er else might chance.
　XV
The council met to whom the chief:
"My words must, gentlemen, be brief:
No time for words but actions this!
The one and only question is
Our hold on Dorset Hill just lost
Re-won must be at any cost;
Re-won must be this very night!
Best now the chances of a fight;
Our enemies need time, and they
Themselves seem waiting for the day.
Attack them ere the daylight rise,
And win, as they won, by surprise.
This, gentlemen, must be your task;
That this be done is all I ask.
The way to carry it safely through,
Being yours to say, I leave to you."
And then the spirit of the man,
As minds, or force electric can—
(This latter flashing from some mass
Surcharged with it and made to pass
Some other, filling it all through
With its own self, will charge it too)
The spirit of the stronger man,
More nervous, more impassioned than
The rest flashed out, and seized and thrilled
The more phlegmatic men, and filled

Them till they glowed (as soon was shown)
With fire and passion like his own:
They closed the council, men of deeds,
And equal to their country's needs.
  XVI
The silent night, no longer young,
Its shades more dense than midnight flung
O'er Town and field. Though no church-tower
Existed then to chime the hour,[104]
The burgher's clock had just struck two,
When panting troops at "double" through
The lampless streets came hurrying down
From Charlotte Fort, to hold the Town;
For those who held the Town before,
A small but smart militia corps,
Had gone already to the front
To bear the coming battle's brunt.
This creole corps is ably led
With gallant Norman at its head,
And Crayton for his subaltern[105]
Who brevet-rank that day shall earn.
'Tis first to leave the bivouac,
And leads as foremost in th' attack.
  XVII
No warning roused the foe to tell
Of danger creeping near; and well
The trusted night the secret kept.
The wind refreshed no longer slept,
But bustling rose; and from the shore
The ocean surf sent friendly roar;
While Arno, swoll'n with mountain rain
Went thundering down the Greathead plain.
Thus under cover of the night
Now many-voiced and dark, the height
Was without let or hindrance climbed;
And so well judged, so aptly timed

The movements of the troops that Day's
First gleam and first prevenient rays
Had just pierced through the yielding East
When Seton's cautious columns ceased
To climb, were formed in line, and found
Brief rest upon the sloping ground—
Some prone, some seated, and just out
Of sight and range of yon redoubt:
Awhile, though eager for the fight
Withheld to wait for better light.

  XVIII

Not long: no sooner could the eye
The loom and frowning front descry
Of yonder grim redoubt, than rang
A bugle's clarion note: then sprang
To feet each eager regiment.
They rush in silence; too intent
On biting now to bark, they go
Like unleashed bloodhounds at the foe.
And not too soon: a Carib's keen
And piercing eyes perhaps had seen
Some movement in the dark, or ears
Had caught enough to wake his fears:
Whate'er it was, that bugle's note
Had scarcely time enough to float
Across the void, when out there burst
A more than ready answer; first
Some volleyed musketry, and then
A rapid fusilade, as men
Came rushing to the rampart wall;
And here and there a soldier falls.

  XIX

But up the British onset came
Silent, like well-trained hounds whose game
Their quickened scent makes known is near;
Not wasting breath on needless cheer;

Not wavering, not halting once,
Not e'en to fire—their sole response
To all that firing fierce but rash
Their levelled bayonet's angry flash;
Intent on grappling with their foe
In hand to hand imbroglio.
  XX
The rampart reached, its breastwork lept,
A line of weltering dead o'erstept,
And then their reeking bayonets pierce
The living walls they meet; and fierce
But brief there wages war within,
And step by step the English win.
Their irresistible attack
Hurls fast the French and Caribs back:
The staggering foe recoils, until
His footsteps cross the narrow hill,
And drive him to its slippery brink.
'Tween that and death the Frenchmen shrink:
They hesitate (as well they might
In that uncertain dawn of light)
But fear and fury drive: they fling
Themselves adown the rocks, or spring
From crag to crag, which morning dew
Has made so slippery that few
Escape from bruisèd limbs or falls.
Some never rise, while musket balls
Come prying round with hissing hate
And seal there many a hapless fate.
'Twas well conceived, 'twas smartly done,
That key-position lost and won:
The foe had won, but ere sunrise.
While gloating o'er had lost the prize.
None know how many wounded fled:
They left behind some sixty dead.

XXI

The beaten foe stayed not their flight
Until they'd neared the Vigie height,
And felt its sheltering guns protect
Their rout; and then pursuit was checked.
Then Vigie felt the battle's rage;
Felt fierce battalions engage—
Not steel with steel, but from afar
In black artillery's sulphurous war;
Her rocks' peaks trembling with the roar,
Her hill-sides dripping red with gore.
No stratagem was there, no night
Surprise, but stubborn open fight.

XXII

Four spurs, or ridges, leave Vigie,
And trend down sharply to the sea:
Four columns marching to th' assault,
And followed by a fifth, to halt
In rear, to watch events, and serve
If need should rise, as strong reserve—
Such Leighton's well directed plan.[106]
One sought the "Ridge" by Carapan,
One sought the Calder's longer curve;
One, where was needed strongest nerve
As winding round some crater's brim;
Toiled up the steepest spur, "The Whim;"
And lastly one essayed to scale
The hills from Arno's watery vale.
And taught by Frenchmen's energy,
Which crowned those heights so manfully
With guns, the columns with them drag
(With ardour which refused to flag,
But fiercer with each hindrance grew)
Field guns, and ponderous mortars too.

XXIII

Now came the crash of war. Where'er
A bank or crag supplied a lair
For crouching men, or fallen stump,
Or patch of canes, or bamboo clump,
(Whose waving crest of feathery bloom
Seems like huge Prince-of-Wales's plume)
Thence poured the fire of musketry.
O'erhead, the fierce-roared artillery,
While from the fort's embrasures flashed
Replies as fierce and fast; or crashed
The plunging cannon-balls, which tore
Their iron way through all, and bore
Huge havoc midst the trees, or mowed
The standing canes, or furrows ploughed
Through living flesh like senseless mould,
Till spent upon the strand they rolled.

XXIV

And thus wore on the fight for hours,
And taxed e'en well-trained veterans' powers
But rawer troops impatient grew,
The Rangers and militia too—
The former, slaves (or Island-bred
Or Afric born) were trained and led
By whites, and excellent soldiers made;[107]
The latter, whites of every grade,
The higher gentry of the Isle
And yeomanry in rank and file
Impatient of restraint these swarmed
The steep hill-sides, rushed on and stormed
With ardour rarely seen excelled
The two redoubts the Caribs held.
The first, commanding Kingstown road,
At cost of blood which freely flowed,
Was won. And when sheer steel had hewed
A path, the Caribs fled, pursued

By those impetuous troops so close
They rushed commingled with their foes
Into, and through, the next redoubt:
And then all fled in broken rout.

  XXV

And now moved out the gallant French
With all their force of arms, to wrench
The hills from English hands, attack
While blood is hot; and win all back.
"Guns! Leighton, guns to keep at bay.
Their force, and hold the half-won day!"
Can cannon up such steeps be dragged,
And that by troops now blown and fagged!
"Up! Up! My lads: it is for you
To show what English pluck can do!"
Two forces meet for mastery,
And wrestle, which shall victor be,
A wrestle of the giants; force
Of human will opposed to course
Of nature's gravitation laws—
That all pervading power, which draws
The apple falling to the ground,
Or rules the rolling spheres around.
They wrestle on till deadweight fails
And stronger human will prevails;
And great twelve-pounder guns, not horsed
But mann'd,' thus inch by inch are forced,
And lifted up the slippery steep,
Where men their footing scarce can keep:
What seemed impossible is done!

  XXVI

And just in time! The foremost gun,
As 't gains the crest hurls down its shot
Upon th' advancing French, then not
Two hundred yards in front; and they
In huge surprise, almost dismay,

Make halt, irresolute in will.
A second gun now gains the hill
And hurls its cataract of fire.
The French, then staggered, quite retire
Regain their own enfortressed height;
And thence maintain the stubborn fight.
  XXVII
For hours, the big artillery played
In one continuous cannonade;
And battle's fire and fury burned
Till evening's shadows long had turned.
Then Barbette, faint and wounded, knew
Defeat and failure round him drew.
Position turned, and every gun
Now silent, ammunition done,
His best artillerymen all killed,
The narrow fighting space quite filled
With dead and dying men, and there
The English pressing everywhere
He'd done his best, and more than most,
But now he owned the day was lost;
So waved the flag and beat chamade[108]
And Leighton ceased his cannonade.
  XXVIII
They met; but while the parley went
Leighton perceived his foe had meant
To 'scape the summons stern to yield
By stealing slily from the field;
So gave the order, "Charge! And show
No mercy to such treacherous foe!"
The French throw down their arms, and fling
Themselves adown the cliff; some cling
Precariously to trees and clumps;
Some, falling, hang impaled on stumps;
And others, falling all the height,
As mangled corpses pass from sight.

But sixty prisoners are secured:
Among them Barbette yields his sword.
Then wearied with the day's fierce work,
(First making sure no Caribs lurk
Near by to force a night attack)
The troops prepare to bivouac
Upon the spot. From chill and damp
Poor shelter in the captured camp,
All shattered, by the war, is found;
So prostrate on the blood-stained ground
Beneath the pale but cloudless star
The soldiers snatch the sleep of war.
  XXIX
Without one wasted hour's delay
Next morning at the break of day
The conquerors leaving force behind
Of line and volunteers combined
To hold the place, marched from Vigie
To follow up their victory,
And, unopposed, reached Biabou;
Of former camp found remnants few,
But halted there that night. Next day
Their slow precarious passage lay
Along those paths, which hang so high
And seem between the sea and sky
Just clinging to the cliffs, rough-hewn
Across their awful front, and strewn
With crags and fallen earth and stones,
And mingling with them, bleaching bones
Of slaughtered men. 'Twas Mass'rica,
Whose jagged peaks and gorges saw
The massacre that fatal eve.
Ah! How those English bosoms heave
With fury, mingled much with shame
For such foul stain on England s name.
They halt to bury there the bones

And build up rough-made cairns of stones;
Then leave the spot with heightened speed,
All vowed avengers of that deed.
  XXX
By noon the heated columns reach
The grassy mead and open beach
Of Colonarie,[109] whose even turf
Is bounded only by the surf.
And storm-line of the sea-fair weald
For stand-up fight, or battle-field,
Should foes by chance encounter there;
So fanned by ocean's bracing air
Which free from o'er th' Atlantic blows
They halt for rations and repose.
At last by evening near Mount Young
They sight their foes. Like clouds they hung
Upon the mountain s brow and crown,
Clouds black with thunder's threatening frown
But threatening only, for no stroke
Was made, no war those wilds awoke.
So on from pass of Biëra.
Throughout the coast to Tourama,[110]
Th' avenging army havoc made
All unopposed, with fire and blade
Destroying everything they found;
Hut, village, or provision-ground;
And, grandest prize, threescore canoes
Left stranded by their flying crews.
  XXXI
While Leighton swept the whole sea-board
Between these points, with fire and sword,
And, master of the pass Biëra,
Held all the Souffrière plain in awe.
An expedition went by sea
To seek the baffled enemy
Where from his stronghold in the North

His flag still flung defiance forth.
Thus once again bluff Owia.
The rush and shock of battle saw.
It was the fierce Duvallè who,
Supported by young Warramou,
Commanded there in chief; and they
Displayed an aptitude that day
And skill of war beyond contempt.
Their cannon foiled the first attempt
The English made to land their troops
While yells defiant, fierce war-whoops
And death they hurled down from their height
Till musket-shot and arrow's flight
And lastly cannon failed to reach
Their foes who now sought sheltered beach
Where safer landing could be gained.
But when, their object now attained,
The English landing made assault,
Their fate or valour was at fault;
The Caribs met their first attack
Unflinchingly, and hurled it back.

  XXXII

'Tis said, (and shame if half be true!)
The baffled troops would not renew
The fight until they all partook
(Not sparkling beverage from the brook,
But) draughts from canteens handed round,
And then fictitious valour found.[III]
Whate'er the evil tale be worth,
Suspense was long ere flashing forth
Old England's banners, blazing red,
Her halting troops to th' onset led.
Like flames which fanned by sudden breeze
(Though till then lying dormant) seize
Upon some hill-side's grassy down
By Autumn's suns now dried and brown—

In spurts of flame or lines of fire
Go creeping, leaping ever higher,
So England's banners' fiery red
And waving lines of scarlet, spread
Across th' opposing hill's ascent,
Now creeping and now leaping went
In streams of living fire, ablaze
In morning's sun's unclouded rays;
And ever mounting upwards, till
They gained the summit of the hill;
And then th' exulting flags flashed high
In blood-red folds across the sky.
  XXXIII
The chiefs did all that chieftains could;
Most bravely but in vain withstood
The fierce assault: they lost the day,
But left small trophies of the fray.
The English on that blood-stained ground
No prisoners made, no dead they found;
For fierce Duvallè though he fled,
Bore off his wounded and his dead:
Bore off, himself though wounded too,
In his own arms young Warramou.
  XXXIV
No foe remained: the war seemed done
The land from end to end re-won.
With one strong grip on Biëra,
And one hand grasping Owia,
And through the coast and hills between
The Carib forces nowhere seen;
While pathless mountains, wild and drear,
'Gainst all retreat their barriers rear—
Th' exulting English deemed their rude
And formidable foes subdued.
They daily looked for them to treat,
And lay submission at their feet.

XXXV

But this once Leighton failed in aim
And hope, for no submission came.
Ten days were passed in waiting, fraught
With dangers Seton little thought;
And then astounding tidings reached
The Town one gala night, and bleached
Once more the pallid cheek with fear
Which music, wine, and festive cheer
Had filled with bloom and love and pride,
The hours in mirth and dance had hied
To past midnight from evening gun
In honour of the victories won,
When tidings reached the blithesome ball
And rushed like whirlwind through the hall;
"That numerous Carib hordes, athirst
For blood, like beasts of prey, had burst
Upon the leeward settlements;
Destroyed their two half regiments,
And now once more with fire and sword
Were ravaging the whole sea-board."
The dance collapsed; the music sank,
The hum of mirth to whisper shrank;
And laughing eyes grew dim with tears
And love's soft murmurings in the ears
Were hushed half said. When fear is master,
And rules by right of dread disaster,
No passion sterner power can wield:
All lighter passions needs must yield.

XXXVI

Duvallè had a feat achieved
Of daring and of skill believed
Impossible, had any dreamt
Despair itself would e'er attempt
What wings not feet were formed to do,
And that where wings e'en seldom flew—

Where Morne Garou and dread Souffrière,
And other rugged mountains rear
The peak, whose wall-like heights sublime
Defy the foot of man to climb.
Those steps are clad with crumpling soil
And struggling trees, and yield to toil.
And vigorous limbs precarious hold;
For loosely sits the treacherous mould
Dispersed with crags and broken blocks
From worn, disintegrating rocks;
And pressure of a foot alone
May hurl a mass of crumbling stone
With death and havoc in its leap
Precipitating down the steep.
And often e'en the voice raised high
Or sharp in sudden call or cry,
By many echoes multiplied,
Its shock also intensified
By very stillness of the air,
Which after rains oft linger there—
The voice itself in such an hour
Attains to such mysterious power,
As from its slumbering lair to drag
Some poised and nicely balanced crag,
To fall, with hundreds more below
Like Alpine avalanche of snow.
There climbers hold their lives at stake
And perils haunt each step they take;
Yet there the Caribs passage sought,
The toil and danger set at nought,
And bore their enterprise of war
Where never man had trod before.
Like tiger-cats in quest of prey,
With hand and foot they won their way:
With regular troops it ill had fared,
If such a passage they had dared!

XXXVII

From windward, summoned thence in haste,
The chafing Leighton now retraced
His conquering steps—his very name
Commanding hope. By sea he came;
Just touched at Kingstown Bay, but cast
No anchor there—no more than passed
To hold a flying half-hour's brief
But needful conference with his chief.
And while still fresh the morning breeze
Swept o'er those tranquil land-locked seas,
His light ships down the leeward shore,
Impatient with their vengeance, bore—
With cumbered decks, by troop and crew;
With hope and promise freighted too—
Bore down, like eagle on their prey,
With outspread wings and proud display.

XXXVIII

With evening sun his ships had gained
Chateaubelair, whose hills blood-stained
Had seen Old England's flag twice trailed
In dust; where twice her troops had failed.
The Carib hordes enmassed lay there;
But Leighton planned to take in rear
His wily dangerous foe; so passed
The fatal Town, and anchor cast
Where night its deepest shadows threw
Athwart the deep-bayed Walliabou;
And fays and ghosts had scarce withdrawn
In flight from now advancing dawn,
Ere sturdy boat and vigorous oar
Had freighted all his force ashore.
And well equipped with light field-guns,
The march went on, long ere the suns
First rays had climbed the lofty hills,
Whose heights luxuriant foliage fills;

And radiant, golden, ruby-hued
Not yet had gilt the forests, strewed
The dew-wet leaves and grass with gems,
Nor lined with gold their moss-clad stems;
For valley, dale and glen yet lay
In gloom of still uncertain day.
  XXXIX
No beat of drum, no bugle's sound
Awoke the tattling echoes round
The English presence to betray,
Should prowling Caribs near-by stray
Scarce tramp of feet, or creak of wheels
On roads o'ergrown with grass, reveals—
(For war since many an idle day
Had chased all traffic far away)
Reveals ten rods beyond their course
Th' advance of this well-handled force.
Yet when the silent column's train
With rising morn now crests the chain
Of hills, which hem in close and cramp
The plain where lies the Carib camp,
Some heavings in the 'campment prove
The foe alert and on the move:
The rumour of th' advancing war
Had somehow winged its way before.
  XL
Soon as those swarthy warriors find
Their foe at hand; and hill-tops lined
With bayonets glittering in the light
Their movements quicken into flight;
And yet no rout: their masses glide
Like shadows up the sunlit side
Of yonder open hill, to where
Those dense primeval forests rear
A barrier safe; wherein pursuit
If ventured on would little boot.

"Now, sirs, ere yonder slippery foe
Elude us, strike one vigorous blow—
And never strike, if strike not now!
Unlimber guns, and from this brow
You'll cannonade them over head
While down the slope the charge is led:
And if their dark battalions
Escape, yet win their lagging guns."
So Leighton spoke, and so 'twas done:
The guns (there were but two) were won.
The Caribs, hesitating, fired
But one rash round, and then retired,
Abandoning the guns—to climb
With them they could not; and the time
Was short to drag them through the weald:
They spiked and left them on the field,
And vanished from the almost bloodless ground
Within the gloomful forest's shades around:
Retreating, yet was theirs no craven flight:
It was not then Duvallè's cue to fight.

XLI

And now those forests depths resound
With tramp of rushing war, with sound
Of axe, and conch, and wild warwhoops
And passage of contending troops.
Duvallè hoping to deceive
His enemy and make believe
He'd led his baffled braves again
Across that frightful mountain chain,
Retreated inwards up the heights
With ostentatious noise, till night's
Intense impenetrable shade
Athwart their path a barrier laid.
And then for days, no less than four—
Duvallè swept in wide detour
To gain Morne Ronde; for there he chose

To turn at bay upon his foes—
Morne Ronde, deemed unassailable.
The one approach available
(As all who know the spot concur)
Was down a winding mountain spur:
Save there, impregnable all round:
And there the big-mouthed cannon frowned.

  XLII

Through gloomsome forest tracts, where never hath
By roving Caribs e'en been traced a path;
Where even tropic sunbeams pierce not through,
To chase the shades and lift the lingering dew;
Where fallen trees, huge forest monarchs, (not
Through man but age supine) lie still and rot—
And ropes of sturdy lianes rest coil on coil—
Untouched, commingling with a virgin soil;
Where neither spade nor hoe had turned the sod,
Where never yet had foot of white man trod;
'Twas there they fled, there Leighton now pursued.
Through obstacles and elements subdued
His iron will laborious passage made
For men and guns, with pick and axe and spade.
Not least of perils, barring thus the way,
An ambuscade of Carib marksmen lay;
In this the leading English column fell,
And lined with gallant dead that treacherous dell.

  XLIII

Now darkening masses sighted through the gloom
Of shadowy woods, and then a cannon's boom
And shot, which through the splintered branches tear,
Reveal the formidable Morne Ronde near.
Then came the cannonade: from either side
As cannon spoke so cannon fierce replied;
And then th' assault—a rush, and cheer, and sheen
Of glistening steel, one moment fierce and keen,
Next moment sheathed in flesh and dimmed in blood—

And Leighton's men once more victorious stood:
The blood-stained hill, and all it held, his gain;
The price of victory sixty good men slain.
  XLIV
Duvallè, worsted once more, fled across
The mountains vowing vengeance for his loss.
But now within his woods on every side
Penned in by foes he had in vain defied,
And driven from his own domain, the sea,
On every point save boisterous Tamatie;
(For English held each strategetic post,
And swift-heeled frigates cruised all round the coast)
The sullen chieftain chafed like lion caged,
To madness roused, to hellish deeds enraged.
His war-boats burned, his bravest warriors slain,
His gallant stroke for freedom struck in vain,
Hiroona seemed to all save him, once more
In England's vengeful grasp from shore to shore.

End of Canto IX

EVENTS OF THE WAR: RANÈE SLAIN

I

Duvallè lost no heart: in him
Grew fierce resolve more fierce and grim
The more that fortune foiled his plan—
Defeat but made him stronger man.
His hate when thwarted of his prey,
Like hunted beast when turned to bay
More dangerous and determined grew;
Keener and more resourceful too;
And caution lent both craft and skill
When fury first supplied the will.

II

He sent his runners through this land,
With urgent haste and stern command,
To bid the tribes all rise as one,
For higher deeds than ought yet done;
With hearts more steeled than heretofore
To force an issue to the war—
To wrench at once from wavering Fate
A victory that should glut their hate;
And hidden under shades of night,
With only stars for guiding light,
Athwart the seas his war canoe
With force of twenty paddles flew:
They sought Sainte Lucie's friendly shore
To urge the Frenchman's aid once more.

III

Duvallè lost no heart—not so
She whom as Hag Nannette we know;
That fierce old hag, who worked so well
Her fiendish craft and hellish spell
To wake Hiroona's sleeping fate,
And goad to war precipitate,
Events for her must rush not creep,
And furies wakened must not sleep;
Impatient hope and envious hate
Her only gauge to measure fate.
When then she saw that grand onslaught,
Victorious once, now come to nought—
Chetwayè, Hiroona's hero, slain,
Duvallè's victories won in vain,
And England's banners float once more
From windward coast to leeward shore,
Her woman's heart and courage failed:
Beneath Qualeva's eye she quailed.

IV

'Twas this, Qualeva's evil-eye
Which all her heart could not defy,
And not defeat alone that broke
That heart, which else were heart of oak.
To see Tamousi, just and good,
She neither thought nor understood—
Her sole religion to disarm
Qualeva, god of wrath and harm.
Even in that her faith was small,
And loss in that were loss of all.
She'd learned the secret of the mere,
The crater-lake of Souffrière—
Learnt how that boyez priest had lied
And tricks to compass fate had tried.
She'd guessed the meaning of that rout
That laughter forced, and rush and shout

The priest had raised, lest should be heard
The warning wail of the mountain bird;
And as the bad will dread the bad,
In her demon-arts she had
Just faith enough to dread the wand
When wielded by another hand.
    V
She gave up hope, but not her hate—
That grew still more infuriate.
And, impotent to break the charm
Which boded Hiroon so much harm,
She now despaired to overthrow
The prowess of her English foe:
By force, or stratagem of war,
Avert the doom approaching, or
By guile her country's fate reverse;
Yet still she held her power of curse,
Drawn from her copious Carib store,
Or negro obeah's darker lore:
Th' invader's aims she yet would foil,
And leave them but a blasted soil -
    VI
Her curse she wrought as hags will do
All o'er the world, whatever their hue,
Or race; for Superstition, bred
Of terror of th' unseen, and fed
On ignorance, all but in name
Is still throughout the world the same.
She wrought with bundle and with bag
Containing feathers, bones, and rag,
Iguana's claw, and lizard's tongue,
And teeth of shark as amulet strung.
With sun-dried caul of vampire bat,
Liver and heart of mouse and rat,
And skin of snake, and centipede,
And poison-bag of wasp, and seed

And bark of deadly manchineel,
And scorpion's sting, and conger-eel.
There too was tusk of mountain hog
And foam from mouth of rabid dog,
Two *wood-slave's*[112] eggs and one of snail,
And rank old ram-goat's hoof and tail.
There too were pots of poisonous plants
Seething with nettle, pepper, ants;
And greatest virtue yet to gain,
The murdered planter's hair and brain.

  VII

A fire of coals was at her feet,
Not smoking but aglow with heat,
On this some mosses pressed and dried.
And virgin sulphur, (both supplied
From Souffrière's crater,) then she threw.
Up sprang the flames all ghastly blue,
And wrapt her round in fire and smoke,
And while her dreadful curse she spoke.
That done, more yet remained—the hag
Had yet to gather up her bag
Of hideous things, and in a hole
Prepared for them to place the whole,
To be her *Obeah*, buried there:
Let them for whom 'twas laid beware!

  VIII

And then her hateful task was done,
Completed with the setting sun:
But yet the hag returned at night,
And twice before the morning light
Revisited the obeahed spot;
As though she thought some spell forgot
Might turn aside th' intended curse,
If not the charm itself reverse.
Perhaps she shrewdly guessed the charm
Might work the white man little harm.

She twice with scrupulous care rehearsed
(With shouts, and menaces at first,
And then in mutterings scarcely heard)
Each cabalistic sign and word;
And yet she lingered still in doubt;
Would turn, as if to go, without
Content: would walk some steps then halt—
Her obeah for this once at fault!

  IX

Till suddenly her eyes flashed bright,
And all her visage gleamed with light;
As when Mount Souffrière's outlines loom,
Scarce visible in mist and gloom
Of thunder-clouds fast settling down
Upon her brow in darkening frown;
Then lightning bursts upon the sight,
And all is quivering with the light—
Some diabolic thought had burst,
More damnable and more accursed
Than all before, like lightning blast
Had burst upon her mind at last.
She sought at once the forest shades,
And soon was lost in gruesome glades;
And day was closing fast before
She reached Taraty's[113] surf-beat shore.
And not alone; for with her two
Like Amazons, huge women who,
Unhelped, had soon with practised hands
Run down o'er rocks, and through the sands,
Down to the beach a large canoe;
And then as deftly launched it through
The boiling surf. Each seized an oar
And soon they'd left the sounding shore
Behind. Into the growing night
They plunged, and soon were lost to sight.

X

They sought across the narrow sea
The Frenchman's island, Sainte Lucie.
The pull across is scarcely more
Than twenty miles from Hiroon's shore.
Like sister isles they stand, each isle
Alike beneath one Heaven's smile;
And yet exists this difference strange,
That while within the whole wide range
Of one no dangerous snakes are found,
In one most deadly kinds abound;
And numbers from the negro gangs
Fell yearly victims to their fangs.
Could then the flight of that canoe
Have ought with that dark fact to do?

XI

Awhile no swift events ensued.
The land was held, but not subdued
By Englan's troops and garrisons,
'Gainst Hiroon's still unconquered sons.
The strongest points were garrison'd; --
The captured Carib post, Morne Ronde,
The strong entrenchment, Owia,
A camp in tents at Biëra
And one in huts at Biabou;
And bristling cannon placed all through
The land on vantage points, until
Was reached the blood-stain'd Dorset Hill:
Not least, by some relied on most,
The Vigie's almost faultless post.

XII

A mountain gorge's deep recess
There was, to which was gained access
By pathway, to Duvallè known
And two most favoured wives alone.
And there, within a splintered cliff,

Whose sides stood steep and sheer, as if
Volcanic powers had rent in twain
A mountain, and had failed again
(When suddenly the huge earth-spasm
Had passed) to close the yawning chasm.
Within the fissure's deepest gloom
Duvallè had discovered room
And level space, contracted, but
Sufficient for a single hut.
There Ranèe pined, unwedded still,
Banished by stern Duvallè's will—
There pined and drooped, like wood-dove caged.
Her father, with her much enraged
For slackness in obedience due
In wedding young chief Warramou,
Had placed her as a prisoner there,
Committed to the women's care;
To wait until the wars should cease,
And calmer times of coming peace
Enable experts in the laws
To deal with such unusual cause.

XIII

Now, since her banishment that day
Ten dreary weeks had passed away.
Her women-guards were hard and stern;
And though her young heart ached to learn
How went the war, 'twas only through
The tenderest hearted of the two
(Not always able to refuse)
She gathered fragments of the news;
And pieced them in her active mind.
From hint and surmise thus she learned
How baneful Nannette had returned
From that mysterious night-voyage o'er
The seas to yonder Island shore,
And brought, in madness of her hate

Two baskets full (most horrid freight)
Of deadliest of the serpents there,
The Island's scourge, the *lance-de-fer*,[114]
She'd landed with her deadly brood,
But torpid then and gorged with food;
Then loosed and flung each deadly coil
On Hiroon's yet untainted soil.
'Twas thus by hellish deed she thought
To make complete the spell she'd wrought,
By this to work the white man harm
More real than all her obeah charm!
  XIV
Duvallè learnt with small content
The tidings of her dark intent;
And hastening forward would frustrate
The hellish deed, but came too late—
'Twas done: and frightful 'twas, ah me!
Duvallè's tempest-rage to see.
It was supreme. All awe and dread
Of witch-craft and of obeah fled,
Vanished from presence of such wrath!
Thus passion, like a madness, hath
Dominion over blinded men—
The woman was but woman then,
The witch, the hag, the fiend forgot!
"Accursèd woman, traitress, what
Is this you've done? Your traitor hand
Is cursing your own native land!"
'Twas thus in words his rage outbroke;
He roared, I scarce can say he spoke.
But Nannette, furious, turned about,
And answered boldly to his shout,
"'Tis well, Duvallè, what I've done,
If traitor be, not I the one!
Hiroon is lost, as all we know:
She's ours no more, I curse her foe."

"Thou fiend, I'll make thee to thy cost
Soon know that Hiroon is not lost.
What's thy one worthless life to all
Of Hiroon's sons who now shall fall
Through this thy curse! On thee thou worse
Than all her en'mies, be my curse!"
  XV
With this his fury burst all bound:
He rushed and felled her to the ground!
And there she bleeding lay, while he
Amazed at his temerity,
Now realizing what he'd done,
Stood pale and horrified, like one
Awakened roughly, who had seemed
Another being while he dreamed.
His rage collapsed: he would have fled,
But that his inborn awe and dread
Of hags and obeah, seizing him,
Had paralized both speech and limb.
A thousand fancies, like a flood
Of icy horrors, chilled his blood:
He crept him off, that stalwart chief,
Like some pursued and skulking thief!
  XVI
But Nannette was not dead; the blow
Had merely stunned the hag—not so
'Twas willed the wretch should meet her doom;
Her own red hand should close her tomb!
She rose with more embittered will
To plan and work more mischief still.
This, Ranèe, in her exile hears,
And builds upon; till gloomy fears
And frightful dreams prognosticate
Her country's and her father's fate.
But soon came tidings, which belied
Her dark presage of ill. The tide

In Hiroon's changeful fate had turned
Once more; and piece by piece she learned
The great events, that swept in grand
Career of victory through the land—
  XVII
The roll of victory had begun,
She learned, with Owia re-won,
Her father's gallant deed. That post
Secured the whole North-eastern coast.
The English opened their campaign
By marching through the sea-board plain—
That fair expanse of open lea,
Which trends from mountain base to sea.
They marched one day and paused for three;
But neither friend nor foe could see.
This column moved from Owia
To meet a force from Biëra:
'Twas planned that when they joined, the two
Should sweep the Carib country through.
Encamped upon the sultry plain,
The column watched three days in vain
For welcome sight of friend or foe;
Disheartened then they turned to go.
  XVIII
Unseen himself, but seeing all,
And biding by his time to fall
Like hurricane upon his foe
Off guard, and deal some crushing blow,
Duvallè, on those hills that would
In forests densely clad all round,
Was hovering near their march by day
And night, his hawk-eye on his prey,
The sequel showed his strength of will,
His tact and military skill.

XIX

Just as the day had changed to night,
And moon, yet young, with fading light
Was lingering, loth to disappear
Beneath yon gorge of Souffrière
Then looming dark in gloom and awe,
The column reached Fort Owia.
They reached, and piled their arms, and deemed
Their vain parade at end, nor dreamed
The foe, they'd nowhere seen, was near,
Was hanging on their straggling rear!
But so it was. Upon their heels
The Caribs crept, and while the wheels
Of creaking carts were toiling through
The open gates, a conch-shell blew,
A preconcerted signal. Then
A rush of Caribs, well-picked men,
A rush through that unguarded gate;
And then? Ah! Then, relentless fate!
A carnage then! All unprepared
To meet such fate, with souls unprayered,
The English soldiers fell; not few
Had fallen ere their comrades knew
What all the huge confusion meant,
Nor how the rush of battle went.
Surprise, so skilful and complete,
Could only issue in defeat
And dread disaster. All in vain
They fought! They bled! That *coup-de-main*,
Most brilliant feat in all the war,
Resistless carried all before.
Some hundreds perished in the fight;
Some few were butchered in their flight,
Still fewer, numbering scarce a score,
Form rocks and caves along the shore
Were picked by frigate-boats, whose crews,

On shore for water learned the news
From friendly blacks—Duvallè's gain
Was vastly more than triumph vain,
Exulting over slaughtered foes—
His gain that great stronghold, which throws
Defiance over sea and land;
Provisions in abundance, and
Vast quantities of warlike stores,
As small-arms, cannon, mules in scores,
And treasure too in much specie—
Such were his fruits of victory.
  XX
That night Duvallè sent canoes,
Across the sea to bear the news;
And favoured by the soft night-breeze
By early morn they reached Castries.
And with next morn the beat of drum
Announced a French brigade had come,
With full supplies of every sort,
To occupy the captured fort.
At once the English troops withdrew
From Biëra, from Biabou,
From every point except Vigie,
And that strong post was known to be
Most ill-provisioned, with no more
That one week's full supplies in store.
  XXI
An escort to the front, and train
Of eighty laden mules; in vain
They toil to reach yon Vigie's height—
In vain, for Caribs are in sight
In force upon the hills; and they
Are bent on bloody work this day;
For Warramou himself commands
Those wild, but far from untrained hands.
If Ritchie[115] is to gain yon height

He first must win in desperate fight.
He fights indeed, but does not win!
The Caribs, fierce and bold, begin
The work of death; and soon the slain—
Poor mangled victims—once again
Have streaked the ghastly field with red,
Where some have died and some have bled.
Now strangely came to pass once more
A foul mischance, which twice before
Old England's meteor-flag[116] befell,
As these our truthful pages tell.
The English troops are owned to be
The stubbornest of soldiery
When matched with European foe;
That they are beaten never know;
And when o'ermatched still hold the field,
When rules of war should bid them yield;
And what they've won will hold it too,
As their own native bull-dogs do.
It much excites out wonder, for
Such troops as these in savage way
To change their nature, miss their forte,
And act like men of baser sort.
Yet so it was. The wild war-whoops,
And Caribs' yells unnerved out troops,
'Twould seem they turned about and fled
In panic, leaving numbers dead!
Behind them flashed the Carib blades
Consigning laggards to the shades.
No limit to the rout was set,
Until the rock-fort Duvernette,
With shot and shell warned Warramou
His beaten for no more pursue.
Yet Ritchie with a gallant band
Of forty men made noble stand;
He seized Bellair's abandoned mill,

And held out splendidly, until
The darkness covered his retreat—
So far retrieving his defeat.
  XXII
This great disaster was not all:
Vigie without supplies must fall.
A gallant deed was done to save
The garrison. A negro slave,
Than whom there breathed no truer man,
Devised and worked the dangerous plan.
While French troops held the open ground
Within the woods and hills around,
The Caribs swarmed like angry bees:
Kodanda, crouched on lofty trees,
And clothed all o'er with leaves, by day
(Disguised in Carib fashion) lay:
By night he crouched, and crawled and crept,
(Because those Caribs scarcely slept.
And watchfires filled the woods with glare.)
He crawled with naked limbs and bare,
And wriggled through as best he could,
As noiseless as a serpent would.
Two days and nights of peril passed,
He reached the leaguered camp at last.
But well nigh perished on the spot
From English sentries' musket-shot.
  XXIII
That day—a thundering gloomy day
It was—the English made display,
As though on succouring Vigie bent;
But what their motions really meant,
The leaguered, through Kodanda, knew
Was but a feint, by which they drew
Their foe's attention from the fort
To cover first and then support,
That difficult and dangerous feat,

Evacuation and retreat.
'Twas done in storm and wind and rain,
Which swept that night o'er hill and plain.
The cannon's roll and tread of men,
Which else had told their tale, were then
Or merged in th' wind, or rain's downpour,
Or lost in thunder's mightier roar.
Vigie abandoned fell once more
To Warramou, as prize of war.
But he who risked his life to save
The garrison, that loyal slave,
Kodanda, by Seton's fair award
Obtained his freedom for reward.[117]

  XXIV

Thus fortune, ever fickle found,
On England's arms once more had frowned,
Once more, in frolic or in spite,
Had left her worsted in the fight—
Twice beaten from the field before,
Beleaguered in the town once more.
But, domineered by Charlotte Fort,
And frigates riding in the Port,
The Town could never have been held,
If captured by their foes; but shell'd
It might have been—or charging down
The hills, they might have fired the town:
And why they never struck the blow
None knew, and none can ever know.

  XXV

When Ranèe in her exile heard
All this, it much within her stirred
The patriot and the maiden too;
But maiden most; for well she knew
Her angry father's stern intent—
Knew well what Hiroon's triumph meant,
What fate with coming peace drew nigh,

To wed chief Warramou, or die!
But Heav'n had willed how this should be,
And surely shaped its own decree.
  XXVI
Now went Duvallè's mandate forth,
To summon men of note and worth,
And knowledge of the ancient ways,
To meet, and say within two days,
"What due those ancient ways decree
For child of chieftain's high degree,
Who dared oppose a father's will,
Not once, but dared oppose it still?"
It was his only child, 'twas true;
But he, as chief, would yield all due
Submission to the law's demands:
He left her freely in their hands.
And came yet sterner words, "Prepare,
Ranèe, to meet thy doom! I swear
That, if thou wilt not now obey,
Although I lift no hand to slay,
To take the wretched life I gave,
I yet will lift no hand to save;
And should the wise men rule it so,
That thou shouldst die, I swear that, though
Thou art my only child, thou'lt die!
Not e'en shalt *thou* our laws defy."
  XXVII
The chiefs and sage experts have met
To solve a question never yet
Before their dark tribunals brought;
For which their sires had ne'er forethought.
Ledru was one, their bearded chief,[118]
Portentous beard, in their belief!
(For Caribs are a beardless race;
In manhood's prime they paint the face.)
Came next an ancient wandering sage,

A warrior once, long bent with age;
A voyager o'er the thousand miles,
Where trend th' Antilles' sunlit isles
From Hayti's northern shore and sea,
Where herds the gentle manatee.[119]
Through Serpent's or through Dragon's Mouth[120]
To fair Iëre in the South;
Had gathered as he went, some store
Of Caribbean's mystic lore—
Abundant once, and erst so rich,
But veriest fragments now of which,
Like voices from the long-gone eld,
Tradition's failing memory held.
Next, one against whose manhood pain
And growing ailments beat in vain,
So vig'rous still, the Boyez priest.
And certain others—last, not least,
The fiery youth of priestly rank—
The same who had not quailed, nor shrank
From bearding in his very den
To dread Qualeva, Scourge of men;
He who in vain presumption lied,
In hope to turn the fates aside.

  XXVIII

And, where the monarchs of the glade
Had cast around their densest shade,
There flitted by from tree to tree
A shadowy form, that seemed to be
The haunting spirit of the place:
'Twas Hag Nannette. Her demon face
And eye malignant glaring there
With mingled mischief, hate, and fear,
Could bode no human being good:
It meant all hurt and blast she could
Against Duvallè wish or do;
And for his sake 'gainst Ranèe too.

Ranèe herself, the culprit fair,
By Carib custom was not there.
  XXIX
The Council met: each gave his word.
The aged Boyez first averred
"That Hiroon's record never knew
(E'en now he scarce could think it true!)
A woman dare defy her lord,
Much less a maid her father's word
Thus stubbornly!" Ledru declared:
"If this a child of his had dared,
No court should need for him decide:
By his own hand she should have died!"
The sage of many voyages, who
Had tread all Caribs legends through,
Believed such thing had never been—
The like himself had never seen;
Believed the maid had Obeah, which
Some Soucouan,[121] or hag, or witch
Had put on her. She should not live.
The meed, he thought, the Tribes would give,
To beat her first with five times five
Lash stripes, then bury her alive.
  XXX
And now the fiery-blooded priest,
The youngest there, would speak, released
From that restraint imposed by age
On youth, as deference due the sage;
"My words," he said, "as brief shall be
As yours. Friends, Chiefs! In this I see
The white man's hand. Ranèe spent years
Amongst those whites, and here appears
The cursèd fruit her exile bore.
True child of Hiroon now no more,
She's bent the knee amongst our foes
To other gods than Hiroon knows.

She did an impious deed, unmatched
For daring—robbed the gods and snatched
The white man's child, the sacrifice
Which gods most love, before our eyes
From off the very altar, then
Insulting gods alike and men.
Her heart is with our enemies:
She's proven it so. My sentence is
By death on Iambou's sacred stone
She do her treason quite atone."
And list! What's that from yonder trees
Like serpent's hiss borne on the breeze?
Was't the Hag's harsh tones we heard?
Was it a human spoken word?
Or demon's murmur from the skies?
"The gods must have their sacrifice!"
  XXXI
Alas! poor Ranèe, noble-souled,
As pure and good as virgin gold!
No pity lifts its voice for thee:
No mercy finds one generous plea!
Thy barbarous people pass thy doom,
And bid thee die in youth's fair bloom
In infamy and foul disgrace,
Thou fairest daughter of thy race,
And worthiest on the country's roll!
Prepare to yield thy fair young soul
To ruthless Death's strong arms, to tear
Thee far from all they best loved here.
To change this glorious light for gloom
Of shadowy paths beyond the tomb,
Which lead to still more shadowy goal—
That spirit-land from whence no soul
Of man, whose life's sun once has set
(At least to thy poor race) has yet
Returned to earth, to bring heart's ease

To those who mourn; to tell of peace
And weal for those gone on before:
To burst the prison gates, and pour
Some light from Heav'n on th' emptied grave,
And tell of One with power to save.
That message has not reached thine ears,
That balm to dry all human tears—
But yet unknown, it surely hath
Some light to shed on e'en thy path!

   XXXII

Sat long those chiefs in warm debate,
No doubting as to what her fate
Should issue in her death—indeed,
In that one point they all agreed—
But *how* or *where* the deed be done
They were by no means all at one;
And such prolonged debate arose
So fierce, it almost came to blows.
In midst of it there came a rout
Of Carib warriors, bursting out
From yonder woods, blood-stained, and soiled
With dust and mud, as though they'd toiled
Through swamp and scrub as well as war.
On seeing chiefs they paused, but for
The briefest space that would avail
For panting breath to tell their tale; -
"A battle had been fought and lost
On Vigie's height at frightful cost
Of blood—all day they'd fought: at night
Their leaders had resolved on flight
The dead were buried on the field,
And then they turned; but day revealed
The English troops in hot pursuit.
Their main corps takes the coast-road route;
But one detachment comes this way
Led through the forest paths, they say,

By negro slave, and close behind!"
The chiefs dispersè: those wise men find
Their safety now of greater weight
And consequence than Ranèe's fate
Could be; and, she forgotten quite,
They seek their safety now in flight.
  XXXIII
The tale they told, that rabble crew
Of Carib fugitives, was true:
The tide of that most fitful war
Which flowed so strong, had ebbed once more.
Fresh troops had come, and with them hope:
And th' English, feeling strong to cope
With such audacious foes, re-formed
Their four attacking columns; stormed
And fighting desperately, won Vigie;
And French and Carib turned to flee.
Her frolic Fortune thus renewed,
And now pursuers were pursued.
The English force, now struggling through
Those forest-paths no white man knew,
A corps of creoles born and bred,
Most gallant volunteers, was led
By youthful Crayton, who now wore
His well-won epaulettes, and bore
A captain's rank: his orders were
To search the woods and, everywhere
He found provision-grounds destroy
Them all, to cripple and annoy
The active foe. The place of guide
Kodanda, quondam slave, supplied.
Now where those chiefs their court had held
Was open space, where trees were felled:
There Crayton guarding 'gainst attack,
Prepared to make night bivouac.

XXXIV

Now Ranèe's woman-guards possessed
That quality with which the rest
Of woman-kind are gifted, or
At least, with men, have credit for;
A wealth of curiosity,
A fond desire to know and see
What may be seen; yet most what men
Would vainly keep beyond their ken.
When then they knew the chiefs had met,
And Justice had her balance set
For Ranèe's fate to be there weighed,
Their restless steps could not be stayed:
They sauntered forth, and left their ward
Left too her prison gates unbarred;
And more! Their garments flitting through
The devious paths, supplied the clue
To Ranèe (who had rightly guessed
Her day had come, and in her breast
Had borne an agony of fears,
And passed her morn in bitter tears)
The clue to exit from the maze
She tracked them where those tortuous ways
In labyrinthic circlets wind,
But following safely far behind;
Through walls of rock, through brake and brae
Where mountain streamlets dance and play,
And creeping oft on hands and knees;
Till glinting through the opening trees
A glimpse of the sea, th' unbounded sea,
With one bright flash proclaimed her free!

XXXV

But free for what? The evening now
Had fallen, yet on Souffrière's brow
A coronet of mellowed light,
Fit symbol of his royal might,

Still rests (although beyond his crest
The day is dying in the West
And night is busy with his shroud)
A coronet of golden cloud.
In yonder East the moon near full
Already's up; though pale and dull,
Scarce waiting yon expiring light
T'assume her sovereignty o'er night.
Silence and calm is everywhere
On land on sea, in th' atmosphere.
Day's last but most impressive hour,
All full of still mysterious power
Of nature, who no tumult needs;
In silence doing her grandest deeds.
  XXXVI
There Ranèe sits on yonder rocks
Like statue motionless; her locks
Of raven hair, her maiden crown,
Have fallen, and droop neglected down.
And long with fixed abstracted air
She sat, like one day-dreaming there;
Her eyes are gazing on the sea
And yet she sees not things that be.
The sea's her home, the sea that gave
Her birth, th' "child of the Ocean wave;"
Buy far beyond its utmost bound
Her eyes have sought, and not yet found
The thing to rest upon—a goal
Whereon to cast her yearning soul.
Beyond the sea's horizon far,
As though she sought some gate ajar
Through which to reach th' unknown abode
The whither trends yon silvery road
Across, whereon the radiance glows
Which now the moon's young light then throws—
Beyond, as though to pierce the skies

Is fixed the gaze of those keen eyes,
Now brighter e'en than wont; for there
Just swells in each one single tear.
  XXXVII
And in her dreamings, with the vast
Unknown commingling, from the past
Forgotten days of childhood, some
Half-formed shadowy mem'ries come
Of old impressions, now grown weak,
Of years once spent in Martinique.
And dim remembrances arise
Of half-learnt Christian verities—
Of great and holy truths, that can
Fulfil the yearning hopes of man;
Of love that stooped from Heav'n to earth,
And gave all human things new worth;
Of One who, gracious, gentle, trod
The earth as man, who yet was God;
Of one on whose most tender breast
The sick and wounded soul can rest;
And who to hungry souls supplies
The food for life that never dies;
Who caused from Heav'n's high mount to burst
A living stream to quench their thirst;
Who gives his peace to souls distressed,
With sin absolved on sin confessed
  XXXVIII
Then from her musings deep and long
Grew other thoughts which half were wrong,
Though half perhaps were right—the thought
That life with all its aims was nought;
The thought to fling away that life
So end her heart's now weary strife,
And longing to be gone, away
From life and change for night her day.
A wild desire to seek and find

The far unseen the undefined;
Some thing to lean upon and love,
Out of herself, beyond, above.
At last with sigh and shivering start
She woke, and did what every heart
That knows its gladness or its grief
And still retains its youth, is lief
To do—pour forth in rhyme and song
Its tale of sorrow, love, or wrong.
And thus her reverie she broke,
And drowsy evening's echoes woke,
While sympathetic moonlight shone;
And thus her song in plaintive tone
(Conversing with a second self,
Or answering some woodland elf)
Went floating o'er the silvered sea
Now calm as tropic seas can be.

  XXXIX

What ails thee, maiden, pray?
Shines not the sun for thee?
This is thy youth's own gala day,
And bright and blithe should be!
What cares can now
Bedim thine eye,
And shadows throw
Across the sky?

What ails? Would that I knew!
The flowers seem dull and pale;
The merry birds sing strangely too;
All bright things seem to fail,
All joy's depart;
And oh! 'Tis long
Since this poor heart
Broke out in song!

Oh maiden, say not so,
There's love that waits on thee;
There's one brave honest heart, I know
Thy life's bright sun would be.
Thy scourge thou art
Thyself alone:
Why break his heart
And break thine own?

Ah! No! For me not this!
I've felt the white man's power
O! Heart! I'd clasp his knee, and kiss
(I ask no other dower)
With reverence deep
The ground he's trod
And then go sleep
Beneath that sod!

XL

Meanwhile, the bearded chief Ledru,
And that young Boyez priest, the two
Most bold by far and competent,
Had planned a skilful ambushment.
Ledru's well-cultured gardens lay
Almost across young Crayton's way:
He guessed such prize for ravage near
Would draw the English leader there
For well the slave, Kodanda, knew
Where all their best provisions grew.
Steep wooded hills there clustered round;
Three mountain streams, not torrents, wound
Their way amongst those hills, to meet
Below in one wide rolling sheet.
The pathway led across the three;
Its length from first to last might be
Six hundred yards but hardly more.

The streams across were scarce a score
Of feet, but swollen now and deep
From rains, with banks all wet and steep.
Between the last two streams the wood
Retired at first, but densest stood
Along the further bank, and there,
Like wild beasts crouching in their lair,
Ledru his warriors placed, to wait
The English marching to their fate;
A spot most aptly chosen for
Such artful stratagem of war.

XLI

That night, although young Crayton placed
Picked men as sentinels, he paced
For hours with restless steps around
The lines that closed his camping ground
Anon within the camp-fires' glow
Would sit, or wearied limbs would throw
One sleepless hour to court repose,
And fight dream-battles with his foes;
But little dreamt what eyes had been
Those hours there gazing on the scene.
Ranèe, poor wanderer of the night,
Attracted by the camp-fires' light,
Past sentinels had crouched, and crept
Quite close; and then her heart had lept
A mighty leap: the sound it made
Well nigh her presence there betrayed;
('Twas so at least she thought) for then
She saw and knew her king of men,
Not heart's, but soul's hero; to kiss
Whose very feet to her were bliss.
Scarce needed she the camp-fire's glow
That manly form and face to know.
And now the sight for hours supplies
A feast for those long-hungering eyes;

Until the signs of coming dawn
Now warn the lingering maid, begone!
 XLII
Next day had reached its noon: by then
Young Crayton with his wearied men
(Their morning's work had been to raze
The Caribs' huts and fields of maize)
Had reached with somewhat straggling ranks
The triple rivers southern banks;
Where mighty trees cast grateful shade,
And formed aloft a grand arcade;
While mosses carpeted the ground,
And waters filled the air with sound.
Such soft sweet things must needs beguile;
So Crayton halted there awhile
His hungering men, to be refreshed
With mid-day meal and needful rest.
And hovering round his flank and rear
Had Ranèe all the morn been near;
Her garments flashing white between
The trees had more than once been seen.
But now, while went that brief repast
Not knowing why herself, she passed
On swiftly to the front; she crossed
The turbid stream by tree-trunks, mossed
With age, and 'thwart the waters thrown,
Yet safe for her as bridge of stone;
And on, till, little thinking what
Before her lay, she reached the spot
Where Ledru's wolves in ambush lay
Just scenting now their coming prey.
 XLIII
Her wits were sharp, her glance was keen;
And quick as thought she grasped the scene,
Portentous with its dark intent;
Not less than Crayton's death it meant.

The shock quite took away her breath;
A very trap it was of death;
And e'en to her young ken 'twas clear,
That none could live who entered there.
A moment stupefied with dread
She turned about and would have fled,
But that her limbs refused to stir.
Two Caribs were confronting her;
Their presence such confusion wrought,
It seemed to her they read her thought;
For sickly conscience, ill at ease,
Creates itself such fears as these.
For none could deem it strange that she,
The daughter of a chief, should be
On passage through those forests wild—
'Twas like Duvallè's wayward child.
No thought to stay her, nor molest
Had they, but greeting words addressed.

   XLIV

Her scattered wits she quickly found,
And courage came back with a bound;
And by her woman's impulse swayed,
Her high resolve at once she made,
To save her friend, cost what it may.
Her terror now was *lest* delay
Should foil her plan, yet dared not run,
Nor take the open road, the one
She came; for that would cause surprise,
And draw upon her queering eyes.
With mastery o'er her self-will proved,
As if with aimless steps she moved,
And feigning play as best she could
Until she gained the denser wood
And then away! Away! Of path
There's none, but Carib instinct hath
No need of road-way through the waste,

So on! As led by hope and chased
By fear. There's work for thew and limb,
O'er hill to mount, through streams to swim:
Her heaving breast and panting breath
Proclaimed a race for life or death.

   XLV

The race is won—most opportune,
And not one moment's space too soon.
Her guide was Heaven's own hand 'twould seem!
The English troops had crossed the stream,
And just commenced their march without
The faintest sign of fear or doubt
That all was well; and Crayton led,
Conspicuous at the column's head.
They thus were marching to their doom,
And in procession to their tomb,
Alive, yet registered to die!
When Ranèe with a strange wild cry
Burst out into the road and flung
Herself across; yet utterance hung
Upon her lips, for breath was gone.
Her very utmost she had done;
She could but fling her arms on high
With frantic signs and speaking eye
To warn that yonder pathway led
To death, for murder lurked ahead.
And Crayton startled, and at fault
What all could mean, at once made halt.
But ere a single word was spoke,
From yonder trees there sudden broke
Some scattered shots of musketry,
And angry balls went screeching by,
Then presently a distant yell,
All told what Ranèe could not tell.

XLVI

Thus Ranèe's venture has availed—
The deadly ambuscade has failed;
Those random shots have lured the foe
To prematurely strike their blow,
And open war must now decide
With whom the mast'ry shall abide.
Swift, fierce and sharp the onslaught came
A die-cast in War's deadly game.
Young Crayton formed the English ranks
As though in square, with both his flanks
Protected by the standing wood:
A with'ring fire point-blank, a crash
Of furious rushing men, a flash
Like lightning from the glittering steel,
And all was o'er; for backward reel
Th' assailants baffled, beaten back
And heartless for a new attack;
And yet one useless volley fire
For hate, then suddenly retire.

XLVII

And Ranèe? Ah! Alas Ranèe!
How bleeds my wounded heart for thee!
Her mission done she turned for flight
At signal of the coming fight.
Alas! Dead beat from toil, she swooned
And fell, and there received a wound;
But whether band of friend or foe
Had dealt it none can ever know.
Alas! So true, so fair, so young,
The cruel ball had pierced her lung.
And weltering now in blood she lay
Her dear life passing fast away.
Her hero's life she saved indeed;
But for that act she now must bleed;

As though for life must life atone
In saving his she gave her own.
  XLVIII
With deep emotion Crayton raised
The prostrate form; and as he gazed
Into those grand though dying eyes,
He could not fail to recognise
The Carib maid, whom once so long
Ago he saved from brutal wrong.
'Twas thus that untaught heathen maid
That kindly act had now repaid.
Can human heart then feel surprise
That tears now filled those manly eyes?
He did his best to stanch the blood;
In vain he stay'd the outward flood,
The hæmorrhage within was past
All cure; Ranèe was dying fast.
  XLIX
Then as the rapid end drew near,
Her swoon was passed her mind grew clear;
She gazed in Crayton's eyes and smiled.
The smile of a guileless happy child,
Which Crayton's heart with anguish wrung;
Then whispered in the soft French tongue,
"Please raise me up." When what was done,
She laid her trembling hands upon
And clasped his knee—her prayer fulfilled
As pitying Heav'n had kindly willed
Then sinking feebly to the ground
Once more, she flung her arms around
His feet imprinting there a kiss,
Murmuring, "I die content with this,"
Then while she held his hand in clasp
Of hers, between each feeble gasp
Of failing breath, she made bequest—
"My spirit now had found its rest:

I yield it to the Christian's God,
The same Who left high Heav'n's abode
And came to earth, I've heard, to save
The spirit of the life He gave.
So lay me in the Christian ground,
That there I may with them be found."

* * * *

So passed her pure young soul away;
Not lost—who that would dare to say?

End of Canto X

HIROONA FALLS

I

Now wanes Hiroona's third long year
Of war: the rueful end draws near;
Portentous thunder-clouds hang low,
Brimm'd with accumulating woe,
Beneath whose ever-deepening gloom
The nation marches to its doom;
Her helpless gods gaze down from high
Aghast at th' coming agony;
And shudderings of some formless dread
Disturb the slumberings of her dead.
Yet Freedom made a gallant stroke
Once more for life, and almost broke
The alien power which strove to place
Slave-fetters on a free-born race.
The all that valour could was done:
All deeds of venture dared—but one!
And Freedom, mad with joy, had wrung
The hand of Valour, then had sprung
To grasp the final victory,
When from her hand Qualeva, he
The demon of Hiroona's fate,
In freak of mischief, if not hate,
There snatched before her very eyes
The almost won, the blood-bought prize.

II

The sun in drenching rains had set,
And night had fallen dark and wet:
The wind and gleet blew cold and raw
Around the bluffs of Biëra.
An English force had long there lain
Inert; yet domineered the plain,
To hold in check and overawe
The country thence to Owia
One mile across, as th' wood-dove flies
Duvallè with his French allies
Had sat down too, to watch his foe
And bide his time to strike a blow.
The night was wretched, as we've told;
The English sentries, wet and cold,
From out the driving rain had crept
To seek some sheltering nook—and slept!
The rain's seductive, drowsy sound
Like spell soon made that sleep profound.

III

Through darkness, dripping woods, and swamp
Two warriors from the Carib camp
Had dared a dangerous feat, had crept
Within the English lines, where slept
Those sentries at their post, and found
Them fast in death-like fetters bound.
Save raindrops falling with a will
The camp, like Midnight's self, was still—
Crept back with noiseless steps till clear
Of dangerous earshot, and all fear
Of an alarm; then sped as fleet
As naked unencumbered feet
O'er slippery rain-clogged soil could go,
With word the hated English foe.
Then slumbering at their mercy lay
And ere one hour had passed away

Since those ill-fated men were found
Asleep like corpses on the ground,
Duvallè, guided by those spies,
Was creeping up with glaring eyes
And cat-like tread, like beast of prey,
To where the sleeping sentries lay;
And following close was motley crew
Of Caribs led by Warramou,
And companies of French allies,
Who gloated o'er th' expected prize.
　IV
Due penalty those sentries pay,
For, bayoneted as they lay,
From sleep to death without a moan
They pass, and so their crime atone—
Then stealthily, and still without
Alarm is gained the first redoubt,
Its holders, as to arms they ran
Half-wakened, slaughtered to a man.
The French then seize the guns, and swing
Them double-shotted round, and bring
Their low-laid muzzles down to bear
Upon the English camp, and tear
With aim and range too deadly true
A gaping path of death right through
The tented mass of sleeping men.
　V
Ah! What awakening was there then!
Confusion rushing to and fro;
Commanders madly wild to know
From whence had come this strange attack,
Till from the front in gallop back
Came mounted officer, with shout
"The French are in our first redoubt,
And turn our guns upon us—Fly!"
And carrying panic, galloped by.

No stand was made, no battle fought;
It was a rout complete, and nought
Was saved; guns, tents, camp equipage
Abandoned all! For fear, which rage
Itself nor shame could turn to bay
Was chasing. Men flung arms away,
And losing even manhood, fled
Into the night; which pitying spread
The mantle of her darkness o'er
Their flight—'Twas well the foe forbore
To add the horrors of pursuit
And strew with dead th' encumbered route,
Content with hurling at their rear
The parting gun and taunting cheer.
And so the mud-stained, routed crew
Came struggling into Biabou,
And brought confusion and dismay.
The night wore on; but break of day
Beheld the fruit of that defeat—
The English were in full retreat;
And men in wonder saw once more
The power of England melt before
The bold onrush of Hiroon's sons,
And terror of her name—so runs
The unreputed tale—Forsooth,
Howe'er it came to pass, 'tis truth
The "broe" and tricolor once more
Were seen soon floating proudly o'er
The oft-recaptured Vigie height
And Dorset stained with many a fight.
And Kingstown's crowded township lay
For fire and sword a tempting prey;
Yet from the hills no outburst broke;
Doubt seemed to hold the Caribs' stroke.
They paused, like leopards ere they leap
Upon some flock of impenned sheep.

VI

'Twas thus that Hiroon's arms had done
All feats that Valour could but one—
Their fortunes brought, as twice before,
The chance to stake of cruel war
On issue, spite of spells and charms,
Of one heroic deed of arms;
While time and chance were theirs they failed;
Before its magnitude they quailed.
"The omens were not good" some said,
"The sun had set in flaming red,"
"Heard rumblings under ground," and far
The worst "was seen a falling star."
So Superstition claimed delay,
When Valour might have won the day.
Alas, Hiroon! Thrice come in vain,
Such chance will never come again:
Thine hour is come and gone!
         Next day

VII

Came proudly sailing in the Bay
A fleet of England's ships. They came
Flushed full of victory and fame,
With colours flying from the mast,
And welcome tidings that at last
Sainte Lucie had surrendered to
The gallant Abercrombie,[122] who
Had thus the Frenchman's base destroyed,
From whence they had so long annoyed
Saint Vincent, pouring in supplies
And men and arms to their allies,
The Caribbees; and thus was free,
With veterans used to victory,
To undertake that task once more,
Which baffled all attempts before,
To save Saint Vincent.

VIII

       'Twas indeed
Her hour of agony and need:
One day's delay had fatal been!
He came as rescuer between
Her ruin and her bitter foe—
But England's weal was Hiroon's woe.
Duvallè saw and Barbette[123] too
From Dorset's vantage point of view
That line of troop and battle-ship;
E'en heard each anchor splash and dip,
And then the loud saluting roar
Resounding both from sea and shore;
Saw pouring from the opened port
In barges, boats of every sort,
Sir Abercrombie's veteran corps,
Old England's blue sea-dogs of war,
And red marines; and brief twilight
Had vanished deepening into night
And lamp and torch had lent their aid,
And flashing far on helm and blade
Made twinkling, scintillations play
Like fire-flies sporting in the Bay,
Or e'er the last boat's labouring oar
Had brought its martial freight to shore.

  IX

Duvallè gazed and Barbette too
Dismayed, for well each leader knew
What all this great arrival meant;
Yet scarcely guessed the whole extent
Of Hiroon's loss, and what would be
Her crushing last calamity:
They knew not yet Sainte Lucie's fall,
That cup to them of bitterest gall!
So held a consultation brief
In which agreed each baffled chief

"That, hope of capturing Kingstown gone,
Nought else remained that could be done,
But seek their hills once more, and thence,
While acting mainly on defence,
Whene'er the chance they waited for
Occurred, wage fierce guerrilla war:
From open war they must desist."

  X

When morning's maids had swept the mist,
Which night with chilly hand distills,
Which settles thick o'er dales and hills—
And chased the timid shades away
With warnings of the coming day,
The scouts, who long with wistful gaze
Had striven to pierce the lingering haze,
Perceived at last with huge surprise,
Yet hardly dared to trust their eyes,
That Dorset camp was gone—nowhere
Was vestige seen of Carib there.
And later, scouts with hurrying feet
Came bringing tidings, "They retreat
To Vigie's fortressed heights, and, there
Enmassed, for vigorous stand prepare;
And gathering hordes are seen to mass
On hills surrounding Iambou Pass."

  XI

By eve Sir Ralph had formed his plan
And moved his troops—Sir Ralph, a man
Of deeds, the future Victor o'er
The French on Egypt's Nile-fed shore,
Who there in smart and brilliant fight
Shall show himself no carpet knight.
The task now waiting to be done
Was not his least of victories won;
For Vigie held commanding height,
Her sides like natural walls were steep;

Some hills were near, with valleys deep
Between, all swept by cannon balls:
Sir Ralph must scale those threatening walls,
Or charge along a winding ridge
No wider than a highway bridge
And much exposed on either flank
To musketry almost point-blank.
The height was held by one great mound
With four supporting works around.
  XII
With morn commenced the great assault,
A feat of arms without a fault,
Where all went right, not one step wrong.
Th' assaulting force four thousand strong
In six attacking columns moved
To salient points the most approved;
Some suiting best for cannonade
Some possible for escalade.
By ten the guns on Carapan
Were placed, and cannonade began
Nor ceased its iron storm until
The "old redoubt" on Vigie Hill
Was battered much and silenced; then
On signal full three thousand men,
With cheer and with resistless rush
O'er ridge, up hill, through scrub and bush,
Made simultaneous dash on three
Outworks—a gallant thing to see,
And each was won. The Caribs fled,
(Yet left some prisoners and their dead,)
And vanished in the neighbouring wood.
The French retired, the few who could,
Into their one remaining fort
To hold it as their last resort.
While yet remained one hour of day,
Sir Ralph had laid his guns to play

Upon this fort, from which had come
No firing yet; when beat of drum
Was heard, and one was seen produce
And wave aloft a flag of truce.
A parley followed, stern and brief;
The only terms the English chief
Would grant, "Surrender this and all
The other forts both great and small:
Those solely held in Frenchman's hand
And those in Caribs' joint command;
And yield as prisoners of war—
Themselves—and half-hour's grace, no more."

 XIII

Ere now Barbette had learned the fall
Of Sainte Lucie, and knew that all
Was lost. Delay could bring no gain,
Could not less bitter terms obtain:
So struck his flag to fate of war,
And England's now ascending star.
Rang out the cheers for battle won,
Good English cheers! And yonder sun,
Just touching now the golden line
Where sea and sky in one combine,
Flung up from thence his parting rays
On England's flag, whose meteor blaze
(Most fitting type of blood-red war!)
Illumined thus flashed bright and far.
The night then came, and Vigie height
Had seen its last, most brilliant fight.

 XIV

Thus Hugues's designs entirely failed,
And Frenchmen's valour nought availed
To drive the English from the land,
As fondly wished and boldly planned.
And well Hiroona's chiefs now knew,
Ledru, Duvallè, Warramou,

That war for them was war to th' knife;
Yet not for victory but for life.
To Caribs' elder instincts true
To forest's depths they then withdrew,
To watch the passage of events,
And wage guerrilla war from thence.
Upon that forest-ocean's verge
Sir Ralph discreetly paused. To urge
His well-drilled veteran soldiers through
Such treacherous awful depths he knew
Were but to lead them to their doom:
To rot in Nature's home-made tomb.
With tactics borrowed from their own,
And troops as free as they, alone
Could England's able General hope
With foes so wild and fierce to cope;
And negro slaves supplied that need
And proved most exc'llent troops indeed.
The warm but simple-hearted slave,
The victim of oppression, gave
Most loyal service to the State—
The slave who, Theorists say, should hate
His white-faced lord, but whom it proved,
When danger's hour had come, he loved.

XV

'Twas one such band young Crayton led,
The smartest of them all 'twas said
Into those forest depths profound,
Where treacherous danger lurks around
Unseen yet never far; where Death,
Like arrow winged on passing breath
As silent and as swift, may strike;
Young Crayton plunged—a plunge much like
The Caribs' own most daring feat,
Who in the ocean dives to meet
And battle with the shark beneath—

Against his formidable teeth
His weapon but a simple knife;
Yet comes victorious from the strife,
And slays the cruel, wily foe
In his own element below.

XVI

Where mountains rise and valleys sink
So dark, so deep, that one might think
An earthquake yesternight had cleft
Them thus asunder, and so left
Them, but that generous Nature had
The gorge and glen in forest clad,
Up mountain side rich verdure led,
And roofed the yawning chasm o'erhead—
In shades where day is almost night,
Where mid-day brings but dubious light,
And guile and treachery love to lurk—
There war now waged his grueful work:
Yet oft 'twas murder dealt the blow,
There Afric met his Carib foe
With guile as dark with wit as keen
And with what issue soon was seen.

XVII

With fire and sword, poignard[124] and dirk
Red Havoc made disastrous work;
Rushed on, nor paused by day nor night;
Swept all by slaughter or by flight—
Swept all that lived and breathed, and turned
To ashes all that could be burned.
From rock and fastness, gorge and glen,
And cavern dark as wild beasts' den
The worsted Caribbees were driven;
No pity asked, no quarter given;
And fair Hiroona weeping stood
Distracted, weeping tears of blood.

XVIII

Along the spurs of Morne Garou,
Along the heights were eagles flew,
Amidst the wilds where oft are heard
The wailings of the Souffrière bird,
Although the eye of man it shuns;
Of routed Warriors, Hiroon's sons,
(Where headlong fall on either hand
The yawning precipice,) a band—
(Their stronghold stormed, their chieftain dead)
Now hot pursued by Crayton, fled.
Crouched low beneath the crumbling edge
Of frightful precipice, on ledge
Of jutting rock, which there by grace
Had formed precarious resting place;
It might, so high it swung in air,
Have held an eagle's eyrie there;
Crouched there, well screened by tufts of grass
Nannette had watched the Rangers pass.
The dangerous spot the hag knew well,
And more than one dark deed could tell
Done there. With eyes of serpent-hate,
Which blood alone could satiate,
On Crayton as he passed she glared,
And slew him with her eyes, but dared
No more, for on the narrow road
Some fifty Rangers with him strode,
But one for evil fate designed,
A straggler, followed far behind
Some fifty yards or so—he came
A stalwart Yoruba, but lame
And limping from a wounded limb
But would not go to rear. On him
The hag now watched her chance to spring
And down the awful fall to fling
Him headlong.

XIX
         Noiseless as the air
She rose, and left her dangerous lair
And followed with her wonted stride
As seeming not to walk but glide,
Then flung her ape-like arms around
The man, and hurled him to the ground
With fierce momentum of her spring;
And falling with him, strove to cling
With arms and legs like huge sloth-bear;
With monstrous nails like claws to tear
His jugular, to choke his breath
And strangulate the man to death.
And he with desperate effort strove
To turn and face his foe, but hove
Himself meanwhile, not heeding, near
The precipice, which fell so sheer
Some twice two hundred yards or so
To rock-hewn river-bed below.
At length by force of will and thew
He turned, and then his peril knew,
Just hanging o'er the jaws of death
There waiting open-mouthed beneath.
Too late! The hag had done her worst:
A cry of horror from him burst
As thus his threatening doom he learned.
His comrades heard that cry and turned
And ran to rescue, but too late
To wrest the awful hand of fate.
Here masculine strength should have prevailed,
But that the wounded limb now failed:
He slipped, and for one moment hung
In blank suspense; but falling flung
Despairing arms around the hag
To save himself, or rather drag
Her down with fierce design of hate,

That dying she must share his fate:
Whate'er th' intent the effect was this,
To drag her with him down th' abyss.
They fell thus fiercely face to face,
Close clasped in awful death-embrace
The 'lated Rangers could but shrink
In horror from the fatal brink;
The torrent, reddened as it rolled
Below, the fearful issue told.
  XX
The "Happy Hill," as hath been told,
Beneath the range of mountains bold
Lay close, protected, and although
Compared with them it seemed but low,
Like buttressed tower 'gainst all foes
From out a circling plain it rose.
In spite of war and tempest still
The sacred hut possessed the Hill;
Aloft still towered those grugru trees,
Whose friends, when gently moved the breeze,
Aye moaned with softened, murmuring wail,
Or howled, when it became a gale.
Thither, as post of strong defence
By nature and by art, from whence
Though foes assail on every side
Attack might almost be defied,
Hiroona's baffled chiefs withdrew,
With troops dejected now and few.
Mount Bentick's neighb'ring heights meanwhile,
Not distant much beyond a mile
As flies the home-bound bird, are white
With English tents: the hills by night
Aglow with glittering fires, by day
With war's red pomp and glare are gay;
And daily wider seem to spread
That sea of white, that mass of red.

XXI

As when a python's coils around
Some forest denizen are wound,
Until, with huge constrictions crushed,
Its struggles gradually are hushed
Beneath that nerve-power's mighty force,
Till life has fled the mangled corse -
So Hiroon, fall'n alas! In foils
Of mastering War, now felt its coils
To tighten evermore their hold
And wrap more close in fold on fold:
Saw no escape, no helping friend
With hand to stay the bitter end;
Saw none to shed the pitying tear,
But saw and felt the grip was near;
So stood at bay to steel her soul
To play at death a hero's role.

XXII

Then Rangers traversing all through
Those forest wilds, (which erstwhile knew,
No feet but Caribs' tread its glades,
No alien venture in its shades,)
Foes, free as Caribs are from fear,
Were pressing fast on flank and rear;
And foes in front on strong array,
And growing bolder every day.
These were the coils of mastering war
Contracting, narrowing more and more:
While war was pressing thus without
Within the Carib camp was doubt,
Divided counsels, and distrust.
The gravest questions were discussed
But no conclusions reached, while yet
The chiefs in daily Council met.

XXIII

Till from the English camp there rode
A horseman all unarmed, who showed
An open parchment in his hand,
And flag of truce; and took his stand
Within a musket's easy range
Of yon hill-fort. None deemed it strange
An English officer should trust
His life in Caribs' hands; for just
It is of Hiroon's sons to say
That, though deemed savages, yet they
Can be to noblest instincts true;
They have their code of honour too,
Nor more would outrage flag of truce
Than Wallace, Hotspur, or the Bruce;[125]
And more than this needs not be told,
That rider was our Norman bold,
And noble Rollo then he rode.
And soon across the open strode,
As brave as he, and unarmed too,
The stalwart chief, young Warramou;
To Norman's flag as some respond
He bore a young palm's feathery frond.
Down to his feet then Norman lept,
And several paces forward stept;
And face to face the two men stood.

 XXIV

So once; before that sea of blood
Had hurled itself on Hiroon's strand,
And deluged the polluted land—
That day when from a cloudless sky
The fierce sun blazed, and earth all dry
And parched lay panting in its thirst;
Yet that one flash of lightning burst,
And that presaging thunder roll'd
Terrific echoes round the wold.

On Norman's mind flashed fresh the scene
When he had almost prophet been,
And warned his youthful Carib friend
How war with England could but end
In ruin to Hiroona's cause,
And bade the rash young chieftain pause
Or ere with fatal hand he flung
Red havoc o'er the land, and wrung
His bleeding country to the core
With agonies of fruitless war:
Now almost all had been fulfilled
As he foresaw, and fate had willed;
And pity rose as Norman thought
On all the wreck that war had wrought.
Awhile emotion held him dumb,
And choked the words which could not come.

 XXV

But Warramou did no way show
The semblance of a humbled foe;
His step as firm, his look as bold,
His air unconquered as of old.
The only change that years had wrought,
And battles fierce and many fought,
Was pride of strength imprinted now
Where pride of *hope* had lined that brow;
The youth as veteran chief now stood,
Whose arms well knew their trade of blood.
Salute the briefest passed between,
As eye met eye with flashes keen.

 XXVI

The first to speak was Warramou;—
"What brings you here? Say, why come you?"
"As harbinger of peace I'm here;
Despatches to your chiefs I bear;
I bring yon England's terms of peace
That useless bloodshed now may cease."

"Peace, stranger, say ye? Peace? Then, No!
If that's your only message, go!"
"Were I your country's foe, I would,
But Hiroon's friend I've always stood;
And friend no less, I'm bold to say,
In this unwelcome act to-day;
For, hark ye, bitt'rer terms than these
Were urged by those in power! I'd please
Our wrathful people better far
To wage exterminating war,
That would not war but slaughter be—
To hunt you down remorselessly
As brutes are hunted in the field.
Now such men would not wish you yield,
But still bear arms, that so might be
For further slaughter some fair plea.
By your own cruel laws, you know,
No mercy may be shown a foe,
Had victory given you the power
There would not now have breathed this hour
One English soul throughout the land:
Indeed, such massacre you planned
When to your demon-gods ye swore
You'd glut them to the full with gore.
But He who wields Creation's powers,
Who willed Himself this life of ours,
And gave this mortal clay its breath,
Must needs delight in life not death;
Be better pleased to see us save
Than take the life He freely gave.
In battle often, Warramou,
Thou'st proven warrior brave and true,
In crash of arms and flash of swords,
A man of deeds and not of words.
No rash and inexperienced youth
But apt to grasp and weigh the truth.

Now placing in your hands this sheet
My mission here would be complete;
But listen, prythee, while I read,
And for thy people's interests plead."
"Read then, O white man, I will hear;
Then to our chiefs they message bear."
So Warramou; and while 'twas read,
Stood listening with averted head.
  XXVII
"By powers to me entrusted by
The King's Britannic Majesty,
I, Seton, Commandant in Chief,
To Carib chieftain's issue brief,
To wit—That further blood-shed cease;
Lay down your arms accept our peace;
And by our Sovereign's royal word,
Although against his crown you've warred
Your fullest pardon is assured,
Your life and liberty secured;
And forfeiture of lands alone
Shall for this wilful war atone;
Yet lands as fair and wide as these
Are granted you beyond the seas,
Where foot of white man never pressed,
And none shall there your peace molest.
The King's own ships of war shall bear
Your tribes to th' homes that wait you there.
Take arms and household goods; but store
Of all you need for passage o'er,
And ample food for sustenance
Until the Season's slow advance
Shall from your own new cultured field
Sufficient grain and produce yield—
All this and more ungrudgingly
The royal bounty shall supply.
Ten days are granted you to bring

Your full submission to the King,
And your acceptance of these terms.
No time, His Majesty affirms,
Beyond t'accept them or refuse
Shall be allowed. Meanwhile a truce
Shall be; hostilities shall cease
Anticipating speedy peace."[126]

  XXVIII

For patriot's, warrior's, Caribs' ear
What words were these! Enough to tear
The very heart-core from its root,
And rouse the lion, noble brute,
Which lurks within the savage breast;
Yet though by furies fiercely pressed,
Young Warramou stood passively;
In dogged silence listened he,
As though he heeded not, nor heard;
As though no breath of passion stirred
The placid surface of his soul;
Nor tremor e'en of feeling stole
In quickened pulse-beats through his frame,
Nor change across his features came,
Although deep down the depths the throes
Of huge convulsions moved, like those
Vast forces, which in Nature make
The cyclones rush or planets quake.
'Twas rage of passion, power of will
As wrestling forces balanced, till
The subtler force of soul excelled;
And will, now proving strongest, held
The partly mastered passion down,
And swept the brow of e'en a frown.

  XXIX

To aid the will came conscious thought
That Fate itself, no doubt, had wrought
By war's unchallenged act this woe,

That truth and right were with the foe;
That all was lost, themselves and land
Were helplessly in England's hand.
So passed the rage and tumult through
The strong, bold heart of Warramou:
He would not, may be, could not, speak
(The strongest man is somewhere weak)
So answering no, as though he spurned
To give one word or look, he turned
Upon his heels, and proudly strode
Away; but on his homeward road
Some hundred yards he turned about
And set afar the echoing shout:
"When shall our chiefs their council hold
Then shall their word and will be told."
  XXX
The Carib camp: more wild each day
The scene. Confusion and dismay
Amongst the gravest chiefs, despair
And helpless rage held revel there.
Then hunger too had come, the gaunt
Dread harbinger of coming want,
And famine, which already through
The ravaged land with wreck and rue
Grim spectres, stalked and threatened death
With touch and blast of withering breath.
Then tidings came that chief Ledru
Had craven proved, and traitor too,
Had fallen to the foes, and turned
King's evidence, and so had earned
Dishonoured freedom, but far worse
Had earned his country's blackest curse.
And prisoners came, who had been freed
By England's well-planned will and deed
From brief and not unkind exile
In Balliceaux' wave-beaten isle.[127]

These tell their tale of England's fair
And even generous treatment there:
Unhurt, unfettered, freely fed
They moved at large. Such things, they said
Had never been; for always war
Had claimed the foes it captured for
Its ban of slavery or of death.
And England more than kept good faith;
Had promised life, but given more;
And gathered on that neighbouring shore
Were men and women, children too
In hundreds, and they daily grew
In numbers, daily more content
That war was gone—that with it went
The misery, want and ceaseless strain
Which many hundreds more had slain
That e'en War's own blood-stained hand
In actual fight, with battle-brand.
These subtle tales, and other such,
Set even brave men thinking much;
And cravens yet more craven grew,
Of whom e'en Hiroon had a few.
  XXXI
When all conflicting speakers ceased
At length up-rose the aged priest,
The father now of th' council ring,
In youth renowned as Black-hawk-wing.
"Chiefs, children, ay! For such are you,
I am and old man now; but few,
Or rather, proudly say I, none,
Have done the deeds that I have done;
And none too loved Hiroon more true
Have better done their service due.
No arm so dreadful in the fight;
No eye could fling so far its sight,
No feet so winged and light to chase

The beaten foe, or climb the face
Of cliff or crag, so swift to seize
The fleetest mountain sheep, as these
Now withered limbs. That rush and spring,
Like hawk descending on the wing,
Was reason why I bore that name
Which never yet assoiled with shame,
In greater honour soon I'll bear
In those bright lands o'er yonder, where,
Amidst the glorious dead, now rest
Hiroona's bravest and her best;
For age, on creeping day by day,
Hath ta'en what youth once gave away;
Hath stiffened limbs, and dimmed the eye,
And warns the old man's end is nigh.

XXXII

But taking much away, yet age
Gives much, gives wisdom, makes the sage;
Gives second sight to pierce e'en through
Those cloudy mists, which close the view,
And spread like curtains dense unfurled,
Across the path to yonder world.
The old man stands between the two,
And sees deep things unseen by you;
Looks down the line of years long past
And memories now receding fast—
Looks forward with the prophet's ken
And sees the things that have not been;
Beholds the formless things that rise,
And shape themselves before his eyes
In gleam which is not day nor night,
Beyond the line which bounds your sight.
The mighty gods who rule above
Are wont to give to those they love,
Who seek their favour, kindly signs,
Freewarnings of their dark designs,

Along the path thus marked by Fate
I sought to guide Hiroona's state;
For well 'tis known that mortal man
The boldest, wisest schemes may plan,
But cannot alter Fate, poor fool!
Nor thwart the will of gods that rule

 XXXIII

Yet this foregone, immortal truth
Was scorned by yon presumptuous youth.
The gods were kindly and benign
And gave, when sought, the warning sign,
That perils hovered in the air,
That blast and bane were lurking near
Should Hiroon then make rising, or
Awaken then the slumbering war.
So spake the signs; but yon rash youth
With impious hand presumed, forsooth,
To set the will of gods aside:
He said the signs were fair—but lied!
And so we rushed to war, deceived
By treacherous tongue; for all believed
That Fate was fighting on our side
And nought but victory could betide.
And so it seemed 'twould be at first;
For scarce broke out this war accursed,
Than lo! Our conquering banner rushed
Throughout the land, and wildly flushed
With seeming victory, bathed in blood,
On verge of final triumph stood.
But all was mockery, now we know,
A swamp-light luring on to woe.
And fallen, now no more to rise
Hiroona, god-forsaken, lies
As conquered slave at white men's feet:
But fate, like brave men, we must meet,
My sentence is submit and go;

Submit, because it must be so,
We're beaten now—no help remains,
No light our feeblest hope sustains;
And *go*, because we will not stay;
We will not stand in England's way.
Hiroon cannot, ourselves have said,
Contain the white man and the red:
The white man now is master, so
Our very manhood bids us go.
But ere we go let vengeance due
Descend on him who wrought our rue—
You traitor to our country's cause
Who dared transverse high Heav'n's laws—
That meddler, who with rash designs
Presumed to handle things divine,
And truth, which gods revealed, to hide
So made it seem that gods had lied—
That man must die. On Iambou stone
He should his impious act alone
As sacrifice to wrath of gods
And those who sleep beneath the sods,
Th' aggrieved spirits of our dead—
His blood should on that stone be shed,
But Fate forbids that vengeance due
The English forces hold Iambou.
But failing that, a lesser stone
Here stands; here let the deed be done
Remember how default hath twice
Withheld th' unfinished Sacrifice.
'Twas here Duvallè's daughter foiled
The sacrificial stroke, and spoiled
The very altar of the child
Outlaid thereon, then fled defiled;
And here our boyez had designed
That guilty Ranèe too should find
Her death, and pay the double die

As culprit and as victim too.
Here, then be made, as is most meet,
Th' unfinished sacrifice complete.
Here pay the penalty of crime
And seizing the propitious time,
With angered gods now make our peace.
I've said an old man's say. I cease."
　XXXIV
The next uprose young Warramou,
Not now the least of chieftains, who
Spoke thus: "The wise old man is right,
We've fought and lost; for England's might
Has proved too strong. Then let us go,
Accepting thus much from our foe.
Hiroon, the mother dear, who bore
Us, now is our Hiroon no more.
Here now the white invader reigns,
And though he threatens not with chains—
If so, a thousand times we'd died
Than yield—yet tamely by his side
We will not live; nor with him own
The land which once were ours alone.
His words, his oath, we will not trust.
Submit, indeed, the vanquished must;
But by his bounty live, that never!
Being foes, for once, we're foes for ever!
Our Hiroon once, we proudly said,
Should hold no white man with the red.
It meant the white must go, we deemed,
Like men who wished it, so we dreamed.
The gods have willed it otherwise,
And now to our astonished eyes
Reveal that fate has willed it so,
That *we* it is, not they, must go.
But no! Let no man die. I too
Forecast a far prophetic view.

It is not Hiroon's gods, who thus
Have false been proved, deserting us,
But we ourselves have failed to act
With vigour, promptitude, and tact,
To seize th' advantage of the hour,
And grasp the victory in our power.

  XXXV

And powers beyond our utmost ken,
O'er-ruling all the tribes of men,
Far higher than Hiroon's gods, there be—
Some glimmerings of that truth I see.
Against the gods I do not rave
Because they could, or would not save.
The Powers have willed it so to be
We must submit to their decree.
But burns my rage at cowardice
Which (shame upon us!) failed us thrice,
When victory hung, as brave men felt,
On one strong blow once boldly dealt;
When England waited thrice in shame
And feared the blow that never came.
On England's name I fling my curse
And France, the cause of our reverse.
But no man dies, is my advice,
To pay a needless sacrifice.
Comrades and fellow chiefs! My word
Is spoken. I sheathe the faithless sword,
That failed before th' insulting foe,
Surrender to King George, and go.
Commit my fate to th' fickle breeze,
And seek new home beyond the seas.
Let those who choose abide here still
But those all follow me who will.
To-morrow eve, ere set the sun
I seek the English camp. I've done."[128]

XXXVI

Then to his feet Duvallè sprang
With words that through the welkin rang:
"O Cowards, dastards, traitors all,
Qualeva's vengeance on you fall
Since faithless to Hiroon are ye,
Yourselves and children cursèd be!
My curse consume your traitor band,
Or ere you reach that mythic land!
But never shall Duvallè yield,
So long as strength remain to wield
My trusty sword; and while I breathe,
That sword, I swear, I'll never sheathe
In craven peace with Hiroon's foe—
My own and nobler way I go!"
He turned and fiercely strode away;
Alas! The fitful legends say
In impotent but ceaseless rage,
Which lessened not with growing age,
He roamed at first in forest wild,
Or where the mount on mount is piled,
Like hunted beast there driv'n to hide;
And then forgotten lived and died—
Forgotten, save that oft the dame
Would use the terror of his name,
As wild old man of th' darksome woods,
To quell her child's rebellious moods.

End of Canto XI

Hiroona's Doom

I
Now dawns Hiroona's day of doom—
Not day of rains, yet deep with gloom:
The sun, long ris'n was veiled from sight.
As though some shadows left by night
Were lingering, vapoury mists which still
O'er vale, and mountain, plain and hill
Hung low, like nether sky of lead
And hid th' ethereal sky o'erhead.
This made the morning sombre-hued;
While crept o'er Nature some subdued
Strange stillness in the atmosphere
Like expectation in the air;
Such stillness as in awe and fear
Makes men to deem an earthquake near.
O'er all a nameless terror broods.
And lo! From yonder gloomy woods
Come issuing forth a trailing line
Of Caribs, winding serpentine
Along the narrow ridge's curve
Which Indians' paths always observe
II
Below on yonder sandy beach
Where line of graceful palm trees reach
In triple rows across the bay

Is drawn in military array
And pomp and panoply of war
The pick of th' Islands army corps;
Whose glare of war and martial sheen
Is th' only bright spot on the scene
And yet but dully real that day
In light so sombre and so grey.

III

Then down the hills, dark-visaged, stern
With eyes that flash with fires, which burn
Within, those doomed to exile come
In sullen silence some; though some
Relieved the anguish in their breast
With sobs which would not be suppressed,
Or mutter vengeance unto death
With bitter curses under breath.
Men, women, children, infants too
They come, in piteous plight to view;
Come warriors first unarmed but bold,
With mien unconquered as of old;
Come others laden, men who bore
Their tools and implements of war;
Come women toiling heavily,
Yet women-like most patiently,
Their babes upon their backs astride
With bands across their bosoms tied.
Some bore their household goods and stuff
In baskets, neither coarse nor rough,
But deftly woven, colour-stained—
Not borne on heads, for they disdained
To ape the mode of slaves, so bore
Them as their mothers did of yore
Upon their backs—(baskets just such
Are used this day, and valued much;)
Come toddling infants at the side,
Poor mites! Though sorely terrified,

Those mites were Caribs, weeping not,
They bravely kept their weary trot;
Come aged men bent down with years,
And women, some of whom in tears,
The only sign or semblance there
Of servile weakness or of fear.

IV

At last the slow and straggling tramp
Has reached the lines of th' English camp.
To meet them coming sallied forth
Some officers of rand and worth,
Men who could speak the Carib tongue,
Or French *patois* at least; among
Whom Crayton, best of linguists, went.
They met the Carib chiefs and spent
Brief space in passing courtesies,
And settling some formalities
Of their surrender; then the doomed
Moved slowly on, while cannon boomed
Salute; but no insulting cheer
Was raised to mock the vanquished ear—
To fallen foes brave men refrain
From giving ought of needless pain:
Misfortune aye commands respect;
And here was noble nation wrecked
By cruel and disastrous war.
They'd nobly fought and lost—yet more
Than battle lost, 'twas country too;
And those stern men, (th' unhappy few
Who fain a warrior's death had died,
But were that patriot's boon denied)
Were now, since death they could not find
For bitterer woe than death designed,
Expatriation, stern exile
For aye from Hiroon's sacred Isle,

And not the captured warriors few:
The nation banned and banished too!
  V
The troops closed round by flank and rear,
With cannon bristling here and there;
And, sweeping round enclosed a space—
An arc, with line of beach for base.
That beach was lined with many a boat,
While close in shore at anchor float
The ships, whose mournful task that day
To freight the banished tribes away.
There, slowly heaving with the sea
On gentle swell, they well might be
Huge monsters of the briny deep,
Just breathing heavily in sleep.
  VI
And how the column passing through
The belt of manchineel, that grew
Along the winding shore, had reached
The open, where the boats were beached
Upon the broad shell-whitened strand;
While stood around, with oar in hand,
Their crews, Old England's dreaded tars,
Her bull-dogs trained in long fierce wars;
And stretching far across the bay
The ships, huge floating castles lay.
  VII
When burst this vision on the view,
The chiefs with start stepped back—they knew
With one keen glance what all this meant,
Those preparations' dark intent.
'Twas such a shock that courage failed
In some, and heart the boldest quailed.
A smothered oath—for *words* none spoke
E'en then—the sullen silence broke
But though half-uttered still it served

To break the spell no longer preserved:
The women caught the muttered sound,
And pent emotion burst all bound.
To th' front with eager feet they pressed
Then saw the waiting boats, and guessed
The truth. Then wildly rose in air
A cry of anguish and despair;
So sudden and so wild it rose.
'Twas like the shriek of death, as those
Who die of ruptured heart will shriek:
And so indeed, in sooth to speak,
A nation's heart it was that broke
In anguish of that cruel stroke!

  VIII

Some flung their frantic arms on high
Assailing Heaven with piercing cry;
Some sat down rocking to and fro,
Expressing thus a speechless woe;
Some sinking down on earth lay prone,
And wailed in long-drawn piteous moan;
While some flung down themselves and rolled
As in convulsions uncontrolled;
Some turned and fled—but wither fled?
On yon encircling line of red,
That living wall of men and steel,
To hurl themselves in vain, and reel
Back helpless, hopeless on their fate,
Aghast with rage, and fear, and hate.

  IX

The women only thus were frail:
The men, surprised, had seemed to fail
One moment in their fortitude;
Next moment manhood had subdued
The passing qualm of shame and pain
And stood forth masterful again.
They bade the prostrate women rise

And cease those worse than useless cries;
And then with firm, though tender, hand
They seized and captive made the band
Of fugitives, who'd vainly thought
To pass the English lines, and bought
Them sobbing much, yet with no lack
Of courtesy, brought them firmly back.

  X

And now the younger men had stept
Down to the boats, and some had lept
On board—alas! that never more
Those feet should press Hiroona's shore!
Some women, wives or lovers, then
Stept in and joined those bolder men—
In climes where gentler custom reigns
Or thinner blood flows through the veins,
Frail women, placed as these, had flung
Themselves impulsively, and clung
Upon their lord's or lover's breast
As on most natural place of rest:
But these were trained in sterner mould.
And so with mien (through seeming cold
For Carib maid and matron meet)
Contented nestled at their feet.

  XI

But only few thus used free-will:
The most refusing, ling'ring still,
When patience passed the limit given
And suasion failed, by force were driven.
Some few lay still upon the ground.
In fetters of their swoon still bound,
With hair all wild and garments torn:
These raised in strong men's arms are borne
Through surf and spray to reach the boats
Where, just in touch of land, each floats,
Each heaving with its human freight.

As loth to move, they lingering wait
The word, to brim the cup of woe
And seal a people's doom, "Let go!"
  XII
'Tis spoken: a hundred oar-blades flash
As one; and as the bending ash
Gives impulse to the boats, they leap
From shore, and breast they swelling deep.
Alas! For with those oars' first stroke
The last remaining link was broke
That bound with Nature's tenderest band
A people to their father-land;
And Hiroon's heart could bear the strain
No more: it shuddering burst in twain.
Beneath a frowning sky, and sun
Who veiled his eyes this deed was done—
Unhallowed deed! For where can cause,
As weighted in Justice' righteous laws,
Be found to justify the deed?
The conqueror's lien, may be, you'll plead,
By right of war to him belongs:
But rights of war are oftenest wrongs.
Væ Vitis![129] Paint it as you will
The old barbaric laws rules still
In these more cultured days, that Might,
If strong to win and hold, is Right.
  XIII
Full long has plied the labouring oar
Between the shipping and the shore.
Until the last of th' exile band
Has left the now deserted strand—
Hiroona's bravest and her best
Torn roughly from her bleeding breast.
In truth no craven heartless crowd
Are they, but fiercely stern and proud,
And vowing, as they pace the deck,

Grim vengeance for their nation's wreck;
But Discipline's strong hand is there
Inspiring prudence if not fear.
Soon Order takes Confusion's place:
The littered decks are cleared apace,
And latest preparations made;
The sails unfurled, and anchors weighed.
  XIV
The floating castles slowly leave
The roadstead one by one, as eve
Comes softly down the hills, whom height
Robs waning day of half the light,
And brings the shades ere yet the West
Has seen the sun sink down to rest;
And all had gone save one, which bore
The pennant of the Commodore.
There on the quarter-deck and poop
Now stand the Governor and group
Of glittering officers and staff,
Who've gaily come on board to quaff
The parting bowl, and bid adieu.
On board are also Warramou
And all the chiefs of note; but he
By Nature's warrant seemed to be
Acknowledged Chieftain of the band,
As born for power and high command.
  XV
Long while he spoke to none, but strode
The deck, with darkening brow which bode
A coming storm, whose swelling wrought
In lines of deep, unuttered thought
Which now across his features crept
Or now like rolling billows swept;
His eyes as though with madness fired,
But gazing far, as one inspired
From hell below, not heaven on high

With awful power of prophecy.
All bent their eyes upon him now
As sterner, darker grew his brow
As longer, quicker grew his stride:
Who thwarts him now shall woe betide.
So all men gaze—not least the group
Of officers upon the poop.
  XVI
When thus he many times had paced
The patient deck, he turned and faced
The knot of Englishmen who stood
Amused as first, but changed their mood
From mirth and bantering laugh to awe,
As now they met those eyes and saw
A flash of fierce intent and glare
Of more than common hatred there.
'Twas though some dangerous beast of prey,
Some royal tiger, turned to bay;
The sentry paused, and stood on guard,
And more than one hand touched the sword.
  XVII
One moment thus opposed they stand;
The Carib, nature's hero, grand
In bearing, splendid in his rage;
The scions of a cultured age,
And sons of England's foremost race;
A tableau worth of a place
In highest art, if found you him
Who could the striking picture limn,
And give dead canvas living form.
One moment thus, then burst the storm
So long pent up, and gathering force
Burst forth and rushed its furious course
Of passion, fire, and righteous wroth
Of patriot and of prophet both.

XVIII

"White men, I curse you to your face,
Curse you and all your hated race!
Great war has placed me in your power;
I am your captive: this your hour
To wreck your bitterest thought of ill;
To bind or slay me as you will;
But speech you cannot bind—'tis free!
Ay! E'en the tongue may severed be,
And torn all bleeding from its root,
And so the lips perforce be mute;
The living thought that makes the speech
Is safe within, beyond all reach
Of all your power to stay or bind—
Free as the unseen boundless wind
Do as your cruel will shall choose:
Whate'er your choice I'll not refuse,
Nor shrink from aught that Fate may bring.
Bind theses poor fettered limbs and fling
Me to the waves, if such your mood,
That sharks may make my flesh their food.
Blow out my brains, or, yet more kind,
To yonder cannon's muzzle bind
Me yet alive, then blow away
My mangled limbs across the bay;
I'd thank you for my freedom, for
Such was the boon I sought from war.
Or bare your blade, and make me feel
The keenest tortures of your steel.
Nought can you do, that I shall fear:
These Carib limbs know well to bear
The sharpest anguish knife can give,
Or flesh endure, and yet to live.
Do what you will; your vengeance wreak:
You cannot stay me—I will speak.
E'en should you slay me in your hate,

You cannot hold the hand of Fate;
And Fate is gathering up for you
The all that Vengeance claims as due—
Has drawn the sword and flung the sheath;
I tell you, white men, to your teeth
No less that robbers, pirates ye,
And plunderers by land and sea.
What restless greed could make you roam,
Has England no waste lands at home?
No treasured hoards of wealth untold?
No mountains of your cursèd gold?
That your great ships should sail the seas
For moons to seek poor isles like these?
What have we here to glut your lust
Or fill your greed, that come you must
To steal from us what gods had given?
You tell of what you call your Heaven,
Where spirits of your best men go
Whene'er they leave this earth below;
Where slave alike and master rest
And have the noblest and the best
Of all your God can give—at least
You send your medicine-men and priest
To tell us so, and bid us take
Your God and heaven for ours; and make
Believe *Bondieu* made you and us:
You lie! It never could be thus!
You spring, you say, from earth's foul sod:
We, offspring of the ocean god!
Your heaven no heaven could be, I swear,
Could white and red men mingle there!
No! Keep your heaven: in deadliest hate
I'd turn me from its very gate,
And hell's own darkest terrors dare
If I on entering found your there!

XIX

We've failed, but never should have failed.
Nor you with all your power prevailed,
Had not our angered gods withheld
Their aid; for we like fools rebelled
Against their rule, forsook the ways
Our fathers walked in better days,
Broke through old customs, changed the times,
And learned from you new ways and crimes,
To steal, and lie, and break one's word,
Drink water-fire, unknown, unheard
Of till accursed for evermore
You set your feet on Hiroon's shore.

XX

Since then our old men and our young
Have lost their manhood, and have flung
Their ancient customs to the wind;
And then our gods, no longer kind
But angered with us much, withdrew
And left us to be crushed by you.
You've won Hiroon, but let me tell
The curse that wrathful powers of hell,
Who love to deal the vengeance due
Are gathering up to hurl on you:—

XXI

This isle of ours, for which you've sold
Your honour in your greed of gold;
On whose fair lands your iron hand
Has stamped and burnt the murderer's brand
In fire and blood, shall be your bane
And all be loss you now think gain.
Though crops may pile the harvest-field
They'll bring no joy, no blessing yield.
For fabled wealth of sugar-cane
You'll spend your strength, but spend in vain,
And all you grasp, and think it gold,

Shall turn to ashes in your hold:
The sweets you laboured for so much
Shall melt and vanish at your touch;
And year by year the gathering curse
Shall make the outlook worst and worse
Till what you deem a paradise
Shall prove the grave where all hope dies!
  XXII
Your England deems these isles so fair
That now she pours her treasures here;
She pays as price her richest blood
And thinks the costly bargain good.
To keep the prize in her sole clutch
She deems no sacrifice too much;
She holds it justified 'fore Heaven,
When war the evil chance had given,
To banish from their native soil
Our lordly tribes—for fear they foil
Her schemes, and one foot's tenure hold
Of what was all their own of old.
The hapless soil with blood they'll drench
Again in battle with the French
Should they once more dispute the prize:
Such now its value in her eyes.
  XXIII
But mark you well the words I say,
There comes, and quickly comes a day
When England's heel shall spurn these isles;
Although she lavish now she smiles
And spend her treasure and her blood
Shall deem them worthless, past all good;
Shall deem their keep not worth the cost;
Her millions spent shall reckon lost;
Regard West Indian tutelage
Not worth a single soldier's wage.
Abandoned all in sheer disgust,

Her stores and guns shall rot and rust,
Her battlements in slow decay
Uncared shall crumble day by day.
Your heartless Mother shall recall
Her best and wealthiest sons, and all
Shall quit the faded land who may—
Except the wretch who needs must stay:
All quit this god-forsaken shore
Where faith and hope are known no more.
  XXIV
Scared hence, as from some deadly sink
Affrighted capital shall shrink.
And enterprise starved out shall die;
What gold remains find wings and fly;
And princely commerce frayed away,
Poor drivelling trade alone shall stay.
Your bravest efforts shall be checked
By cold contempt or stern neglect,
Or crushed by unjust, cruel laws—
For England's lion has it claws!
Ah! Wronged Hiroon, my country, then
Shall Heaven be known as just—white men
Flung forth from thee, O ocean gem,
As we are now flung forth by them!
Your very negro-slaves shall gain
Their freedom, fling away the chain
And claim to shake your by the hand,
And strut your equals in the land:
Ay! Revolution strange and new,
Becomes its lord and master too.
  XXV
Ha! Ha! Great *Bondieu* gives me eyes
To see what in the future lies;
And on them visions vast have broke.
See! See! Yon mountain burst in smoke
And flame, which fiercely leaps and flays,

And all the mountain's sides ablaze:
No earthly flames! For see they spurn
The forest trees—'tis rocks that burn!
And fire rolls down the mountain's side
And streams of flame like rivers glide.
And while the fiery torrents pour
Tremendous peals of thunder roar;
And up leaps lightning everywhere
Vile smells of sulphur choke the air
Deep down its sides the mountain moans,
In pain and loud unearthly groans.
And all the hills rounds quake with fear
At th' agony of dread Souffrière.
And while the fierce, terrific glow
Fills all with hellish glare below
Above no sky is seen o'erheard;
But heavy mass of darkness spread,
'Gainst which the demon flames in hate
Spring up but cannot penetrate;
Through which no opening cleft is riven
To let descend one smile from Heaven.
The very sun sends through no light;
But for th' unearthly glare, 'twere night!
Such night above such glare below,
'Twould seem the gods had meant it so—
'Twixt heaven and earth such barrier thrown
As left the earth to hell alone!
Yet deathlier shudderings through me thrill
And horrors crowd on horrors still!
See! Can it be? God! Can we trust
Our startled senses? Yet we must!
See! Heaven no longer pours its rain
To bless the thirsty waiting plain;
But from that lurid darkness pour
Such showers as none e'er knew before
Of stones and rocks, and dust and mud

Which strike the earth with heavy thud:
Trees, houses perish, and not least
Your harvests—perish man and beast.
  XXVI
Confusion, terror and dismay!
Hiroona never saw such day.
And yet that day yourselves shall see;
And when it comes remember me:
Accept it as a pledge that all
That I foretell you shall befall
Hiroon—but now Hiroon no more
Since all her sons have left her shore—
All come to pass and nothing fail.
  XXVII
Now weigh your anchor, hoist your sail;
The hour has come to go; but first
Receive my curse—already cursed,
Thrice-cursed by Heav'n, Hiroon, and hell
With blast and power no force can quell:
Now fill it, demons, to the brim
May fevers burn your every limb;
May raving madness seize your brains
May agues pierce you through with pains.
May ache and anguish gnaw your bones
Till Heaven is weary with your groans,
Yet every day bring something fresh!
May cramp and tremblings seize your flesh!
May pining sickness day by day,
By wasting steal your life away;
To poison Obi turn your food,
And leprous taint befoul your blood.
Your children die as soon as breath
They draw; or live for worse than death.
Of all the ills you yet have known
May more in thousands press your down:
Of all the ills you now most dread

Ten thousand more beat down your head,
Until in densest night below
  XXVIII
Sink down your souls in endless woe!"
When now was reached the highest stage
And climax of his maniac rage,
He ceased to speak, and with a yell
Staggered, flung up his arms and fell.
His heart had failed—it almost broke,
With swelling feelings seemed to choke,
Too full of words or further breath!
He fell in swoon, which seemed like death;
And there unheeded on the deck
He lay, a stranded human wreck.
  XXIX
Meanwhile the ships were heading West,
Whither yon sun had sunk to rest.
Alas! Hiroon, in endless night
Thy sun has quenched its glorious light:
The pledge that earth again shall see
Its sun affirms no hope for thee!
The ships go freighting on the band
Of exiles far from Hiroon's strand,
To Rattan Island, round whose shore
With ever ceaseless roll and roar,
Far in the Bight of Mexico
The great Gulf-stream's strong currents flow.
And when ere long the slumberer broke
The thraldom of his swoon and woke,
Hiroon had vanished far from sight:
The ship was plunging into night.
And thus, in anguish, Warramou
Had bid his last and long adieu.

The End

THE HOLIDAY

DEDICATION
To Mother, Brothers, Sisters and other
Kinsmen, In the Island of St Vincent, this
little volume of verse In Memory of a visit
to them in August 1877, which although it
should be followed by others equally
pleasant, must remain in its antecedents and
its memories unique, is affectionately
dedicated
BY ITS AUTHOR
H.N.H.

THE HOLIDAY

Calm was the sea, and clear the sky
With fleecy cloudlets floating high;
We seemed to've left for aye behind
The murky clouds and gustful wind.
The ceaseless rain, the lightning flash
The frequent thunder's rolling crash
That, now for dreary weeks, had thrown
An aspect quite unlike thine own
O'er thee, Iëre, claimed to be
Gem of the Caribbean sea.
Now all was bright, that glorious day,

As on we steamed our easy way
O'er tranquil waves, through lambent air
A fragrance sweet that seemed to bear.
I norward strained mine eyes to see
The loom of land right dear to me;
And soon it came—mere haze at first,
Anon it seemed at once to burst
From out th' invisible, or rise
From Ocean's depth to meet mine eyes;
And peaks and mounts to come to me
From dim and far off memory.
Heart swelled; I sprang upon my feet;
I felt all through the quickened beat
Of leaping pulse within my veins,
Almost a whirl amidst my brains.
No common day was that which sped
So swiftly, brightly, o'er my head;
No stranger land before me grew;
For there my life's first breath I drew,
And there my childhood's earliest years
Were passed; thence, 'midst a mother's tears,
I crossed the seas for Home and school;
For such was then th' accepted rule
And there returned, my school days o'er
Bright happy days I spent once more;
A spot well named "The Happy Hill",
A name I find it bearing still.
And holier mem'ry yet! 'twas there
As priest of God, year after year,
With many failures, doubtless yes,
And yet with very much to bless,
I strove—I fearlessly avow,
Reflecting back as I do now—
I strove with every power and nerve
As faithful priest my Church to serve,
A flock by pastor much beloved

And true (as after years have proved)
I'd left, now sixteen years ago—
So swift the stream of life doth flow!
And stronger still than all yet told
Of such associations old,
A tie of nature and of blood,
Which neither time, nor fire, nor flood,
Nor all the haps of life's turmoil
Can break, fast bound me to that soil;
A mother, stricken now in years,
Advancing down this vale of tears,
Dwelt there; and sisters, brothers too,
And other kinsmen not a few;
And years, long years had passed away,
And locks of youth had turned to grey,
Since they and I, by Heaven's grace
Had looked each other in the face.
To meet again had come to seem
The vanished image of a dream.
But sickly, weary, needing rest,
(From evils worst come gifts the best!)
From work now grown beyond my strength
I'm forced to seek repose at length—
My first real holiday, first "leave";
Indeed, from work first real reprieve—
And five-and-twenty years 'tis now
I've borne my ordination vow.
'Tis wonder small my heart should leap.
And surge and swell with feelings deep!
Fast sped the steamer on, and clear
Through cloudless tropic atmosphere
Came hill and dale, and mountain peak,
Down whose wooded sides a streak
Of golden light from evening sun
With flash of seeming joy, would run;
Came field and rock, and bay and beach,

And town, low stretching round the reach;
Came swiftly each remembered spot,
Familiar once, forgotten not.
It seemed, delusion strange and fond!
So calm the sea, like placid pond,
So motionless her onward way,
The ship herself at anchorage lay,
The land to hasted forth to meet,
And, sailing "welcome home", to greet
Her son! At length, with rush and roar,
The anchor joined us to the shore;
And there she stood, sublime and grand,
And beautiful, my native land!

That other welcome home—words fail
To tell of that; I draw a veil
O'er scenes where son and mother met;
Where brothers clasped the hand, and yet
More tender welcome sisters gave,
And youthful daughter too. (I crave
A brief parenthesis, to say
A child of mine was there that day,
An inmate of my mother's home.
To which a year ago she'd come),
Methinks such homely meetings are
For other's eyes too sacred far.
Enough! Let night her gentle mantle spread
And close a day to hallowed.

And now I will, in lighter vein,
Resume my interrupted strain;
How fared my kins on there my page
Shall now record—how youth and age,
The one hath ripened on through time,
The other blossomed into prime.
The Mother first. Of good old stuff

She must have been, so well to rough
The tempests and the storms of life,
And hold her own in lengthened strife
And battle with the world; not few
Her cares, and toils and ailments too
Have been. Of children twelve have known
Her moth'ring care, and all but one
A babe, their pride of manhood gained,
Or bloom of womanhood attained.
And now rightly nobly she well she wears
The honour of increasing years;
Of which near threescore now and ten
She counts with dignity—but then
A Crichton and Macdowell she,
Right noble branch of noble tree!
With lines of age but few, and brow
Scarce furrowed more than mine is now;
Her hair not silvered yet, but grey;
Far off, God grant, that be the day
Ere on that head be crown of snow;
God grant her years of peace to know!

Of sisters now what can I say?
Not grave and serious things to say.
There's one, a travelled one, who knows
A thing or two, a quelquechose
Of this and that—so much she knew,
'Twas thought her stockings would be blue,
A trainer of little dears
From alphabet through all the spheres.
She learning's shaky ladder mounts,
Sums well, and "casteth up accounts"!
She's slender, slight and fair; her waist
Would suit the most exacting taste.
She dons a most peculiar hat;
Is fond of parrot, chick and cat;

Is great at women's argument,
And much on deputations bent.
A right good soul she is, I say,
A little fond of her own way.
A second's tall; it is her pride
To stand at some short brother's side,
And something reach from off some shelf
Which he can't reach, poor man, himself!
A great housekeeper—she can make
A pudding, pastry, pie or cake;
Can mend a buttonhole at need;
Her needles ply with skill and speed;
Flags, scrolls and banners has supplied
At Christmas and at Eastertide,
Well finished with minutest care,
Exact, and measured to a hair.
Sedate, not often making jokes,
Content with those of other folkes;
Good-natured, easy, seldom cross,
For kindness never at a loss.
She leads a gentle useful life,
For peace created, not for strife;
In word not great, but great in deed
She's everybody's help and need.

Who's next? A busy little bee—
No drone, you easily can see;
A busy bee without a sting,
She's ever flitting on the wing.
Comptroller of the household too,
Makes money last as few can do.
Half comical and half demure,
She's full of frolic, and you're sure
When e'er that serious phiz is on,
Some little mischief has been done—
Live kittens served you in a pie,

Your pockets filled with sand or rye,
A horseshoe given you to eat,
Or some such pleasant trick or treat!
Yet would not hurt a fly; you'll find
Her fun the laughing harmless kind.
Chief helper she at Church—there's nought
That there is said or done or taught
But she is there to hear or do
Her part in aisle, or choir, or pew.
Her sisters call her Deaconess,
While Pastor loves, and people bless.
A brother next, in honest truth
A pattern son, pattern youth;
Of all the sons the only one
That from the homestead has not gone,
And of that Home, who can gainsay?
He's now the "house-band" and the stay.
He serves the Queen, and in her cause
Maintains her rights in Excise laws.
Right good at everything he is,
The 'onimies and 'ologies;
Can tell of fishes, tell of birds,
Can give you hard botanic words;
Can tell of heraldry, of crest,
Of shield, and gules and all the rest;
Excels in pyrotechnic art,
Can bid the mimic Etna start
The hissing rocket soar on high,
Or wheels of fire revolving fly;
Can handle well the workman's tool,
And make a table chair or stool;
Can order well the scenic stage,
Or e'en supply the drama's page;
Can tell in Fancy's highest flights
How Englishmen are Israelites!
A volunteer, a first class shot—

There's scarce a thing that he is not;
But Nature would not grant him all
Her gifts—she fixed his stature small!
These four still linger at the nest;
My rhyme must follow now the rest.
A stately matron first demands
Attention at my willing hands.
The world, methinks, at her has smiled
No rush of floods, nor tempest wild
Have beat upon her house, it stands
As on a rock, not on the sands.
Of good strong sense, and sure if staid,
She's gone serenely on, and made
The country's highest state her own,
And e'en vice-regal honours known;
But bears her years and honours well.
No stranger guest, I'm sure, could tell
That living children twelve she has,
And two asleep! There never was
Such clustering circle, even round
Our mother's spacious table, found
Of olive branches—sure I am
That even Japhet, Shem or Ham
Those great progenitors of yore,
A finer cluster never bore!
Had all the others mated been,
What prodigies we might have seen!
My Heaven's favour on them rest,
And she in them be doubly blest!
One sister more there yet remains,
And still my lingering pen detains;
The youngest born, but strongest built,
True gold is she, not silver gilt.
Of habits active, spirits light,
Of disposition warm and bright;
Strong sens'd, and clever quite enough,

And ruddy without rouge or puff;
With figure more than average high,
With merry, laughing, twinkling eye;
The light of home when there; one who
The young ones round her every drew;
Who, sane in mind and body sane
Seems scarce to know of ache or pain.
In pantry good, or kitchen range,
Or hall, or drawing room—'tis strange
The blinded planters cannot see
What glorious housewife she would be!

A brother last, but not the least—
One who in climes of sunny East
A wealthy man would be a great;
For there his healthy children eight
(And many more approaching fast,
And none can yet forsee the last!)
A source of power would be and gain—
The sons to scour the laden plain;
The girls for pelf; for there, 'tis said,
The maids are priced before they wed;
But in the unromantic West
He's only passing rich at best.
In open air and sunny meads
The good old planter's life he leads.
Full round and rubicund his face,
In him 'tis pleasant now to trace
The powers that to our race belong;
Like them robust, full bodied, strong,
With rich blood bounding through the veins
With all too vigorous health pertains;
Of all the sons in form and frame
Most like the honour'd sire, the fame
Of th' ancient sturdy Huggins race,
Gone down in those degenerate days,

Upholding best . . . Our martyred king
Once knew that metal's honest ring.
When rebels rolled their traitor horde
Against their Church, their realm and lord,
A Huggins fought for Charles' right,
In fatal Naseby's ill-starred fight,
A Colonel in the Royal ranks—
His only need his master's thanks.
When all was lost; the Throne and Crown
And Church by Cromwell trampled down;
The sturdy Colonel turned to roam,
And seek o'er western seas a home.
To his old fashioned ken
Old England was no England then;
His country, ruled by rebel hand,
A dark, blood-stained, polluted land.
He left; no serf of Cromwell he!
Nor traitor's henchman e'er could be!
From him we spring, we proudly say,
Who bear his honoured name to-day.
('Twas spelt as Huygens once, 'tis said.
'Tis so in old traditions read,)
But changed, no matter when or how,
To more euphonic Huggins now.
'Tis even said, of course a joke,
The sturdy English Huggins oak
Was strong in even Roman times,
And flourished in Italian climes.
There was Huginus, Pope of Rome,
The Ninth, as ancient records come.
You know the Popes were married then,
And well Huginus might have been
Himself a patriarchal man,
And founder of a Huggins clan.
But from this "jeu d'esprit" lets turn,
And sober fact, not fiction learn.

In Nevis' Isle a home he sought,
And with his shattered fortune bought
Plantations. There he lived, and there
With high repute and honour fair,
Have lived two centuries and more,
Like him their ancestor of yore,
His sons, the children as the sires,
Rich feudal lords and country squires,
In days when these were isles of gold,
And rich in fabled wealth untold.
Half Nevis owned them lords, and few
As good a portion saw or knew.
'Tis known in these West Indian Isles,
Were sunny summer ever smiles,
But treacherous fevers ever lurk
To hasten Death's o'er speedy work,
That men of English blood, as soon
As they have drawn the golden boon
The willing soil so freely yields
From out her sugar laden fields,
Turn homewards fast; and there at ease
Enjoy their grains, while o'er the seas
Their hirelings toil and die, where seldom dwell
A landed gentry; there, 'tis good to tell
The Huggins' have dwelt, and been
A fair exception rarely seen;
A dew in colonies there are
Can trace fair pedigrees so far.
And though not few have wandered forth,
To East, to further West, to North,
And times have sadly changed, yet some
E'en now in their old island home,
With 'minished fortune, still retain
Some fragments of their old domain.
A strong limbed, long lived race they've been
Acclimatised through years I ween;

Broad shouldered, tall, six feet or more,
And living oft to years fourscore.
The family legends tell of sires
Outliving long their youthfull fires,
With silvery hair where once was jet,
O'er thee score years and ten, and yet
Hale, vig'rous, cheery, straight and sage,
While younger men were broken with age;
Of ladies, who at ninety still
Could mount their palfreys, and o'er hill
And dale all unattended ride
Save by a serving man beside.
My father's sire myself I knew,
A grand old man at eighty-two.
A fine old squire he was, upright,
Of noble and commanding height.
A open house he kept, and hall
And bed, for gentle strangers all;
And many noble guests and great
Oft entered through that far famed gate;
And Englan's best loved son was one,
Hero of hundred victories won.
Immortal Nelson oft was guest;
At lordly feast, or come to rest
From war, and there his days to spend
An old familiar welcome friend.
In brief repose from mortal strife,
'Twas there Lord Nelson found a wife;
And thus his kin by marriage tie,
Was bound to his friend more tenderly.
He gave his own ennobled name
To one of Huggins's sons, the same
Who founded with his own strong hands
Estates, and "Bronte" named his lands.
'Twas on those famous days of Punch,
When weary travellers turned for lunch,

Of heartiest welcome ever sure
At that inviting open door;
And England's "mighty Nelson" knew
Right well the strength of "Huggins brew".

The squire's wife, by Heaven's grace,
Was worthy if her lord and race;
Could ever faithful wife do more?
Of children TWENTY-ONE she bore!
Of those our sire was seventh son;
Was clever, vig'rous, hearty; one
With close knit frame, and nerves well strung
He died at sixty-three, still young,
And with the young in death he slept.
That scourge of deadly fever swept
The land, that spurns decrepit years,
That spares the tender infant's tears,
That scorns the sickly and the weak;
The young and strong alone to seek;
With such, as young himself, he went.

From long digression now I turn
But could I help my spirit burn,
When once again, are close to life
My father's sons, my father's wife
Mine eyes beheld, and footsteps trod
My native isle's paternal sod?

How fared the Holiday, how well
It went, my freshened pen must tell.
Right pleasant were each night and day
And swift the hours have fled away;
Sometimes in pleasant rustic walk,
Sometimes in pleasant homely talk
Of other days, and olden times,
Or stories told of other climes;

Or cheerful games went laughing round,
And merry Mirth and Frolic found.
Each day was sought some new pursuit,
Some thing to please, some luscious fruit
Some flower strange, or something new
To see or seek, to try or do.
And then the Flock that once I taught
Abundant joy and pleasure brought;
They came in scores to welcome me,
Right glad their priest again to see
Returned once more to the fatherland;
To shake again their Pastor's hand.
To hear once more his voice, they said—
I loved that flock that once I fed;
And mine it was to feed anew
From pulpit, and from altar too.
When light the waves and soft the breeze
We ventured oft o'er tranquil seas,
To skirt the rocks to hoar and grey,
Or scull the boat o'er placid bay,
Midst coral reefs, where feed and sleep
Bright sunny creatures of the deep;
Of red and green, or gold and blue,
That flash the deepest waters though.
Sometimes we flung them on the land,
With barbed hook, and sleight of hand;
Or plunged, on cooling luxury bent,
And shared with them their element.
I've gazed from heights with raptures glow
Where calm, serene, reposing low,
And exquisitely soft and sweet,
Some hundred yards beneath my feet,
Some lovely vale, at eve of day,
Like sleeping, smiling beauty lay.
Or rode along those famous ways,
Where erst, in olden Carib days,

Was war, and many soldiers brave
Found fierce, relentless death and grave;
Where paths are hewn on slippery scarp
Of solid rock, round angles sharp;
Where cliffs above straight, towering soar,
Below the foaming waters roar.
'Twas here our soldiers got their foes
In cruel war's most anguished throes.
Like demons from the nether world
The savage Caribs shrieked, and hurled
Great crags on the helpless troops below,
And buried all in huge o'erthrow.
We shudder as we hurry on,
Most thankful that such days are gone
I've stood on th' Isle's North-eastern shore,
To hear th' Imperial ocean roar,
Midst granite boulders turned and ground,
By restless waters beaten round.
And oh! 'twas great and grand to see
(And more than grand, 'twas joy to me)
Those mighty waves come rolling on,
And leap and cast themselves upon
The shore, with wide unbroken sweep
From o'er the vast Atlantic deep.
And oh! 'twas sweet indeed to stand,
And there, on that sea-beaten strand
Inhale and drink the ocean breeze;
(My native air and breath are these!)
I felt my lungs with life re-filled;
I felt a longing with fulfilled.
'Twas thus no doubt Old Homer stood,
And watched the ocean's rolling flood;
And told, in grand euphonious Greek,
Which seems its sense in sound to speak[1]
How surges, breaking on the shore
With romping, rolling, boist'rous roar,

(To express it better I would wish)
Recede with sullen hissing swish.
I've stood at sombre Soufrière's base;
I could not climb, I did but gaze.
Here now there seems profound repose,
Where erst in huge Titanic throes
Upheaved the mighty mount, and burst
In fire and flame and smoke at first,
And then in showers of falling stones.
While streams of fiery lava glide
Down the trembling mountain's side,
Portending death and ruin and woe
To peaceful vale and plain below.
Th' astonished Island shook with fear,
And thought the Judgement self was near,
And near one hundred miles away
Grenada, fearful, heard all day
The strange unearthly sound—they thought
The French and British navies fought,
And trembled for the issue. Right
A new alarm revealed to sight—
From out a blood red northern sky
What flashed aloft, and brandished high,
Like sabres, swords and brands of fire,
As heralding just Heaven's ire,
Some dread even's portentous birth,
Some coming down to guilty earth.
But on Barbadian shores next day
The greatest mass and horror lay,
There too was 'twas deemed they heard from far
The thunder loud of England's war,
And anxious night was passed. Next morn
No day had come! And terror born
Of doubt and darkness, bred in hell
All o'er a wailing island fell.
"Great God! What does this darkness mean,

Egyptian like both felt and seen?"
"Is't night?" "The clocks say day." "Eclipse?"
"This moon is old," from trembling lips
The whispered word and answers pass
"What's that now patt'ring on the glass?
And this? O horror! This that just
Has passed and swept my face? This crust
That covers all I touch? 'Tis here!
'Tis there! It chokes the very air!"
"It thickens fast! And can we trust
Our sense? The Heavens are raining DUST!"
Slow, slowly dragged that awful day
Its terror-laden hours away;
Grew on the darkness more intense;
Fell on the shower of dust more dense;
Grew dull the candle's feeble light
In struggle with unnat'ral night;
Grew on a silence still and death,
As men could hear their bated breath.
Sudden, as seen through smokened glass,
Which boys before their eyes will pass,
The zenith seeking sun, no more
Himself, but changed as though to gore
Midst unillumined blackness stood
And glared, a rayless orb of blood!
"'Tis Sodom's doom! To prayer, to prayer!"
The tremblers cry in wild despair;
The bells are toll'd, and thousands rush
And churches fill with crowd and crush;
And litanies to Heaven bore
Their prayer, who never prayed before.
By noon the showers of dust were o'er,
And those who prayed could smile once more.
But inches deep it lay; it filled
The plains, all vegetation killed;
And where the ashes thickest lay

Sepulchral famine rose to slay.
It was not all then baseless fear
That shook the Isles, thou dread Soufrière
But placid, calm, supremely still
Now rests the huge volcanic hill,
With mien as innocent, as mild,
'Twould seem as harmless as child.
Above its wooded belt are seen,
Savannah like and softly green,
And gently sloping down the steep,
That look like peaceful downs for sheep;
While dewy, soft, perpetual cloud
Obscured his head in cowl or shroud.
Yet oft a tremor shakes the ground,
And sulph'rous smells are wafted round.
Soon may its dormant horrors wake:
A day or hour may sudden break
The silent monster's treach'rous sleep,
And raise them from their vastly deep.
In many tropic isles I've been,
But quieter spot, or lovelier scene
To calm and fascinate the eyes,
Transfix with pleasure and surprise;
And hold the captive gazer's sight
In dreamy trance, or rapt delight.
Than that in soft repose and rest,
Neath Virgie's eyrie ridge and crest,
Which lies—its Indian name Iambou—
More peerless vale, or perfect view,
I n'ere have seen. The hills stand round
In changing cloud and sunshine crowned,
In an unbroken circling sweep,
As though to form a lake, while deep
And rapid streams across the vale
In waving lines of silver trail,
Till all, converging, meet below

Through gorge of riven mount to flow—
More cleft through upright walls of rock,
As rent in twain by earthquakes shock.
Through clouds, that mass themselves upon
The mountain tops, the struggling sun,
Himself unseen, through unseen reft
In high aerial regions cleft,
Pours slanting down diverging rays
Of softened light through mist and haze,
And gilds the lower clouds in streaks,
While darkness veils the higher peaks;
He flings his partial light on hill,
Or cultured field, or resting mill,
Or village nestling midst the trees,
Or palm tree waving in the breeze;
Or sends illumined air, which seems,
Quite visible in golden gleams,
To penetrate some deep recess,
To hold it in its warm caress,
And throw, in an unearthly sheen,
Strange spell all o'er the silent scene;
Which seems to come and go, and fade
In wondrous change of light and shade.
Here too was war; and while men slept
Secure, the prowling Caribs crept.
With neither moon to guide, nor star,
The bloody footsteps of the war—
They crept like midnight beasts of prey,
And sprang, as savage and as wild,
On helpless woman, maid and child;
They sprang, ferocious in attack,
Alike on white man and on black.
Ah! then from out that startled vale
Now rose to Heav'n a midnight wail
Of vengeance and of woe! Next morn
Appeared in Town a slave, all torn

And soiled, and haggard, and footsore;
In bleeding arms a babe she bore.
She'd snatched him from amid the dead,
Her master's infant child, and fled
The vale of massacre, through blood,
And flame, and night, and river flood,
And mountain-pass and wood, her prize
The babe, the darling of her eyes,
Held firm, and clinging to her neck,
The sole survivors from the wreck;
And brave and faithful, thus had won
Her way, and saved the white man's son.

But Virgie's narrow ridge and height
Saw once a fair and gallant fight.
The French with mighty toil and skill
Had dragged and planted on the hill,
With valour worthy of their foe,
Some guns to sweep both vales below,
And sweep with grape the winding-ridge,
Where man could rush, as on a bridge,
But two or three abreast. Our men
With cheers charged up the narrow glen
And gained the height through scrub and bush
With gallant climb and head-long rush;
A few fierce blows, and all was won—
In splendid pluck the thing was done.
I passed a wild yet lovely spot,
Where blood was poured, yet not forgot.
Sweet hills and forests cluster round,
Three rivers blend harmonious sound,
And murmur softly still their tale
Of blood to listening hill and dale.
In those dense forests' darkened shade
Fierce Caribs lay in ambuscade.
The narrow path went through; our troops

In broken ranks, and struggling groups,
(A sad necessity it was,
The uncleared way the fatal cause)
An escort to the front, marched through.
A moment more, and war shells blew
From every side, and Caribs poured
With poisoned dart, and blood-stained sword
In swarming multitudes. The fight
Was fierce and long. Who dreamt of flight
E'en then from such tremendous odds?
'Twas Englishmen who fought, ye gods!
Each man his life for ten he sold,
But yet the saddened tale is told
That from that wood, when evening fell,
But three or four emerged to tell—
Our mother's father, Crichton,—me—
How that dark deed was fiercely done,

A rough adventure crossed my way
One stormy, dark, and gloomy day;
A hurricane, the seaman said.
Was likely brooding overhead:
The crazy boat, the "Pioneer,"
Lay rocking roughly at the pier;
Was't wise to tempt the threatening flood?
I'd given my work, and go I would.
Just off; when down from hill and cloud
There burst, with roarings wild and loud,
A fiercely rampant, rushing squall,
Of deathlike black, like funeral pall,
With driving rain and blinding sleet,
As only in these seas we meet.
It seized us in its folds—all sight
Was gone, and day was turned to night!
The wheezing engine fails to urge
The boat, 'tis driven through the surge

By rushing winds; while close ahead
We knew, as on we wildly sped,
Were dreaded rocks, where oft the drowned
A sudden watery grave have found.
What is our course? Not one can see,
Or on those rocks, or out to sea!
When sudden lifts th' impervious cloud,
And then, with acclamations loud,
We see the cliff, and feel the swell;
"Luff! Luff! My man, quick" ah 'Tis,
Thank God! We've shunned the fatal shock,
And safely passed the dangerous rock!
I've seen those lovely Leeward bays,
When morning sun, or evening rays
Were soft and mild, and air was still,
And Nature seemed to drink her fill
Of peace—the sea profoundly blue
And rippleless, save where we drew,
With reverent oar and silent skiff,
'Neath darkening shade of hanging cliff,
And there 'twas black, yet brightly black
Like burnished jet, reflecting back.
'Twas from the dark and threatening deep
From which they rise upright and steep,
And deep below as high above,
With cavern grim, and darkness cove,
And rocks, where ironclads might moor,
And with their yard arms touch the shore;
And where Geology's delight,
Primeval strata meet the sight,
In wonderous order strongly laid,
And easy traced from grade to grade;
And round those bare and slippery sides
The treach'rous cold iguana glides;[2]
Or clinging aloes, here and there
Lift high and lofty crown and spear;

But round whose bases hoar and grim
The fish in teeming myriads swim.
O'er tiny bay, through narrow glen
Where scarce are seen abodes of men,
Through long defile of light and shade,
'Tween green clad hills, or opening glade,
The grateful eye, well pleased, would roam.
Sure this is solitude, the home
Of peace, seclusion from the world!
But no! some coils of wire unfurl'd
On yon secluded beach, invade
Its sanctity, and thus is made
The sea girt isle but one with wide
And bustling, busy worlds outside;
Knit close by nerves of quivering wire
To th' heart of England's vast Empire.

In scenes like these I could unbend
From self and thought, and hours could spend,
And yield to uncontrolled dream
The less of earth than Heav'n would seem.
And swiftly fades the distant scene,
The soft dissolving blue and green,
And grey and purple hue of land;
Till nought is seen, from where I stand,
Save something dimly traced by eye,
That mythlike floats 'tween sea and sky,
So visionary and ideal,
I ask, is't false? Or is it real?
Not so from mem'ry o'er can fade
(So strong the fond impressions made)
The vision bright of those bright days,
Bright in Affection's purest rays.
That visit, printed deep and fast
In th' unobliterated past,
A clear bright spot must ever be,

And never fade from memory!

Now southward, that is homeward, bound,
I go with thankfulness profound,
A wife and home await me there,
And loving little ones most dear;
Besides, my life's great care and love,
My Church and work, all else above.
My longing little ones, I know
Full well (my heart now tells me so).
Though little more than babes they are,
Have deck'd the home in loving care
With flowers and wreaths, and garlands gay
To mark the bright and welcome day,
When home again, with childish glee,
They welcome me most joyfully.

Thus leaving part myself behind
In th' land I quit, I'll surely find
E'en greater part myself with you,
My Church, my wife, and children true.

The End

Notes

Introduction

1. The copy at the Cambridge University Library came courtesy of the university's purchase of the complete collection of the Royal Commonwealth Society's library and archives in the early 1990s. According to the log book, this copy arrived in London as a donation to the Royal Empire Society Library from a Huggins family member, likely George F. Huggins, on 9 December 1930. While the initials in the society's log are indistinguishable, it is probable that Charlotte and Evelyn brought the book with them earlier in the year and were present for the donation, as the two made a trip to London from Trinidad in August 1930 and remained in Exmouth during their stay. The British Library acquired its copy in November 1931. A copy of *Hiroona* is in the Kingstown Public Library in St Vincent, which was last located in storage and has since gone missing. One copy is located in the closed stacks of the library at the University of the West Indies, St Augustine, and in the Trinidad Public Library.

2. Paula Burnett, *The Penguin Book of Caribbean Verse in English* (Harmondsworth: Penguin, 1986); Louis James, *Caribbean Literature in English* (New York: Longman, 1999); Edward Baugh, "A History of Poetry", in *A History of Literature in the Caribbean*, ed. Albert James Arnold and Vera M. Kutzinki (Amsterdam: J. Benjamins, 2001); Selwyn Cudjoe, *Beyond Boundaries: The Intellectual Tradition of Trinidad and Tobago in the Nineteenth Century* (Wellesley, MA: Calaloux, 2003).

3. This is the accepted history. One of the earliest English records of this is in Sir William Young, *Considerations Which May Tend to Promote the Settlement of Our New West-India Colonies* (London: James Robson, 1764), 9; Charles Shephard, *An Historical Account of the Island of Saint Vincent* (London: W. Nicol, 1831), 22. According to Governor James Seton, the ship was wrecked in 1734; another governor put the date around 1712, while Young put the date at 1675, which correlated to an actual hurricane in Barbados in the same year. Christopher Taylor, *The Black Carib Wars: Freedom, Survival, and the Making of the Garifuna* (Jackson: University Press of Mississippi, 2012), 15.

4.   Nancie L. Solien Gonzalez, *Sojourners of the Caribbean: Ethnogenesis and Ethnohistory of the Garifuna* (Urbana: University of Illinois Press, 1988), 8.

5.   Sir William Young, Bart., *An Account of the Black Charibs of St Vincent with the Charaib Treaty of 1773, and other Original Documents* (London: Frank Cass, 1971 [1795]), 23.

6.   This account of the start of the war is first documented in Bryan Edwards, and then elaborated in Sir William Young and Charles Shephard. *Hiroona* also follows this account. Bryan Edwards, *History Civil and Commercial of the British West Indies*, 4 vols (London: J. Stockdale, 1793–1801).

7.   Sources from the eighteenth and nineteenth century like Shephard and Young cite this encounter as a duel.

8.   Eduard Conzemius, "Ethnographical Notes on the Black Carib (Garif)", *American Anthropologist* 30, no. 2 (April–June 1928): 189. Of the original 4,338 who were captured and taken to Baliceaux in February 1797, 2,026 men, women and children arrived at Roatan in April 1797. Gonzalez, *Sojourners of the Caribbean*, 21.

9.   T.B.C. Musgrave, *Historical and Descriptive Sketch of the Colony of St Vincent, W.I.* (St Vincent: Gardener's, 1891), 25.

10.   Michael Huggins, personal interviews, 24 February 2008; 3 October 2011. Michael provided me with a patrilineal family tree, which is the source for names and dates where no other reference could be found.

11.   John Huggins was involved in a famous duel with Walter Maynard, resulting in John's death in 1822. Joyce Gordon, *Nevis, Queen of the Caribbees* (London: Macmillan Caribbean, 1993), 16. Even more grievous misconduct is documented in *Case in Nevis*, the report of the trial of Edward Jr in 1817 for the excessive punishment dealt to female slaves on the Nevis plantation belonging to T.J. Cottle, president of the island. In the anonymously written report, the two slaves, Thisbe and Christiana, were said to have been beaten (one later died of her injuries) following their vocal objection to the excessive flogging of three younger slaves for receiving stolen goods. Although he had been put on trial before in 1810 for similar behaviour, Edward was later acquitted due to eyewitness testimony that both women were seen relatively unharmed days after the incident, even attending a ball over the weekend. Attention was paid to this trial in the aftermath of the execution of Honourable Arthur William Hodge in 1811 for the murder of one of his slaves on Tortola in the British Virgin Islands. *Case in Nevis, 1817* (London: Whitmore and Fenn, 1818).

12.   Thomas Liburd, "Lord Nelson and the Island of Nevis", *West India Committee Circular* 16 (13 October 1905): 412.

13.   "Graduations at Edinburgh in 1809", *Edinburgh Medical and Surgical Journal* 5 (1809): 487. Daniel W. Huggins, "Dissertatio medica inauguralis quædam de hepatitide complectens" (Excudebat Gulielmus Creech, 1809). Daniel was a classmate and friend to James Cowles Prichard, physician and early ethnologist/proto-

evolutionist and author of the study *Researches into the Physical History of Mankind*, which argues for an early unity of the species theory and accounts for variation among the races. Evidence of this can be found in Prichard's *Researches*, which includes an interview with Daniel comparing certain trends in the mortality rates and the onset of menstruation in black and white women in the West Indies, using St Vincent as an example. James Cowles Prichard, *Researches into the Physical History of Mankind* (London: Sherwood, Gilbert, and Piper, 1836), 1:161. The third edition includes Prichard's correspondence with Dr Huggins.

14. Frank Wesley Pitman, "Slavery on the British West India Plantations in the Eighteenth Century", *Journal of Negro History* 11, no. 4 (October 1926): 599.

15. Shephard, *Historical Account*, appendix 19.

16. The Crichtons were a lowland Scottish family who traced their lineage back to the fourteenth century. Patrick's uncle Patrick Crichton is the alleged author of the famous Woodhouselee manuscript, an eyewitness account of the Jacobite Rebellion in Edinburgh from September to November 1745. Patrick's father William Crichton was a successful merchant and alderman of Cheap ward in the City of London. "The Monthly Chronologer", *London Magazine, or, Gentleman's Monthly Intelligencer* (September 1780): 49; 435. W. Cramond, Patrick Crichton and A.W. Crichton, "Crichton Papers", *The Scottish Antiquary, or, Notes and Queries*, ed. J.H. Stevenson (Edinburgh: George P. Johnston, 1899), 13.

17. Paula Burnett incorrectly states that the author of *Hiroona* is the son of this H.N. Huggins. The first Horatio Nelson Huggins had moved to Trinidad in 1820 where he became the proprietor of the Bronte estate, and half-proprietor of Nassau estate and Union Hall plantation in South Naparima (*Penguin Book of Caribbean Verse*, 399). Donald Wood, *Trinidad in Transition: The Years after Slavery* (London: Oxford University Press, 1968), 114. *Papers Relative to the West Indies: Antigua, Trinidad, St Lucia, Grenada 1841–1842* (London: William Clowes, 1842), 91.

18. Antonio Benítez-Rojo, *The Repeating Island: The Caribbean and the Postmodern Perspective* (Durham: Duke University Press, 1992), 64.

19. "Death of the Reverend Canon Huggins", *San Fernando Gazette*, 2 August 1895.

20. A.C. Carmichael, *Tales of a Grandmother* (London: Richard Bentley, 1841), 113. Karina Williamson, "Mrs. Carmichael: A Scotswoman in the West Indies, 1820–1826", *International Journal of Scottish Literature* 4 (Spring–Summer 2004): 12. The Carmichaels were also close to the Huggins family, as Alison's husband John was Patrick Crichton's ensign in the Queen's Companies of 1828.

21. The college was founded in 1710 through the will of Sir Christopher Codrington (the same will that endowed the Codrington Library at All Souls, Oxford), who bequeathed two of his plantation estates in Barbados to the Society for the Propagation of the Gospel.

22. Thomas Parry, *Codrington College, in the island of Barbados* (London: Society for the Propagation of the Gospel, 1847), 23.

23. "In 1834 Mr Henry Carpenter, of Nevis, presented some volumes, Bishop Coleridge was also generous, Dr Bray's Associates gave some sixty volumes, valued at £35, and the University of Oxford made a munificent donation in 1842 of books printed at the Clarendon Press to the value of £150." Herbert T. Bindley, *Annals of Codrington College Barbados, 1710–1910* (London: Batten and Davies, 1911), 49.

24. Examples in *Hiroona* are the introduction, v and I, i.

25. *Copy of Papers relating to the State of various Religious Bodies in the West Indies, in return to a Circular issued to the Governors of the West India Colonies in 1864* (London, 1867), 34–53; *Laws of St Vincent* (London: Edward Stanford, 1864), 366.

26. "La Croix", *Encyclopedia of Massachusetts* (New York: American Historical Society, 1916), 8:411.

27. Shephard, *Historical Account*, appendix 4. James Huggins Lacroix spent another twenty years on St Vincent before moving to Trinidad where he became a convert to Swedenborganism and moved to Springfield, Massachusetts, in 1878.

28. Charlotte Wemyss's father Otho Hamilton Wemyss was a captain of the First West India Regiment and her uncle Francis Courtney was a famous stage actor in America and friend of Charles Dickens.

29. Bridget Brereton, *Race Relations in Colonial Trinidad, 1870–1900* (Cambridge: Cambridge University Press, 1979), 34, 96.

30. Faith Smith, *Creole Recitations: John Jacob Thomas and Colonial Formation in the Late Nineteenth-Century Caribbean* (Charlottesville: University of Virginia Press, 2002), x.

31. J.H. Collens, *Guide to Trinidad* (London: Elliot Stock, 1888), 228.

32. *San Fernando Gazette*, 26 January 1884; 1 March 1884; 30 October 1884; 15 November 1884. Michael Anthony, "Hosein Riots of 1884", in *Historical Dictionary of Trinidad and Tobago* (London: Scarecrow, 1997), 289–90; "Canboulay Riots", 97.

33. Marion O'Callaghan, "Composite Culture in Trinidad", in *Composite Culture in a Multicultural Eociety*, ed. Bipan Chandra and Sucheta Mahajan (New Delhi: Pearson Education, 2008), 70.

34. Belinda Edmondson, *Caribbean Middlebrow: Leisure Culture and the Middle Class* (Ithaca: Cornell University Press, 2009), 30.

35. J.H. Collens, *The Trinidad and Tobago Official and Commercial Register and Almanack 1894* (Port of Spain: Government Printing Office, 1893), 74, 78–79.

36. J.H. Collens, *Guide to Trinidad*, 148. Collens also includes a description of the church: "It consists of [a] nave with two aisles, and chancel, the total length being 114 feet, and width 28 feet. Both aisles and clerestory are lighted by double lancet windows." Its interior presented "a rather felicitous adaptation of material, the

prevailing features being its roof, the many columns and light arches, and general airiness", 147–48.

37. Collens, *Trinidad Almanack*, 67, 71.

38. Evidence for this can be found in the autograph book of Evelyn Huggins, one of Huggins's daughters, and one of the editors of *Hiroona*. Although done a few years after Canon Huggins's death, a simple drawing and signature of Robert J.L. Guppy can be found.

39. Oldfield Thomas, "A Preliminary List of the Mammals of Trinidad", *Journal of the Trinidad Field Naturalists' Club* 1, no. 3 (April 1892): 159.

40. Michael Anthony, *Anaparima: The History of San Fernando and Its Environs*, vol. 1, *1595–1900* (Laventille, Trinidad: City Council of San Fernando/Zenith, 2001), 500.

41. Anthony mentions the dispute twice, this time claiming that the dispute was between Huggins and the borough council, not the police inspector; in both cases, however, Huggins lost the argument. Ibid., 595, 602.

42. According to Michael Huggins, who provided it from memory, the poem was originally published in 1883 in the *Port-of-Spain Gazette*.

43. The Free Church was the evangelical branch of the Church of Scotland, led by Thomas Chalmers, Robert S. Candish and forty-six other ministers and laypeople, that broke away from the established Church in 1843; it was reincorporated in 1900. Sandy Finlayson, *Unity and Diversity: The Founders of the Free Church* (Fearn, UK: Christian Focus, 2010).

44. Rev. A.M. Ramsay, "Presbyterianism", *San Fernando Gazette*, 17 May 1890.

45. Letter to the editor, *San Fernando Gazette*, 31 May 1890.

46. Letter to the editor, *San Fernando Gazette*, 7 June 1890. Huggins follows with a response on 14 June, and Ramsay offers a final response on 28 June 1890.

47. "Jubilee Day in St Paul's Church", *San Fernando Gazette*, 11 August 1888.

48. "Jubilee Hymn", *San Fernando Gazette* 4 August 1888.

49. *San Fernando Gazette*, 9 June 1888.

50. Bridget Brereton, "Birthday of Our Race: A Social History of Emancipation Day in Trinidad, 1838–88", in *Trade, Government and Society in Caribbean History, 1700–1920*, ed. Barry Higman (Kingston: Heineman, 1983), 70.

51. *San Fernando Gazette and Trinidad News*, 31 May 1893.

52. "Revd Canon Huggins Ill", *San Fernando Gazette*, 18 April 1895.

53. Interview with Michael Huggins, 24 February 2008.

54. Anthony, *Anaparima*, 327.

55. *San Fernando Gazette*, 9 August 1895.

56. *San Fernando Gazette*, 11 October 1895.

57. *Hiroona*, foreword.

58. Michael Anthony, *Historical Dictionary*, 292–93.

59. Michael Huggins estimates that the number of copies printed was between twenty

and twenty-five, while Alfred "Sutty" Huggins believes the number was exactly twelve.

60.   An original copy of the published poem exists in the possession of the Huggins family in the United Kingdom.

61.   There is a discrepancy in the dating of this poem. Although no specific dates are mentioned, Huggins says that it has been sixteen years since his last visit to St Vincent, placing his original departure around 1861. However, the Baptism records located at St Paul's Calliaqua list Reverend Huggins as performing baptisms there until 1863. Also, he mentions that it has been twenty-five years since his ordination, which was in 1853, placing a more likely date for *The Holiday* around 1878. See *Papers relating to the State of various Religious Bodies*, 49.

62.   Elias Lönnrot, *The Kalevala*, trans. Keith Bosley (Oxford: Oxford University Press, 2008), xiii.

63.   "Published in November 1855 both in Boston and London, it sold 4,000 copies the first day in Boston alone; 100,000 in the first two years. After eighty years a million copies had been sold, but long before then, as the poem went into numerous editions and adaptations it was hailed as the 'literary triumph' of the century." Helen Carr, *Inventing the American Primitive: Politics, Gender and the Representations of Native American Literary Traditions, 1789–1936* (New York: New York University Press, 1996), 106.

64.   F.P.L. Josa, *"The Apostle of the Indians of Guiana": A Memoir of the Life and Labours of the Rev. W.H. Brett, B.D.* (London: Wells Gardner, Darton, 1888), 1–4.

65.   William Henry Brett, *Legends and Myths of the Aboriginal Indians of British Guiana* (London: W.W. Gardner, 1880), V.

66.   Henry H. Breen, *Warrawarra, the Carib Chief: A Tale of 1770*, 2 vols (London: Tinsley Bros., 1876).

67.   Nathaniel Weekes, *Barbados, A Poem* (London: R and J Dodsley, 1754); M.J. Chapman, *Barbadoes and other poems* (London: James Fraser, 1833); Henry G. Dalton, *Tropical lays and other poems* (London: J. Evans, 1853); Egbert Martin, *Poetical Works* (London: WH Collingridge, 1883).

68.   Laurence Breiner, *An Introduction to West Indian Poetry* (Cambridge: Cambridge University Press, 1998), ix.

69.   Burnett, *Penguin Book of Caribbean Verse*, xliii.

70.   Ibid., li.

71.   E.L. Risden, *Heroes, Gods, and the Role of Epiphany in English Epic Poetry* (Jefferson, NC: McFarland, 2008), 1.

72.   Louis James, *Caribbean Literature in English* (New York: Longman, 1999), 17.

73.   Cudjoe, *Beyond Boundaries*, 294.

74.   Ibid., 290.

75.   Ibid. 291.

76.   Ibid., 275.

77.   Leah Reade Rosenberg, *Nationalism and the Formation of Caribbean Literature* (New York: Palgrave Macmillan, 2007), 1.

78.   Edmondson, *Caribbean Middlebrow*, 23.

79.   Albert Gomes, "A West Indian Literature", in *From Trinidad: An Anthology of Early West Indian Writing*, ed. Reinhard Sander (New York: Africana Publishing, 1978), 31. First published in the *Beacon*, 12 (June 1933).

80.   Belinda J. Edmondson, *Caribbean Romances: The Politics of Regional Representation* (Charlottesville: University Press of Virginia, 1999), 4.

81.   Rachel Ley, "A Man Out of His Time: A Personal Reading of Literary History" (BA thesis, University of Exeter, 2001); Nan Peacocke, "Subject Matters: *Hiroona*, re-reading an Atlantic Epic" (MA thesis, Trent University, 2006). Rachel is the great-great-great granddaughter and Nan is the great-great granddaughter of Horatio Nelson Huggins.

82.   Daryl Cumber Dance, ed., *Fifty Caribbean Writers: A Bio-bibliographical Critical Sourcebook* (New York: Greenwood, 1986), 1.

83.   Thomas Coke, *A History of the West Indies*, 3 vols (London: Nuttall, Fisher and Dixon, 1810) 2:262.

84.   Taylor, *Black Carib Wars*, 108–9. Governor Seton wrote in a letter that two of Chatoyer's sons were living with the family of a "gentleman" who had intended to take them to Europe but, detained on business, had been prevented from doing so. Ibid., 110. Seton letter, CO 280/9.

85.   CO 260/19, Seton letter. Quoted in Taylor, *Black Carib Wars*, 110.

86.   Interestingly, this is the same action done by Warrawarra in Breen's novel, *Warrawarra, the Carib Chief*.

87.   F.W.N. Bayley, *Four Years' Residence in the West Indies* (London: W. Kidd, 1830), 245.

88.   By the time of the *Registry of Slaves* was produced on 31 May 1834 in St Vincent, Daniel's household included Antoine, a fifty-eight-year-old gardener; Marie Victoire, a forty-five-year-old cook; Codanda (Isaac), aged thirty-three; Clare, the twenty-eight-year-old domestic (also shares a name with one of Norman's slaves in *Hiroona*); Mary, a twenty-year-old domestic; and two children, John Logan aged nine and Robert aged six. Daniel had joint ownership with his brother Horatio Nelson Huggins of Nanny, a fifty-year-old midwife and assistant. *Slave Registers of Former British Colonial Dependencies, 1812–1834*, Registry of Colonial Slaves and Slave Compensation Commission (National Archives Microfilm Publication) T71; piece 500, 123.

89   Since the British Army never kept enlistment records for the "black regiments", it is impossible to determine if another soldier with the same or similar name served in the St Vincent Rangers. A.B. Ellis, *The History of the First West India Regiment* (London: Chapman and Hall, 1885), 78.

90. Leila Caroline Russell (1875 or 1879–1977), one of Huggins's granddaughters through his son Henry Daniel, made the note (found in her nephew Peter Seymour Huggins's copy of *Hiroona* in 2011) to remind future readers that Ranèe's story is based on a "family history in the West Indies", and that her rescue of Crayton was a real incident. Russell also connects the rescue of the child in the poem to a real-life rescue of a child belonging to the Laborde family. Henry William Laborde was rector of St George's Anglican cathedral in Kingstown. He baptized Horatio's children born in St Vincent. Horatio's sister Lucy and his cousin Horatio James were married to members of the Laborde family.

91. Taylor, *Black Carib Wars*, 115.

92. Prichard, *Researches into the Physical History of Mankind* (London: Sherwood, Gilbert, and Piper, 1836), 1:161.

93. Harry Johnston, *The Negro in the New World* (New York: Macmillan, 1910), 309n.

94. Alan Burns, *History of the British West Indies* (London: Allen and Unwin, 1954), 567. C.L.R. James, *The Black Jacobins: Toussaint L'Ouverture and the San Domingo Revolution* (New York: Vintage, 1964), 143; 161.

95. Peter Hulme and Neil L. Whitehead, eds., *Wild Majesty: Encounters with Caribs from Columbus to the Present Day: An Anthology* (Oxford: Clarendon, 1992), 212.

96. Sir William Young, *A tour through the several islands of Barbadoes, St. Vincent, Antigua, Tobago, and Grenada, in the years 1791–1792*, 210–14.

HIROONA

1. Huggins's footnote: "*January* the books say; one copying from another, misled by the name 'S. Vincent', oblivious of the fact that Colon was still in Spain in January, and discovered S. Vincent after leaving Trinidad, which latter was the first land he made that voyage, on Trinity Sunday." Huggins's correction is also inaccurate, as several corroborating accounts document that Columbus set sail on 30 May 1498 and recorded the discovery of Trinidad on 31 July 1498 in his log book. According to Columbus's journal and contemporary biographers, he professed a special devotion to the Holy Trinity, and named the island based on the appearance of three mountains in line together. Trinity Sunday, which is the Sunday after Pentecost, occurred on 10 June in 1498.

2. Leapt.

3. Huggins's footnote: "Early Spanish accounts speak of flamingoes in these Islands, now only seen to the South."

4. Huggins's footnote: "Banyan branches send down shoots which form columns."

5. Plantains were not planted in the West Indies until after the introduction of plantation slavery.

6.   Huggins's footnote: " 'Mahaut', local name for a formidable whip, used by cattle-drivers, made from the bark of a tree so called."

7.   St Vincent is named after the fourth-century martyr Vincent of Saragossa. This is only one of three times Huggins calls the island by its colonized name.

8.   Opossum: A term borrowed from the Algonquin language used to describe members of the marsupial family Didelphidae found in the southern United States. In the Lesser Antilles, the species of common opossum (*Didelphis marsupialis*) is known by the local name "Manicou".

9.   Goutie: A reference to the *Dasyprocta leporina*, a species of agouti common in the Lesser Antilles.

10. Guana: A reference to either the common green iguana or the Lesser Antillean iguana.

11. This refers to the belief that St Vincent had no snakes during this period, unlike neighbouring St Lucia.

12. The ancient people of the Balearic Islands in the Mediterranean were known for their skill with slings as a weapon.

13. Arawak peoples were one of the many indigenous Amerindian groups inhabiting several of the Caribbean islands. The pre-Columbian Amerindian people of St Vincent, although identified as "Carib", spoke a variation of the Arawakan language.

14. Local tree found in both America and the Caribbean whose apple-like fruit and leaves are poisonous.

15. This is the only reference to the origins of the Black Caribs. Arguably, Huggins avoids mentioning the group's African origin in order to separate their later fight with the British on the grounds of indigeneity.

16. Division of St Vincent between black and yellow/red Caribs and French settlers.

17. The river and village on the windward side of St Vincent that, according to the treaty of 1773, marked the boundary of Carib lands. In modern times spelled "Byrea", and alternately spelled "Byeira" or "Bieria". The spelling "Byëra" is used in cantos I, III and IV, while the spelling "Biëra" is used in cantos II, V, VIII, IX, X and XI. This might be an indication of the different periods during which Huggins wrote each canto.

18. Tarraty (or Tarratee Point) and Owia are northern villages located in the Carib lands.

19. Souffrière bird: *Myadestes genibarbis sibilano*, also known as the Rufous-throated or St Vincent Solitaire. See note 34.

20. French missionaries arrived in the eastern Caribbean islands since the sixteenth century.

21. Victor Hugues: See discussion in the introduction.

22. Happy Hill is located 1.6 miles southwest of Rabaca at the base of the eastern side of the Morne Garu Mountains, near Langley Park.

23. Morne Garou (or Garu) is the name of the mountain chain that runs down the length of St Vincent. La Soufrière volcano is its hightest peak, at 4,173 feet.

24. Grugru: Species of palm tree found in the Caribbean and South America.

25. Huggins's footnote: "The French made the name into *Chattoyen*. The Carib sound for the letter *a* was very broad, almost equivalent to *aw*. The chief's name was pronounced as if Chet-*waw*-yé."

26. Shephard, *Historical Account*, 45; John Anderson, *Between Slavery and Freedom: Special Magistrate John Anderson's Journal of St Vincent during the Apprenticeship*, ed. Roderick McDonald (Philadelphia: University of Pennsylvania Press, 2001), 128.

27. See description of the Carib chief in Alexandre Moreau de Jonnès, *Adventures in Wars of the Republic and Consulate*, trans. A.J. Abdy (London: John Murray, 1920), 106; 112–15.

28. In the engraving of Agostinio Brunias, Chatoyer is clutching his hilt.

29. Jumbie: Supernatural spirit; derived from the Kikongo word *nzumbi* (also the origin of the word *zombie*) meaning spirit of a dead person. The word began appearing in print from the 1830s, with E.L. Jospeh's novel *Warner Arundell* one of the earliest examples. Lise Winer, *Dictionary of the English/Creole of Trinidad and Tobago: On Historical Principles* (Montreal: McGill-Queen's University Press, 2009), 474.

30. Huggins's footnote: "Or Mapapire—local West Indian name for a deadly serpent. The animals here named, though not found in S. Vincent, are common in more Southern islands, and in S. Lucia."

31. This speech is based on Hugues's alleged letter to Chatoyer. See Lionel Mordaunt Fraser, *History of Trinidad: From 1781 to 1813* (Port of Spain: Government Printing Office, 1891), 89. Taylor, *Black Carib Wars*, 117n6.

32. "Chatoyer" in French means "cat-like eyes".

33. One of the deported Black Caribs transferred to Trujillo, Honduras in October 1797 was named "Nanete". Nancie L. Solien Gonzalez, *Sojourners of the Caribbean*, 66, quoted in *Archive General de Centro América* A3.16/2025/194(4) Honduras 16 Octubre 1797. CO 260/19.

34. An image reminiscent of Rintrah in William Blake's poem *The Marriage of Heaven and Hell*.

35. This describes what happened in the eruption of 1812, when a lake formed in the crater.

36. Huggins's footnote: " 'The Souffrière bird'. Much mystery even yet hangs about the existence of this bird. Its peculiar notes, described as exquisitely sweet and plaintive, are occasionally heard in the upper heights of the Souffrière, but of the bird itself few, if any, specimens have ever been seen. The late Governor Dundas camped on the mountain for several days, determined, if possible, to solve the mystery; and in his Précis of the History of S. Vincent states that he shot several, and determined their species, but withholds all further information, 'lest he should dispel the mys-

tery which has so long made famous the Souffrière bird'." Dundas (1819–1880) was lieutenant governor of St Vincent from 1875 to 1880. George Dundas, *Précis of information concerning the colony of Saint Vincent, West Indies* (St Vincent: Government Printing Office, 1880). See note 19.

37.   Balak, king of the Moabites, in fear of the approaching Israelites, asks the prophet Balaam to curse the Israelites, to which Balaam refuses. Numbers 22-24.

38.   The sibyls are a group of ten (or twelve in Christian myth) prophetesses of classical mythology who had the ability to see the future and usually offered their visions to kings and military leaders.

39.   An interesting note to the legend of a Carib woman holding a place similar to Nannette's is contained in a fragment of a Garifuna song transcribed by the anthropologist Donald Taylor that places the blame for the start of the war on Chatoyer trusting the advice of a woman. Donald Taylor, "Lines by a Black Carib", *International Journal of American Linguistics* 24 (October 1958): 325.

40.   There is a Carib named Joyett, aged thirty-six, among those who surrendered and taken on 28 May 1805. CO 260/19. Taylor, *Black Carib Wars*, 167.

41.   Grand Sable, located in present-day Charlotte parish. At the time of the war, Grand Sable was part of Carib territory. By the 1830s it became the largest sugar estate on the island.

42.   Mount Young and Mount Bentick (also spelled Bentinck), both named after former governors, are located in Grand Sable, near the area that is now Georgetown.

43.   Huggins's footnote: "Pronounced 'By-e-raw'." See note 17 for Byëra in canto I.

44.   Another British military post, located in Grand Sable. It was the site of the attack on 8 January 1796, when fifty-four British soldiers were killed, one hundred were wounded and two hundred went missing.

45.   Huggins's footnote: "Pronounced 'Yamboo'."

46.   The Bonhomme Peaks, located in the Mesopotamia Valley.

47.   The Vigie, located less than two miles from Kingstown and one mile from Dorsetshire Hill.

48.   Manicou: see note 8 for I, iv. Conger snake: type of aquatic salamander that resembles a snake or eel; also commonly referred to as conger eel, congo snake or congo eel. It is often confused with the blind eel or hag fish.

49.   Warrawarrow River, which starts at Mount St Andrew and flows into Greathead Bay.

50.   See introduction for a discussion of Warramou.

51.   Norman is referring to the Carib Treaty of 1773, signed by thirty Carib chiefs, including Chatoyer and Du Vallet.

52.   The American Revolutionary War, 1775–1783.

53.   Owia.

54.   Huggins's footnote: "Iëre. The aborigines' name for Trinidad. Trinidad has never

been known to have been visited by a hurricane. According to Reid's Law of Storms the West Indian hurricane has its origin in latitudes but little lower than Trinidad: It follows the course of a parabola trending towards the coast of the United States. By the time it has reached the latitude of Barbados, the storm is at its full swing. A hurricane may sometimes pass over Trinidad, but the monster is then but in infancy. No Island in the West Indian Tropics can compare with Iëre in the richness of its animal and vegetable kingdoms."

55. Huggins's footnote: " 'Sauteurs'. The name remains in Grenada, and History records the fact as here related." Frederick Albion Ober explains that "[a]t the northern end of Grenada is a high bluff, descending to the sea in a precipice, over which, tradition relates, the last of the Caribs leaped in despair when pursued by their enemies. The cliff is yet known as the Hill of the Leapers—Le Morne des Sauteurs." *Camps in the Caribbees: The Adventures of a Naturalist in the Lesser Antilles* (Edinburgh: David Douglass, 1880), 268.

56. The warning given to Norman is reminiscent of the experience of William Grieg, who, "with his family arrived in town Marriaqua . . . informed the Governor and Council, that he had been strongly urged by a neighbouring Carib to withdraw himself from the Island without delay, as it was the unanimous intention of his Countrymen to proclaim war against the English". Shephard, *Historical Account*, 59.

57. Huggins's footnote: "Pronounced as if written "Conarie"." At the time of the war, this area would have been called Calonery Point or Point Calonery.

58. Archaic form of corpse.

59. Huggins's footnote: "A dark and terrible superstition, imported by the slaves from Africa. Some hag from the lower world is supposed to come from underground, like a vampire to suck blood; but is under the necessity of leaving her skin at the place of exit. Could anyone carry off the skin, the Soucouan would be helpless. Her feast of blood over, the Soucouan recovers her skin and vanishes."

60. Biabou, windward coastal village six miles from Kingstown and five and a half miles from Grand Sable.

61. Couboumarou, located in what is now Stubbs, five miles from Kingstown and less than four miles south of Biabou.

62. Huggins's footnote: "Labelle—the country name for the beautiful *elater nocti-lucus*—called also firefly. In the text the smaller insect, like the female glow-worm, is the 'fire-fly'."

63. Massy: An area called Massey is located near South Union.

64. Isaac Walton, *The Compleat Angler; Or, The Contemplative Man's Recreation*. Originally published in 1653.

65. The leaves are known as elephant ears, and produce a tuber called tannia.

66. Rabacca River.

67. Huggins's footnote: "A fine bird (genus *pelicanus,*) called locally 'Man-of-war Bird' from its stately and magnificent motion through the air."

68. Washilabo, located on the northwest leeward side of the island. The Washilabo River empties into Cumberland Bay.

69. Battowia, one of the Grenadine islands.

70. Wallibou, north leeward village located in the area of Chateaubelair and Richmond. The leeward side of the Carib boundary was marked with the Walliabou River.

71. Dorsetshire Hill, located one and a half miles northeast of Kingstown. It reaches a height of over nine hundred feet.

72. Massarica or Massaricaw, windward village now known as North Union, was the site of several battles during the war.

73. Chateaubelair, located in the north leeward, two miles south of the Carib boundary.

74. Misspelling of Couboumarou, which was also spelled Cubamarou, Cubiamairou and Cubaimarou.

75. Marriaqua, located near the Mesopotamian Valley.

76. Huggins's footnote: "This records an historic fact: The rout or massacre of 'Massarica'. This disaster was more discreditable to the British arms than even the text describes it. Their hasty retreat at the first sight of the Caribs, till they were brought up by the ambuscade, which had outrun them, and from being in their rear had established themselves in front, survived in the memory of the colonists, long after the horrors of the tragedy had ceased to be talked of. The 'Massarica Races' as this retreat was facetiously named, are even yet heard of—the comic thus outliving the tragic." This event is described in detail in Shephard, *Historical Account*, 64–66.

77. Sepulcher.

78. Huggins's footnote: "This was a Carib stratagem in war. They would fasten branches around their bodies in such a manner as to look like innocent shrubs. This was better than to conceal themselves in trees, as it enabled them to shift their position as they pleased."

79. Mount St Andrew, a 2,413-foot mountain three miles from Kingstown.

80. Frangipani flower.

81. Spelled "jumbie" in II, x.

82. Fancy, northernmost village on the island.

83. Morne Ronde Carib fort located north leeward, three and a half miles from Chateaubelair.

84. James Seton, governor of St Vincent from 1787 to 1798.

85. Fort Charlotte is located one and a half miles west of Kingstown Bay and reaches over six hundred feet in height. The groundwork for the original fort was begun in the mid-1790s and completed in 1806. It mounted thirty-four guns that were situated to defend landward approaches.

86. Sion Hill was a British post located one mile of Dorsetshire Hill. It reaches a height of between four hundred and five hundred feet.

87. Brae: Scottish word for a steep bank.

88. Hecate is the Greek goddess of the magic and the underworld. The line is a possible reference to *Hamlet* III, ii: "With Hecate's ban thrice blasted, thrice infected", spoken by Lucianus, one of the actors in the staged play.

89. Variant spelling of "barracuda". It is also the name of a pacific fish.

90. Huggins's footnote: "From mid-night (2 am)."

91. Major Alexander Leith.

92. This depiction is similar to all of the nineteenth-century accounts of this encounter between Leith and Chatoyer. See the Introduction for further discussion.

93. See II, v.

94. An earthenware container.

95. Fort Duvernette, island and fort 250 feet above sea level located close to Young's Island.

96. This story is retold in *The Holiday*.

97. Carapan is located on the windward side, south of the Mesopotamia Valley, three miles from Kingstown. Ribishi is located near present-day Diamond. The Ribishi River flows into the Diamond River.

98. Arnos Vale, located two miles east of Kingstown, was once one of the largest sugar estates in St George's Parish.

99. The term "Campbell's Highlanders" refers to the Eighty-Eighth, One Hundreth (and sometimes the Seventy-Fourth and Ninety-First) Regiment of Foot. The Forty-Second, or Royal Highland Regiment, was the only military formation with the Highland title that fought in the war. This is likely Dugald Campbell, captain, later colonel then major-genera,l of the Forty-Sixth Regiment of Foot, who commanded a formation in St Vincent from March to December 1795 when it was dispatched from Martinique. Shephard, *Historical Account*, 70. Richard Cannon, *Historical Record of the Forty-Sixth, or The South Devonshire, Regiment of Foot* (London: Parker, Furnival, and Parker, 1851), 30–34.

100. Sandy Bay. The original Sandy Bay was located in an area once called Warigara Bay, less than a mile south of Owia.

101. In the original text, this was spelled "troup".

102. Molesworth: Calliaqua was under his command; this skirmish being described occurred on 7 May 1795.

103. Ratho-Mill.

104. St George's Anglican Cathedral was completed in 1820.

105. There was nothing linking the two before this.

106. Leighton: Lieutenant-Colonel Baldwin Leighton (1747–1828).

107. The St Vincent Rangers were a regiment of foot made up entirely of slaves cre-

ated in 1795 in response to the Carib attacks. It was drafted into Sir William, Brigadier-General Myers's Regiment of Foot in 1796 and 1797 to form the Second West Indian Regiment, whose first campaign was in St Vincent. A.B. Ellis, *The History of the First West India Regiment* (London: Chapman and Hall, 1885), 69–77.

108. The beating of a drum that indicates an invitation to parley.

109. Huggins's footnote: "Pronounced *conaree.*" A note on this is provided in IV, v, where it is pronounced "Conarie".

110. Tourama, called "Imayarow" on pre-1795 maps.

111. Huggins was one of the leaders of the temperance movement in San Fernando.

112. Huggins's footnote: "Local name for hideous reptile of the lizard kind." A gecko.

113. Spelled "Tarraty" in I, xvi.

114. Lance-de-fer, *Bothrops Caribbaeus,* a species of viper snakes only found in St Lucia. There was a long-held belief that St Lucia was the only island in the Lesser Antilles that had poisonous snakes,

115. Lieutenant-Colonel John Ritchie, of the Sixtieth Royal American Regiment of Foot. While fighting in St Vincent, he died from wounds sustained in battle on 11 October 1795. Nesbit Willoughby Wallace, *A Regimental Chronicle and List of Officers of the 60th, or the King's Royal Rifle Corps, formerly the 62nd, or the Royal Regiment of Foot* (London: Harrison, 1879), 124; *Edinburgh Magazine, or Literary Miscellany* (London: Murray and Highley, 1796), 78.

116. Also called the British or Colonial Red Ensign, it was the flag adopted between 1707 and 1801 that represented the union of the kingdoms of England and Scotland.

117. This story is similar to that of the slave Tamaun, as first told by Thomas Coke in *A History of the West Indies, II* (1810), 232–33.

118. This name does not appear in any account or record.

119. Huggins's footnote: "These mammalia used to abound in these Seas, though seldom seen now."

120. Huggins's footnote: " 'Serpent's Mouth', 'Dragon's Mouth', the passages, so named, by which the Gulf of Paria is entered, and Trinidad (Iëre) reached from the Ocean."

121. In the original text, this is misspelled as "succouan".

122. Lieutenant-General Sir Ralph Abercrombie, 1734–1801, commanded the British forces in the West Indies during the Napoleonic Wars, recapturing St Lucia, Grenada, St Vincent and Trinidad, where he served as governor in 1797. He died fighting in the Mediterranean.

123. Huggins appears to have forgotten that Barbette was captured in IX, xxviii.

124. Poignard: A long, lightweight thrusting knife with a tapering pointed blade

125. William Wallace (d. 1305), leader of Scottish rebellion beginning in the late thirteenth century against Edward I, and executed in London. He was the subject of a popular epic poem *The Wallace* by Blind Harry and *Exploits and Death of William Wallace, the 'Hero of Scotland'* by Sir Walter Scott. Sir Henry Percy (1364–1403)

English nobleman famously characterized in *Henry IV, Part I*; Robert I "the Bruce" (1274–1329), King of the Scots from 1306 to 1329.

126. Taylor, *Black Carib Wars*, 154.

127. Baliceaux, Grenadine island and the first destination for the nearly five thousand Garifuna exiled to Central America. The conditions there were severe and many died due to famine and disease.

128. Compare with the words of "the son of Chatoyer": "It is no disgrace to us to surrender to a great nation, the subjects of France and all great nations, even of England, are obliged to submit to each other, when there no longer remains the means of resistance. What else is now left for us? have we power to continue the war? No! to-morrow morning I will set you the example of submission, by bringing my family to Colonel Haffey, that he may send us to the General, you may do as you please, I can only be accountable for myself and my family." CO 260/13: 250, quoted in Shephard, *Historical Account*, 164–65 and Taylor, *Black Carib Wars*, 137–38.

129. A possible misspelling of the phrase *vae victis*, meaning "woe to the conquered".

THE HOLIDAY

1. Huggins's footnote: "Poluphloisboic thalasses."

2. An allusion to the belief to the iguana assimilates its colour to brown rock, or green leaves, as it may be, around it. Huggins's footnote.

SELECTED BIBLIOGRAPHY

Anderson, John. *Between Slavery and Freedom: Special Magistrate John Anderson's Journal of St Vincent during the Apprenticeship*. Edited by Roderick McDonald. Philadelphia: University of Pennsylvania Press, 2001.

Anthony, Michael. *Anaparima: The History of San Fernando and Its Environs*, vol. 1: *1595–1900*. Laventille, Trinidad: City Council of San Fernando/Zenith, 2001.

———. "Hosein Riots of 1884". In *Historical Dictionary of Trinidad and Tobago*, 289–90. London: Scarecrow, 1997.

Baugh, Edward. "A History of Poetry". In *A History of Literature in the Caribbean*, edited by Albert James Arnold and Vera M. Kutzinki, 227–84. Amsterdam: J. Benjamins, 2001.

Bayley, F.W.N. *Four Years' Residence in the West Indies*. London: W. Kidd, 1830.

Benítez-Rojo, Antonio. *The Repeating Island: The Caribbean and the Postmodern Perspective*. Durham: Duke University Press, 1992.

Bindley, Herbert T. *Annals of Codrington College Barbados, 1710–1910*. London: Batten and Davies, 1911.

Bodleian Library. MSS W. Ind. S 41, Papers Relating to Bishop Rawle.

Breen, Henry Hegart. *Warrawarra, the Carib Chief: A Tale of 1770*. London: Tinsley Bros., 1876.

Breiner, Laurence. *An Introduction to West Indian Poetry*. Cambridge: Cambridge University Press, 1998.

Brereton, Bridget. *A History of Modern Trinidad, 1783–1962*. Kingston: Heinemann, 1981.

———. *Race Relations in Colonial Trinidad, 1870–1900*. Cambridge: Cambridge University Press, 1979.

———. "Birthday of Our Race: A Social History of Emancipation Day in Trinidad, 1838-88". In *Trade, Government and Society in Caribbean History, 1700–1920*, edited by Barry Higman, 69–83. Kingston: Heineman, 1983.

Brett, William Henry. *Legends and myths of the aboriginal Indians of British Guiana*. London: W.W. Gardner, 1880.

Buckley, Roger Norman. *The British Army in the West Indies: Society and the Military in the Revolutionary Age*. Gainesville: University Press of Florida, 1998.

Burnett, Paula. *The Penguin Book of Caribbean Verse in English*. Harmondsworth: Penguin, 1986.

Cannon, Richard. *Historical Record of the Forty-Sixth, or The South Devonshire, Regiment of Foot*. London: Parker, Furnival, and Parker, 1851.

Carmichael, A.C. *Domestic Manners and Social Conditions of the White, Coloured and Negro Population of the West Indies*. 2 vols. London: Whittaker, 1834.

———. *Tales of a Grandmother*. London: Richard Bentley, 1841.

Carr, Helen. *Inventing the American Primitive: Politics, Gender and the Representations of Native American Literary Traditions, 1789–1936*. New York: New York University Press, 1996.

Case in Nevis, 1817. London: Whitmore and Fenn, 1818.

Chapman, M.J. *Barbadoes, and other poems*. London: James Fraser, 1833.

Coke, Thomas. *A History of the West Indies*. 3 vols. London: Nuttall, Fisher and Dixon, 1810.

Collens, J.H. *Guide to Trinidad*. London: Elliot Stock, 1888.

———. *The Trinidad and Tobago Official and Commercial Register and Almanack 1894*. Port of Spain: Government Printing Office, 1893.

Conzemius, Eduard. "Ethnographical Notes on the Black Carib (Garif)". *American Anthropologist* 30, no. 2 (April–June 1928): 183–205.

Cramond, W., Patrick Crichton and A.W. Crichton. "Crichton Papers". *The Scottish Antiquary, or, Notes and Queries*, edited by J.H. Stevenson, 12–16. Edinburgh: George P. Johnston, 1899.

Craton, Michael. *Testing the Chains: Resistance to Slavery in the British West Indies*. Ithaca: Cornell University Press, 1982.

———. "The Black Caribs of St Vincent". In *The Lesser Antilles in the Age of European Expansion*, edited by Robert L. Paquette and Stanley L. Engerman, 71–85. Gainsville: University Press of Florida, 1996.

———. "From Caribs to Black Caribs: The Amerindian Roots of Servile Resistance in the Caribbean". In *In Resistance: Studies in African, Caribbean, and Afro-American History*, edited by Gary Y. Okihro, 96–116. Amherst: University of Massachusetts Press, 1986.

Cudjoe, Selwyn. *Beyond Boundaries: The Intellectual Tradition of Trinidad and Tobago in the Nineteenth Century*. Wellesley, MA: Calaloux, 2003.

Dalton, Henry G. *Tropical Lays and Other Poems*. London: J. Evans, 1853.

Dance, Daryl Cumber, ed. *Fifty Caribbean Writers: A Bio-bibliographical Critical Sourcebook*. New York: Greenwood, 1986.

Dundas, George. *Précis of information concerning the colony of Saint Vincent, West Indies*. St Vincent: Government Printing Office, 1880.

Edinburgh Magazine, or Literary Miscellany. London: Murray and Highley, 1796.

Edmondson, Belinda. *Caribbean Middlebrow: Leisure Culture and the Middle Class*. Ithaca: Cornell University Press, 2009.

———, ed. *Caribbean Romances: The Politics of Regional Representation*. Charlottesville: University Press of Virginia, 1999.

Edwards, Bryan. *History Civil and Commercial of the British West Indies*. 4 vols. London: J. Stockdale, 1793–1801.

Ellis, A.B. *The History of the First West India Regiment*. London: Chapman and Hall, 1885.

Ellis, Godsman. *The Garinagu of Belize*. Belize: The Mainan, 1997.

Finlayson, Sandy. *Unity and Diversity: The Founders of the Free Church*. Fearn, UK: Christian Focus, 2010.

Fraser, Adrian. *Chatoyer (Chatawae): National Hero of St Vincent and the Grenadines*. Kingstown, St Vincent: Galaxy, 2002.

Fraser, Lionel Mordaunt. *History of Trinidad: From 1781 to 1813*. Port of Spain: Government Printing Office, 1891.

Gomes, Albert. "A West Indian Literature". In *From Trinidad: An Anthology of Early West Indian Writing*, edited by Reinhard Sander, 30–31. New York: Africana Publishing, 1978.

Gonzalez, Nancie L. Solien. *Sojourners of the Caribbean: Ethnogenesis and Ethnohistory of the Garifuna*. Urbana: University of Illinois Press, 1988.

———. "From Cannibals to Mercenaries: Carib Militarism, 1600–1800". *Journal of Anthropological Research* 46, no. 1 (Spring 1990): 25–39.

Gordon, Joyce. *Nevis, Queen of the Caribbees*. London: Macmillan, 1993.

"Graduations at Edinburgh in 1809". *Edinburgh Medical and Surgical Journal* 5 (1809).

Hulme, Peter. *Colonial Encounters: Europe and the Native Caribbean 1492–1797*. London: Methuen, 1986.

———. "French Accounts of the Vincentian Caribs". In *The Garifuna: A Nation Across Borders: Essays in Social Anthropology*, edited by Joseph O Palacio, 21–42. Belize: Cubola Productions, 2005.

———. *Remnants of Conquest: The Island Caribs and Their Visitors, 1877–1998*. Oxford: Oxford University Press, 2000.

———. "Travel, Ethnography, Transculturation: St Vincent in the 1790s". Paper presented at the conference Contextualizing the Caribbean: New Eras in an Approaching Era of Globalization, University of Miami, Coral Gables, 29–30 September 2000.

Hulme, Peter, and Neil L. Whitehead, eds. *Wild Majesty: Encounters with Caribs from Columbus to the Present Day: An Anthology*. Oxford: Clarendon, 1992.

James, Louis. *Caribbean Literature in English*. New York: Longman, 1999.

Josa, F.P.L. *"The Apostle of the Indians of Guiana": A Memoir of the Life and Labours of the Rev. W.H. Brett, B.D.* London: Wells Gardner, Darton, 1888.

Kirby, I.E., and C.I. Martin. *The Rise and Fall of the Black Caribs*. Toronto: Cybercom, 2004.

Krise, Thomas W. *Caribbeana: An Anthology of English Literature of the West Indies 1657–1777*. Chicago: University of Chicago Press, 1999.

Laws of St Vincent. London: Edward Stanford, 1864.

Le Breton, Adrien Fr. *The Caribs of St Vincent: Historic Account of St Vincent, the Indian Youroumayn, the Island of the Karaybes*. Edited by Fr. Mark De Silva. Kingstown: Mayreau Environmental Development Organization, 1998.

Ley, Rachel. "A Man Out of His Time: A Personal Reading of Literary History". BA thesis, University of Exeter, 2001.

Liburd, Thomas. "Lord Nelson and the Island of Nevis". *West India Committee Circular* 16 (13 October 1905): 412–13.

Ligon, Richard. *A True and Exact History of the Island of Barbadoes*. Edited by Karen Ordahl Kupperman. Indianapolis: Hackett, 2011.

Lönnrot, Elias. *The Kalevala*. Translated by Keith Bosley. Oxford: Oxford University Press, 2008.

Martin, Egbert. *Poetical Works*. London: W.H. Collingridge, 1883.

Moreau de Jonnès, Alexandre. *Adventures in the Wars of the Republic and the Consulate*. Translated by A.J. Abdy. London: John Murray, 1920.

"The Monthly Chronologer". *London Magazine, or, Gentleman's Monthly Intelligencer* (September 1780): 49; 435.

Musgrave, T.B.C. *Historical and Descriptive Sketch of the Colony of St Vincent, W.I.* Kingstown, St Vincent: Gardener's, 1891.

Ober, Frederick Albion. *Camps in the Caribbees: The Adventures of a Naturalist in the Lesser Antilles*. Edinburgh: David Douglass, 1880.

O'Callaghan, Marion. "Composite Culture in Trinidad". In *Composite Culture in a Multicultural Society*, edited by Bipan Chandra and Sucheta Mahajan. New Delhi: Pearson Education, 2008.

Palacio, Joseph O. "Reconstructing Garifuna Oral History: Techniques and Methods in the Story of a Caribbean People". In *The Garifuna, a Nation across Borders: Essays in Social Anthropology*, edited by Joseph O. Palacio, 43–63. Belize: Cubola Productions, 2005.

Papers Relative to Codrington College, Barbados. London: R. Gilbert, 1828.

Papers Relative to the West Indies: Antigua, Trinidad, St. Lucia, Grenada 1841–1842. London: William Clowes, 1842.

Parry, Thomas. *Codrington College, in the island of Barbados*. London: Society for the Propagation of the Gospel, 1847.

Peacocke, Nan. "Subject Matters: *Hiroona*, re-reading an Atlantic Epic". MA thesis, Trent University, Canada, 2006.

Pitman, Frank Wesley. "Slavery on the British West India Plantations in the Eighteenth Century". *Journal of Negro History* 11, no. 4 (October 1926): 584–669.

Prichard, James Cowles. *Researches into the Physical History of Mankind*. London: Sherwood, Gilbert and Piper, 1836.

Ramchand, Kenneth. *The West Indian Novel and Its Background*. London: Faber, 1970.

Risden, E.L. *Heroes, Gods, and the Role of Epiphany in English Epic Poetry*. Jefferson, NC: McFarland, 2008.

Rosenberg, Leah Reade. *Nationalism and the Formation of Caribbean Literature*. New York: Palgrave Macmillan, 2007.

Sander, Reinhard W, editor. *From Trinidad: An Anthology of Early West Indian Writing*. New York: Africana, 1978.

———. *The Trinidad Awakening: West Indian Literature of the Nineteen-Thirties*. New York: Greenwood, 1988.

Shephard, Charles. *An Historical Account of the Island of Saint Vincent*. London: W. Nicol, 1831.

Slave Registers of Former British Colonial Dependencies, 1812–1834. http://search.ancestry.ca/search/db.aspx?dbid=1129.

Smith, Faith. *Creole Recitations: John Jacob Thomas and Colonial Formation in the Late Nineteenth-Century Caribbean*. Charlottesville: University of Virginia Press, 2002.

Taylor, Christopher. *The Black Carib Wars: Freedom, Survival, and the Making of the Garifuna*. Jackson: University Press of Mississippi, 2012.

Taylor, Donald. "Lines by a Black Carib". *International Journal of American Linguistics* 24 (October 1958): 324–25.

Thomas, J.J. *Froudacity: West Indian Fables by James Anthony Froude*. Philadelphia: Gebbie and Company, 1890.

Thomas, Oldfield. "A Preliminary List of the Mammals of Trinidad". *Journal of the Trinidad Field Naturalists' Club* 1, no. 3 (April 1892): 158-68.

Trachtenberg, Alan. *Shades of Hiawatha: Staging Indians, Making Americans 1880–1930*. New York: Hill and Wang, 2004.

Wallace, Nesbit Willoughby. *A Regimental Chronicle and List of Officers of the 60th, or the King's Royal Rifle Corps, formerly the 62nd, or the Royal Regiment of Foot*. London: Harrison, 1879.

Walton, Izaak. *The Compleat Angler 1653–1676*. Edited by Jonquil Bevan. Oxford: Clarendon, 1983.

West Indies. *Copy of Papers relating to the State of various Religious Bodies in the West Indies, in return to a Circular issued to the Governors of the West India Colonies in 1864*. London, 1867.

Williamson, Karina. "Mrs Carmichael: A Scotswoman in the West Indies, 1820–1826". *International Journal of Scottish Literature* 4 (Spring–Summer 2004): 1–17

Winer, Lise. *Dictionary of the English/Creole of Trinidad and Tobago: On Historical Principles*. Montreal: McGill-Queen's Press, 2009.

Wood, Donald. *Trinidad in Transition: The Years after Slavery*. London: Oxford University Press, 1968.

Young, Sir William, Bart. *An Account of the Black Charibs of St. Vincent with Charaib treaty of 1773, and other original documents*. London: Frank Cass, 1971 [1795].

Young, Sir William. *Considerations Which May Tend to Promote the Settlement of Our New West-India Colonies*. London: James Robson, 1764.

———. *Some Observations; Which May Contribute to Afford a Just Idea of the Nature, Importance and Settlement, of Our New West-India Colonies*. London, 1764.

Acknowledgements

This book is the result of years of dedication to seeing that more people throughout the Caribbean and beyond might enjoy its pages and glimpse a little further into the rich culture of St Vincent and the Grenadines. I am indebted to my supervisor at Cambridge, Tim Cribb, for his knowledge, guidance, enthusiasm and patience throughout this project. At the start of my research, I travelled to Devon, England, to meet Huggins's great-great-grandson Michael Huggins, who first set the record straight. I have benefited from Michael's friendship, along with that of his wife, Pauline, and their children. Of the people I met in St Vincent on my research trip in 2010, I would like to thank Alfred "Sutty" Huggins of Golden Vale, Canon Patrick McIntosh of St George's Anglican Cathedral, and the staff of the parish office at St Paul's Church, Calliaqua.

I am grateful to the University of Cambridge English faculty, Cambridge Overseas Trust, Smuts Fund, Santander Trust and Clare Hall, Cambridge, for funding my studies and research trips. I owe thanks to the staff at the Cambridge University Library; the St Vincent National Archives; the Kingstown Public Library; and the library at Codrington College, Barbados. I appreciate the help in my research from Priyamvada Gopal, Selwyn Cudjoe, Adrian Chatfield, Peter Hulme and Sarah Meer. I also thank Alex, Quillan and Jihan for their technical support; Clare, Richard, Pelly, Nik and Christian for balance; and Aleeia Abraham for help with the geography of St Vincent. The initial idea for my research on *Hiroona* began by asking my parents, Clarence and Soleitor Osborne, about the literature and history of our island home. It was their encouragement that pushed me first through the dissertation and now this publication, and I thank them.